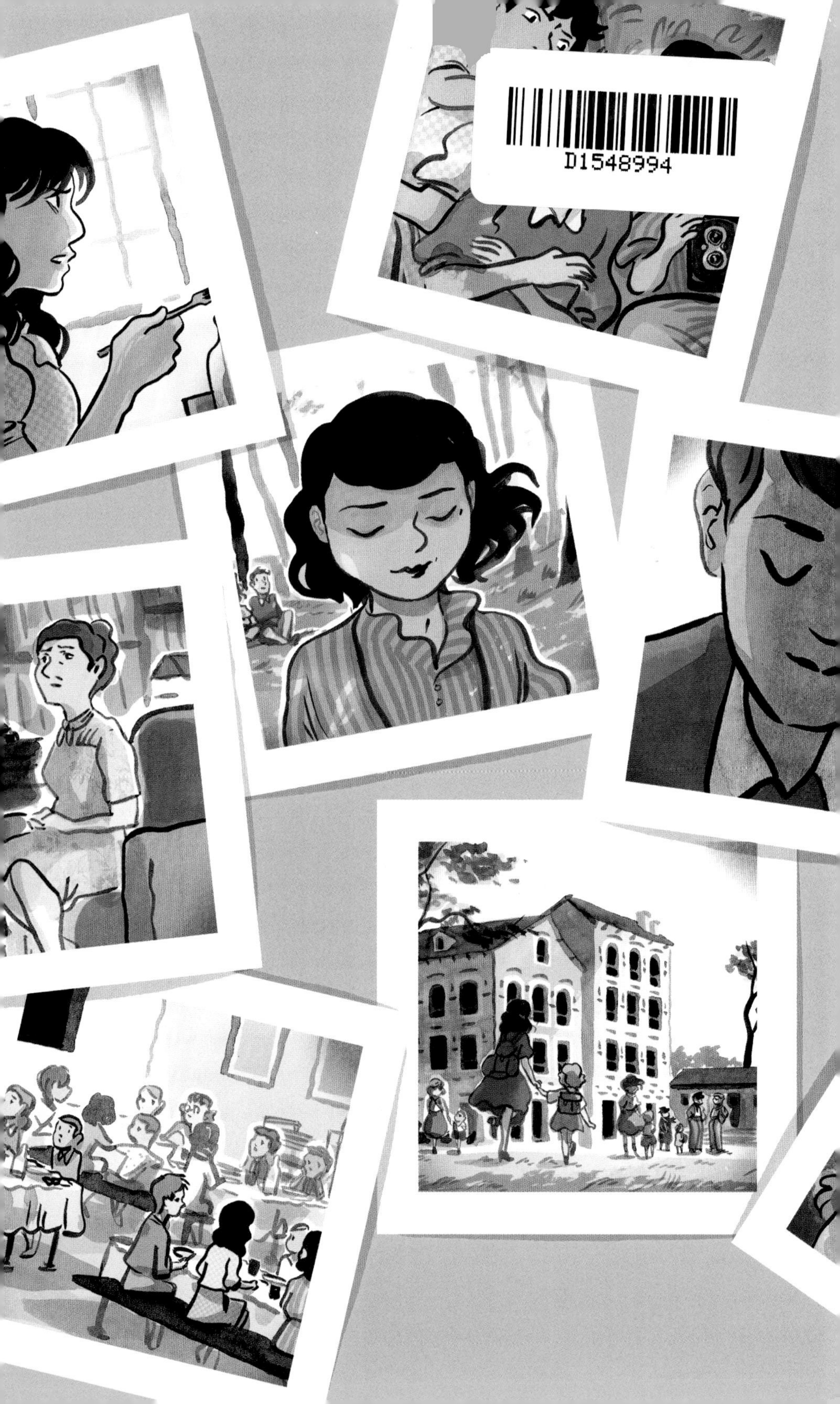

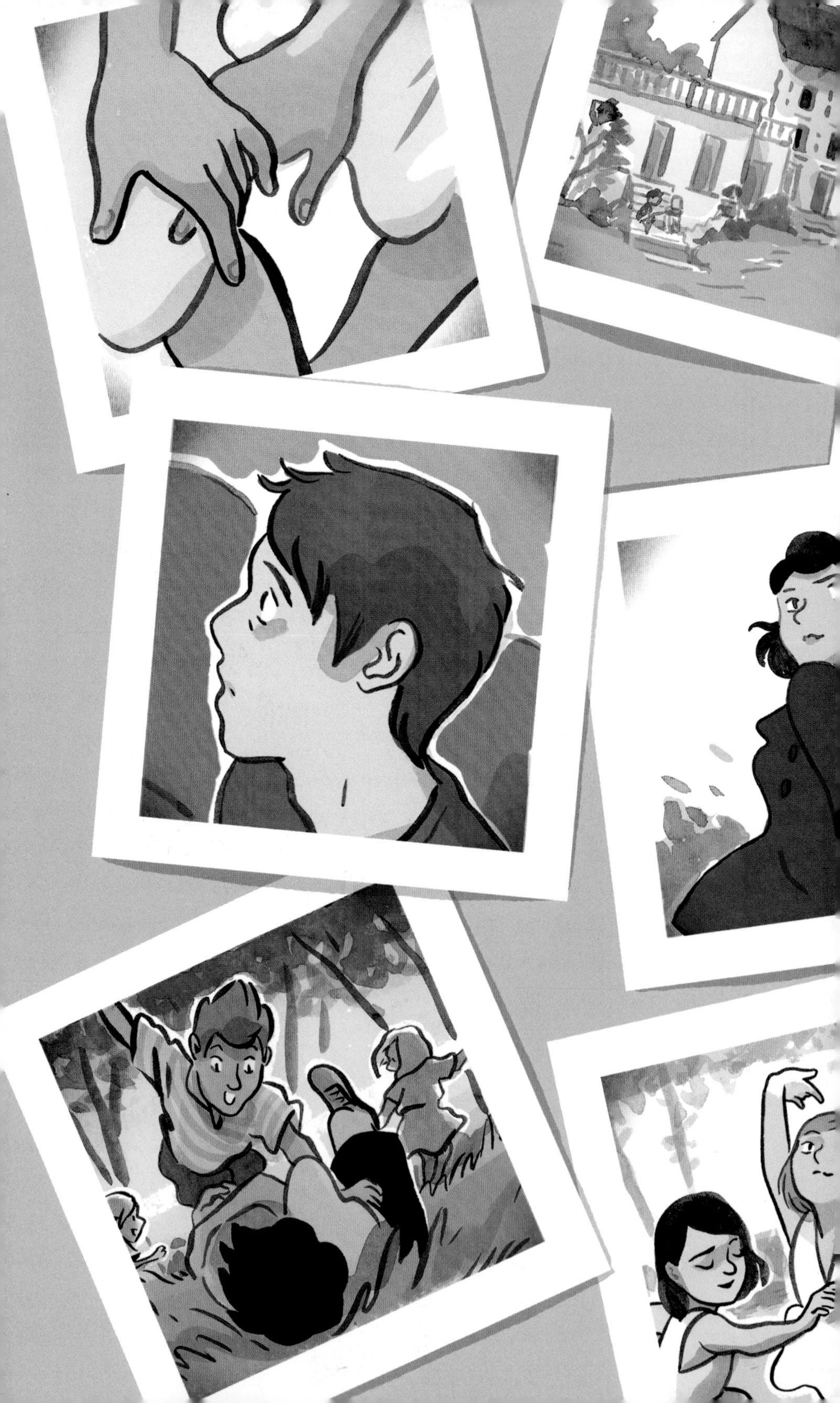

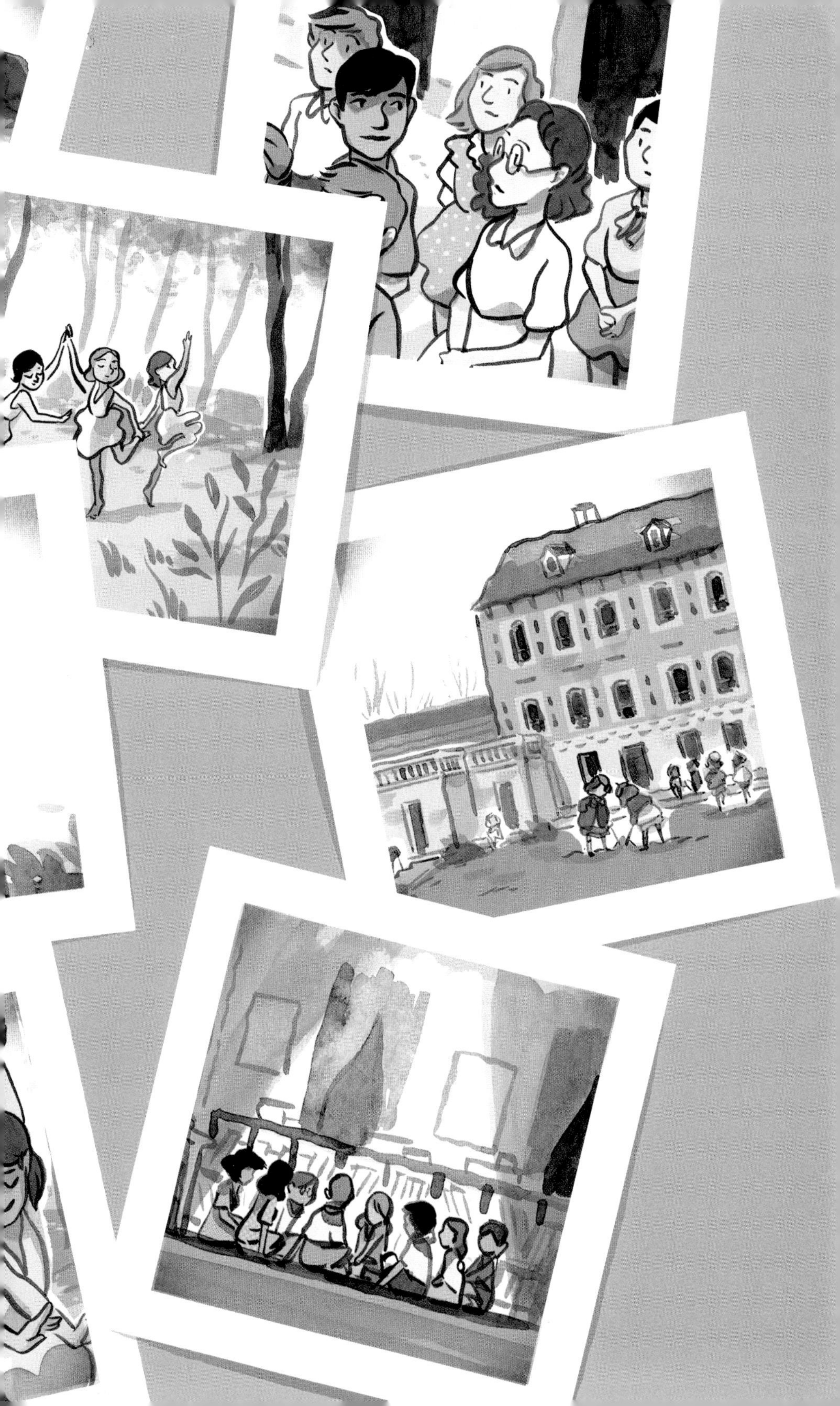

Catherine's War

JULIA BILLET

CLAIRE FAUVEL

Translation by Ivanka Hahnenberger

HARPER alley

An Imprint of HarperCollins*Publishers*

HarperAlley is an imprint of HarperCollins Publishers.

Catherine's War
Text by Julia Billet, art by Claire Fauvel © 2017 by Rue de Sèvres, Paris.
Originally published in 2017 in French by Rue de Sèvres as La guerre de Catherine.
English translation copyright © 2020 by HarperCollins Publishers

For information address HarperCollins Children's Books, a division of HarperCollins Publishers, 195 Broadway, New York, NY 10007.
www.harpercollinschildrens.com
Library of Congress Control Number: 2019941457
ISBN 978-0-06-291560-3 — ISBN 978-0-06-291559-7 (paperback)
Typography by David DeWitt
21 22 23 24 PC/LSCC 10 9 8 7 6 5 4 3
❖
First U.S. edition, 2020

To my mother and her life force, and also to Seagull and Penguin, without whom this Grande Histoire would have been even more horrible than it was. I would like to thank Marija Gaudry for allowing Catherine to fly to the United States and Jill Davis and Ivanka Hahnenberger for all the attention, rigor, and generosity they have brought to the translation. And thank you to Michel Schwab for his precious help.

—J. B.

A big thank-you to Charlotte Moundlic for initiating this project, and to Julia Billet for her involvement and kindness. A special thanks to my muse, Christophe!

—C. F.

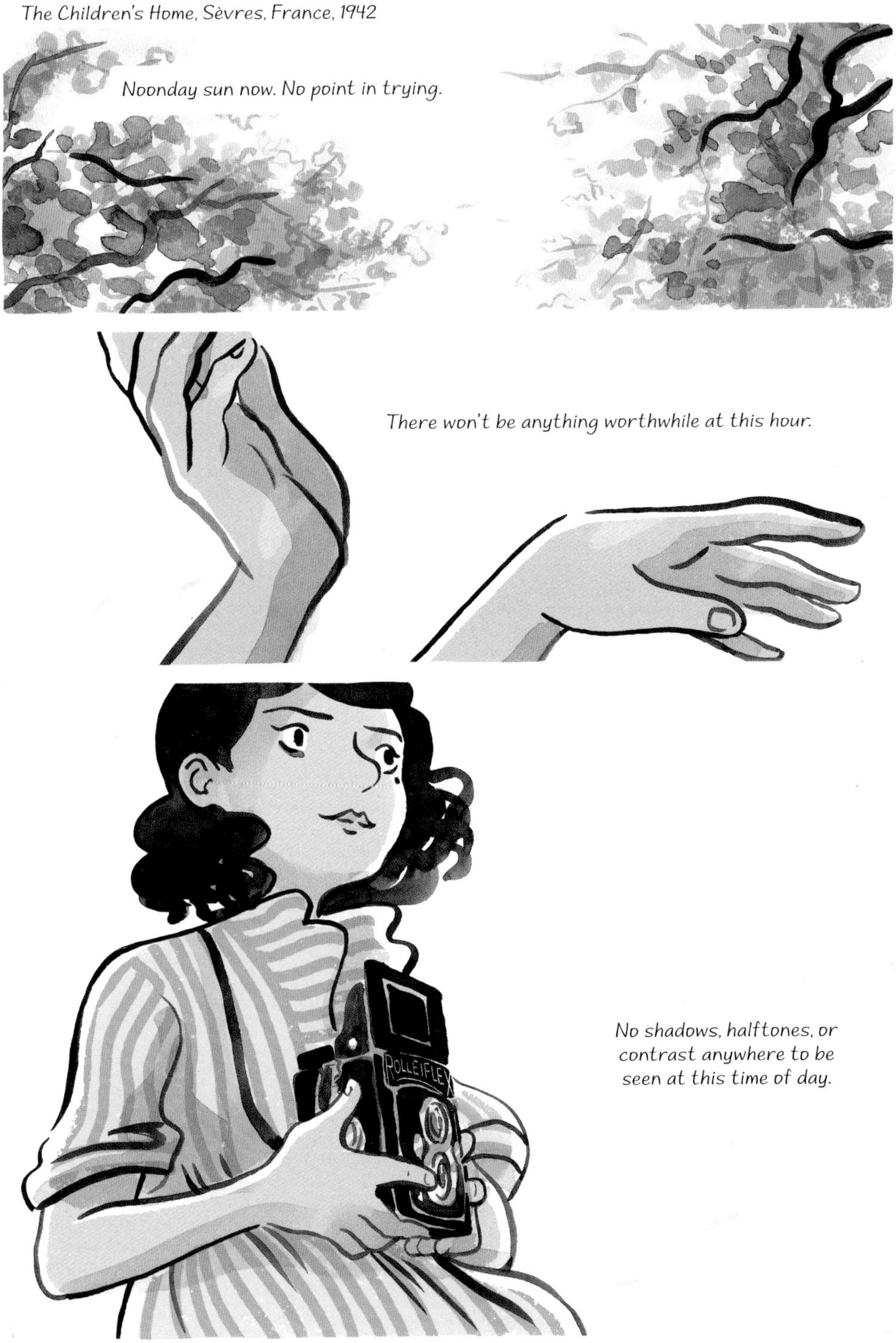
The Children's Home, Sèvres, France, 1942
Noonday sun now. No point in trying.
There won't be anything worthwhile at this hour.
ROLLEIFLEX
No shadows, halftones, or contrast anywhere to be seen at this time of day.

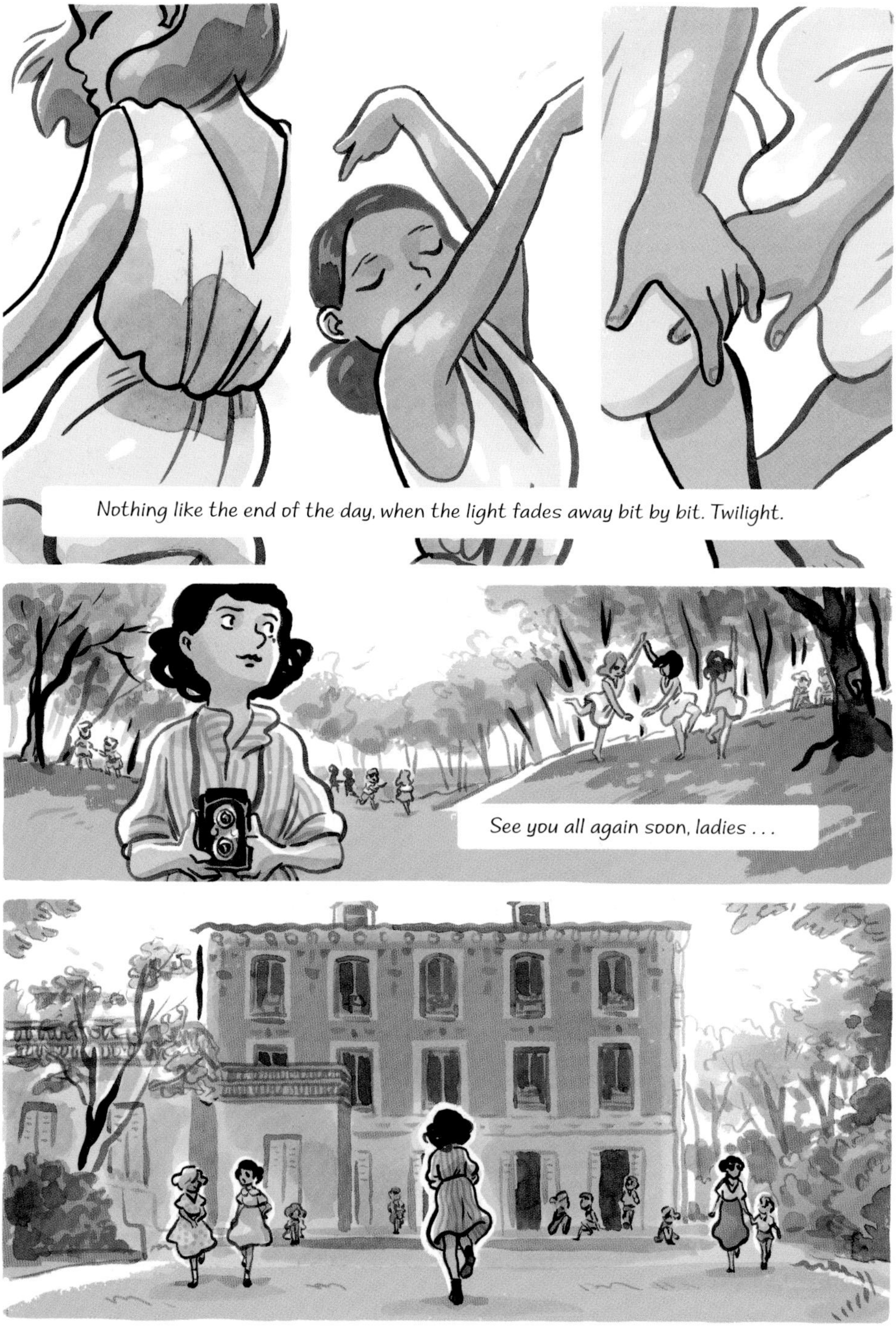
Nothing like the end of the day, when the light fades away bit by bit. Twilight.
See you all again soon, ladies . . .

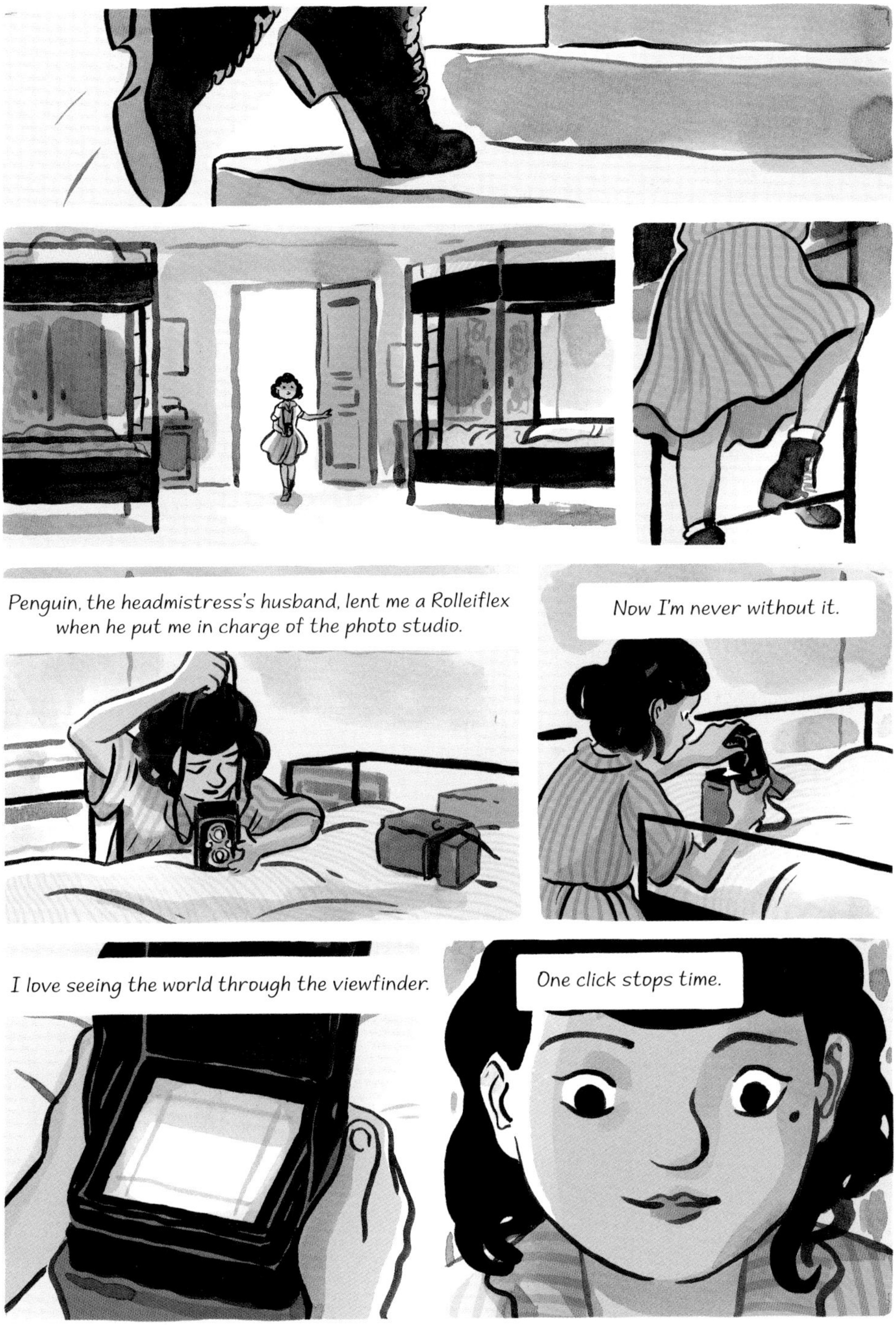
Penguin, the headmistress's husband, lent me a Rolleiflex when he put me in charge of the photo studio.
Now I'm never without it.
I love seeing the world through the viewfinder.
One click stops time.

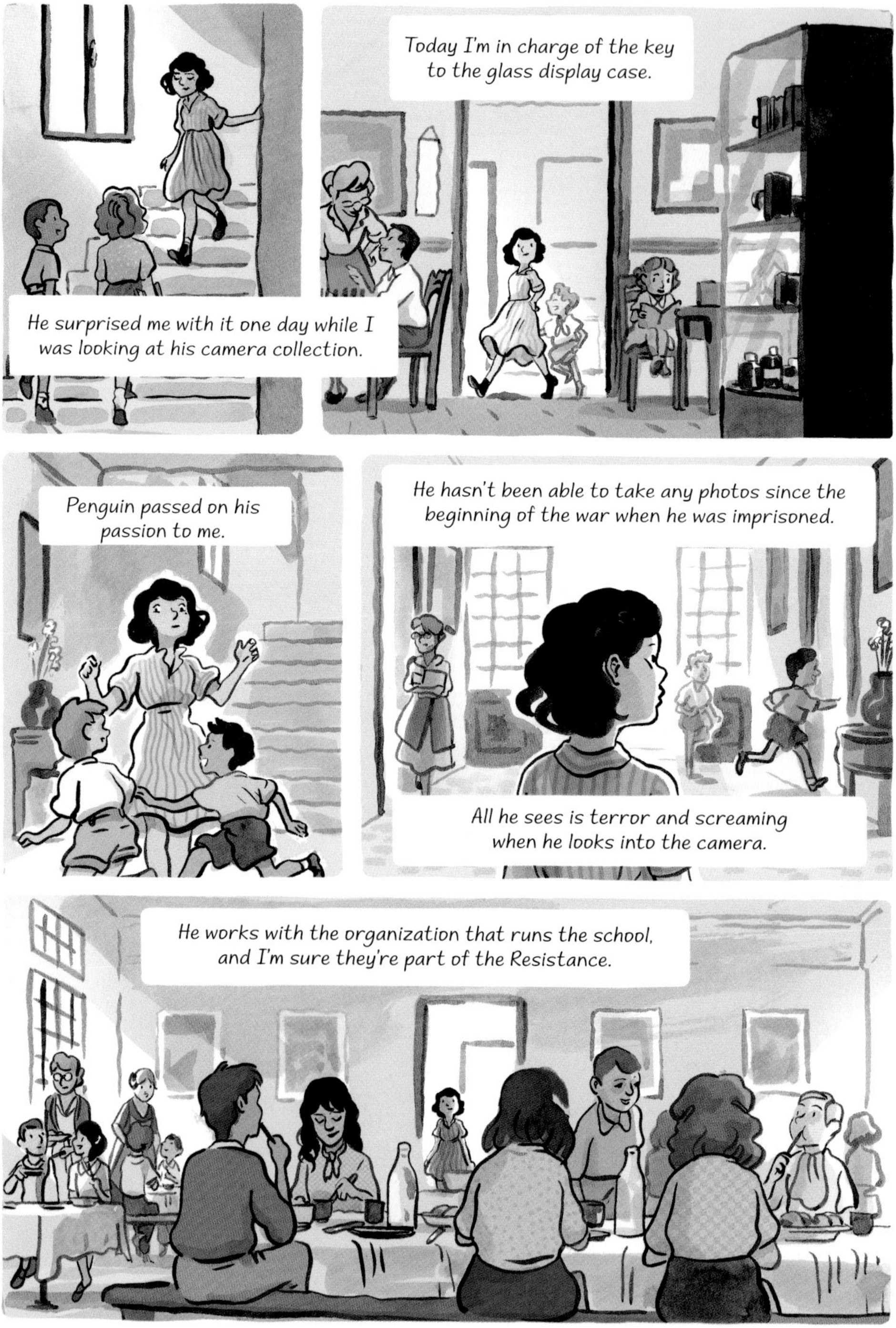
He surprised me with it one day while I was looking at his camera collection.
Today I'm in charge of the key to the glass display case.
Penguin passed on his passion to me.
He hasn't been able to take any photos since the beginning of the war when he was imprisoned.
All he sees is terror and screaming when he looks into the camera.
He works with the organization that runs the school, and I'm sure they're part of the Resistance.

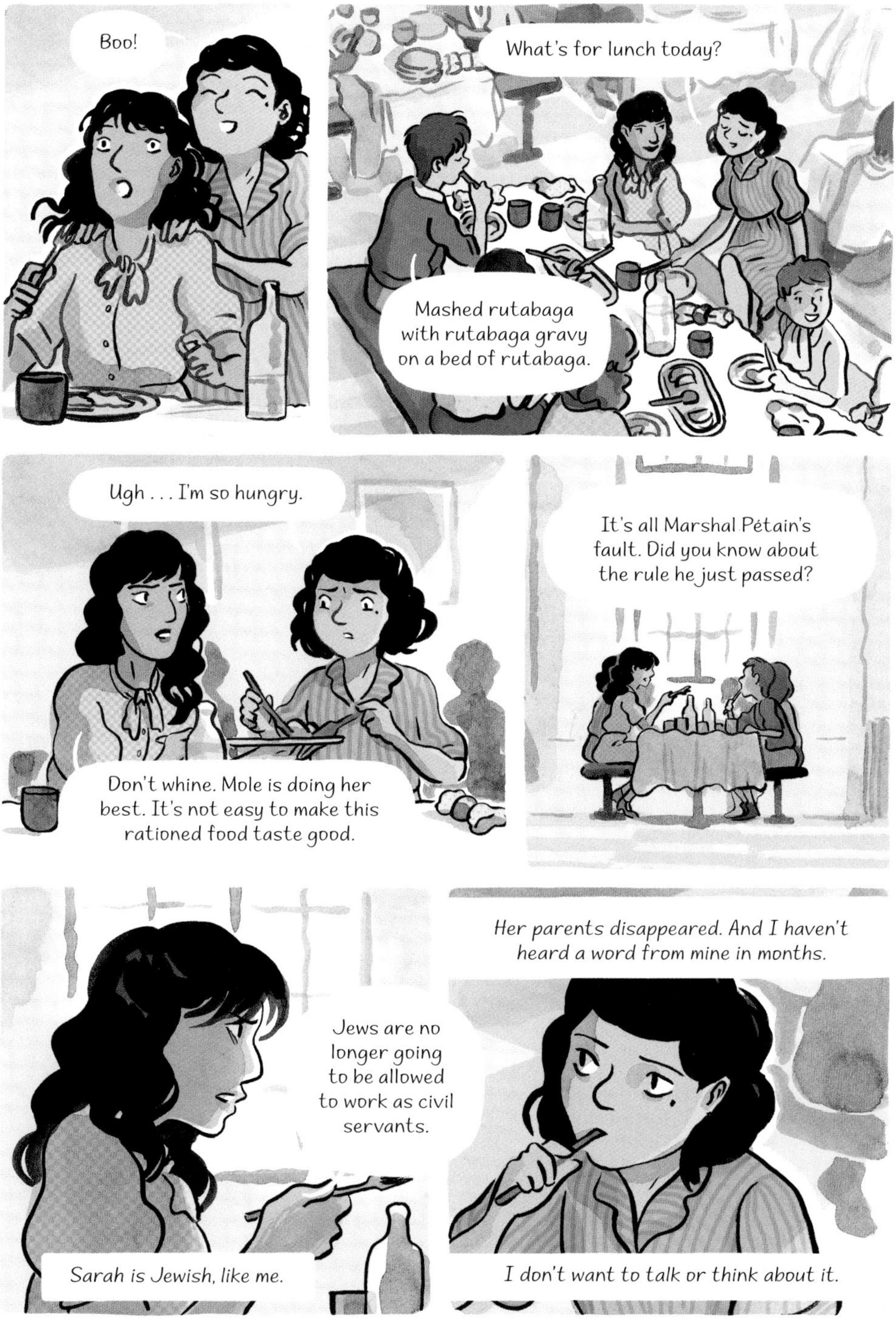
Boo!
What's for lunch today?
Mashed rutabaga with rutabaga gravy on a bed of rutabaga.
Ugh . . . I'm so hungry.
Don't whine. Mole is doing her best. It's not easy to make this rationed food taste good.
It's all Marshal Pétain's fault. Did you know about the rule he just passed?
Jews are no longer going to be allowed to work as civil servants.
Sarah is Jewish, like me.
Her parents disappeared. And I haven't heard a word from mine in months.
I don't want to talk or think about it.

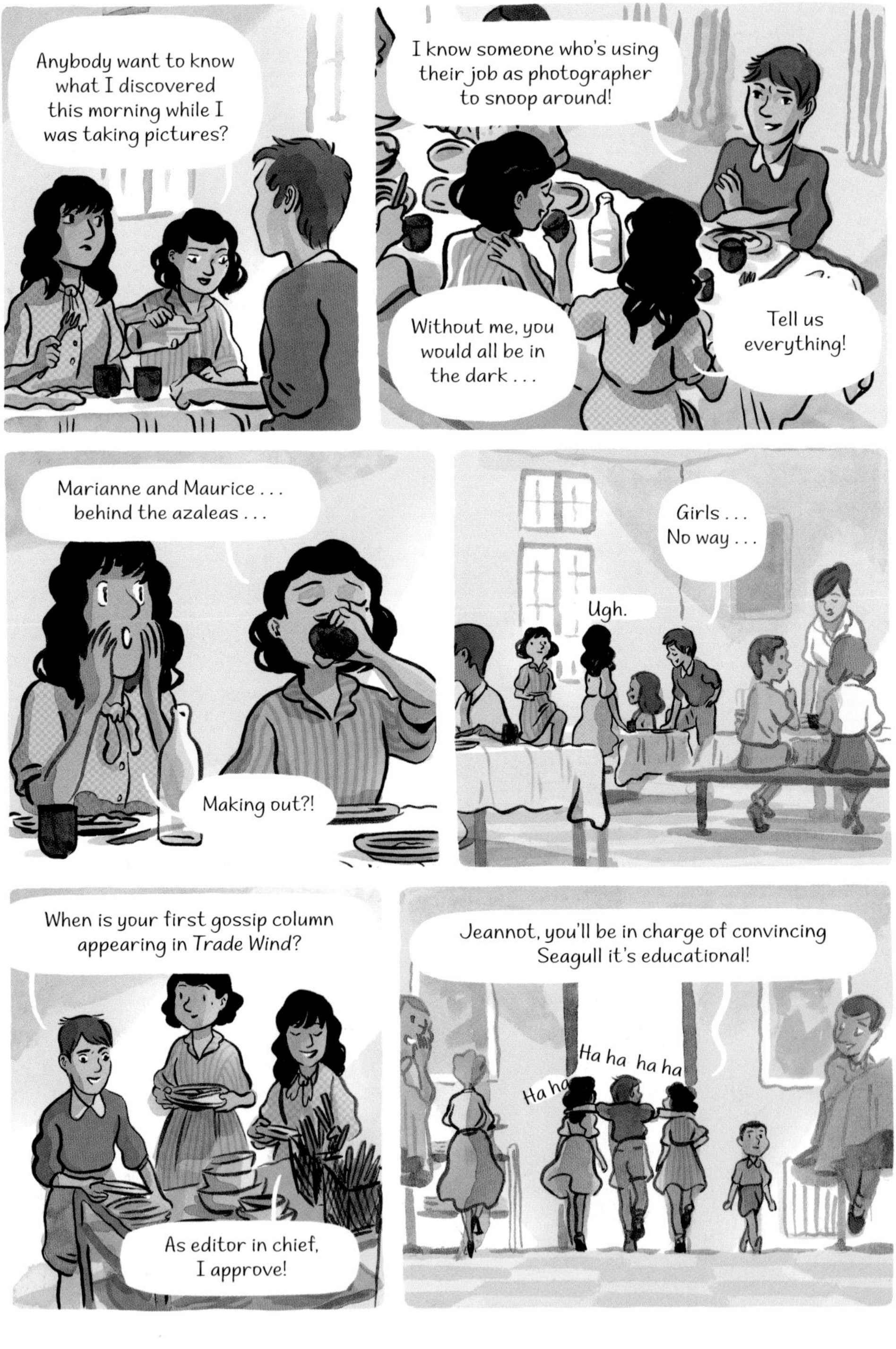
Anybody want to know what I discovered this morning while I was taking pictures?
I know someone who's using their job as photographer to snoop around!
Without me, you would all be in the dark . . .
Tell us everything!
Marianne and Maurice . . . behind the azaleas . . .
Making out?!
Girls . . . No way . . .
Ugh.
When is your first gossip column appearing in Trade Wind?
As editor in chief, I approve!
Jeannot, you'll be in charge of convincing Seagull it's educational!
Ha ha
Ha ha ha ha

At two o'clock our class gathers to discuss the upcoming week.

The Children's Home is a special place.

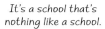

It's a school that's nothing like a school.

Students decide, themselves, how to spend their time. The teachers encourage us to read books and learn on our own.

I found myself in this universe a few months ago and still can't believe I'm actually here.

I really suffered at my school in Paris. "Talks too much, doesn't try hard enough."

Everything here is different.

For the first time, someone cares about my work.

7

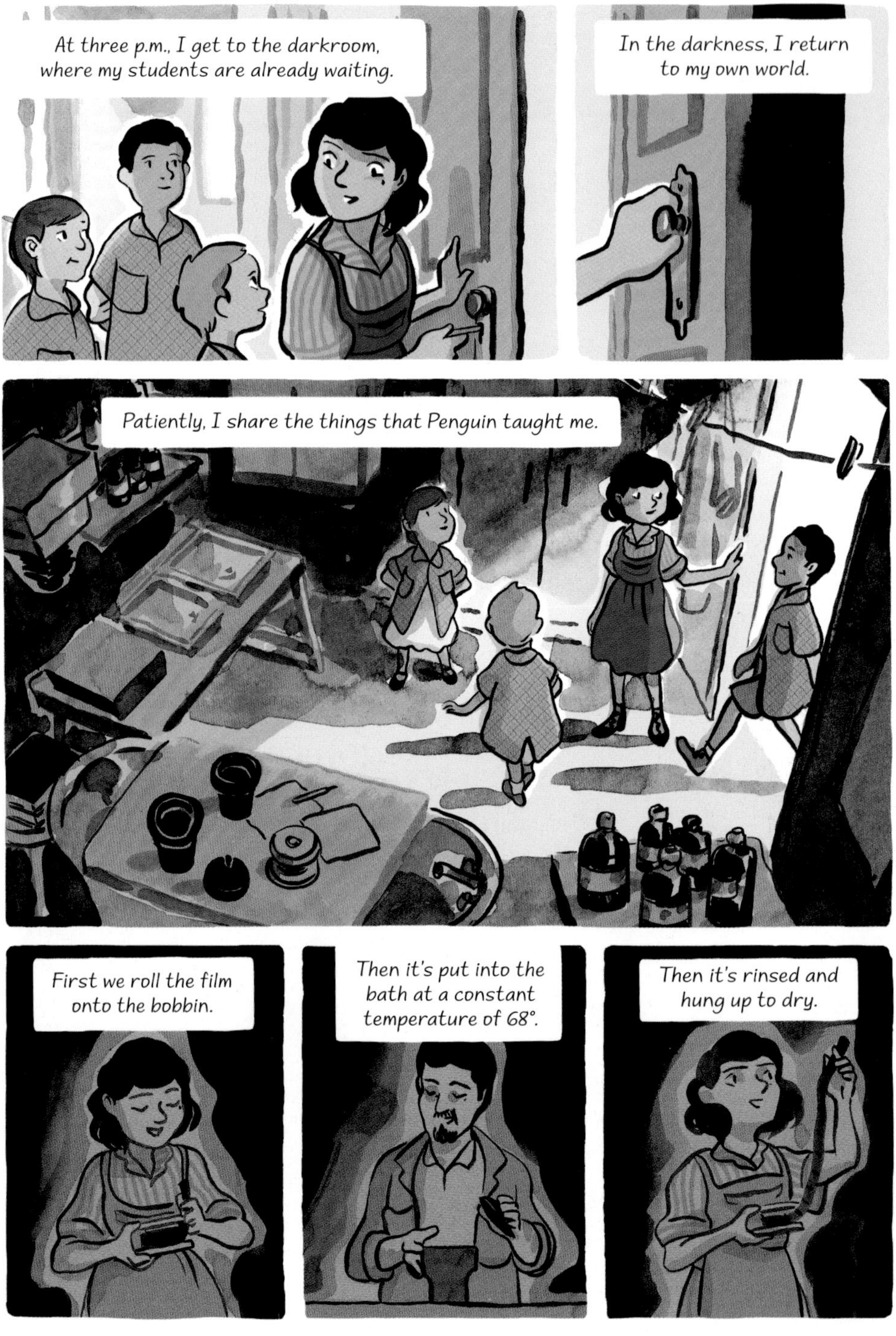
At three p.m., I get to the darkroom, where my students are already waiting.
In the darkness, I return to my own world.
Patiently, I share the things that Penguin taught me.
First we roll the film onto the bobbin.
Then it's put into the bath at a constant temperature of 68°.
Then it's rinsed and hung up to dry.

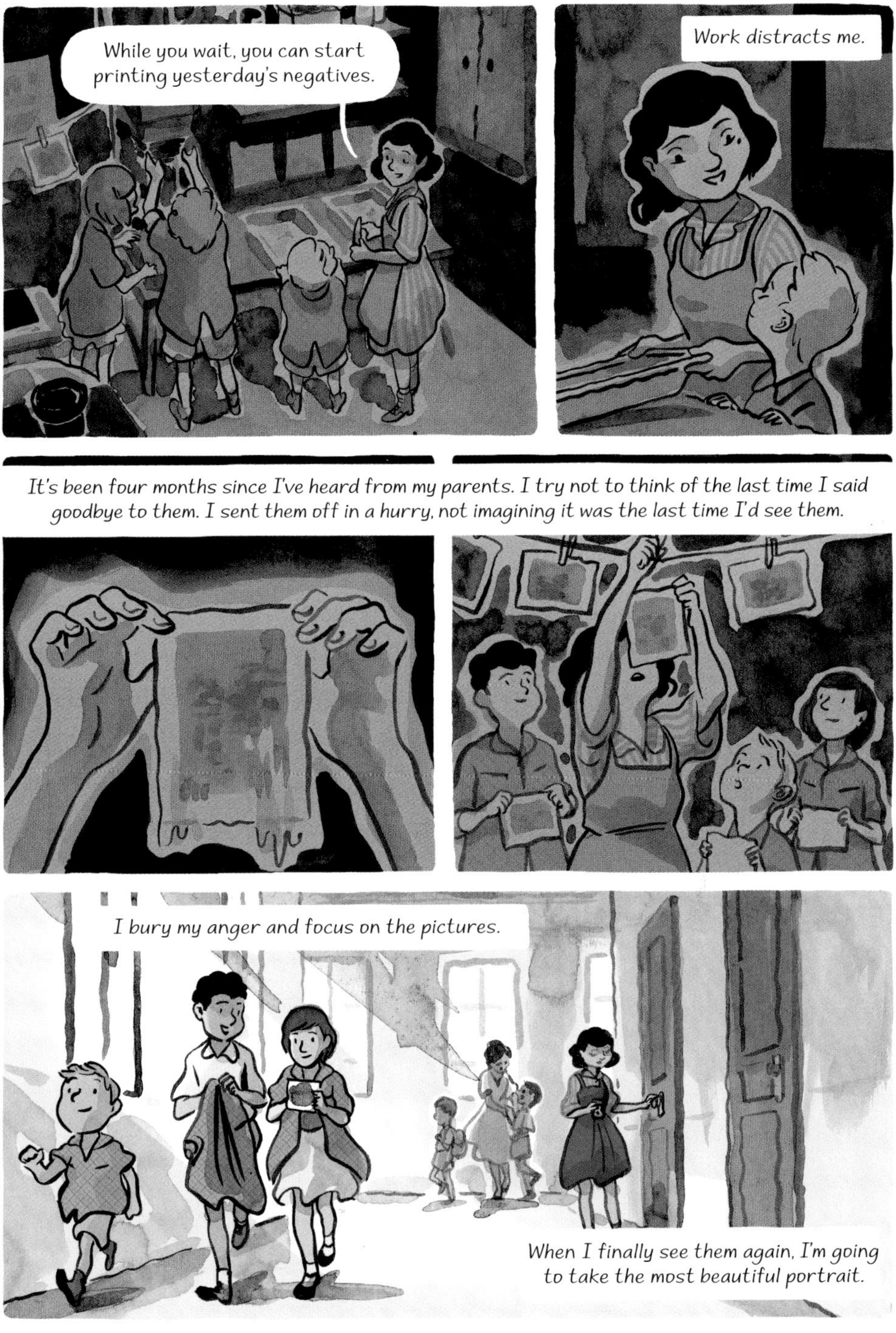
While you wait, you can start printing yesterday's negatives.
Work distracts me.
It's been four months since I've heard from my parents. I try not to think of the last time I said goodbye to them. I sent them off in a hurry, not imagining it was the last time I'd see them.
I bury my anger and focus on the pictures.
When I finally see them again, I'm going to take the most beautiful portrait.

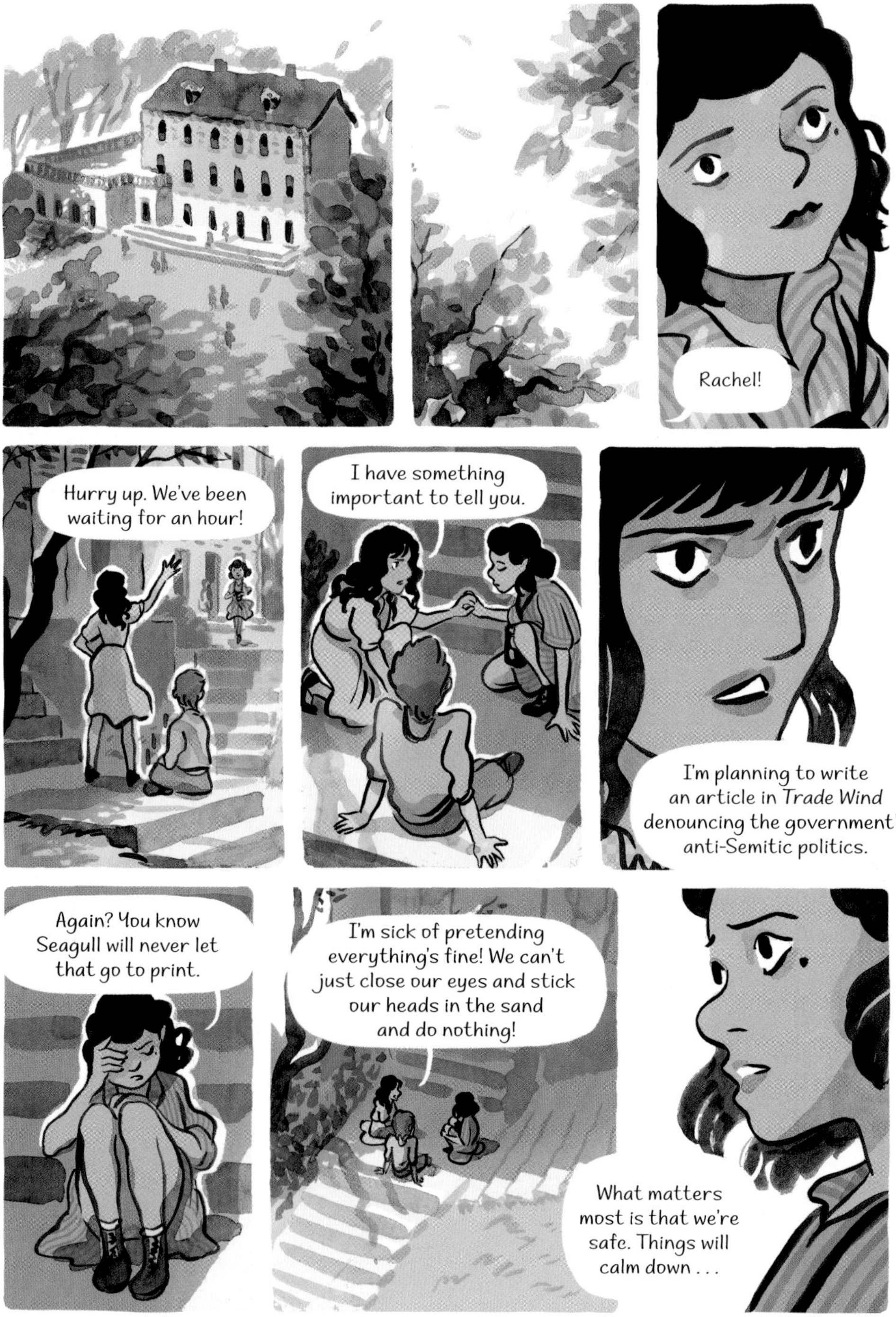
Rachel!
Hurry up. We've been waiting for an hour!
I have something important to tell you.
I'm planning to write an article in *Trade Wind* denouncing the government's anti-Semitic politics.
Again? You know Seagull will never let that go to print.
I'm sick of pretending everything's fine! We can't just close our eyes and stick our heads in the sand and do nothing!
What matters most is that we're safe. Things will calm down . . .

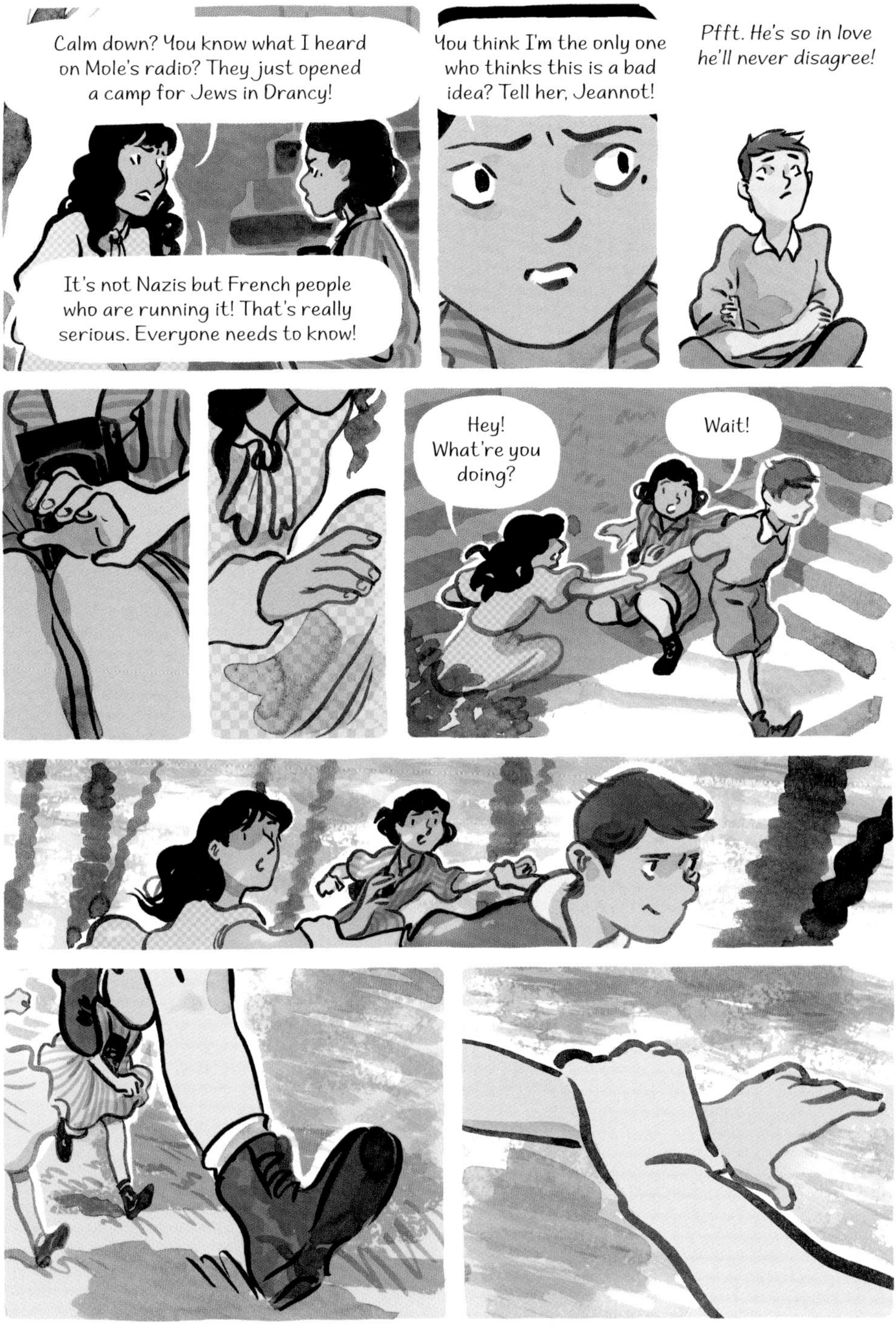
Calm down? You know what I heard on Mole's radio? They just opened a camp for Jews in Drancy!
It's not Nazis but French people who are running it! That's really serious. Everyone needs to know!
You think I'm the only one who thinks this is a bad idea? Tell her, Jeannot!
Pfft. He's so in love he'll never disagree!
Hey! What're you doing?
Wait!

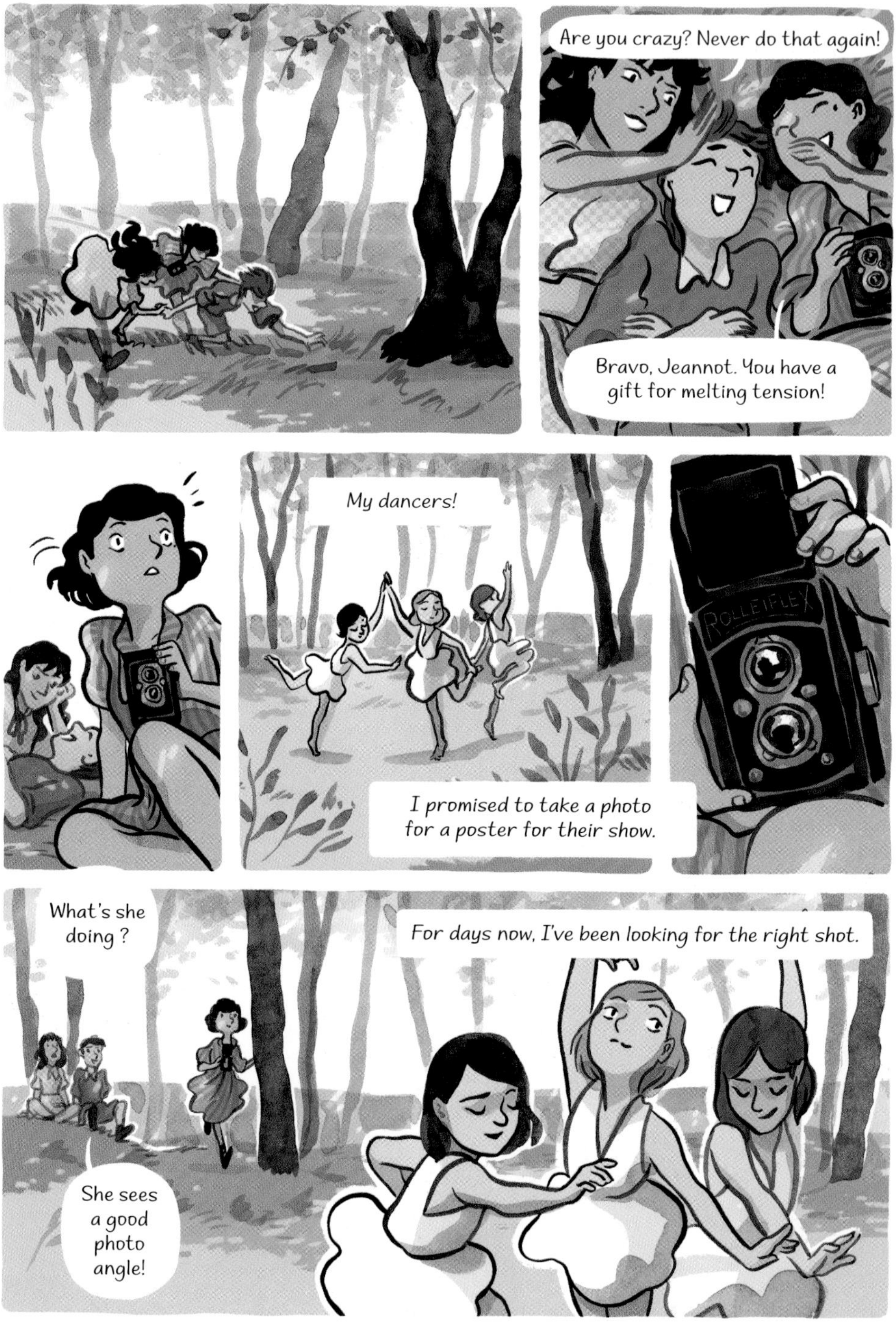
Are you crazy? Never do that again!
Bravo, Jeannot. You have a gift for melting tension!
My dancers!
I promised to take a photo for a poster for their show.
ROLLEIFLEX
What's she doing ?
For days now, I've been looking for the right shot.
She sees a good photo angle!

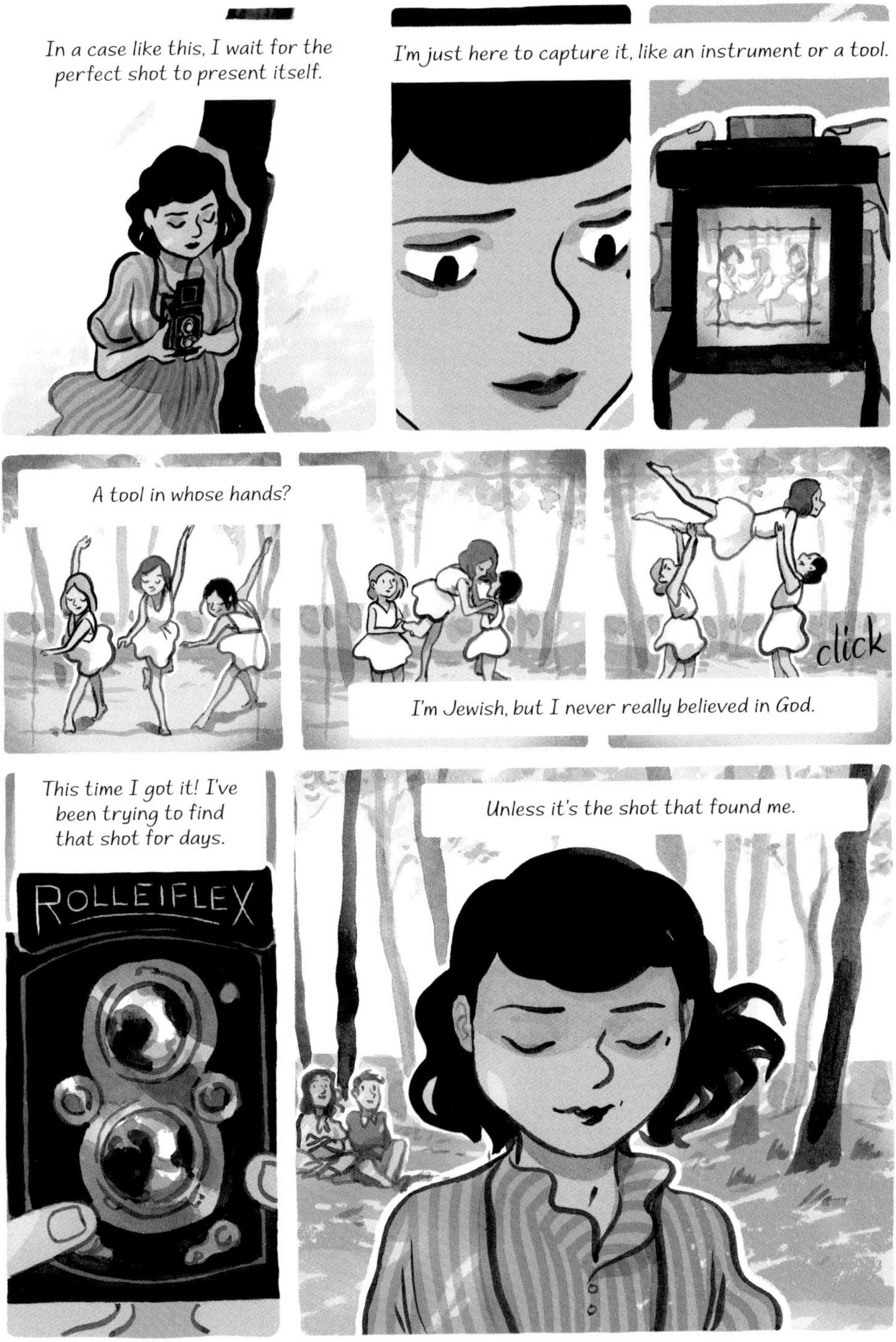
In a case like this, I wait for the perfect shot to present itself.
I'm just here to capture it, like an instrument or a tool.
A tool in whose hands?
I'm Jewish, but I never really believed in God.
click
This time I got it! I've been trying to find that shot for days.
ROLLEIFLEX
Unless it's the shot that found me.

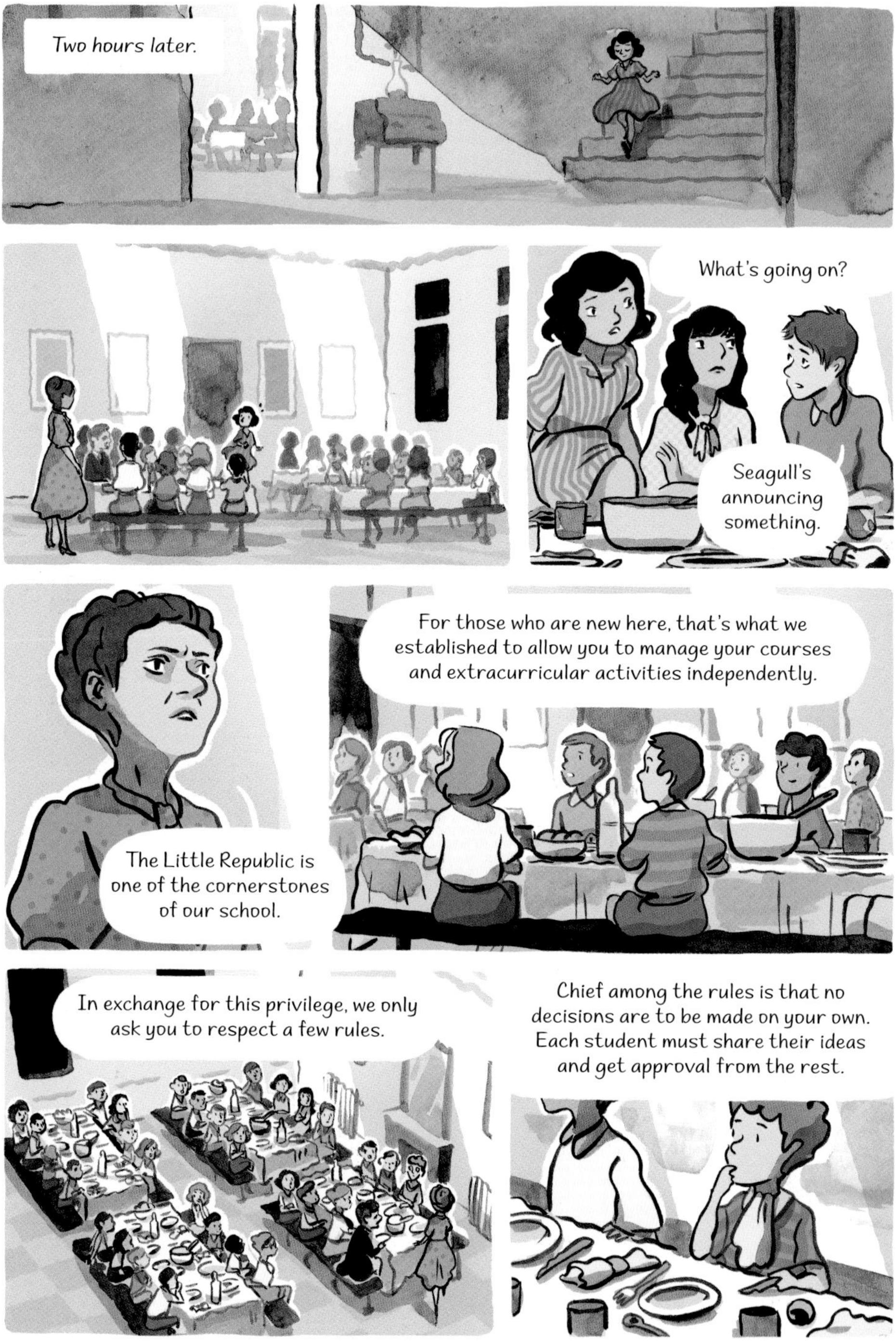
Two hours later.
What's going on?
Seagull's announcing something.
The Little Republic is one of the cornerstones of our school.
For those who are new here, that's what we established to allow you to manage your courses and extracurricular activities independently.
In exchange for this privilege, we only ask you to respect a few rules.
Chief among the rules is that no decisions are to be made on your own. Each student must share their ideas and get approval from the rest.

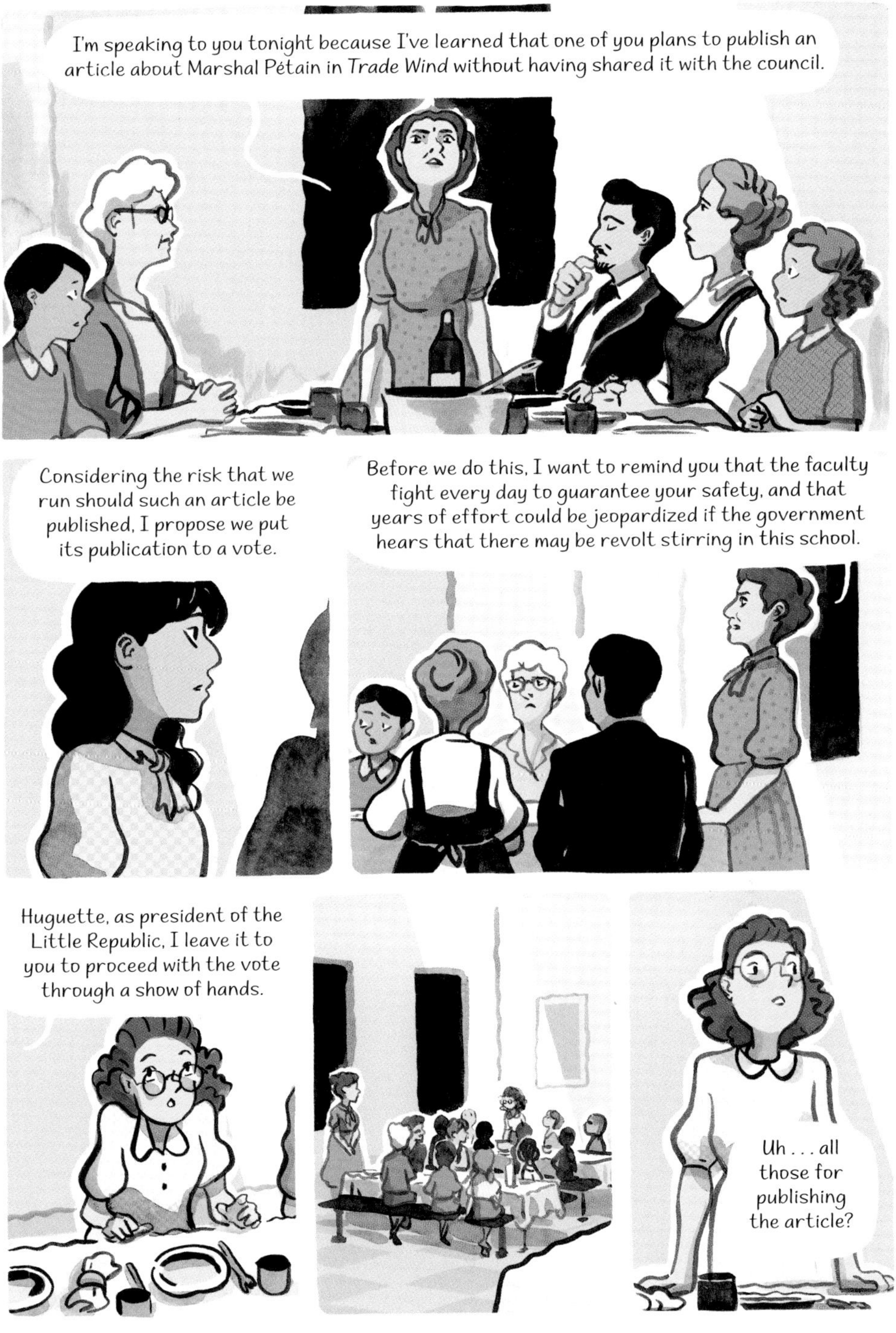
I'm speaking to you tonight because I've learned that one of you plans to publish an article about Marshal Pétain in *Trade Wind* without having shared it with the council.
Considering the risk that we run should such an article be published, I propose we put its publication to a vote.
Before we do this, I want to remind you that the faculty fight every day to guarantee your safety, and that years of effort could be jeopardized if the government hears that there may be revolt stirring in this school.
Huguette, as president of the Little Republic, I leave it to you to proceed with the vote through a show of hands.
Uh . . . all those for publishing the article?

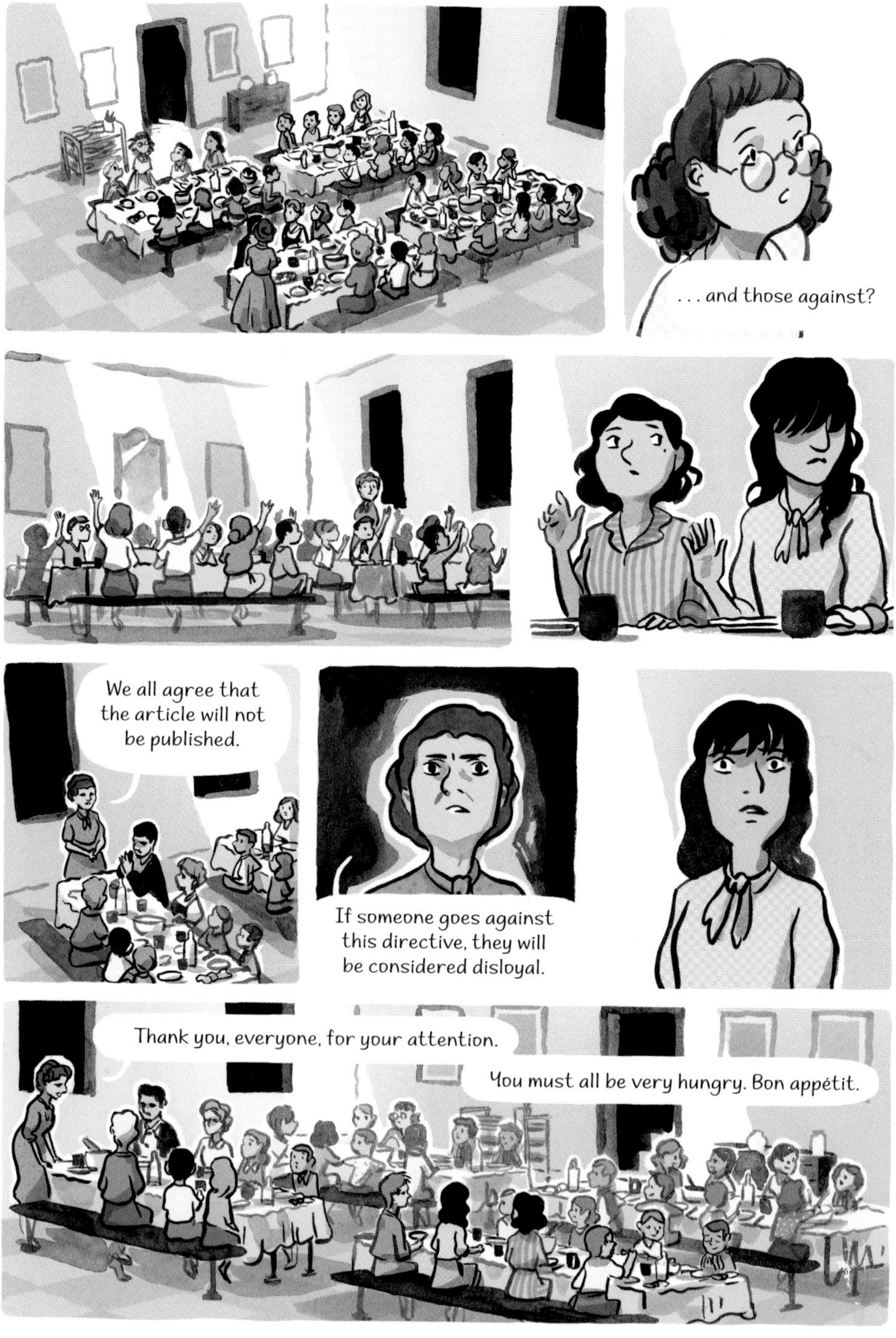

. . . and those against?
We all agree that the article will not be published.
If someone goes against this directive, they will be considered disloyal.
Thank you, everyone, for your attention.
You must all be very hungry. Bon appétit.

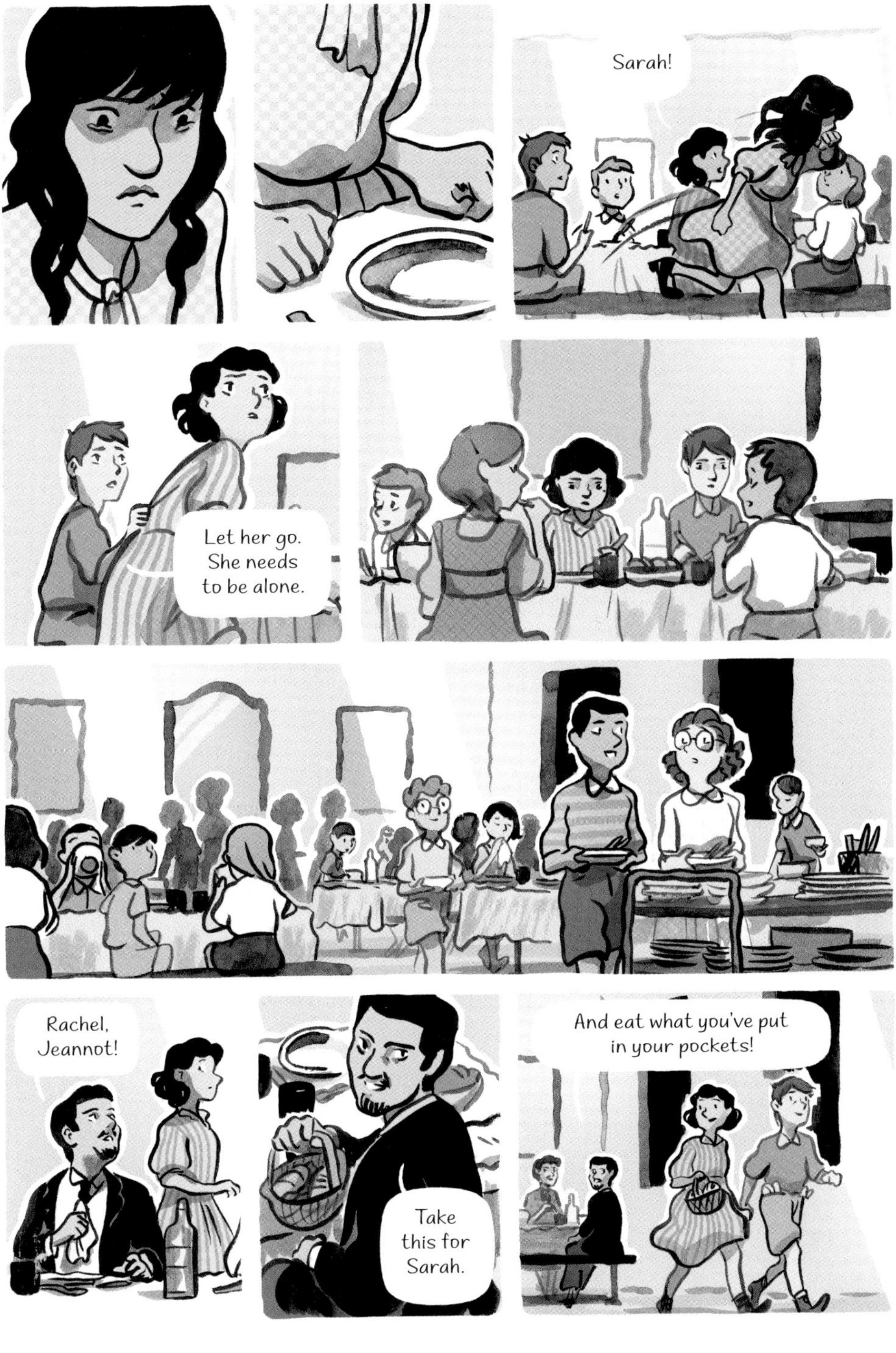
Sarah!
Let her go. She needs to be alone.
Rachel, Jeannot!
Take this for Sarah.
And eat what you've put in your pockets!

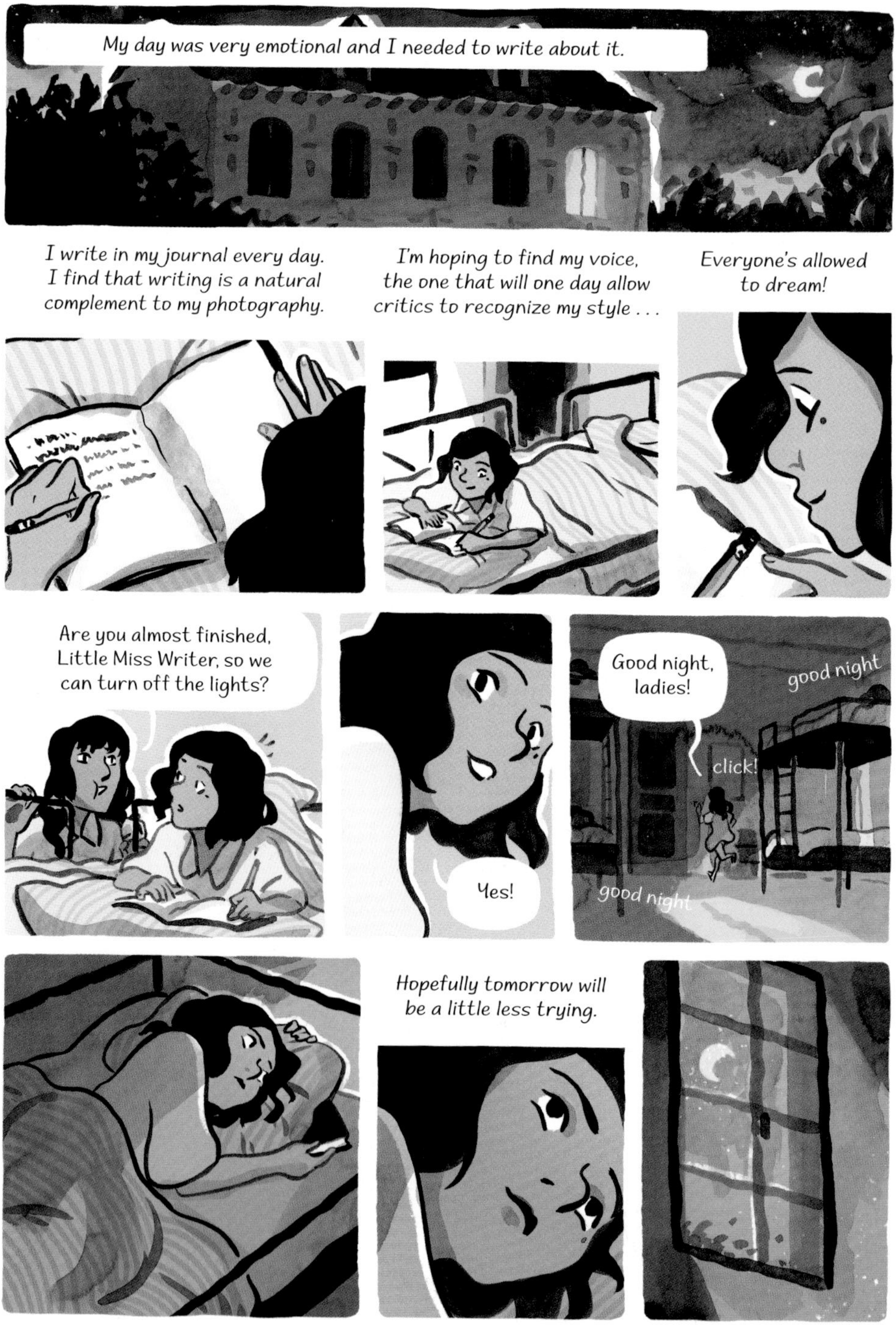
My day was very emotional and I needed to write about it.
I write in my journal every day. I find that writing is a natural complement to my photography.
I'm hoping to find my voice, the one that will one day allow critics to recognize my style . . .
Everyone's allowed to dream!
Are you almost finished, Little Miss Writer, so we can turn off the lights?
Yes!
Good night, ladies!
good night
click!
good night
Hopefully tomorrow will be a little less trying.

What's going on?

General assembly!

Excuse me, sorry . . .

My dear students, it is a pleasure to be here today and to finally see the Sèvres Children's Home.

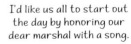

I'd like us all to start out the day by honoring our dear marshal with a song.

19

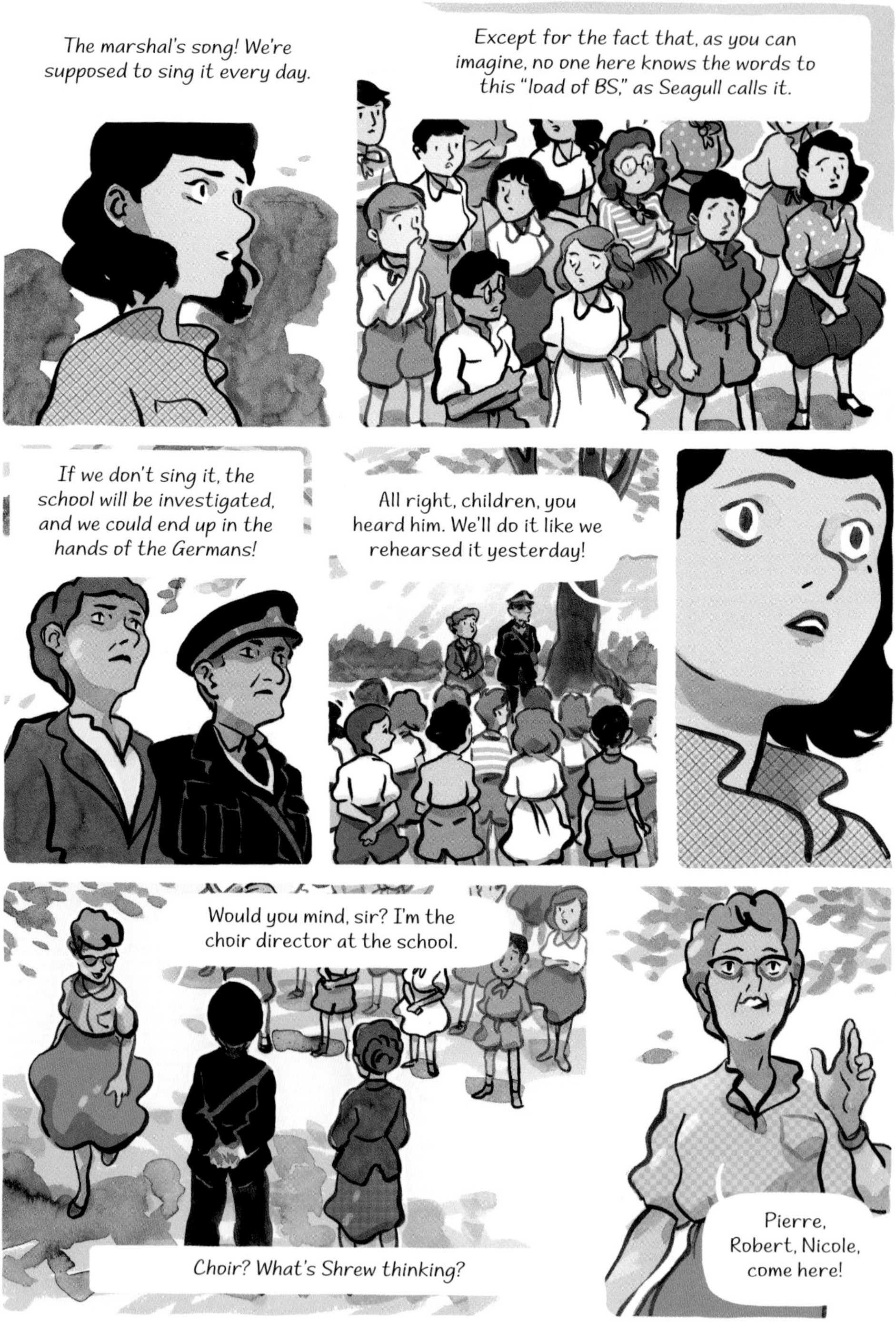

The marshal's song! We're supposed to sing it every day.
Except for the fact that, as you can imagine, no one here knows the words to this "load of BS," as Seagull calls it.
If we don't sing it, the school will be investigated, and we could end up in the hands of the Germans!
All right, children, you heard him. We'll do it like we rehearsed it yesterday!
Would you mind, sir? I'm the choir director at the school.
Choir? What's Shrew thinking?
Pierre, Robert, Nicole, come here!

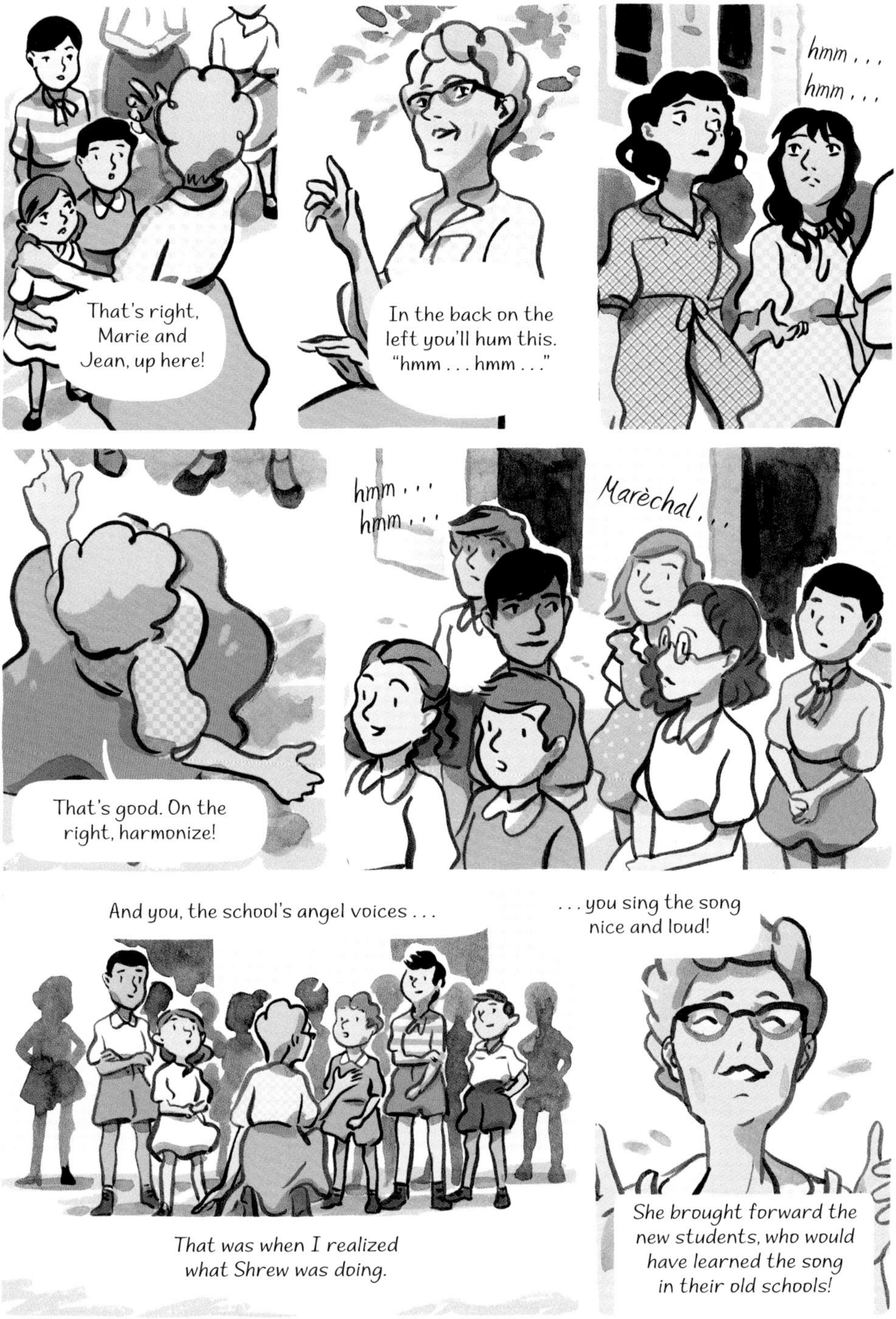
That's right, Marie and Jean, up here!
In the back on the left you'll hum this. "hmm . . . hmm . . ."
hmm . . .
hmm . . .
That's good. On the right, harmonize!
hmm . . .
hmm . . .
Marèchal . . .
And you, the school's angel voices . . .
That was when I realized what Shrew was doing.
. . . you sing the song nice and loud!
She brought forward the new students, who would have learned the song in their old schools!

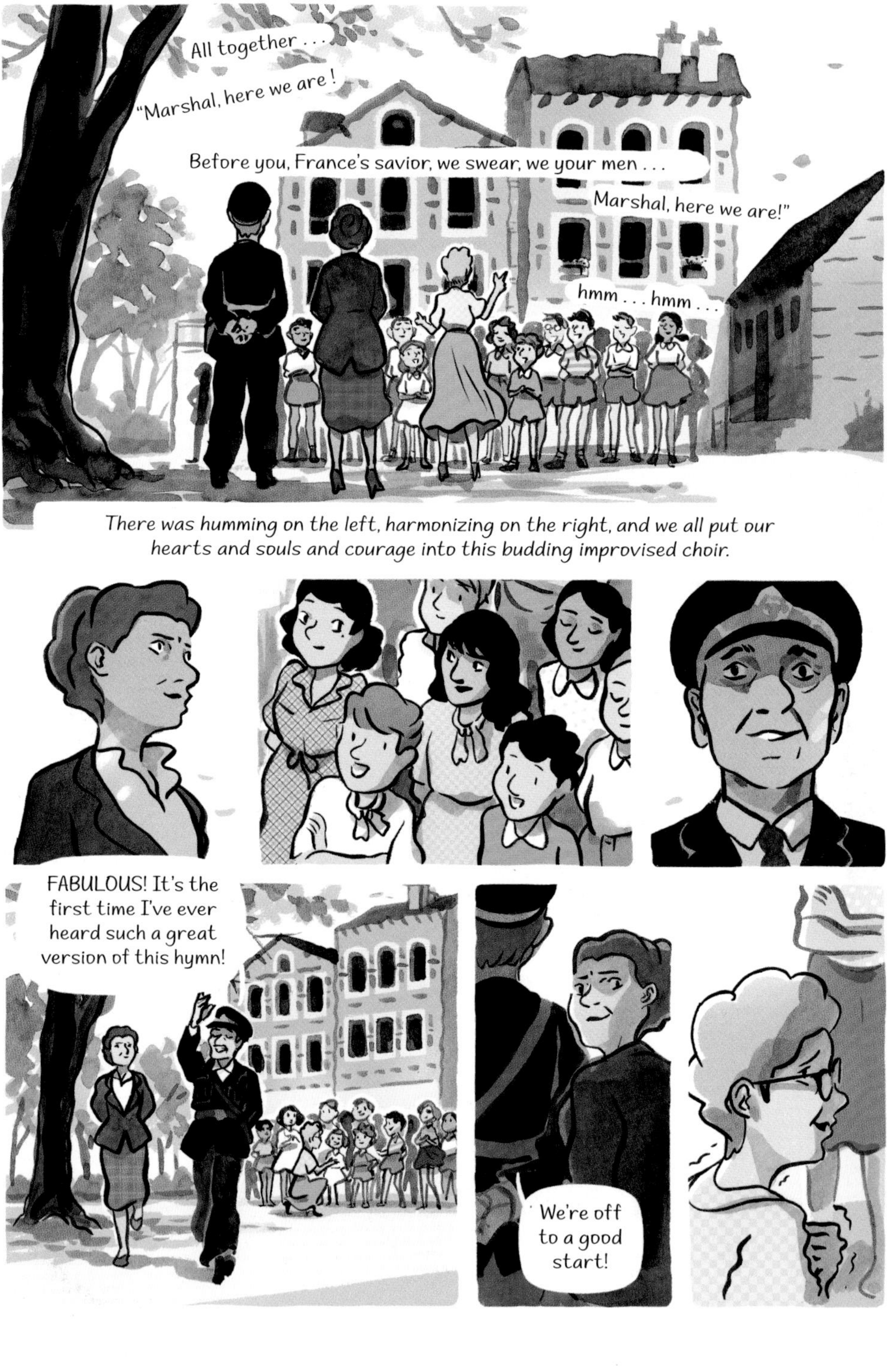
All together . . .
"Marshal, here we are!
Before you, France's savior, we swear, we your men . . .
Marshal, here we are!"
hmm . . . hmm . . .
There was humming on the left, harmonizing on the right, and we all put our hearts and souls and courage into this budding improvised choir.
FABULOUS! It's the first time I've ever heard such a great version of this hymn!
We're off to a good start!

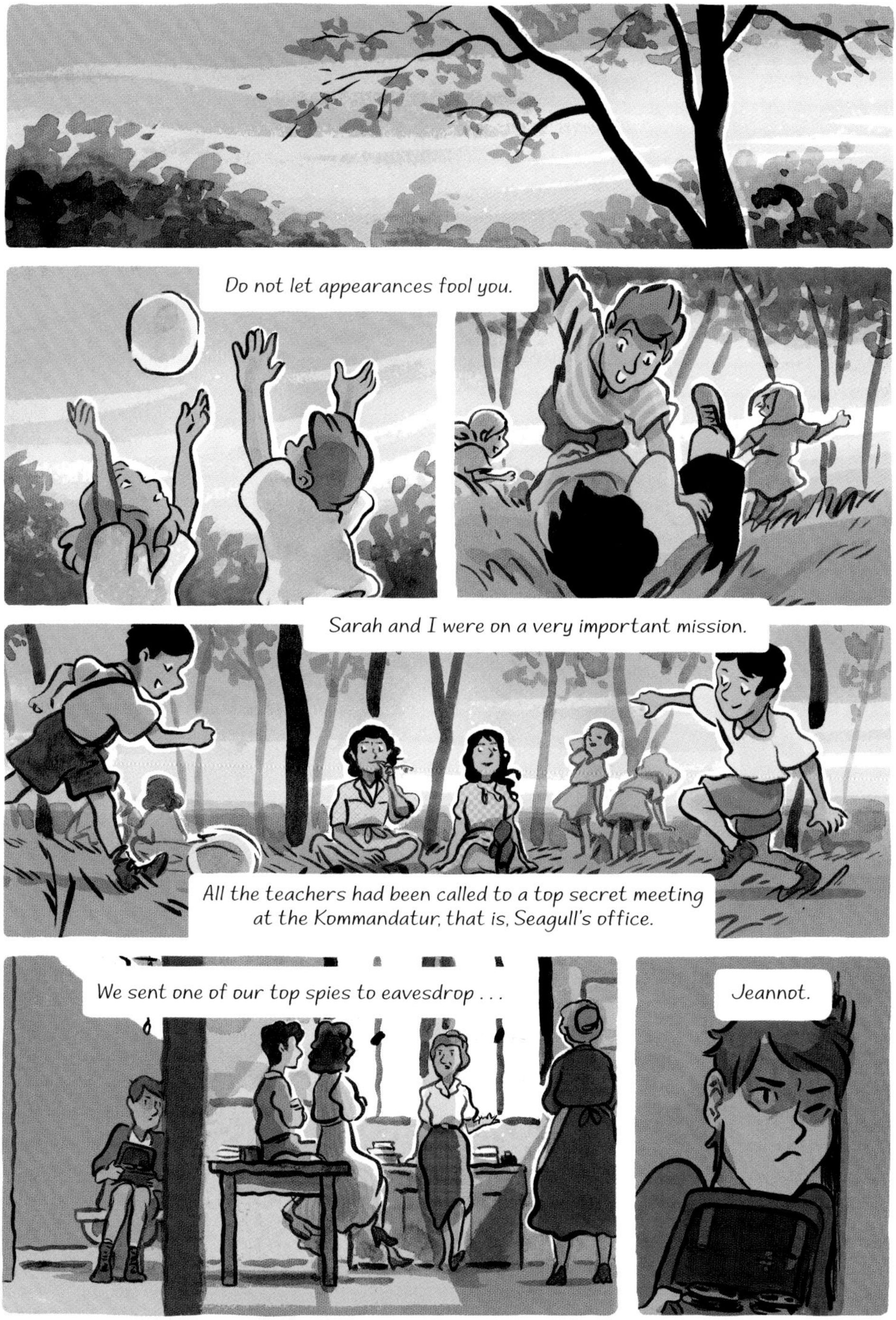
Do not let appearances fool you.
Sarah and I were on a very important mission.
All the teachers had been called to a top secret meeting at the Kommandatur, that is, Seagull's office.
We sent one of our top spies to eavesdrop . . .
Jeannot.

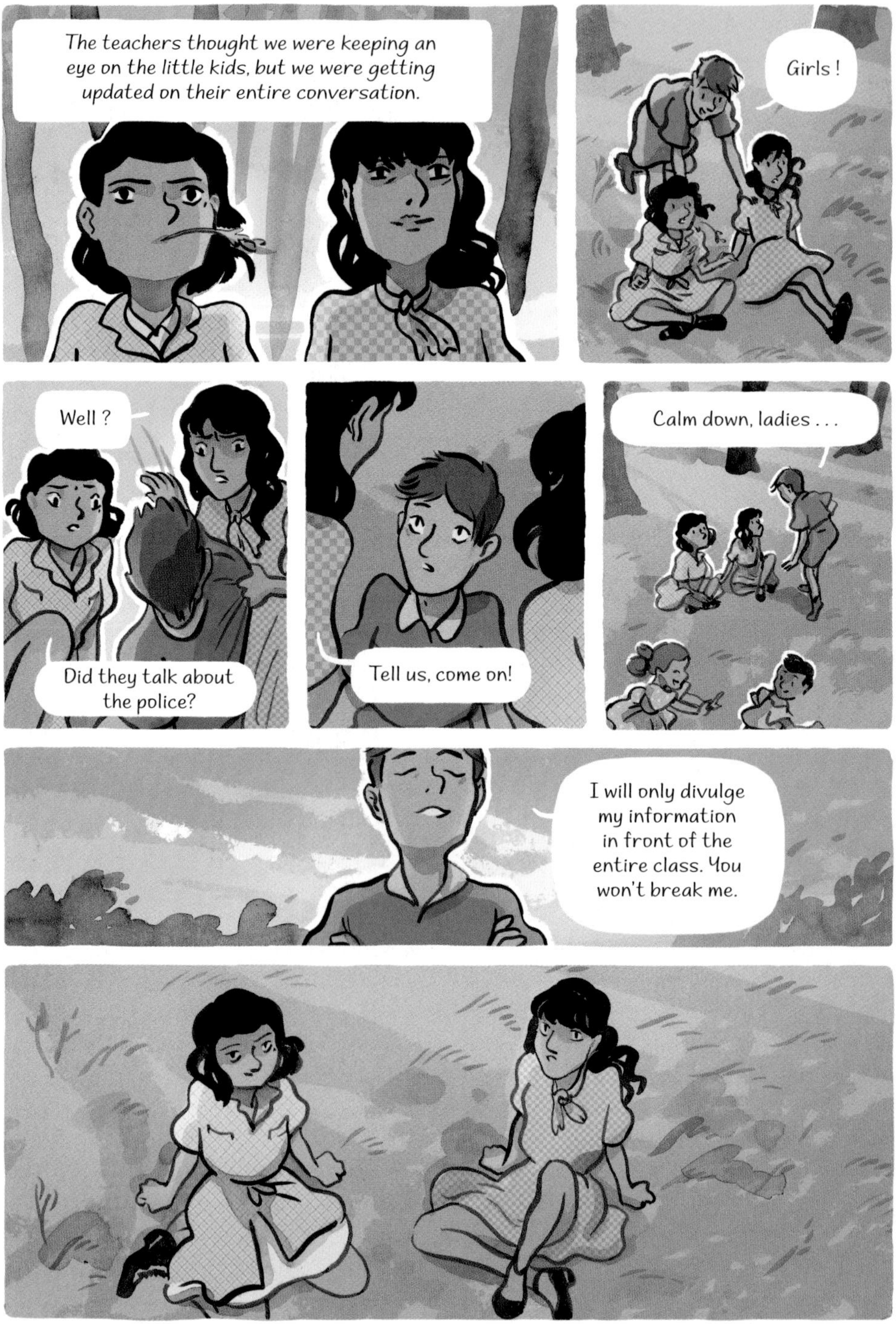
The teachers thought we were keeping an eye on the little kids, but we were getting updated on their entire conversation.
Girls!
Well?
Did they talk about the police?
Tell us, come on!
Calm down, ladies . . .
I will only divulge my information in front of the entire class. You won't break me.

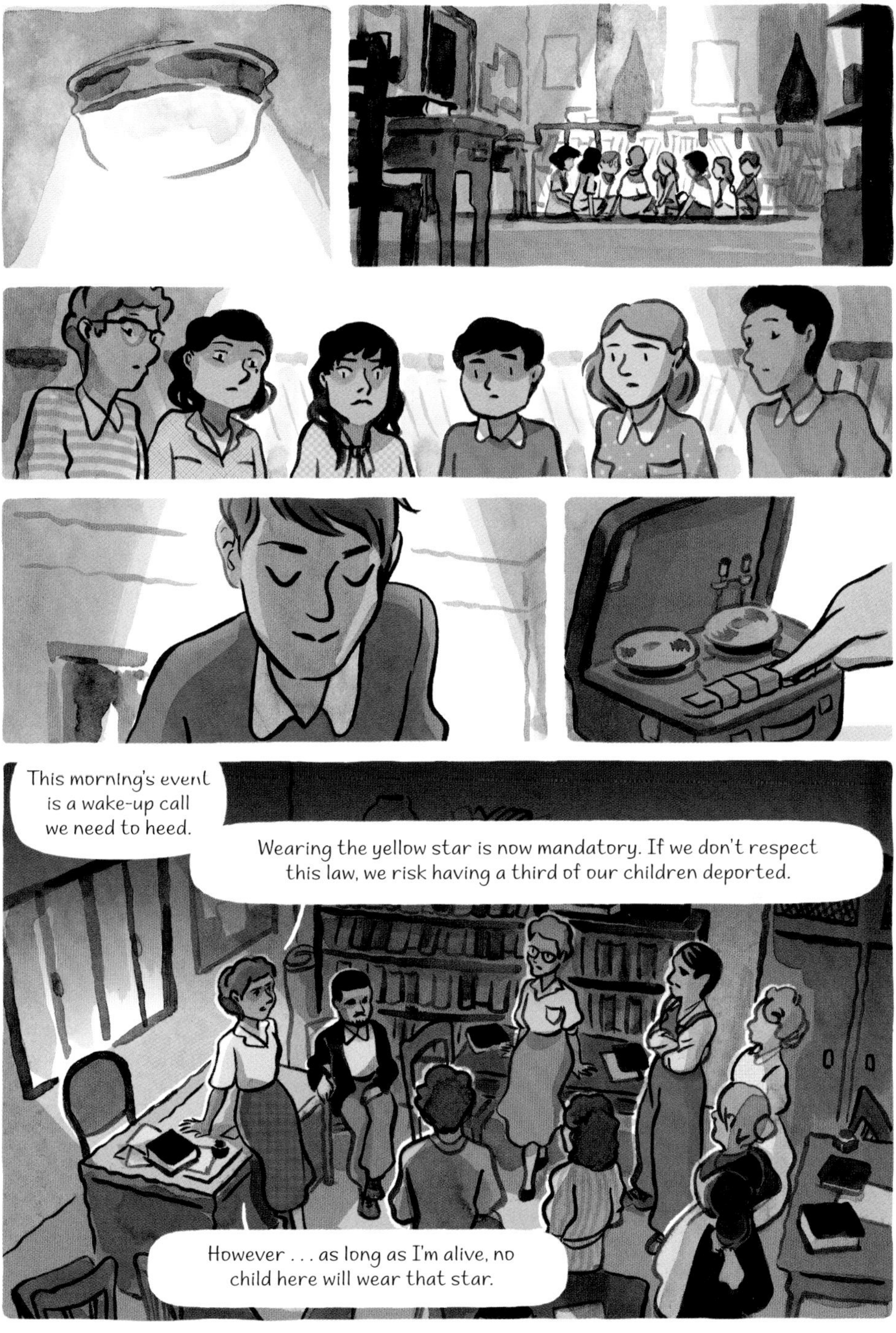
This morning's event is a wake-up call we need to heed.
Wearing the yellow star is now mandatory. If we don't respect this law, we risk having a third of our children deported.
However . . . as long as I'm alive, no child here will wear that star.

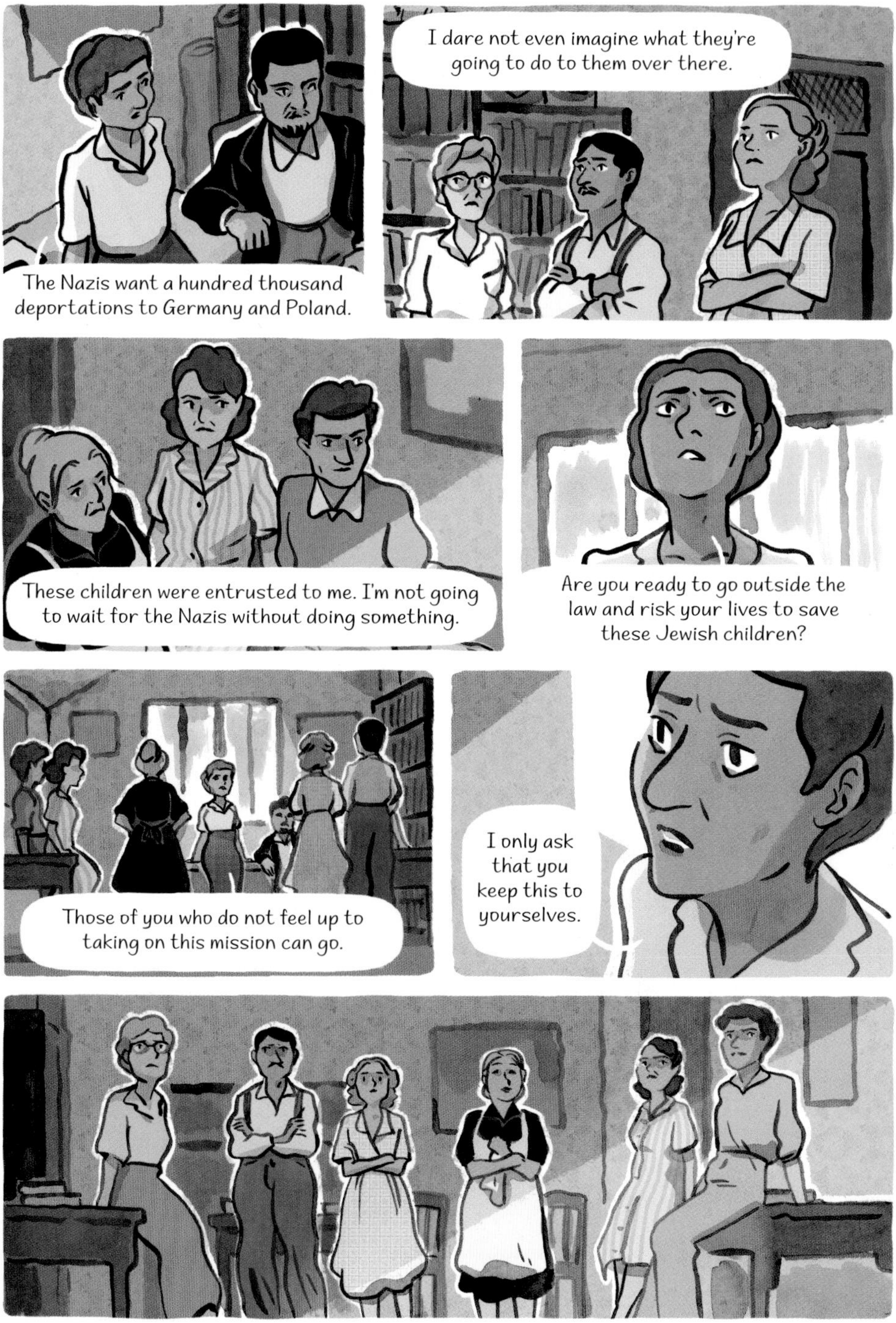
The Nazis want a hundred thousand deportations to Germany and Poland.
I dare not even imagine what they're going to do to them over there.
These children were entrusted to me. I'm not going to wait for the Nazis without doing something.
Are you ready to go outside the law and risk your lives to save these Jewish children?
Those of you who do not feel up to taking on this mission can go.
I only ask that you keep this to yourselves.

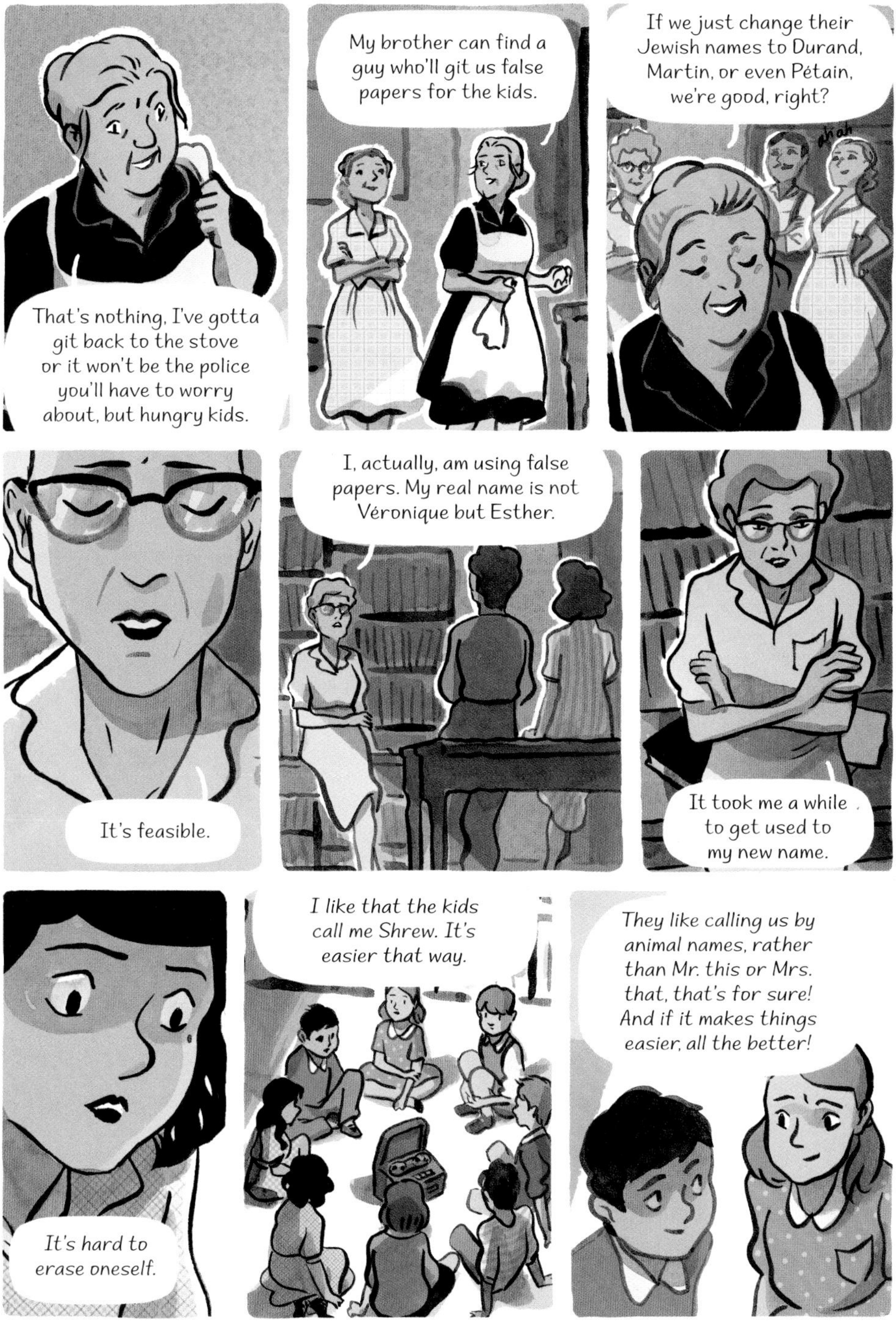
That's nothing, I've gotta git back to the stove or it won't be the police you'll have to worry about, but hungry kids.
My brother can find a guy who'll git us false papers for the kids.
If we just change their Jewish names to Durand, Martin, or even Pétain, we're good, right?
It's feasible.
I, actually, am using false papers. My real name is not Véronique but Esther.
It took me a while to get used to my new name.
It's hard to erase oneself.
I like that the kids call me Shrew. It's easier that way.
They like calling us by animal names, rather than Mr. this or Mrs. that, that's for sure! And if it makes things easier, all the better!

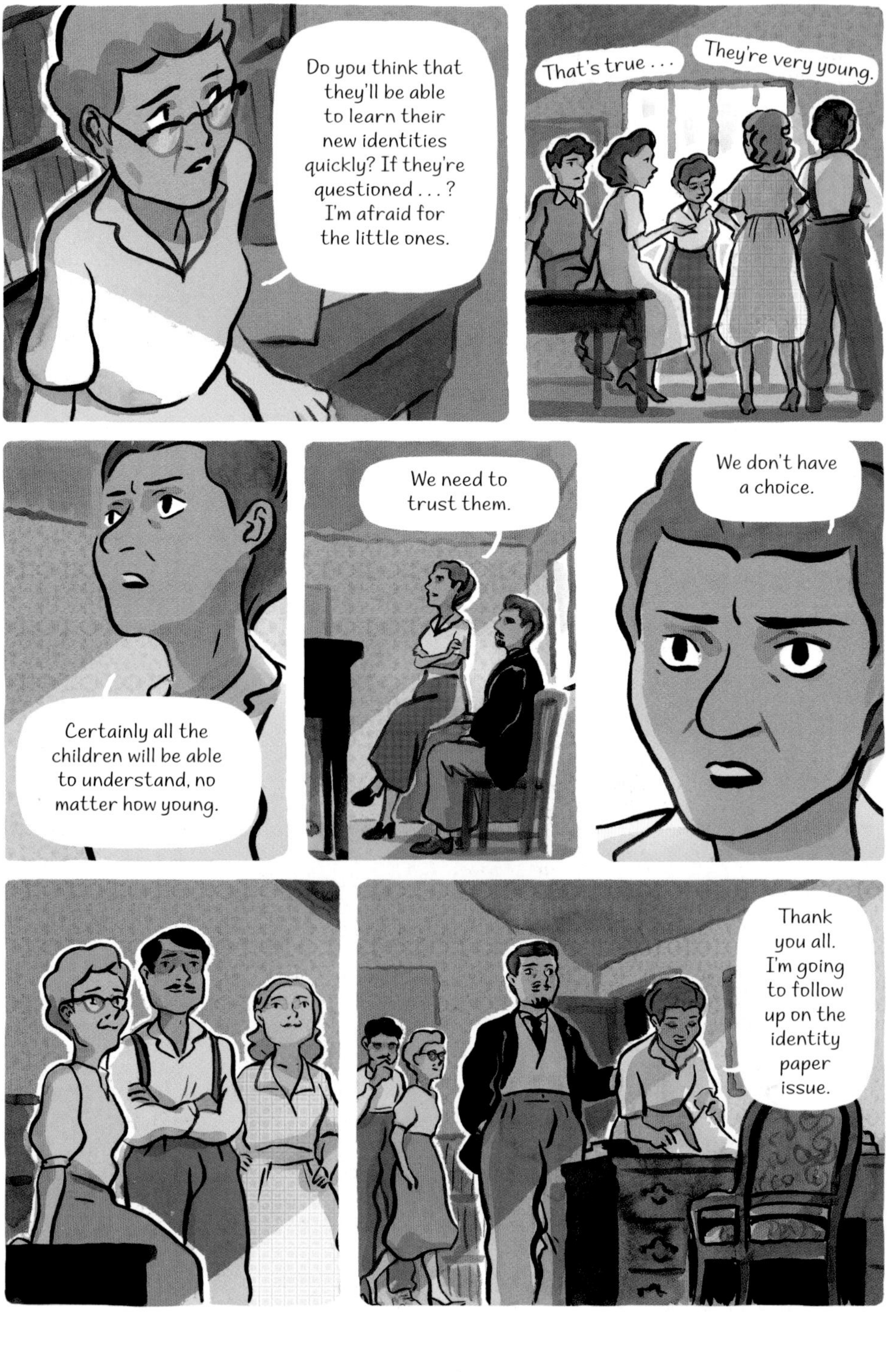

Do you think that they'll be able to learn their new identities quickly? If they're questioned . . . ? I'm afraid for the little ones.
That's true . . .
They're very young.
Certainly all the children will be able to understand, no matter how young.
We need to trust them.
We don't have a choice.
Thank you all. I'm going to follow up on the identity paper issue.

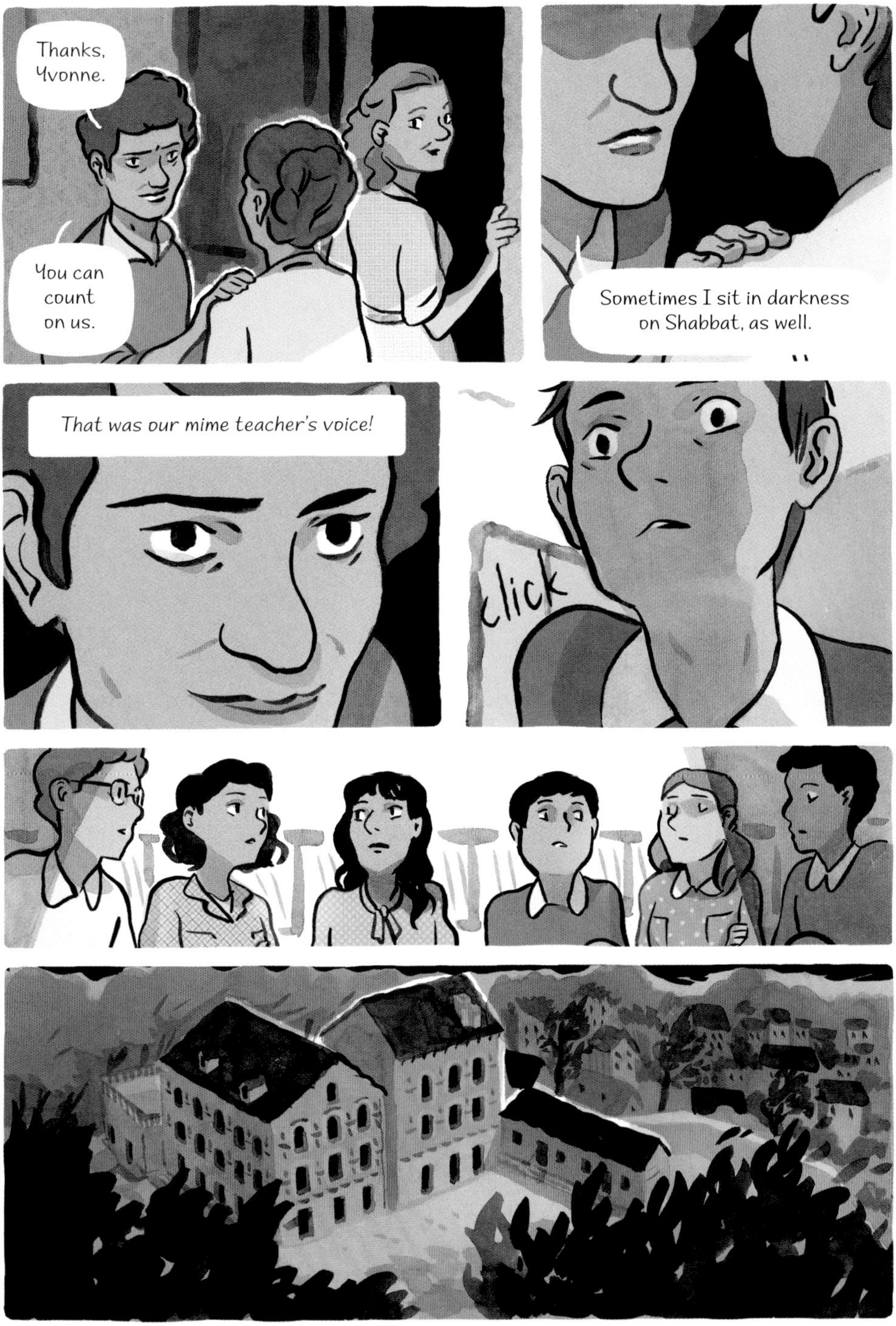

Thanks, Yvonne.
You can count on us.
Sometimes I sit in darkness on Shabbat, as well.
That was our mime teacher's voice!
click

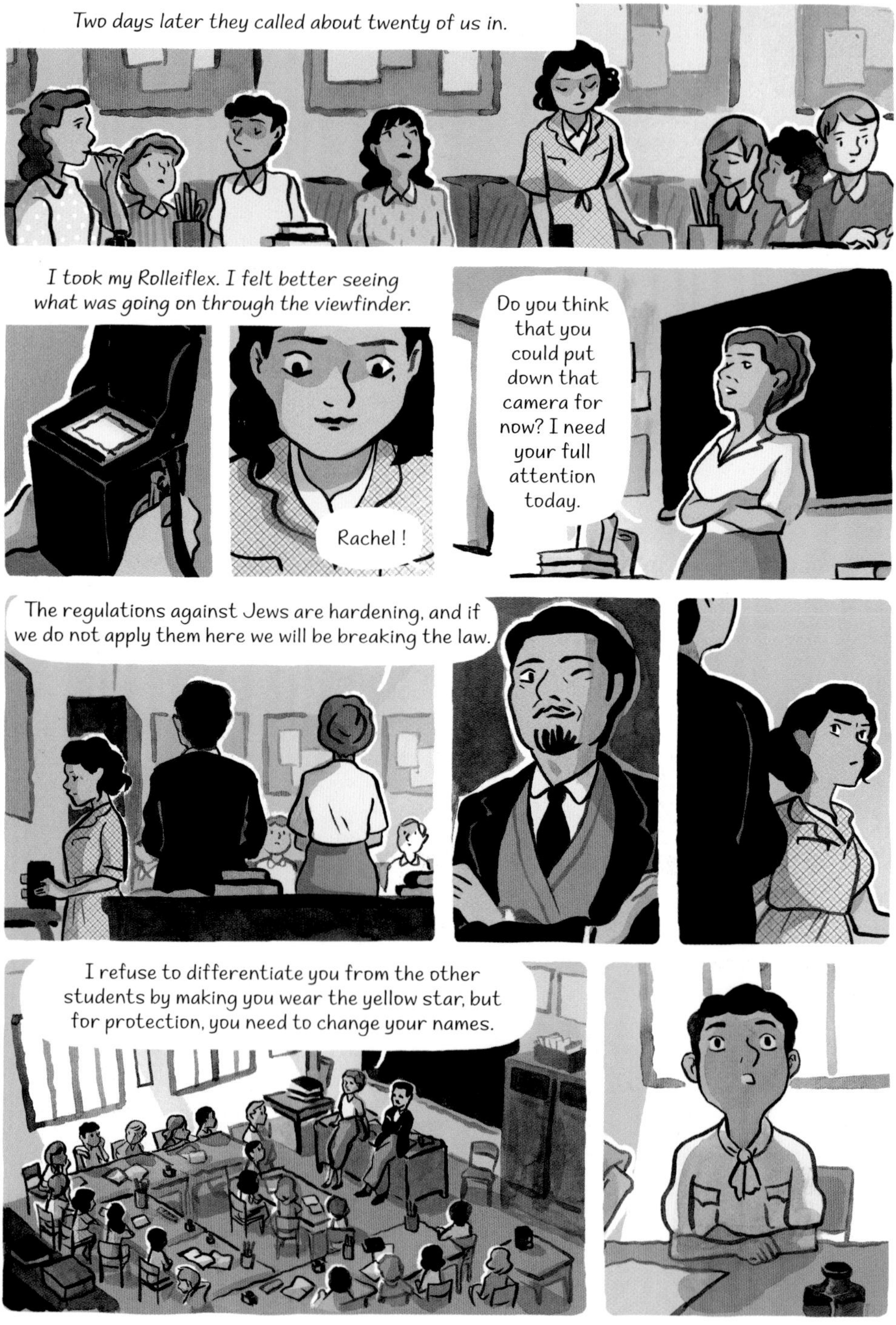
Two days later they called about twenty of us in.
I took my Rolleiflex. I felt better seeing what was going on through the viewfinder.
Rachel !
Do you think that you could put down that camera for now? I need your full attention today.
The regulations against Jews are hardening, and if we do not apply them here we will be breaking the law.
I refuse to differentiate you from the other students by making you wear the yellow star, but for protection, you need to change your names.

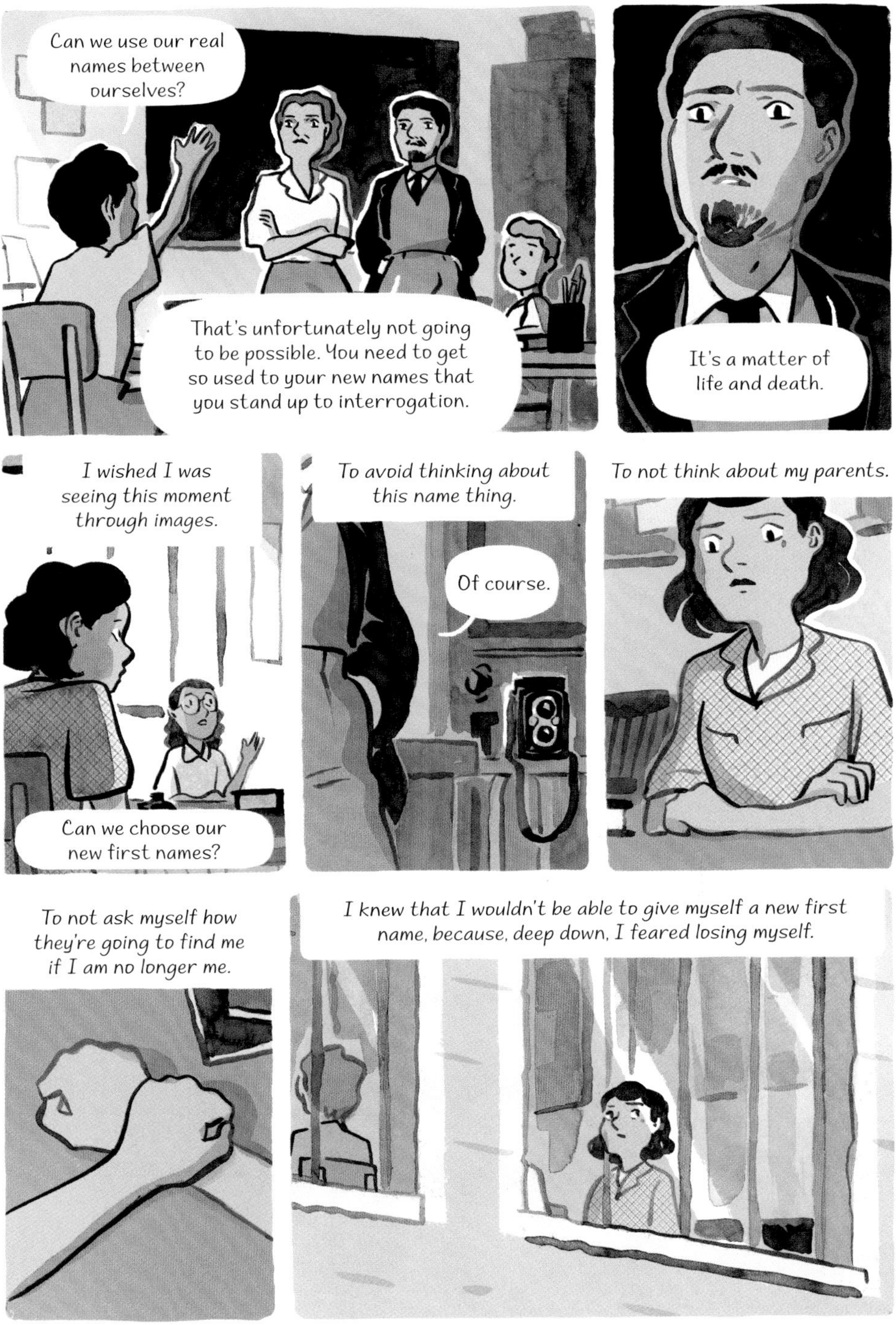
Can we use our real names between ourselves?
That's unfortunately not going to be possible. You need to get so used to your new names that you stand up to interrogation.
It's a matter of life and death.
I wished I was seeing this moment through images.
Can we choose our new first names?
To avoid thinking about this name thing.
Of course.
To not think about my parents.
To not ask myself how they're going to find me if I am no longer me.
I knew that I wouldn't be able to give myself a new first name, because, deep down, I feared losing myself.

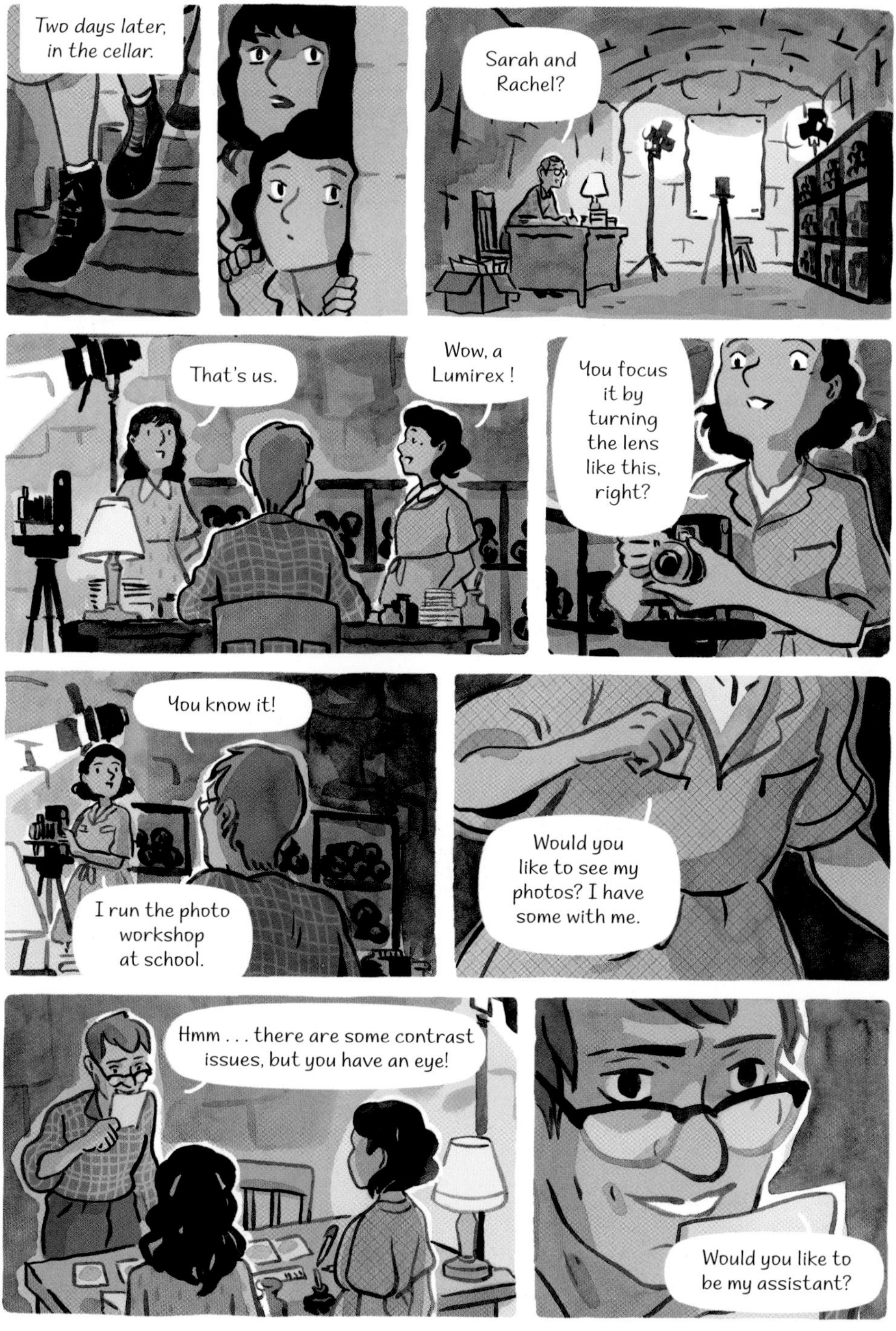
Two days later, in the cellar.
Sarah and Rachel?
That's us.
Wow, a Lumirex!
You focus it by turning the lens like this, right?
You know it!
I run the photo workshop at school.
Would you like to see my photos? I have some with me.
Hmm . . . there are some contrast issues, but you have an eye!
Would you like to be my assistant?

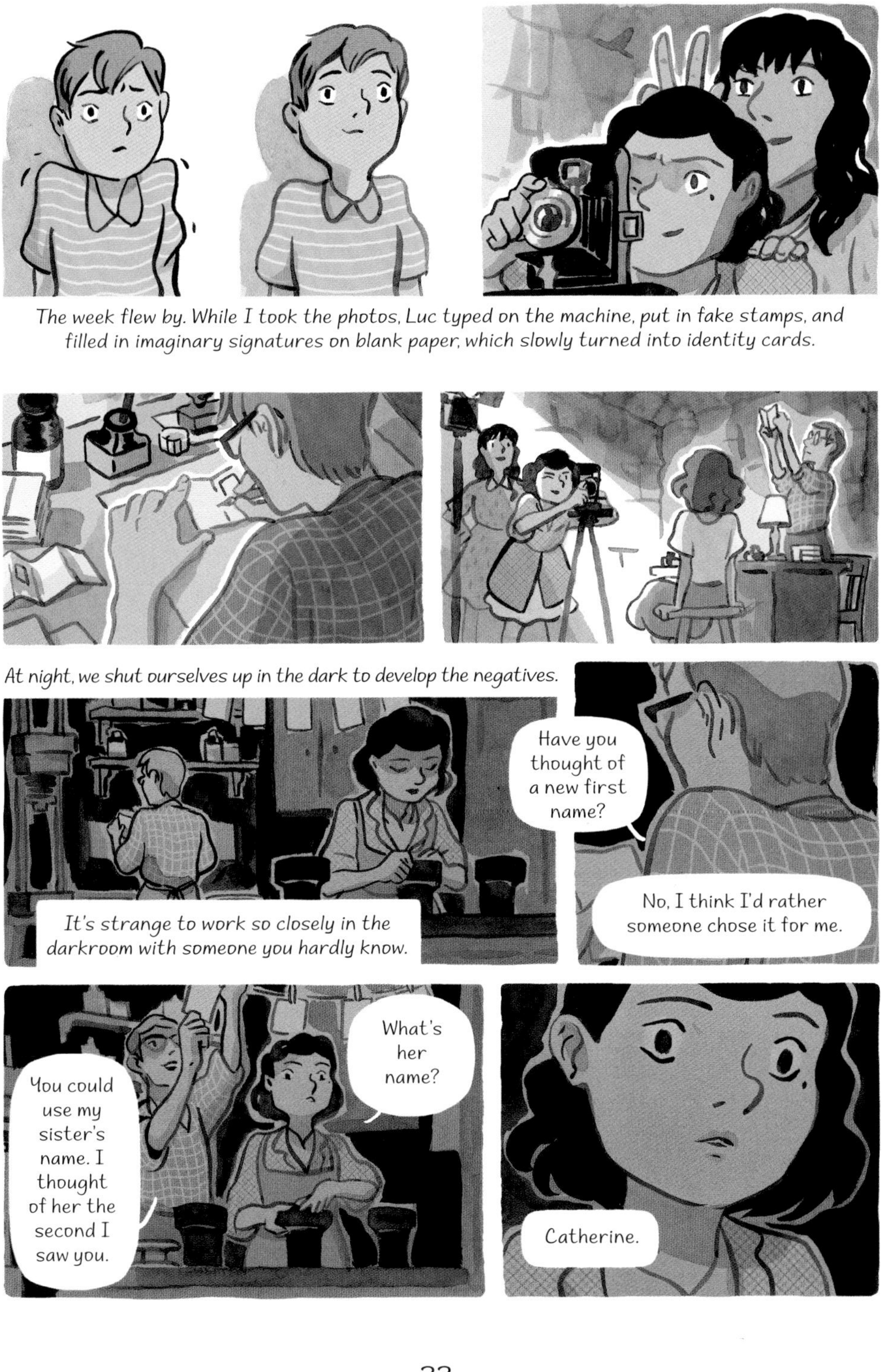
The week flew by. While I took the photos, Luc typed on the machine, put in fake stamps, and filled in imaginary signatures on blank paper, which slowly turned into identity cards.
At night, we shut ourselves up in the dark to develop the negatives.
It's strange to work so closely in the darkroom with someone you hardly know.
Have you thought of a new first name?
No, I think I'd rather someone chose it for me.
You could use my sister's name. I thought of her the second I saw you.
What's her name?
Catherine.

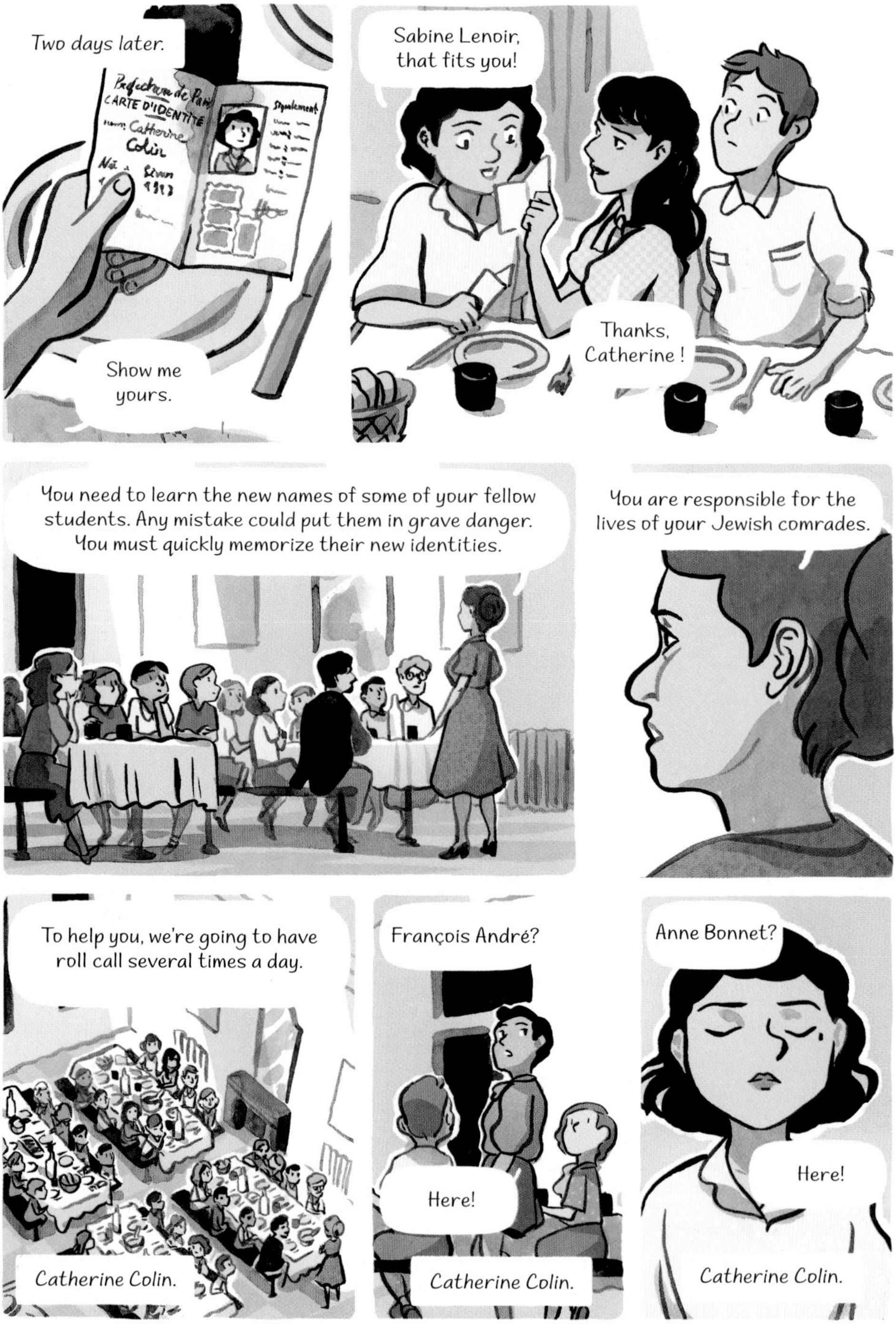
Two days later.
Prefecture de Paris
CARTE D'IDENTITÉ
Catherine Colin
Show me yours.
Sabine Lenoir, that fits you!
Thanks, Catherine!
You need to learn the new names of some of your fellow students. Any mistake could put them in grave danger. You must quickly memorize their new identities.
You are responsible for the lives of your Jewish comrades.
To help you, we're going to have roll call several times a day.
Catherine Colin.
François André?
Here!
Catherine Colin.
Anne Bonnet?
Here!
Catherine Colin.

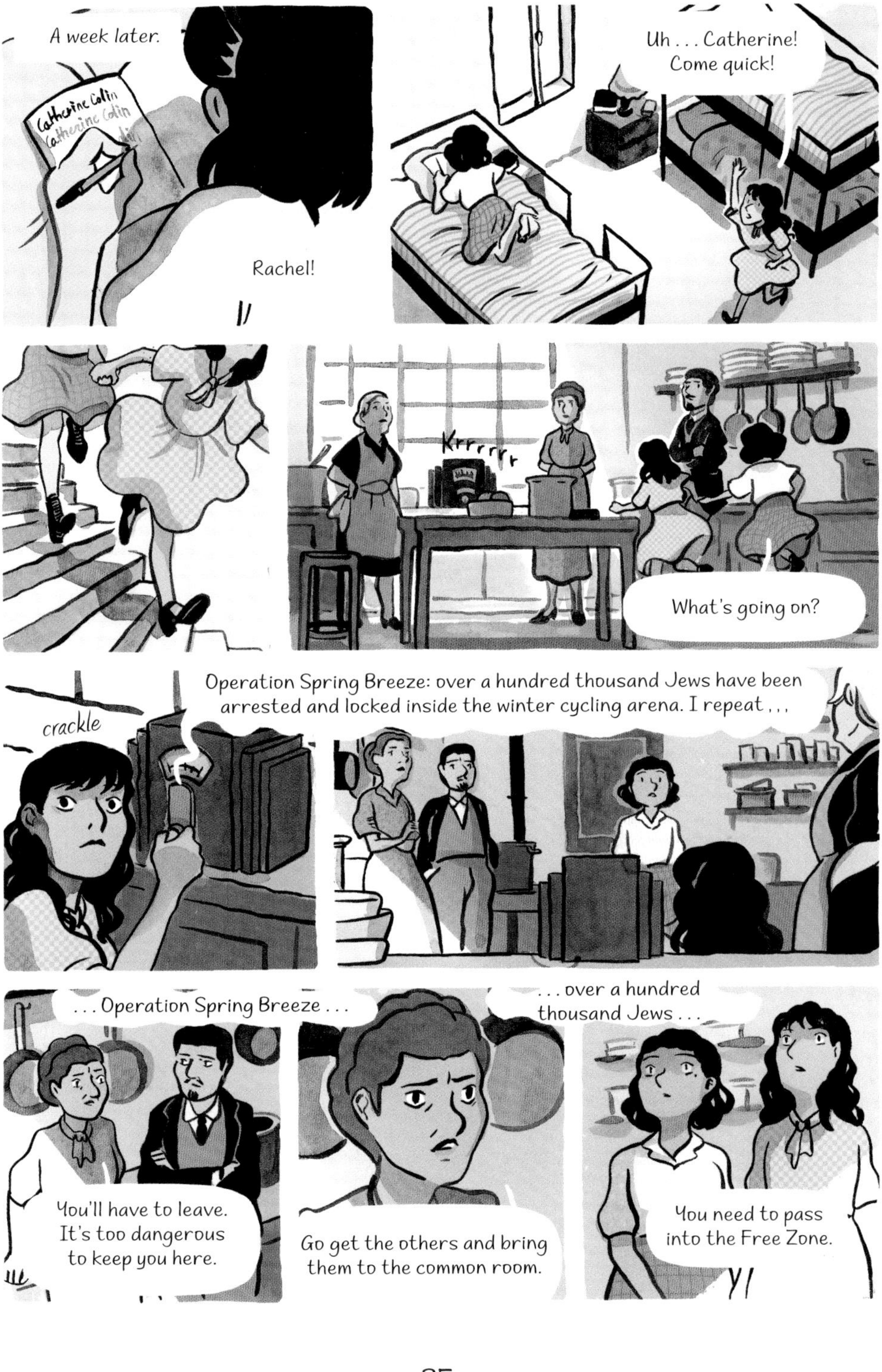
A week later.
Catherine Colin
Catherine Colin
Rachel!
Uh . . . Catherine! Come quick!
Krrrrrr
What's going on?
Operation Spring Breeze: over a hundred thousand Jews have been arrested and locked inside the winter cycling arena. I repeat . . .
crackle
. . . Operation Spring Breeze . . .
. . . over a hundred thousand Jews . . .
You'll have to leave. It's too dangerous to keep you here.
Go get the others and bring them to the common room.
You need to pass into the Free Zone.

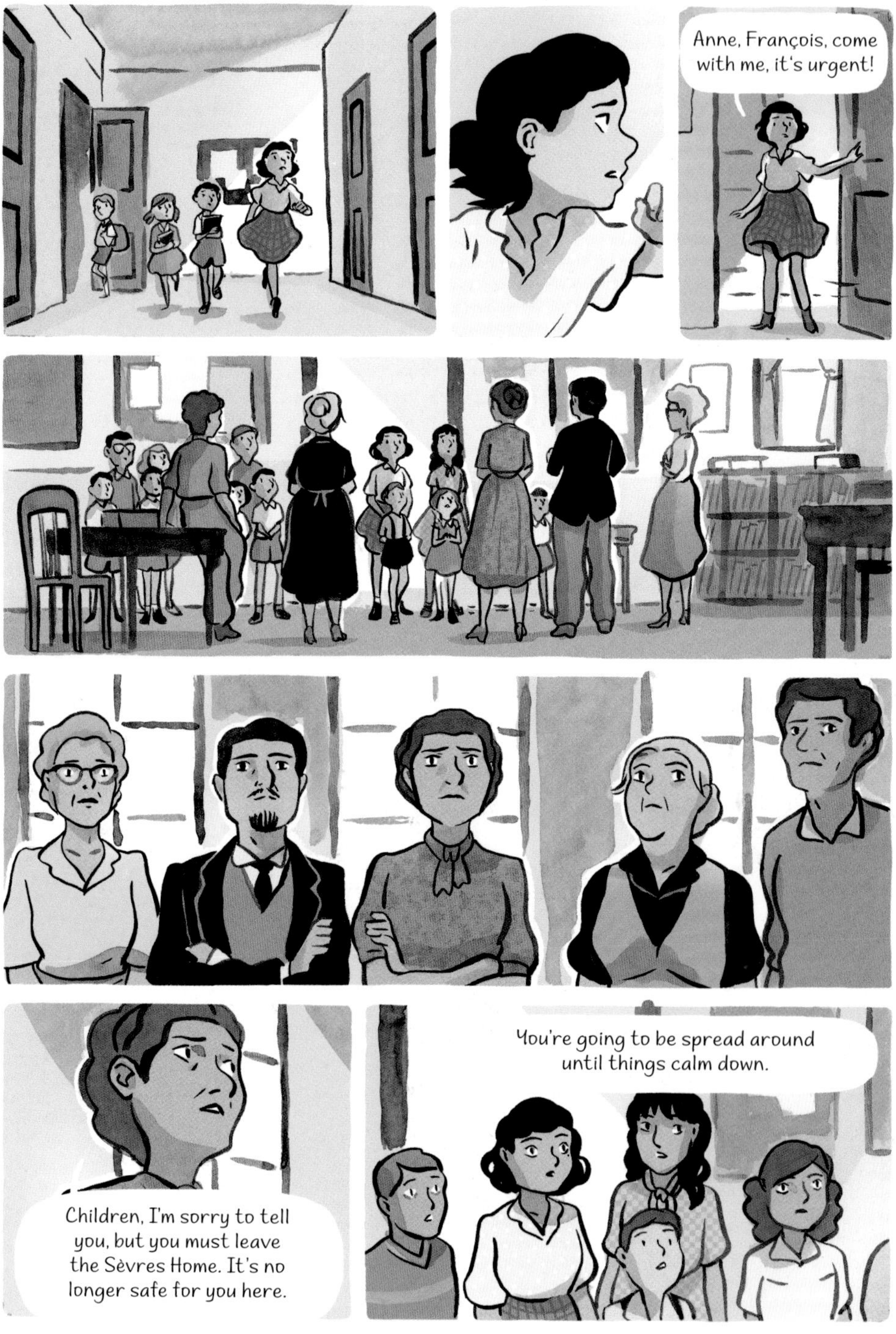
Anne, François, come with me, it's urgent!
Children, I'm sorry to tell you, but you must leave the Sèvres Home. It's no longer safe for you here.
You're going to be spread around until things calm down.

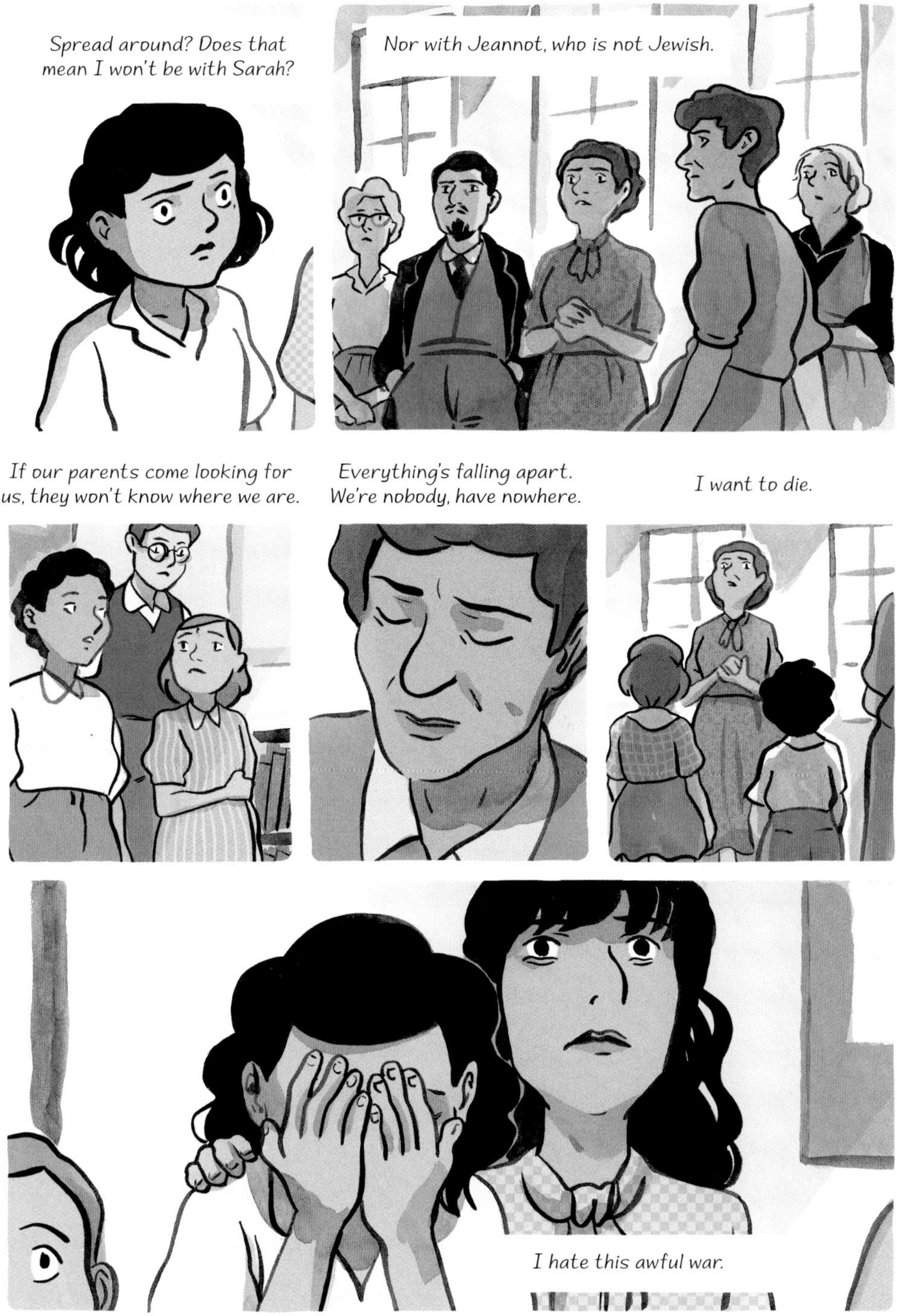
Spread around? Does that mean I won't be with Sarah?
Nor with Jeannot, who is not Jewish.
If our parents come looking for us, they won't know where we are.
Everything's falling apart. We're nobody, have nowhere.
I want to die.
I hate this awful war.

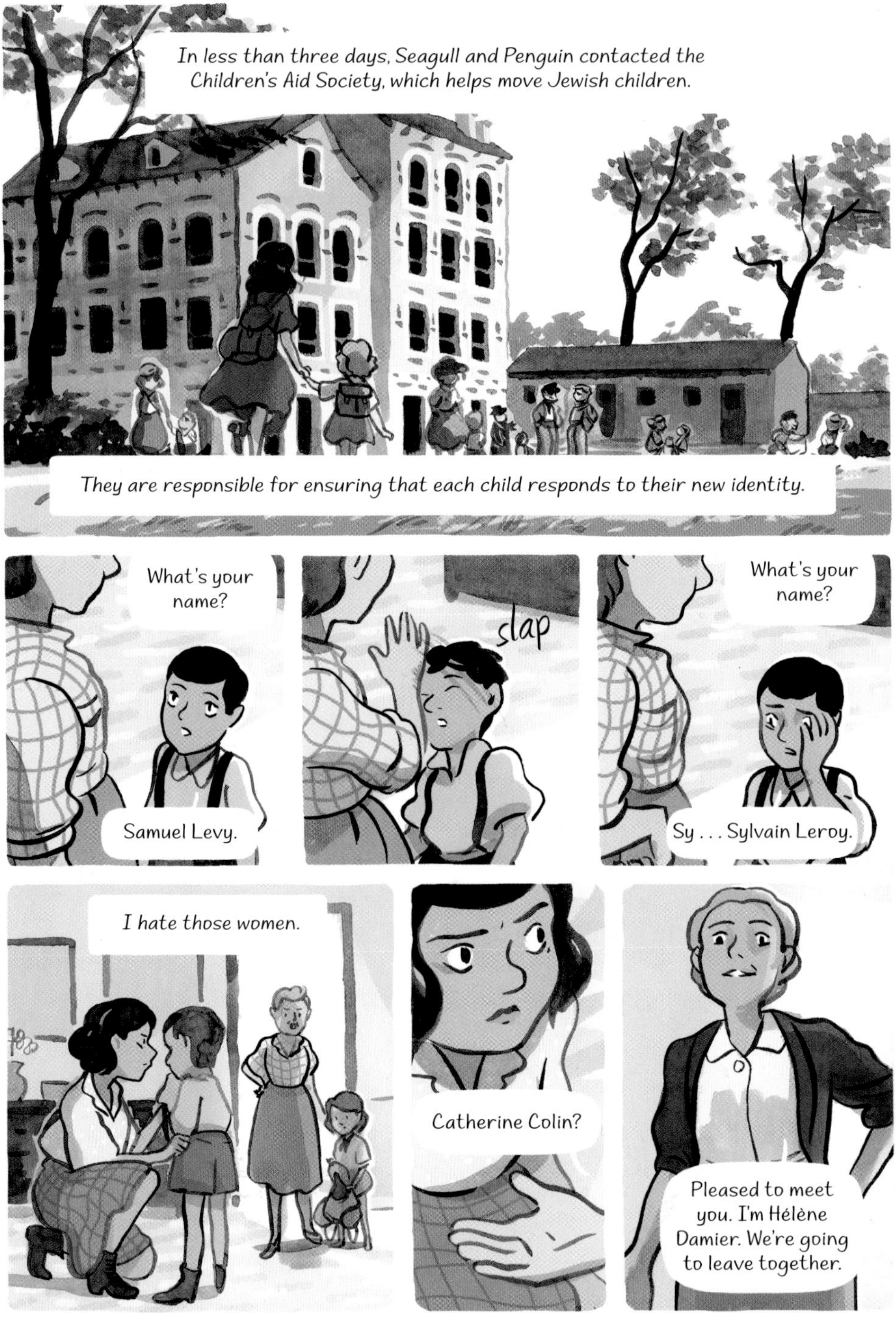
In less than three days, Seagull and Penguin contacted the Children's Aid Society, which helps move Jewish children.
They are responsible for ensuring that each child responds to their new identity.
What's your name?
Samuel Levy.
slap
What's your name?
Sy . . . Sylvain Leroy.
I hate those women.
Catherine Colin?
Pleased to meet you. I'm Hélène Damier. We're going to leave together.

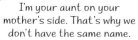

I'm your aunt on your mother's side. That's why we don't have the same name.

She asked me to accompany you because I live on the family farm near the convent where you're going to stay.

I can't tell you where it is. It's best to know as little as possible in the event that we're arrested.

That's a rule of the Resistance,

The Resistance! And I criticized these women.

I suddenly felt like an idiot.

We'll leave tomorrow. Don't take too much, but do bring warm clothes.

We have a long road ahead . . .

Leave anything that will weigh you down.

What're you doing?

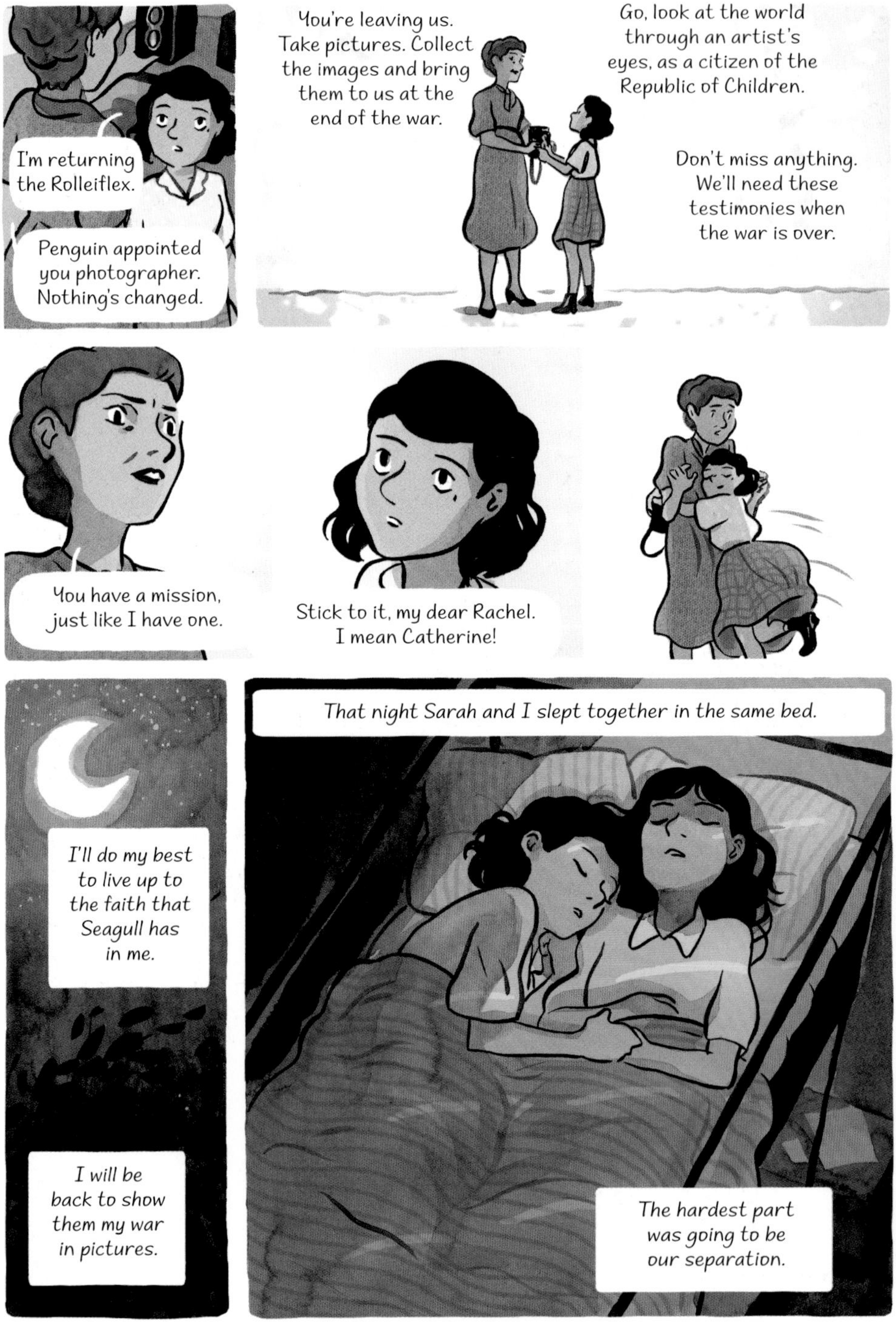
I'm returning the Rolleiflex.
Penguin appointed you photographer. Nothing's changed.
You're leaving us. Take pictures. Collect the images and bring them to us at the end of the war.
Go, look at the world through an artist's eyes, as a citizen of the Republic of Children.
Don't miss anything. We'll need these testimonies when the war is over.
You have a mission, just like I have one.
Stick to it, my dear Rachel. I mean Catherine!
I'll do my best to live up to the faith that Seagull has in me.
I will be back to show them my war in pictures.
That night Sarah and I slept together in the same bed.
The hardest part was going to be our separation.

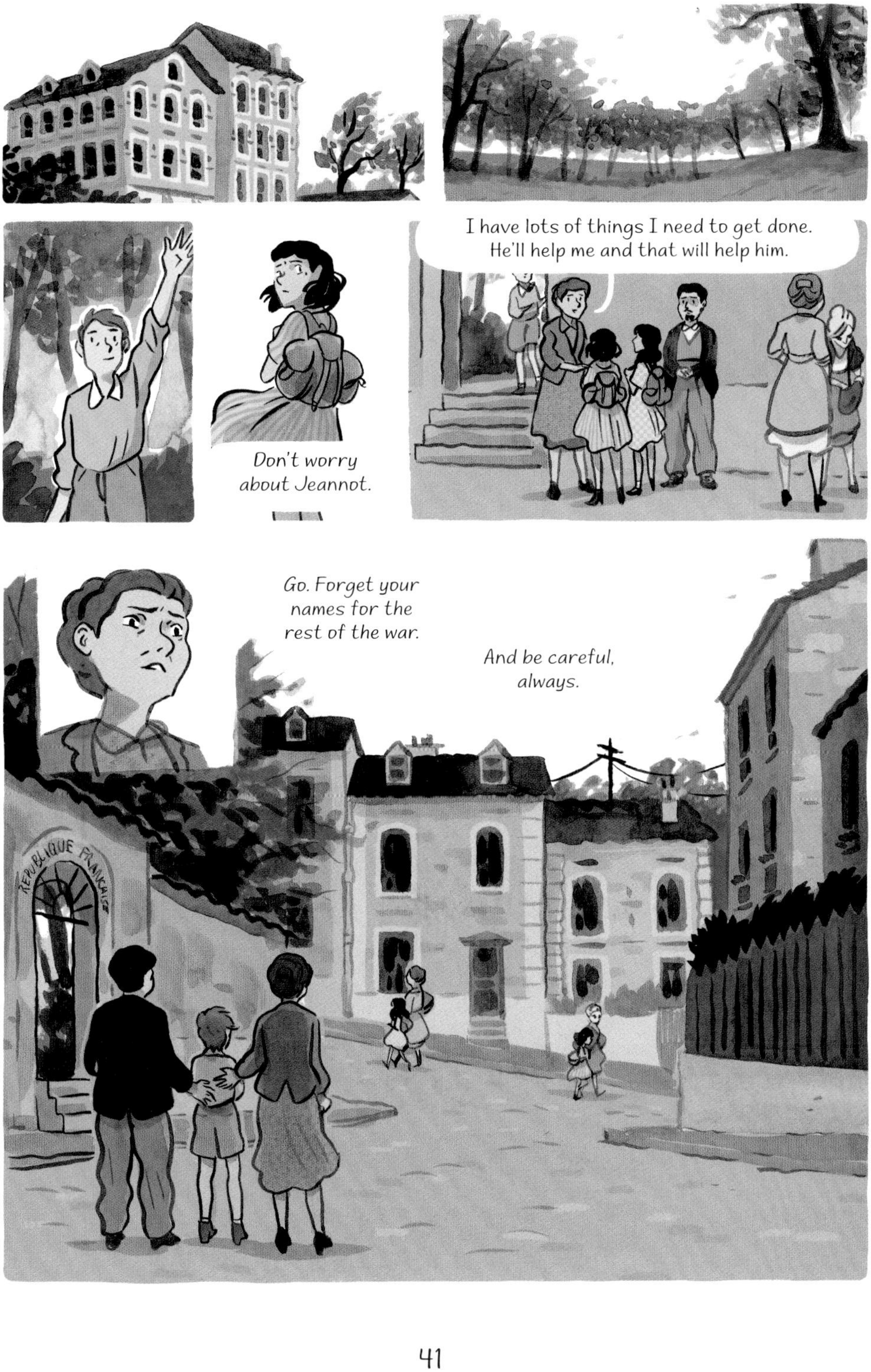
Don't worry
about Jeannot.
I have lots of things I need to get done.
He'll help me and that will help him.
Go. Forget your
names for the
rest of the war.
And be careful,
always.
REPUBLIQUE FRANCAISE

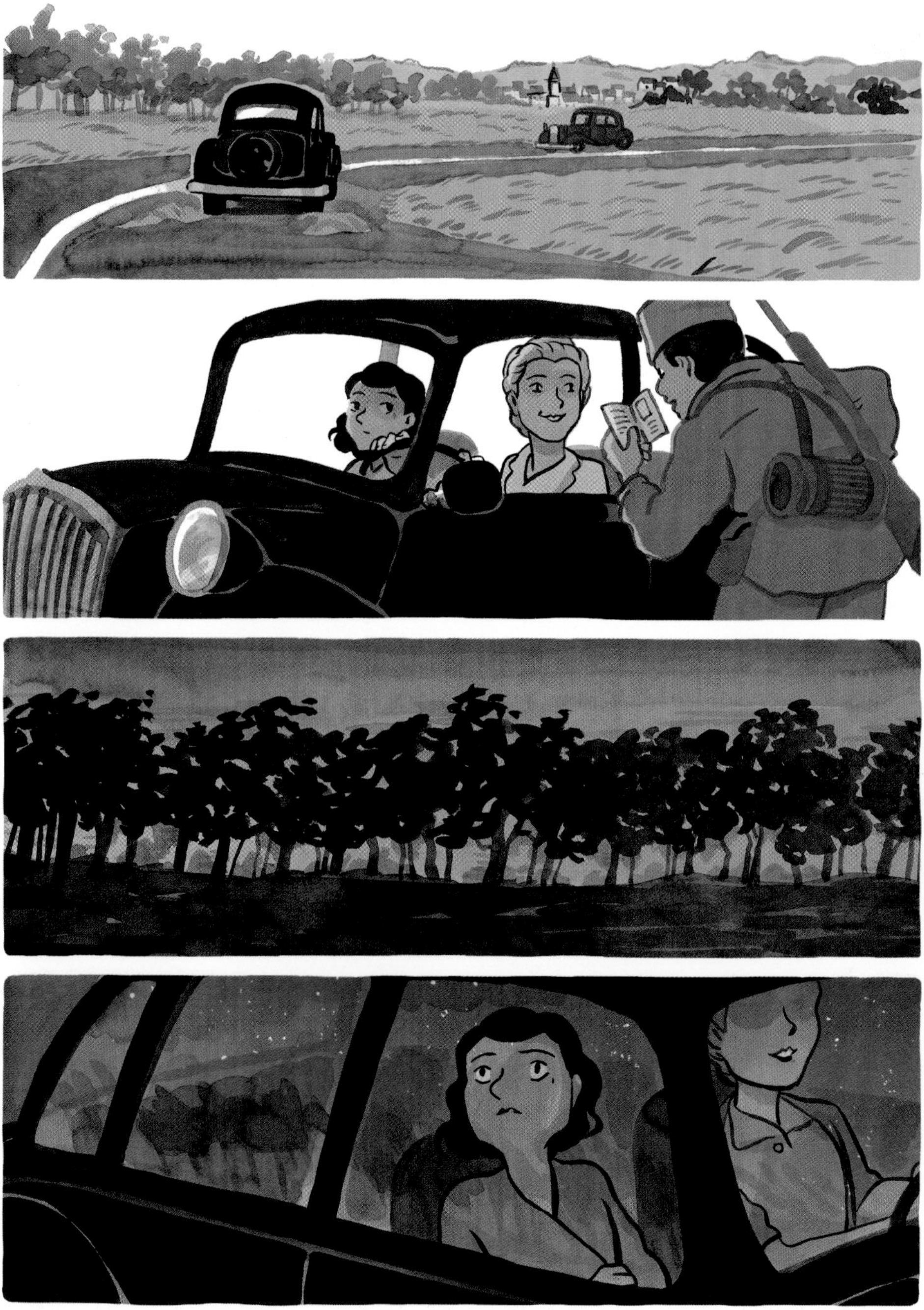

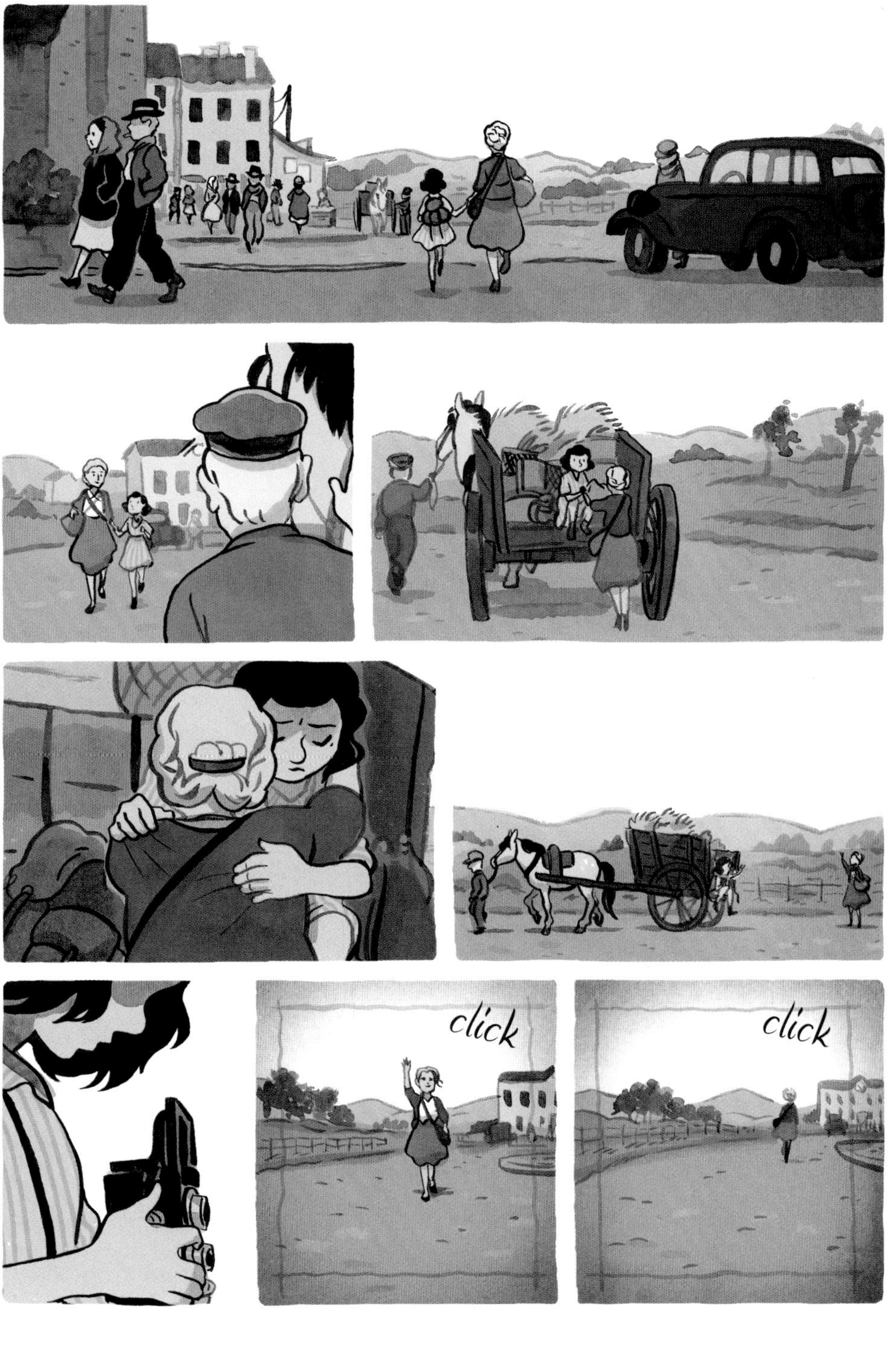
click
click

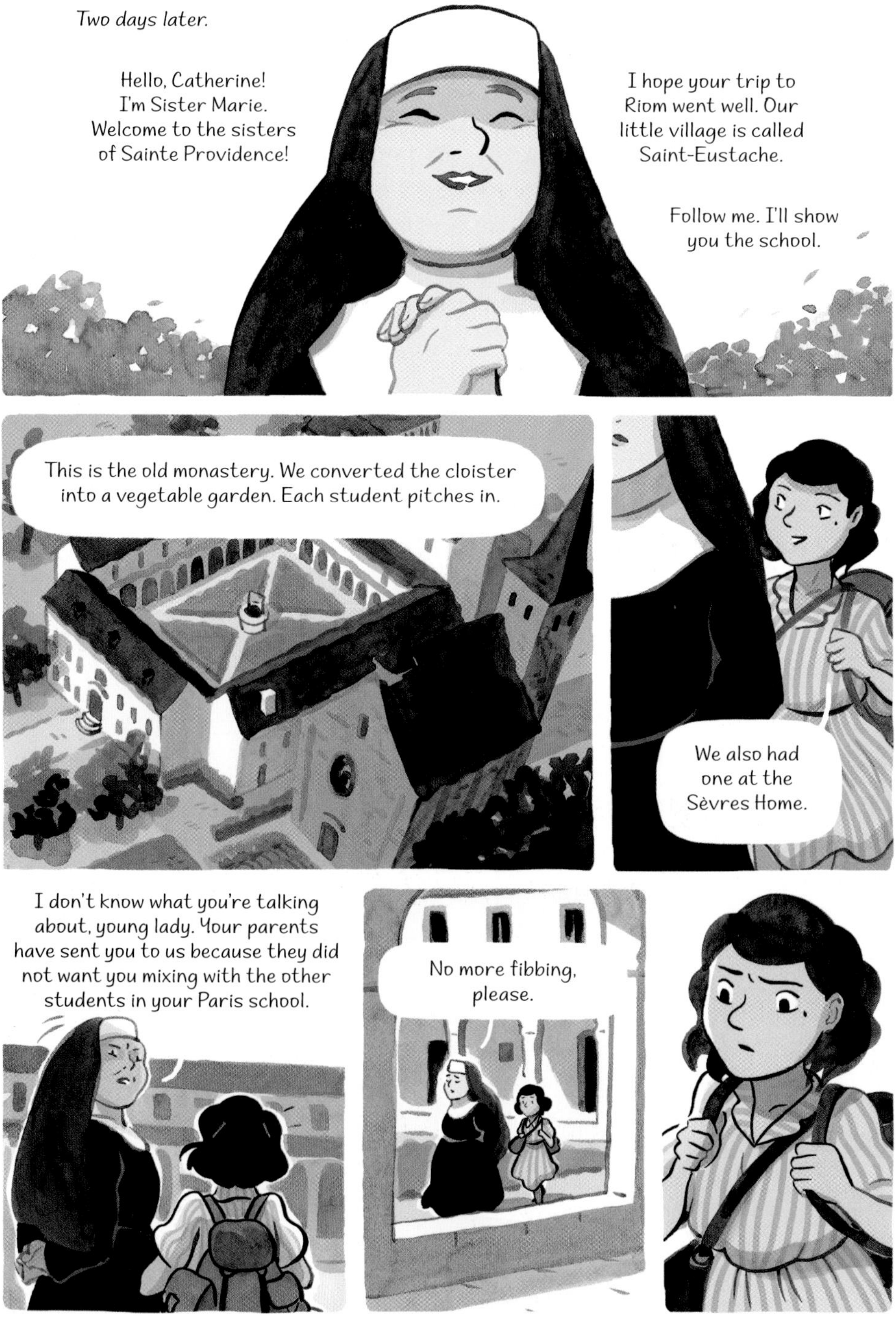
Two days later.
Hello, Catherine! I'm Sister Marie. Welcome to the sisters of Sainte Providence!
I hope your trip to Riom went well. Our little village is called Saint-Eustache.
Follow me. I'll show you the school.
This is the old monastery. We converted the cloister into a vegetable garden. Each student pitches in.
We also had one at the Sèvres Home.
I don't know what you're talking about, young lady. Your parents have sent you to us because they did not want you mixing with the other students in your Paris school.
No more fibbing, please.

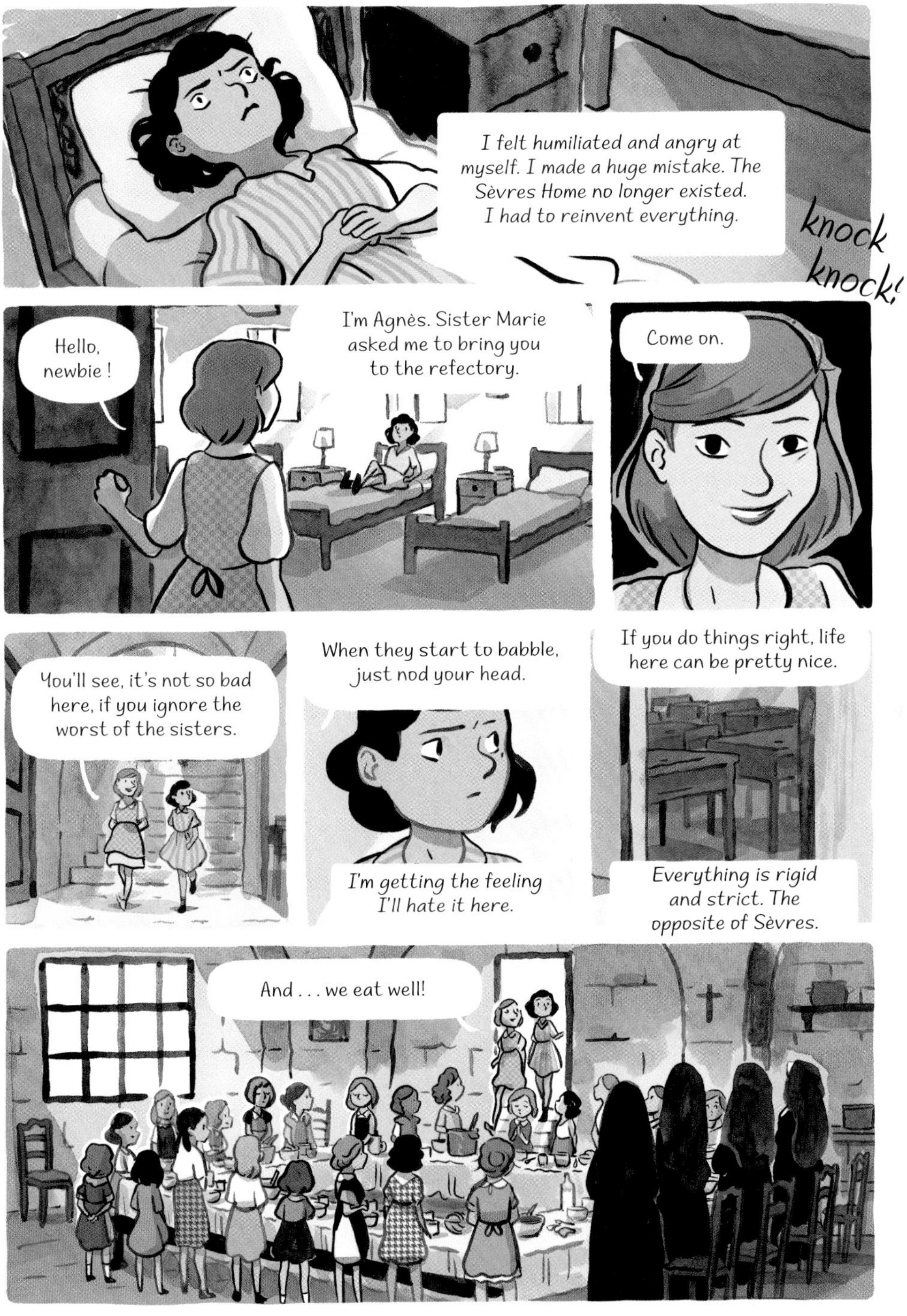
I felt humiliated and angry at myself. I made a huge mistake. The Sèvres Home no longer existed. I had to reinvent everything.
knock knock!
Hello, newbie !
I'm Agnès. Sister Marie asked me to bring you to the refectory.
Come on.
You'll see, it's not so bad here, if you ignore the worst of the sisters.
When they start to babble, just nod your head.
I'm getting the feeling I'll hate it here.
If you do things right, life here can be pretty nice.
Everything is rigid and strict. The opposite of Sèvres.
And . . . we eat well!

I would like to welcome our new student, Catherine Colin, who comes to us from Paris. I'm counting on all of you to give her a warm welcome.

That's the old lady. Mother Superior. Keep your head down when she talks to you or she'll humiliate you in front of everyone.

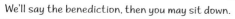

We'll say the benediction, then you may sit down.

Bless us, Lord, and bless this meal . . .

. . . Amen.

The soup smells good. What is it?

Uh, lard!

Oh no, I'm not supposed to eat pork!

Too bad, I have no choice.

It's pretty good!

Soup, salad, applesauce with cake. It's been a long time since I've left the table feeling so full.

46

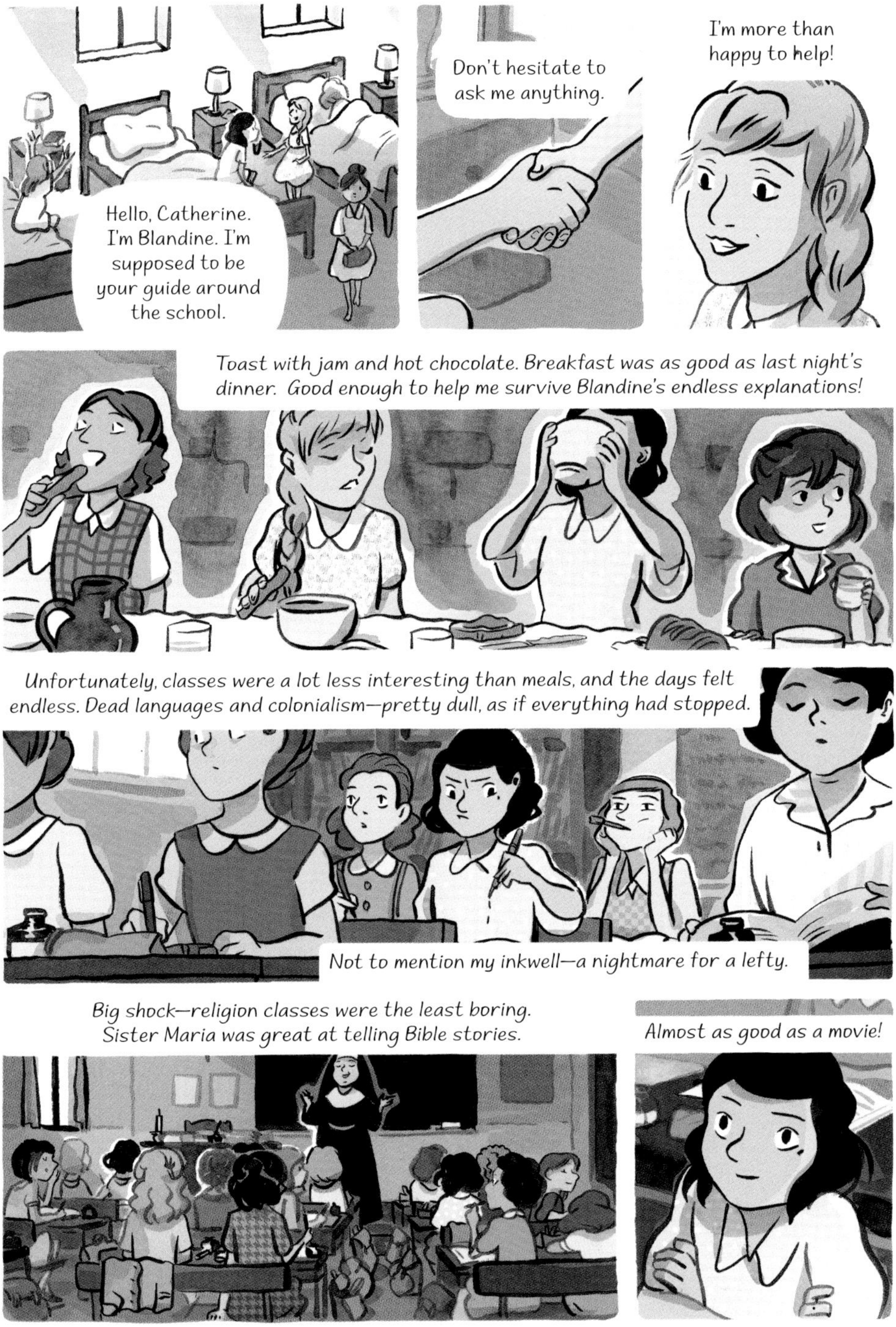
Hello, Catherine. I'm Blandine. I'm supposed to be your guide around the school.
Don't hesitate to ask me anything.
I'm more than happy to help!
Toast with jam and hot chocolate. Breakfast was as good as last night's dinner. Good enough to help me survive Blandine's endless explanations!
Unfortunately, classes were a lot less interesting than meals, and the days felt endless. Dead languages and colonialism—pretty dull, as if everything had stopped.
Not to mention my inkwell—a nightmare for a lefty.
Big shock—religion classes were the least boring. Sister Maria was great at telling Bible stories.
Almost as good as a movie!

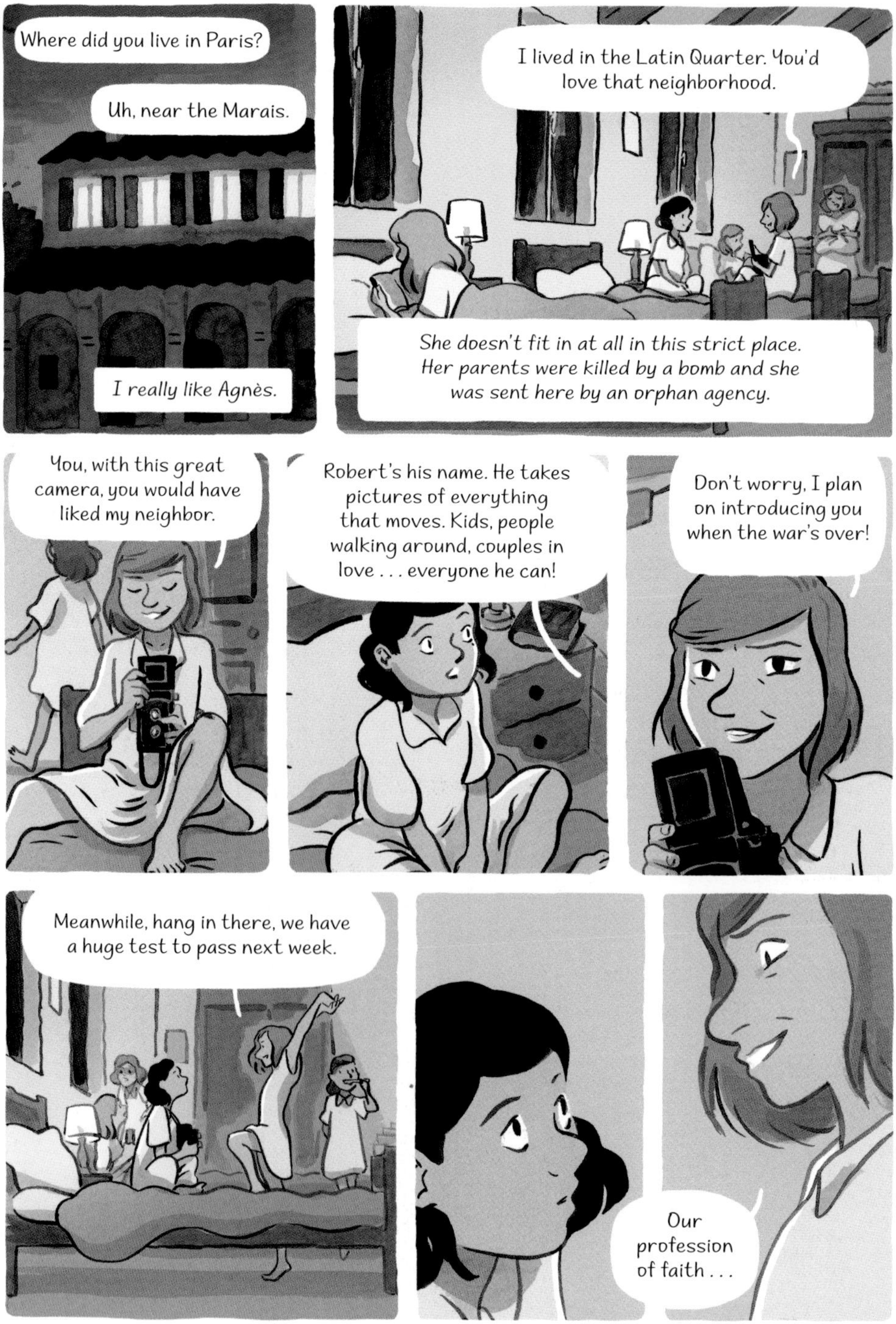
Where did you live in Paris?
Uh, near the Marais.
I really like Agnès.
I lived in the Latin Quarter. You'd love that neighborhood.
She doesn't fit in at all in this strict place. Her parents were killed by a bomb and she was sent here by an orphan agency.
You, with this great camera, you would have liked my neighbor.
Robert's his name. He takes pictures of everything that moves. Kids, people walking around, couples in love . . . everyone he can!
Don't worry, I plan on introducing you when the war's over!
Meanwhile, hang in there, we have a huge test to pass next week.
Our profession of faith . . .

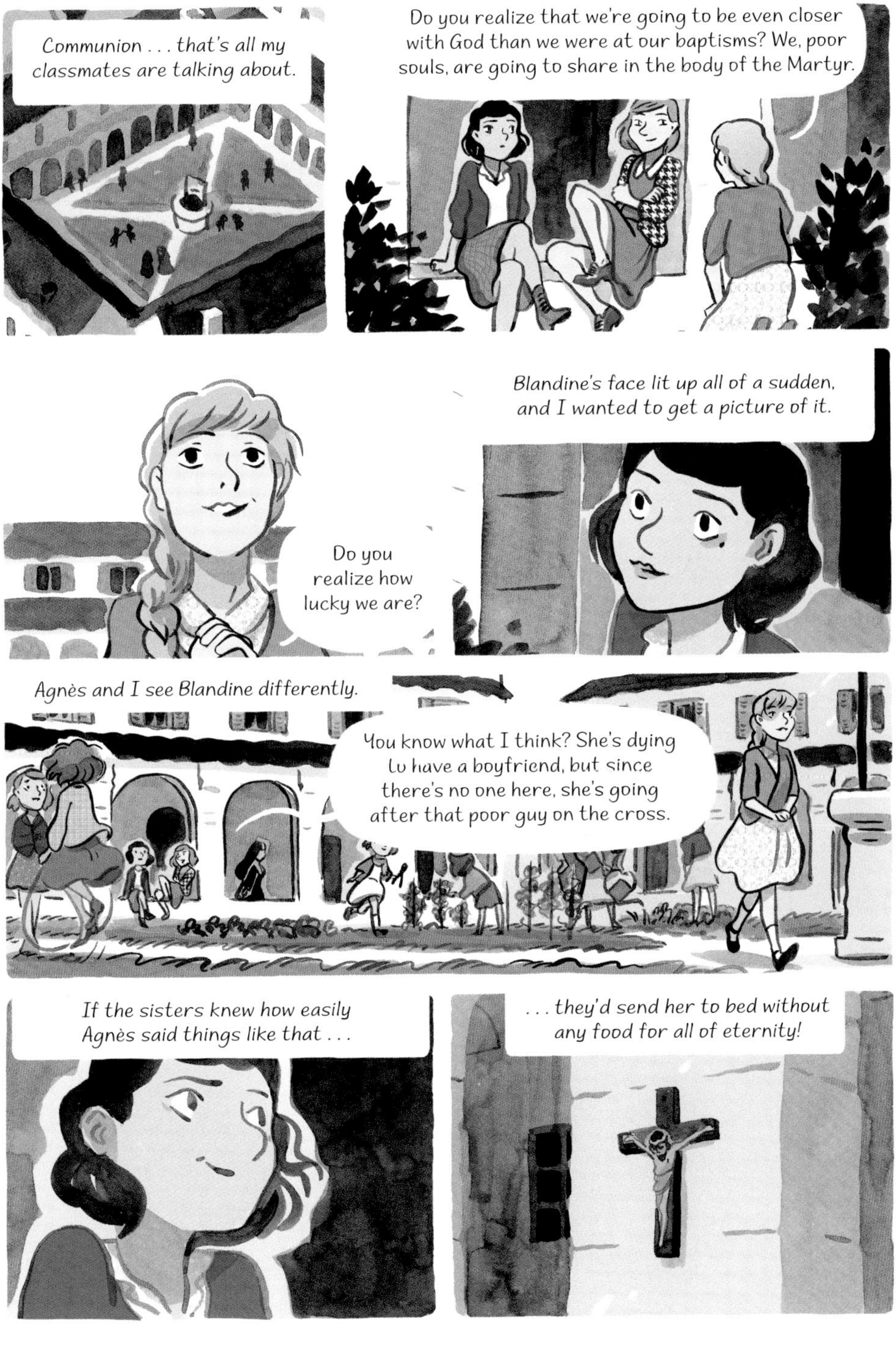
Communion . . . that's all my classmates are talking about.
Do you realize that we're going to be even closer with God than we were at our baptisms? We, poor souls, are going to share in the body of the Martyr.
Blandine's face lit up all of a sudden, and I wanted to get a picture of it.
Do you realize how lucky we are?
Agnès and I see Blandine differently.
You know what I think? She's dying to have a boyfriend, but since there's no one here, she's going after that poor guy on the cross.
If the sisters knew how easily Agnès said things like that . . .
. . . they'd send her to bed without any food for all of eternity!

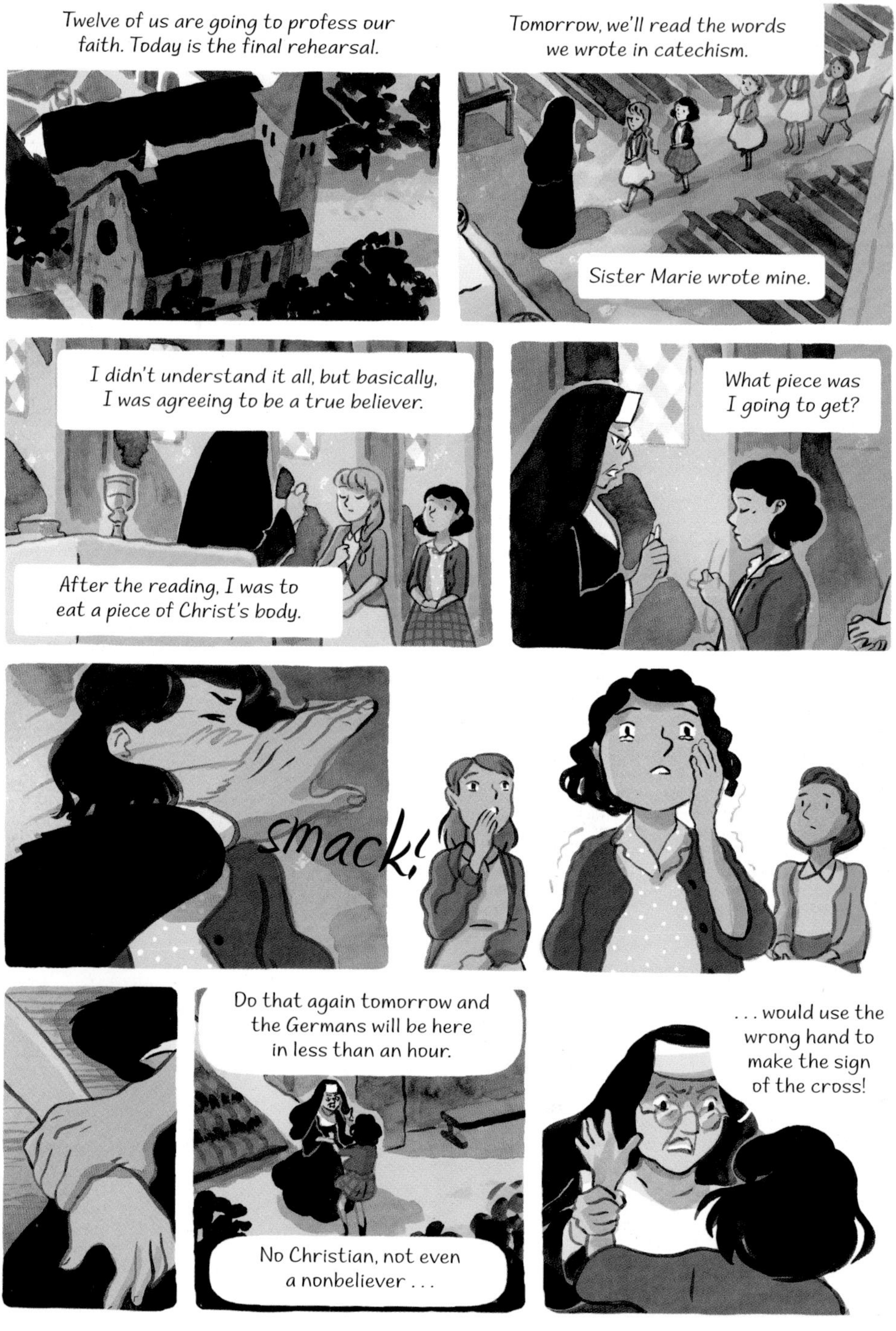
Twelve of us are going to profess our faith. Today is the final rehearsal.
Tomorrow, we'll read the words we wrote in catechism.
Sister Marie wrote mine.
I didn't understand it all, but basically, I was agreeing to be a true believer.
After the reading, I was to eat a piece of Christ's body.
What piece was I going to get?
smack!
Do that again tomorrow and the Germans will be here in less than an hour.
No Christian, not even a nonbeliever . . .
. . . would use the wrong hand to make the sign of the cross!

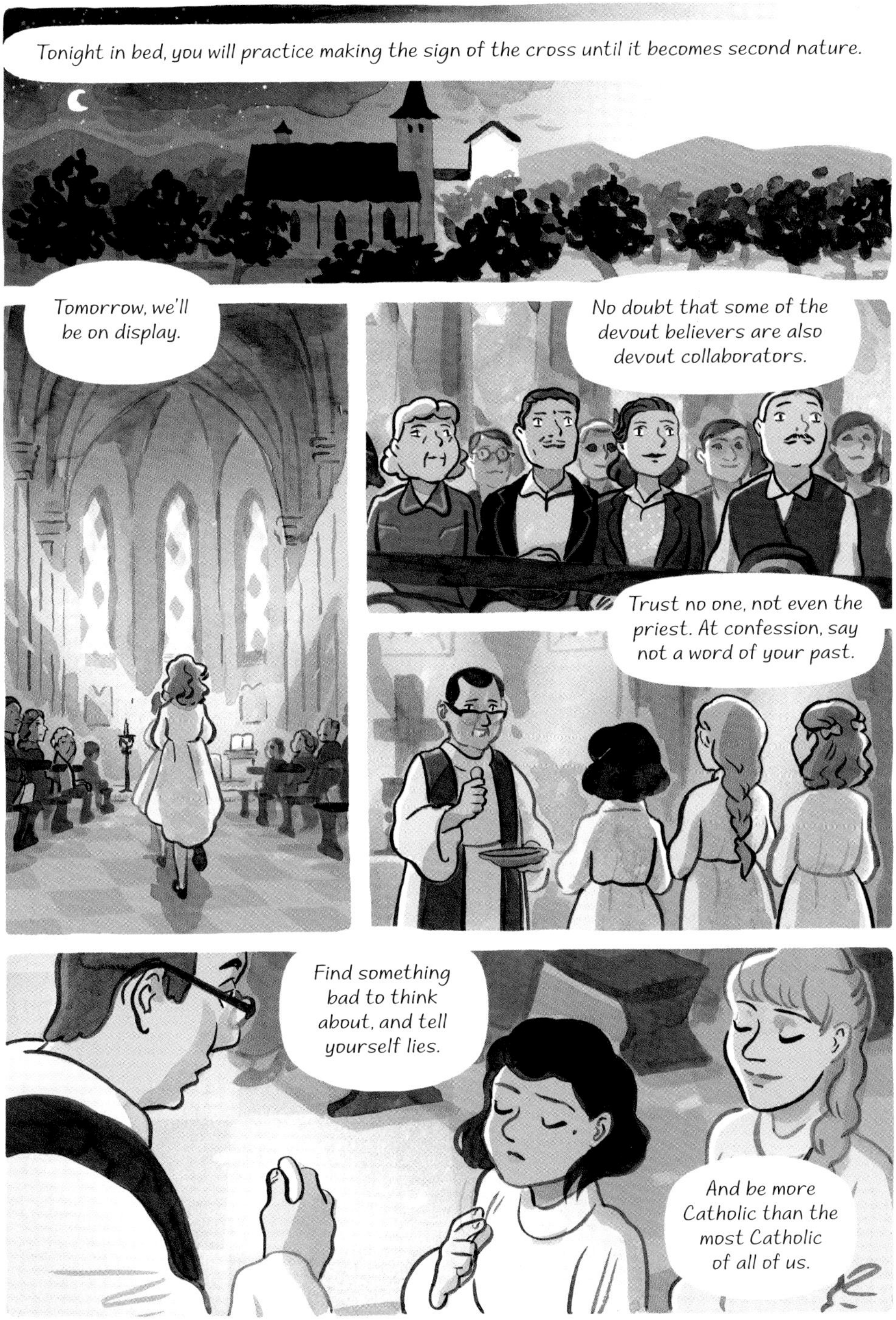
Tonight in bed, you will practice making the sign of the cross until it becomes second nature.
Tomorrow, we'll be on display.
No doubt that some of the devout believers are also devout collaborators.
Trust no one, not even the priest. At confession, say not a word of your past.
Find something bad to think about, and tell yourself lies.
And be more Catholic than the most Catholic of all of us.

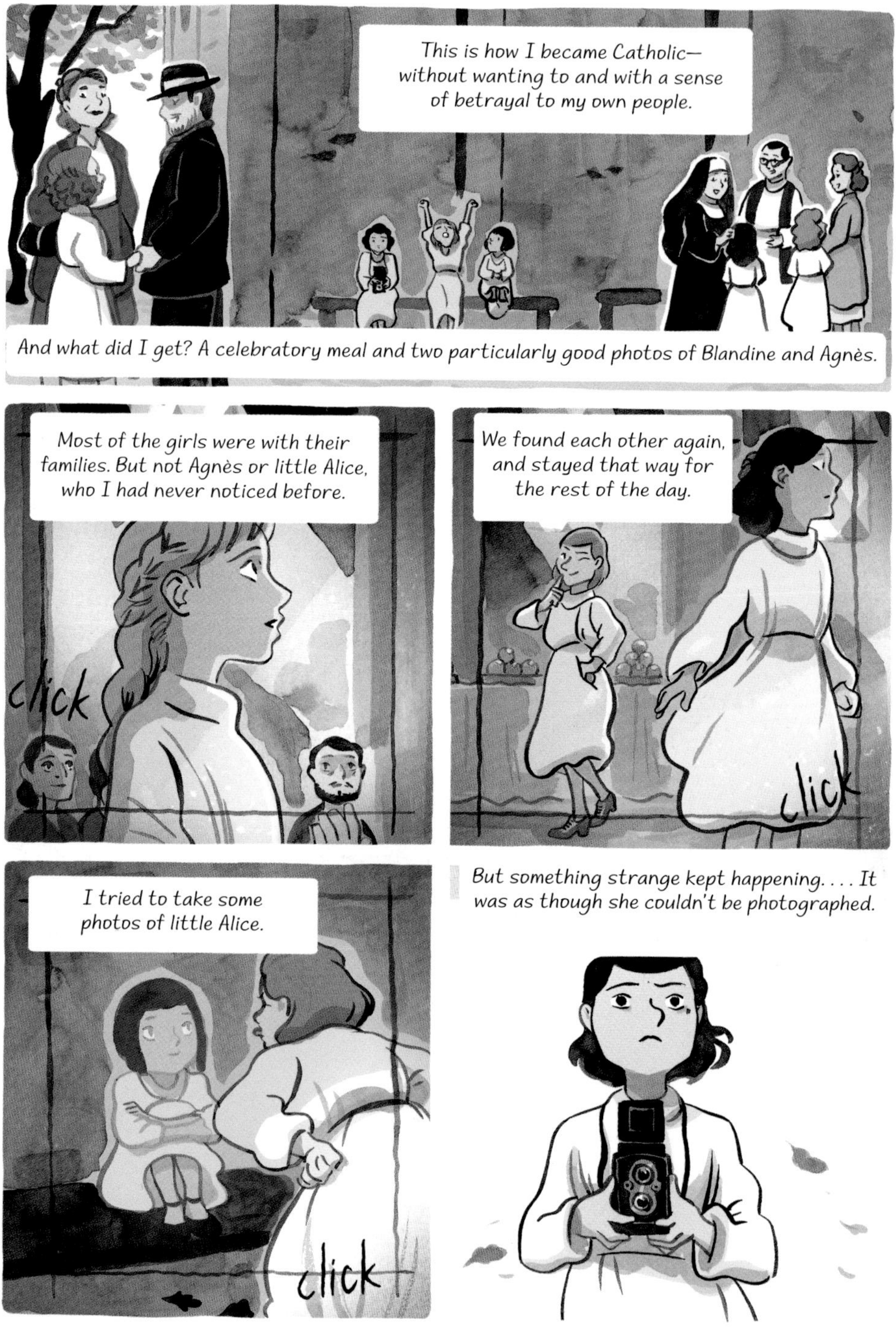
This is how I became Catholic—without wanting to and with a sense of betrayal to my own people.
And what did I get? A celebratory meal and two particularly good photos of Blandine and Agnès.
Most of the girls were with their families. But not Agnès or little Alice, who I had never noticed before.
click
We found each other again, and stayed that way for the rest of the day.
click
I tried to take some photos of little Alice.
click
But something strange kept happening. . . . It was as though she couldn't be photographed.

Seeing me take pictures at the ceremony, Mother Superior asked me if I would take a portrait of her to hang in her office.

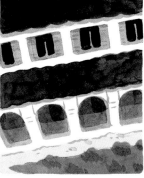

I suspected her of a sin—vanity!

Mother, may I ask a favor?

Would you let me go to the village with Father Lucas to develop my photos?

I'm good at printing pictures, so I can help. I took excellent classes in Paris.

It's a very important part of the process, especially for large portraits.

All right, you can go with him next Monday. But be careful. And you'll make up the classes, understood?

Thank you, Mother!

I would have hugged her, but we didn't do that here.

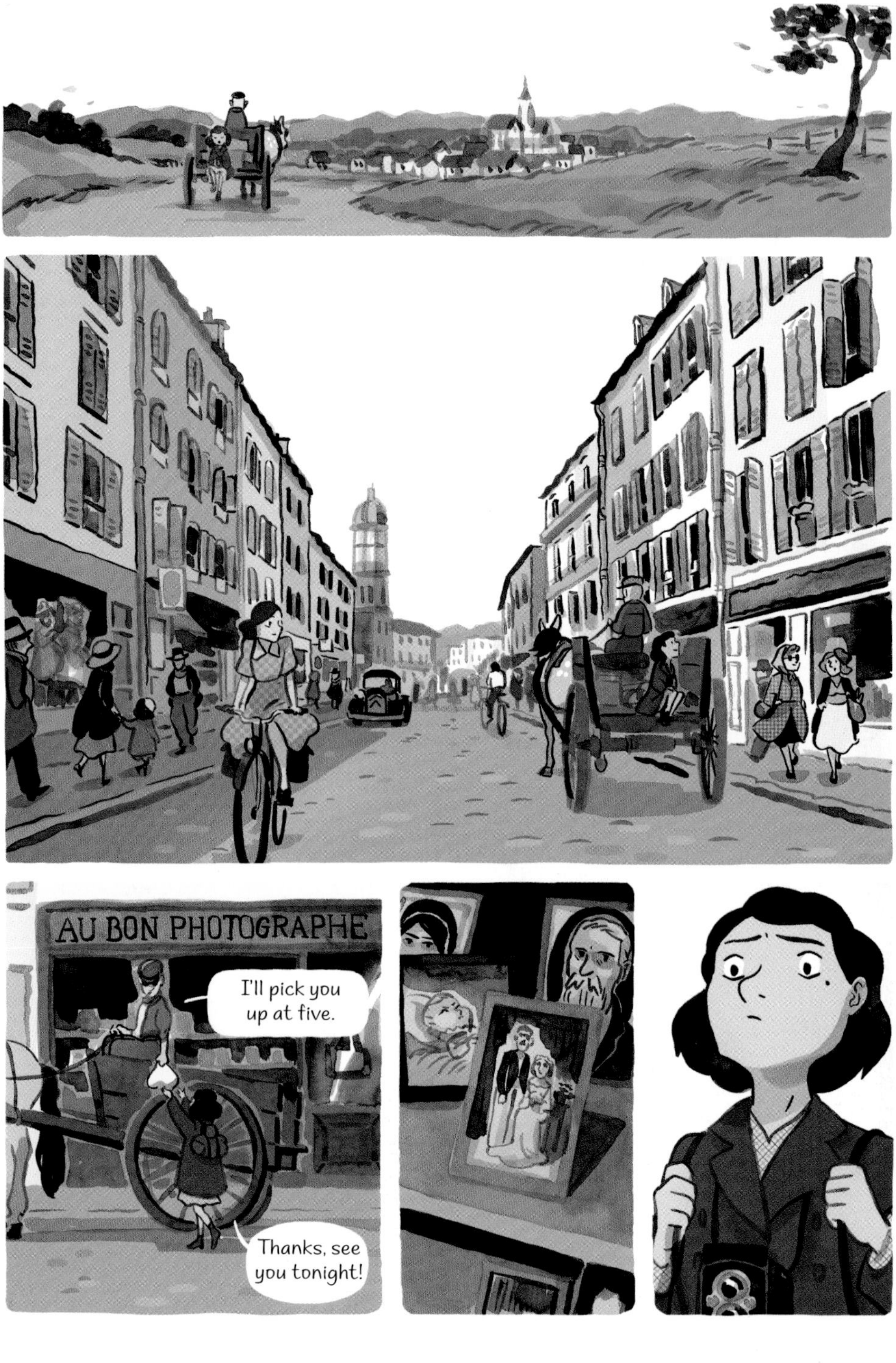
AU BON PHOTOGRAPHE
I'll pick you up at five.
Thanks, see you tonight!

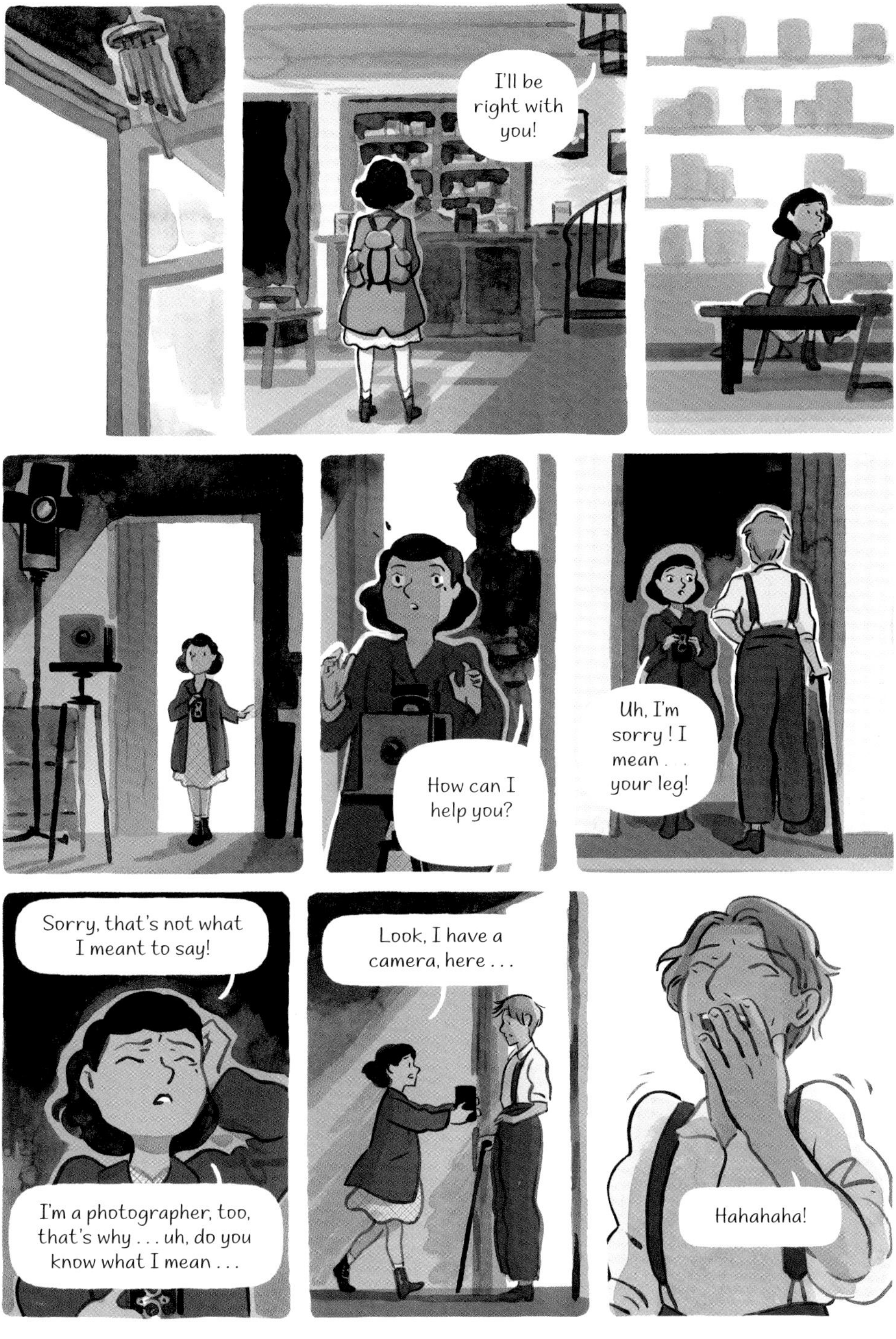
I'll be right with you!
How can I help you?
Uh, I'm sorry! I mean . . . your leg!
Sorry, that's not what I meant to say!
I'm a photographer, too, that's why . . . uh, do you know what I mean . . .
Look, I have a camera, here . . .
Hahahaha!

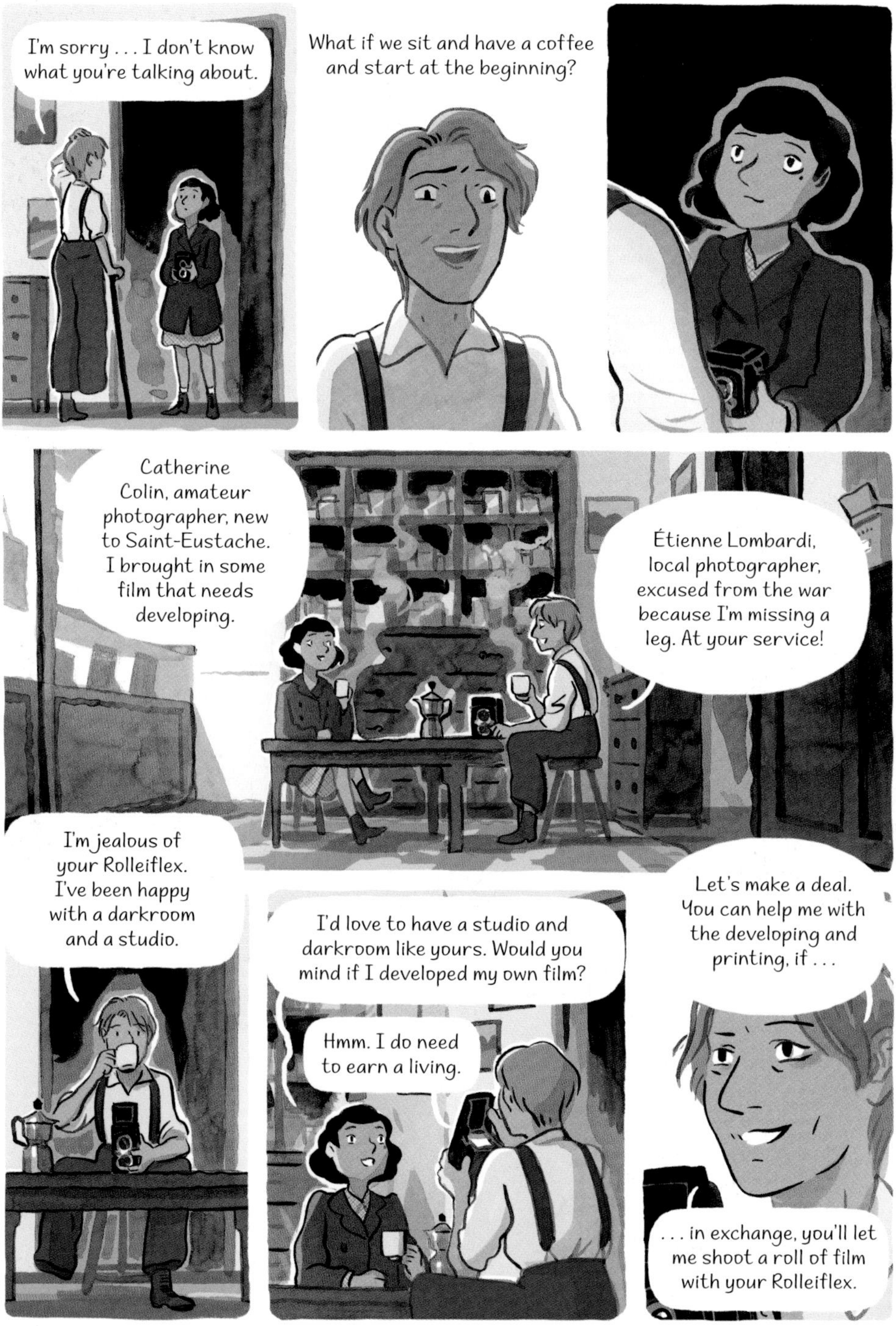
I'm sorry . . . I don't know what you're talking about.
What if we sit and have a coffee and start at the beginning?
Catherine Colin, amateur photographer, new to Saint-Eustache. I brought in some film that needs developing.
Étienne Lombardi, local photographer, excused from the war because I'm missing a leg. At your service!
I'm jealous of your Rolleiflex. I've been happy with a darkroom and a studio.
I'd love to have a studio and darkroom like yours. Would you mind if I developed my own film?
Hmm. I do need to earn a living.
Let's make a deal. You can help me with the developing and printing, if . . .
. . . in exchange, you'll let me shoot a roll of film with your Rolleiflex.

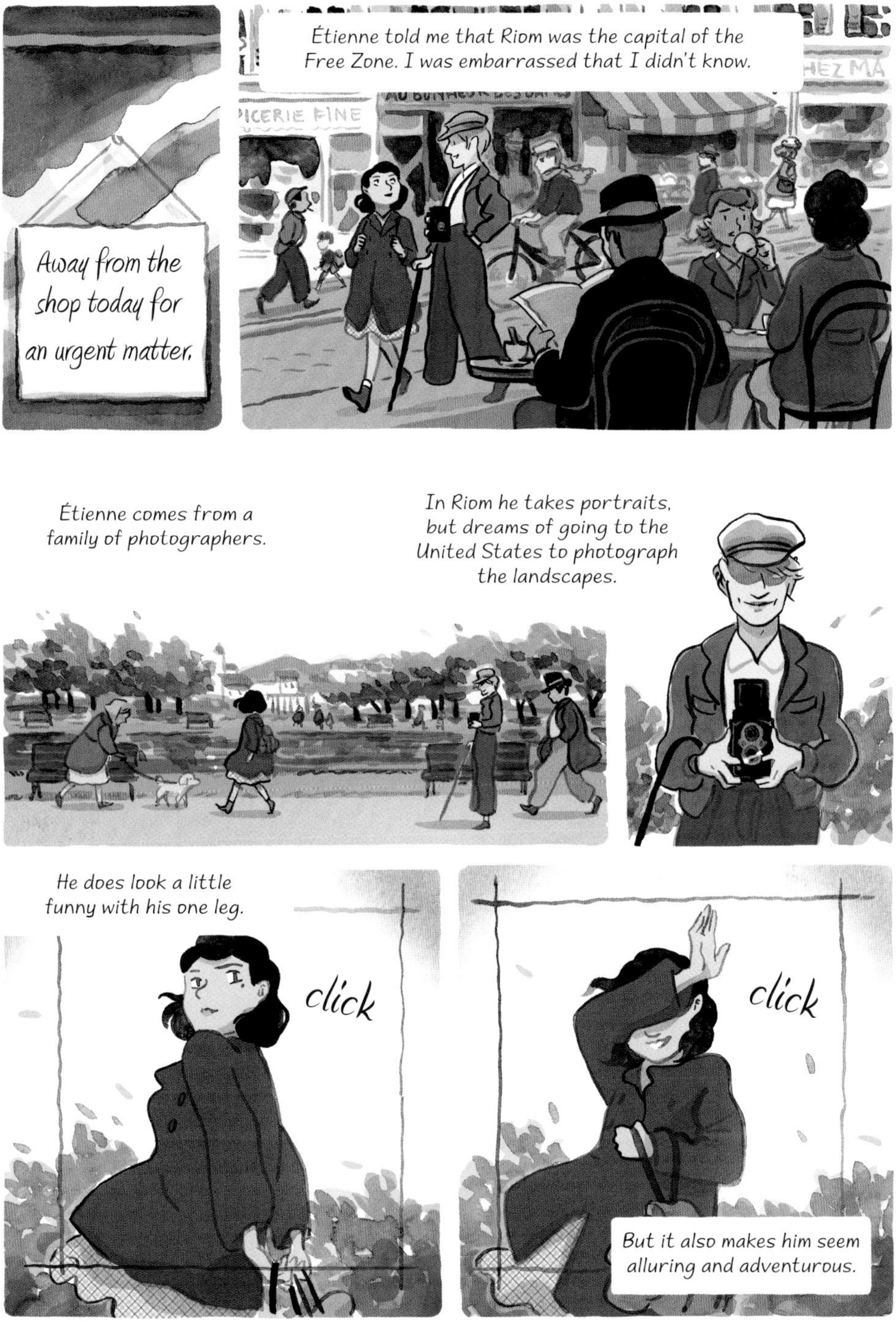

Away from the shop today for an urgent matter.
Étienne told me that Riom was the capital of the Free Zone. I was embarrassed that I didn't know.
Étienne comes from a family of photographers.
In Riom he takes portraits, but dreams of going to the United States to photograph the landscapes.
He does look a little funny with his one leg.
click
click
But it also makes him seem alluring and adventurous.

And you? What kind of photos do you like to take?

I guess I like taking photos of everyday life.

Capturing people's movements . . .

. . . or the moment when an emotion registers on a face.

Sometimes I get the feeling that the images exist already in some invisible world.

We're just here to wake them up.

That's nice. You capture the extraordinary moments, while I stage everything I shoot.

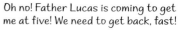

Because of you, even my landscapes seem fake.

Oh no! Father Lucas is coming to get me at five! We need to get back, fast!

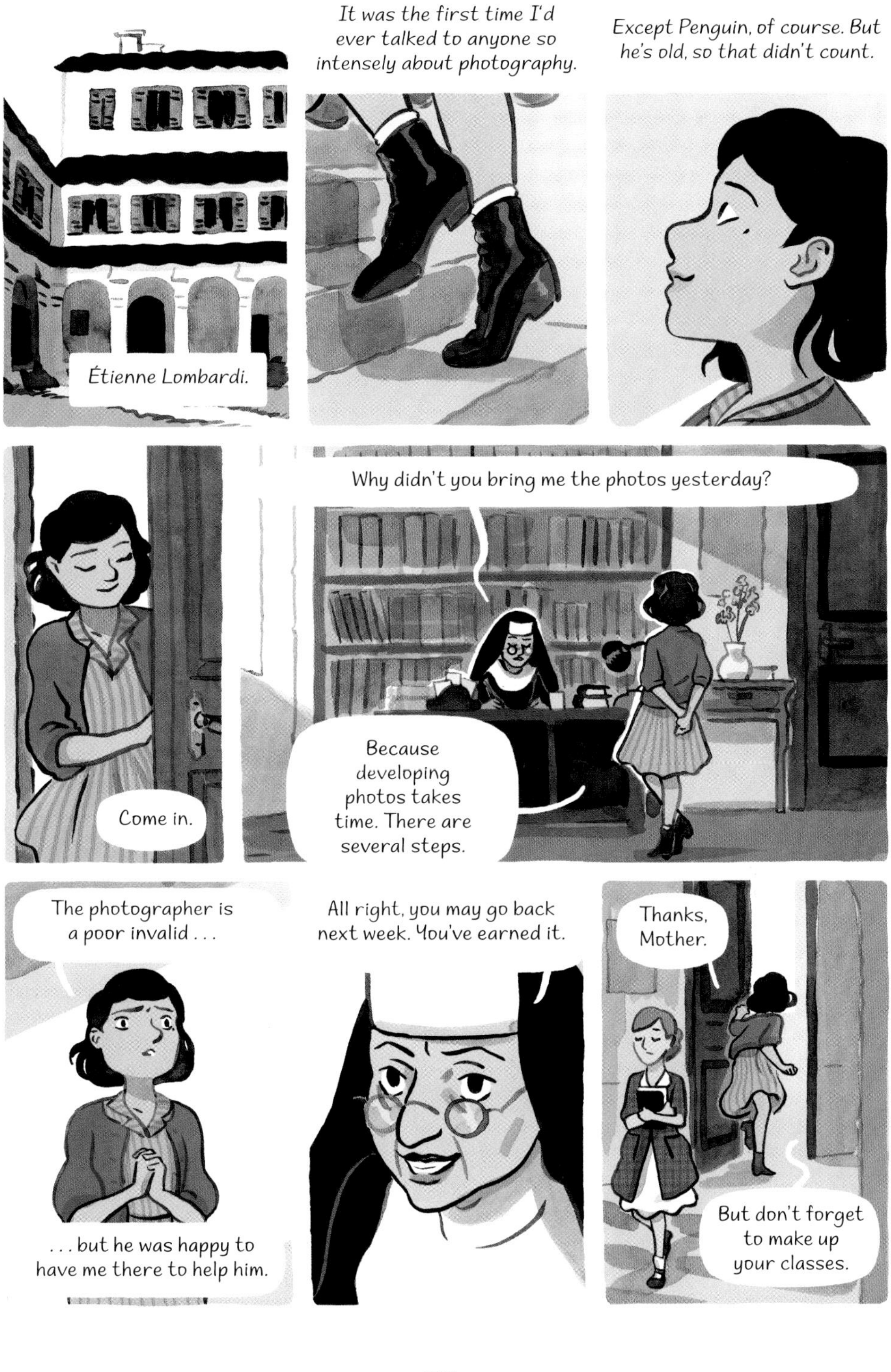

It was the first time I'd ever talked to anyone so intensely about photography.
Except Penguin, of course. But he's old, so that didn't count.
Étienne Lombardi.
Come in.
Why didn't you bring me the photos yesterday?
Because developing photos takes time. There are several steps.
The photographer is a poor invalid . . .
. . . but he was happy to have me there to help him.
All right, you may go back next week. You've earned it.
Thanks, Mother.
But don't forget to make up your classes.

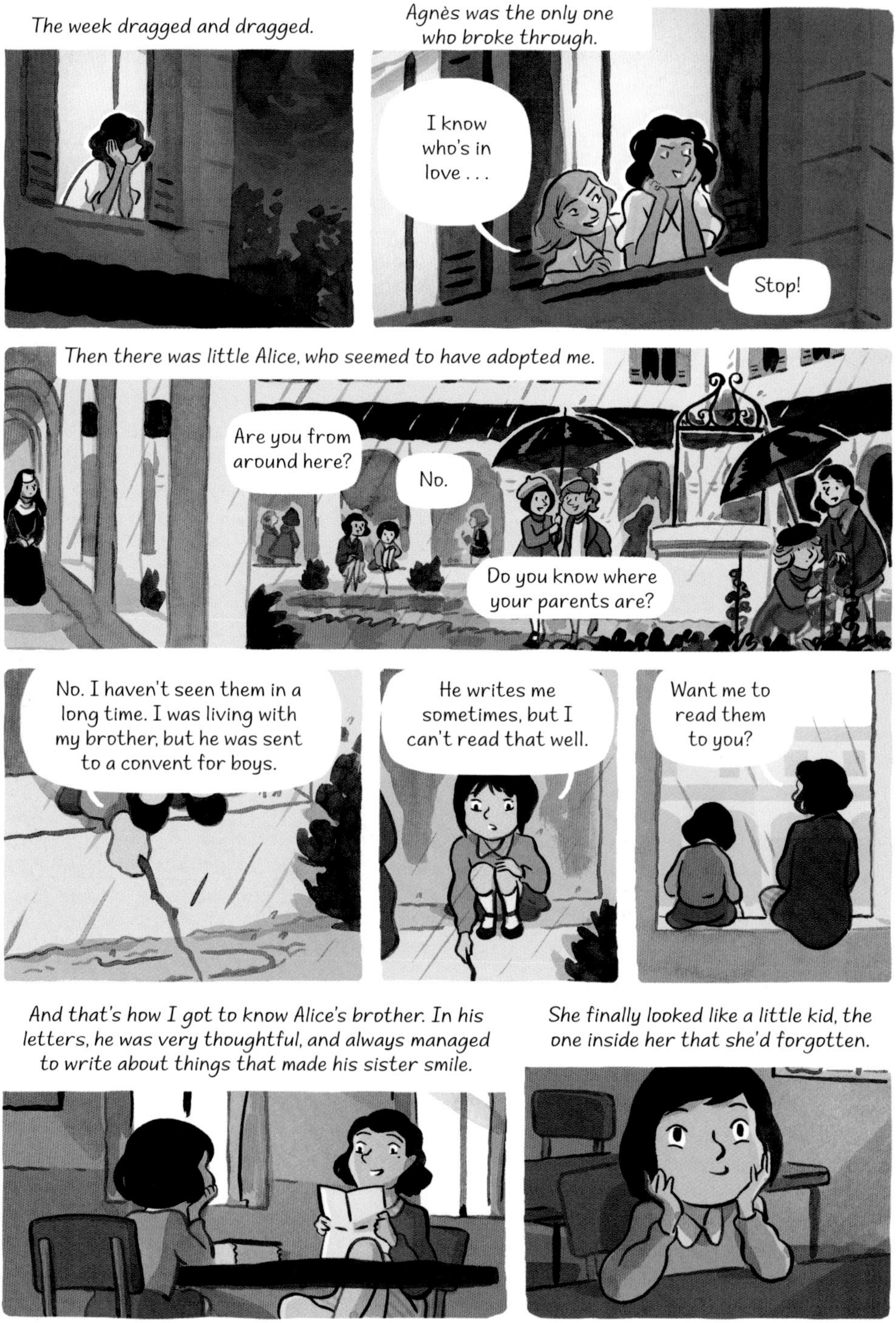
The week dragged and dragged.
Agnès was the only one who broke through.
I know who's in love . . .
Stop!
Then there was little Alice, who seemed to have adopted me.
Are you from around here?
No.
Do you know where your parents are?
No. I haven't seen them in a long time. I was living with my brother, but he was sent to a convent for boys.
He writes me sometimes, but I can't read that well.
Want me to read them to you?
And that's how I got to know Alice's brother. In his letters, he was very thoughtful, and always managed to write about things that made his sister smile.
She finally looked like a little kid, the one inside her that she'd forgotten.

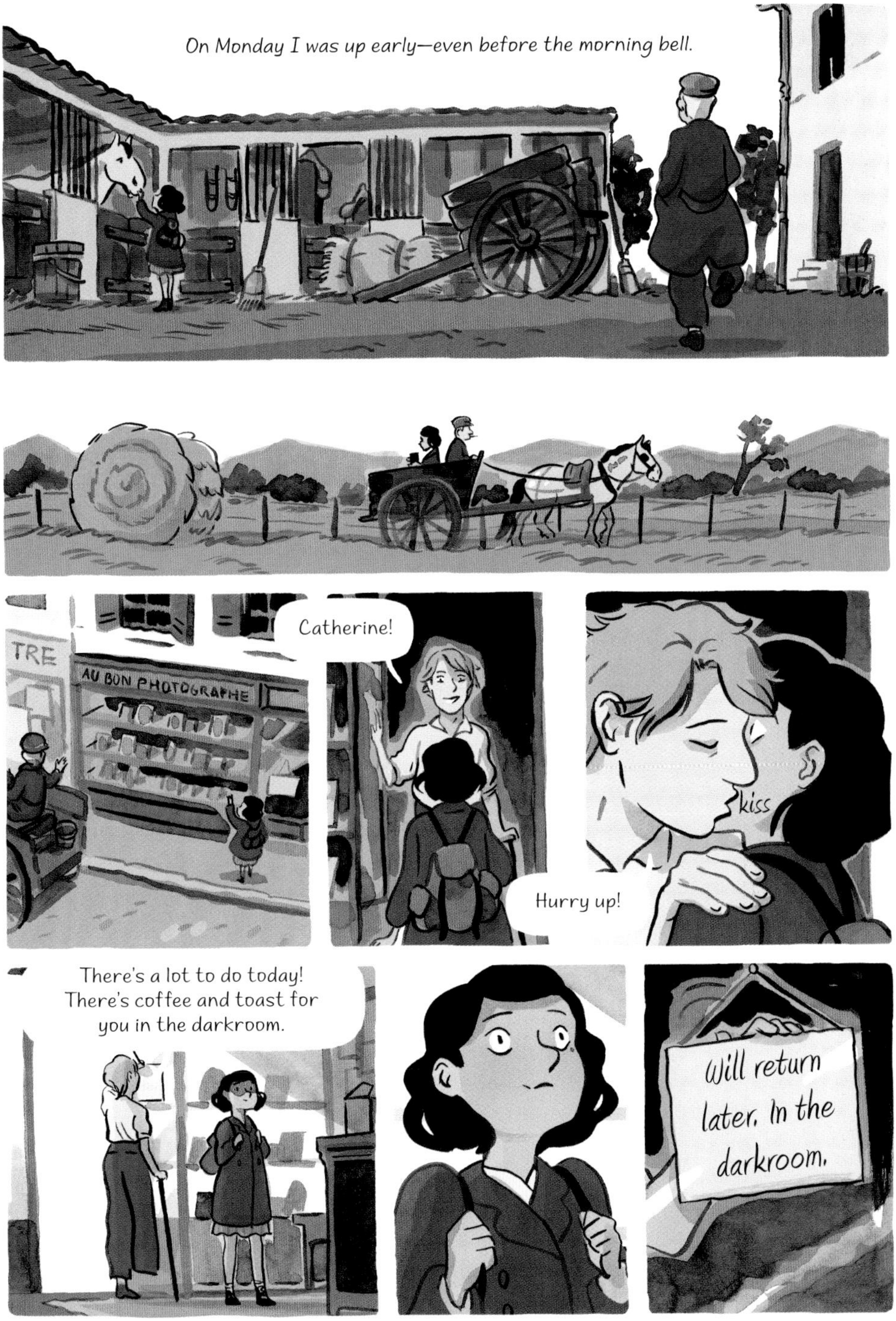
On Monday I was up early—even before the morning bell.
TRE
AU BON PHOTOGRAPHE
Catherine!
kiss
Hurry up!
There's a lot to do today! There's coffee and toast for you in the darkroom.
Will return later. In the darkroom.

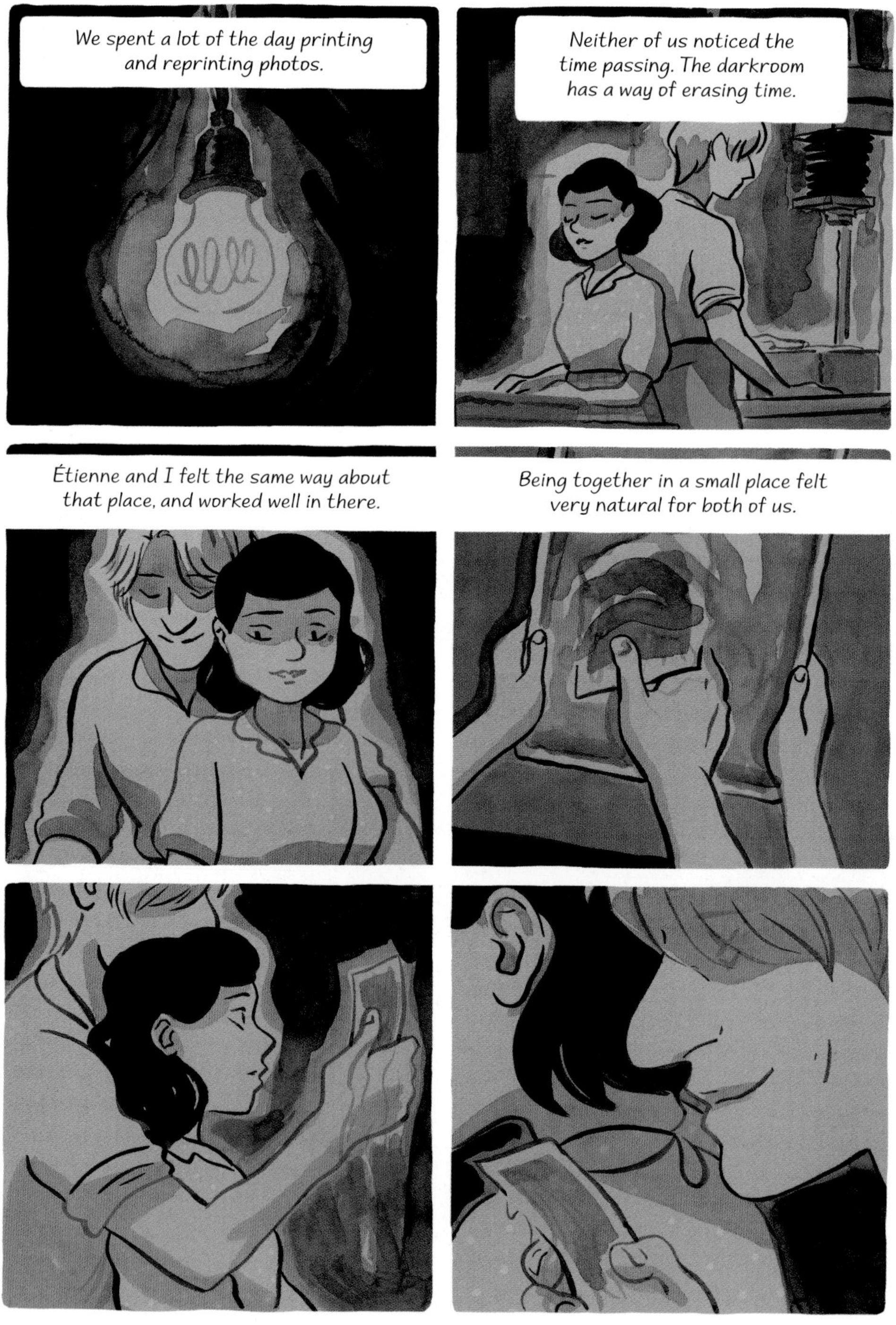
We spent a lot of the day printing and reprinting photos.
Neither of us noticed the time passing. The darkroom has a way of erasing time.
Étienne and I felt the same way about that place, and worked well in there.
Being together in a small place felt very natural for both of us.

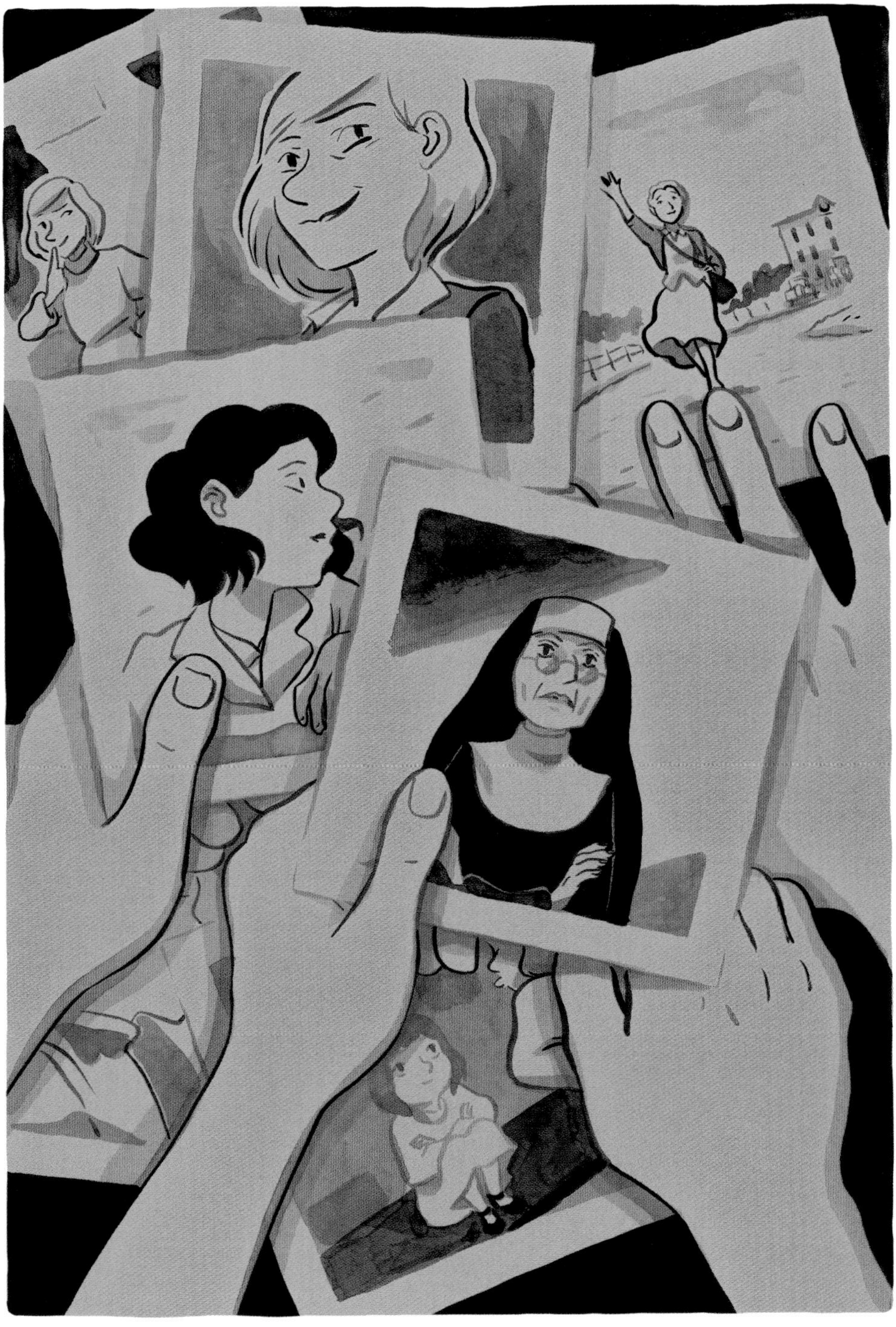

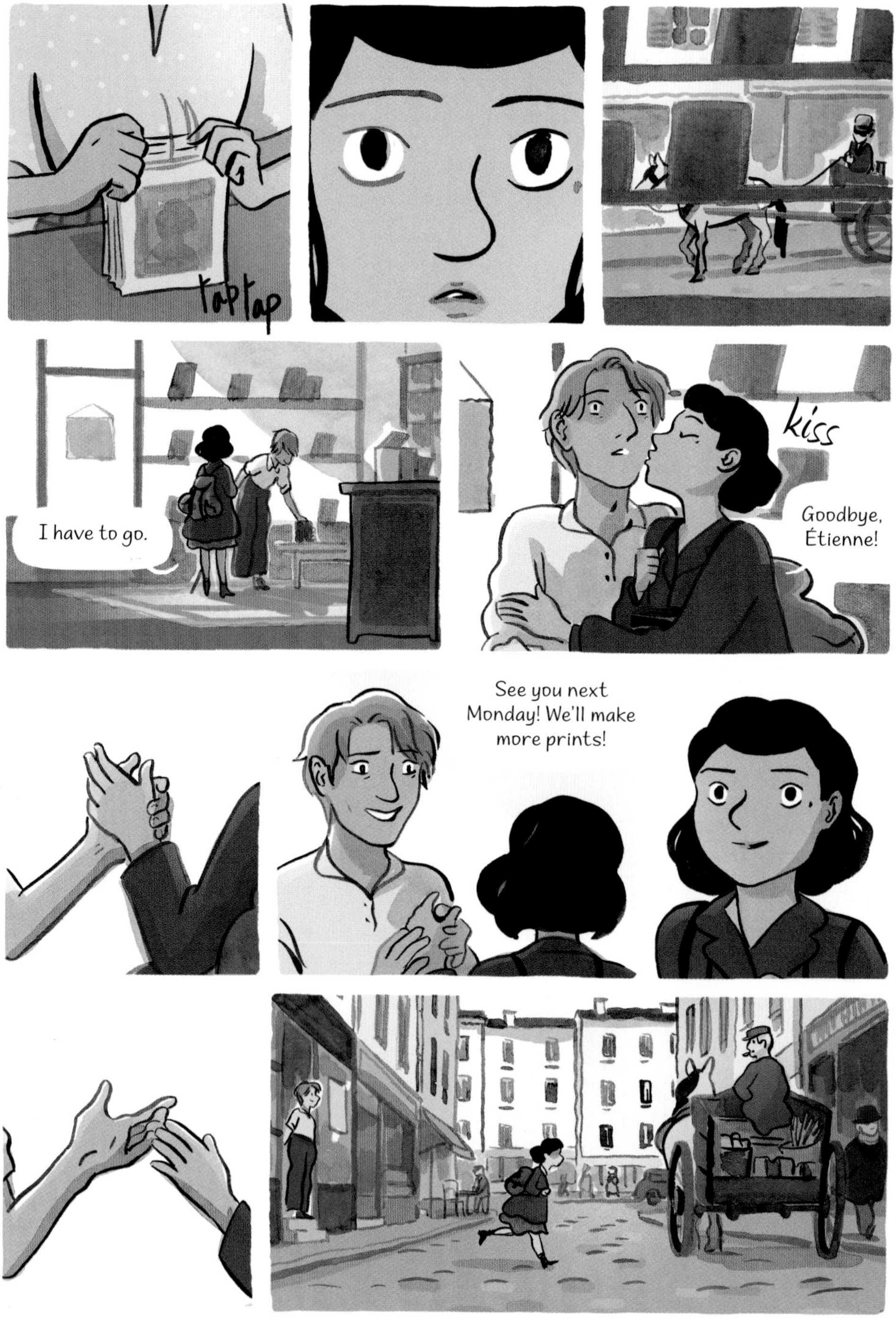
tap tap
I have to go.
kiss
Goodbye, Étienne!
See you next Monday! We'll make more prints!

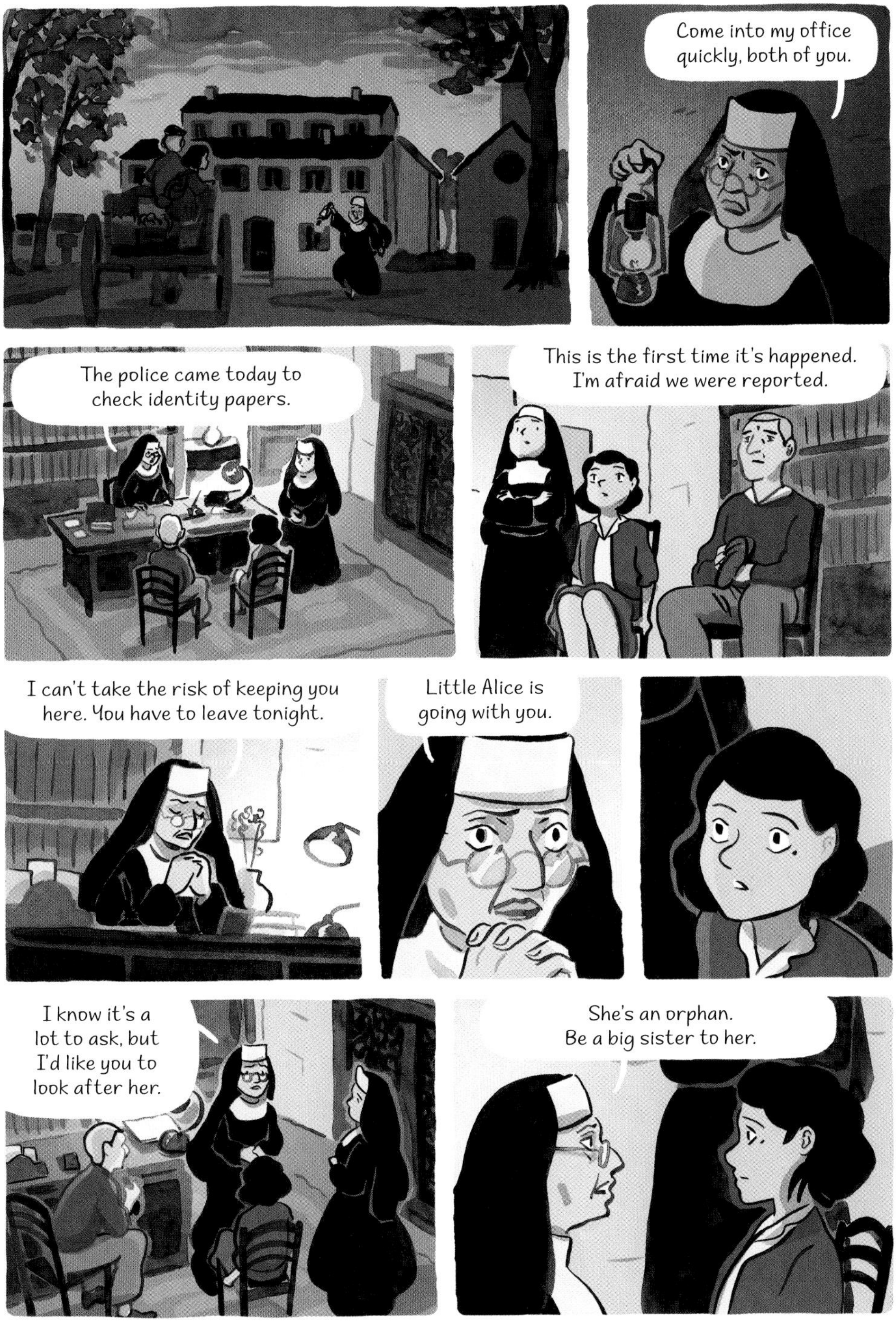
Come into my office quickly, both of you.
The police came today to check identity papers.
This is the first time it's happened. I'm afraid we were reported.
I can't take the risk of keeping you here. You have to leave tonight.
Little Alice is going with you.
I know it's a lot to ask, but I'd like you to look after her.
She's an orphan. Be a big sister to her.

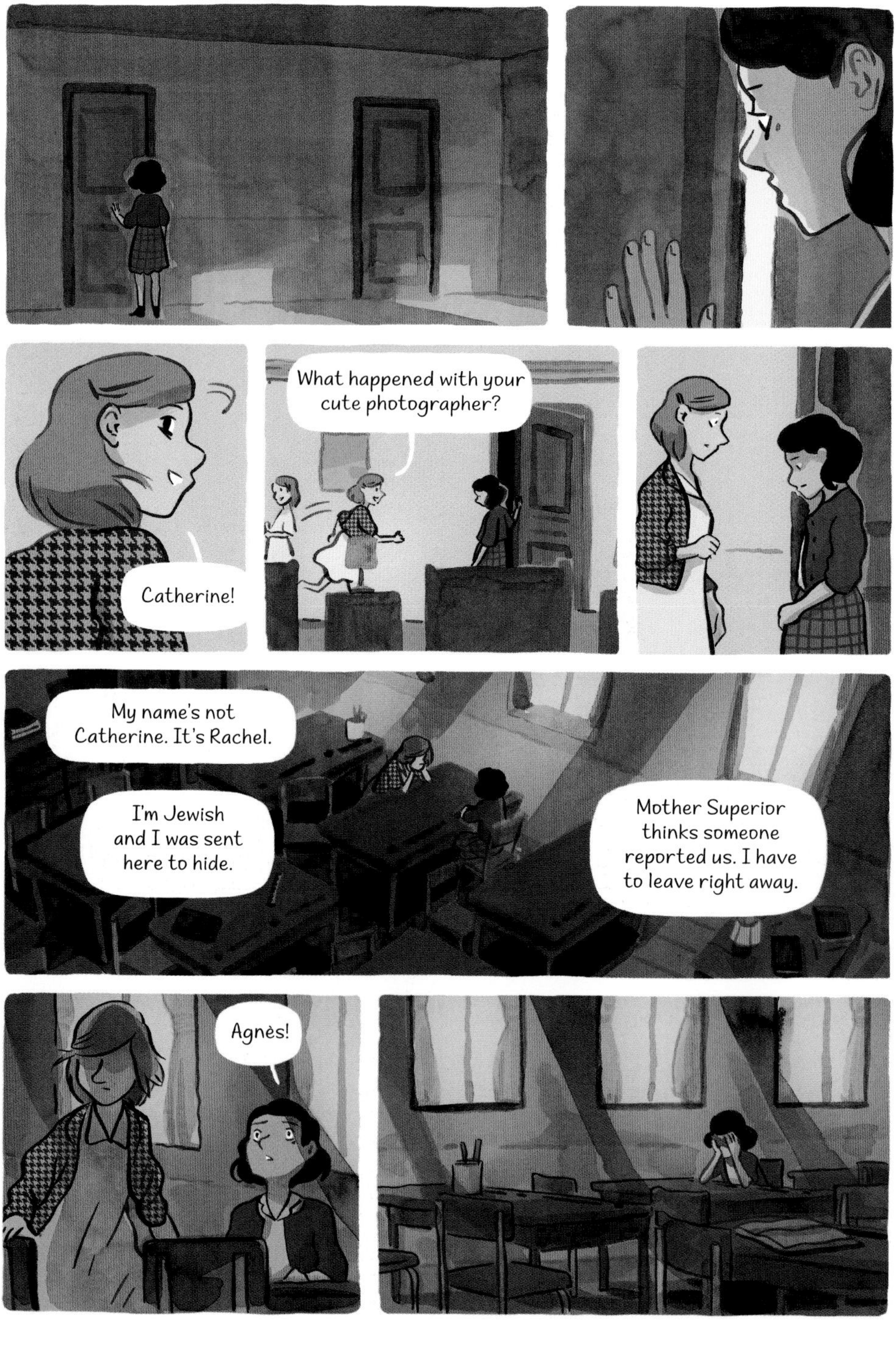
Catherine!
What happened with your cute photographer?
My name's not Catherine. It's Rachel.
I'm Jewish and I was sent here to hide.
Mother Superior thinks someone reported us. I have to leave right away.
Agnès!

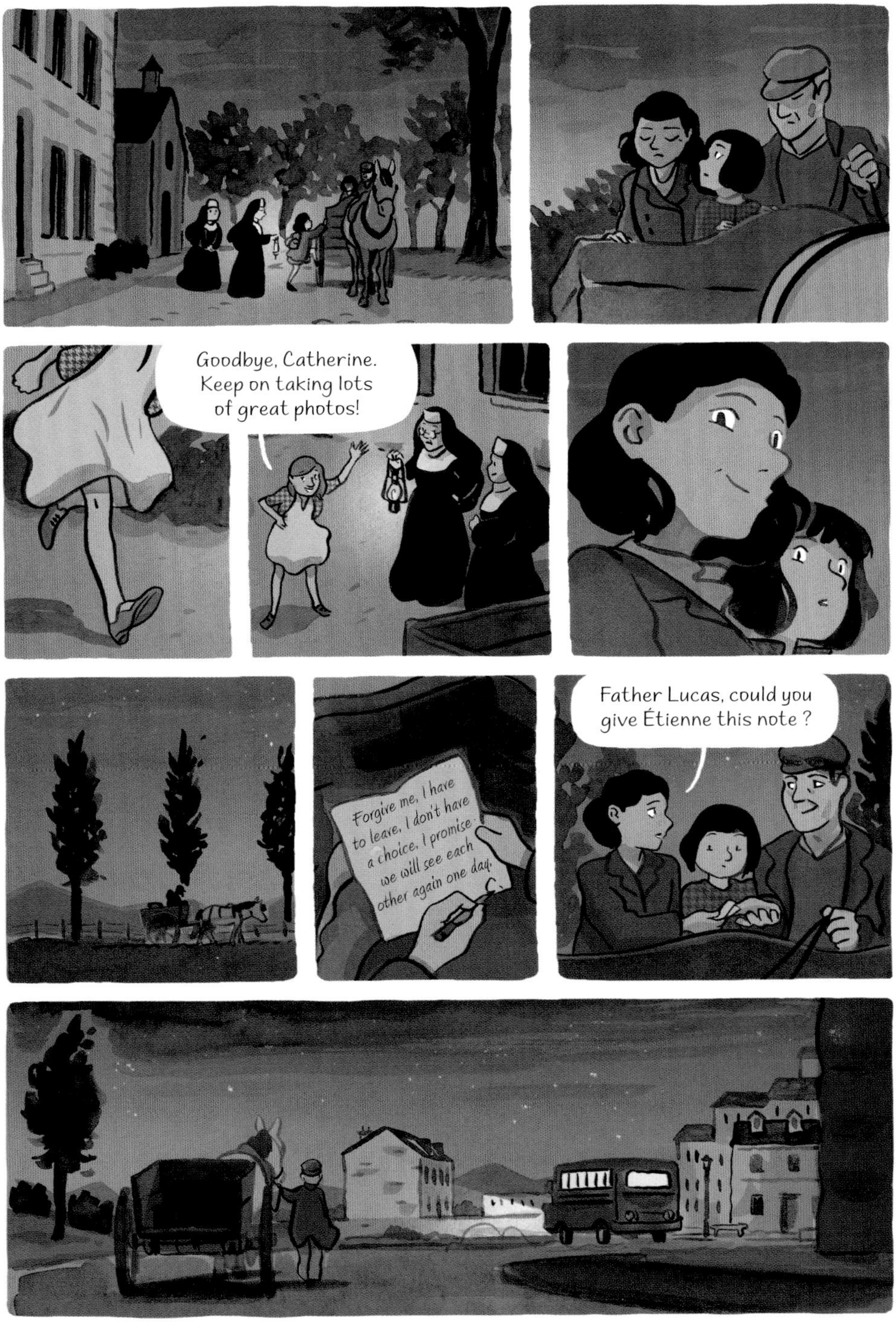

Goodbye, Catherine. Keep on taking lots of great photos!
Forgive me, I have to leave, I don't have a choice. I promise we will see each other again one day.
C.
Father Lucas, could you give Étienne this note ?

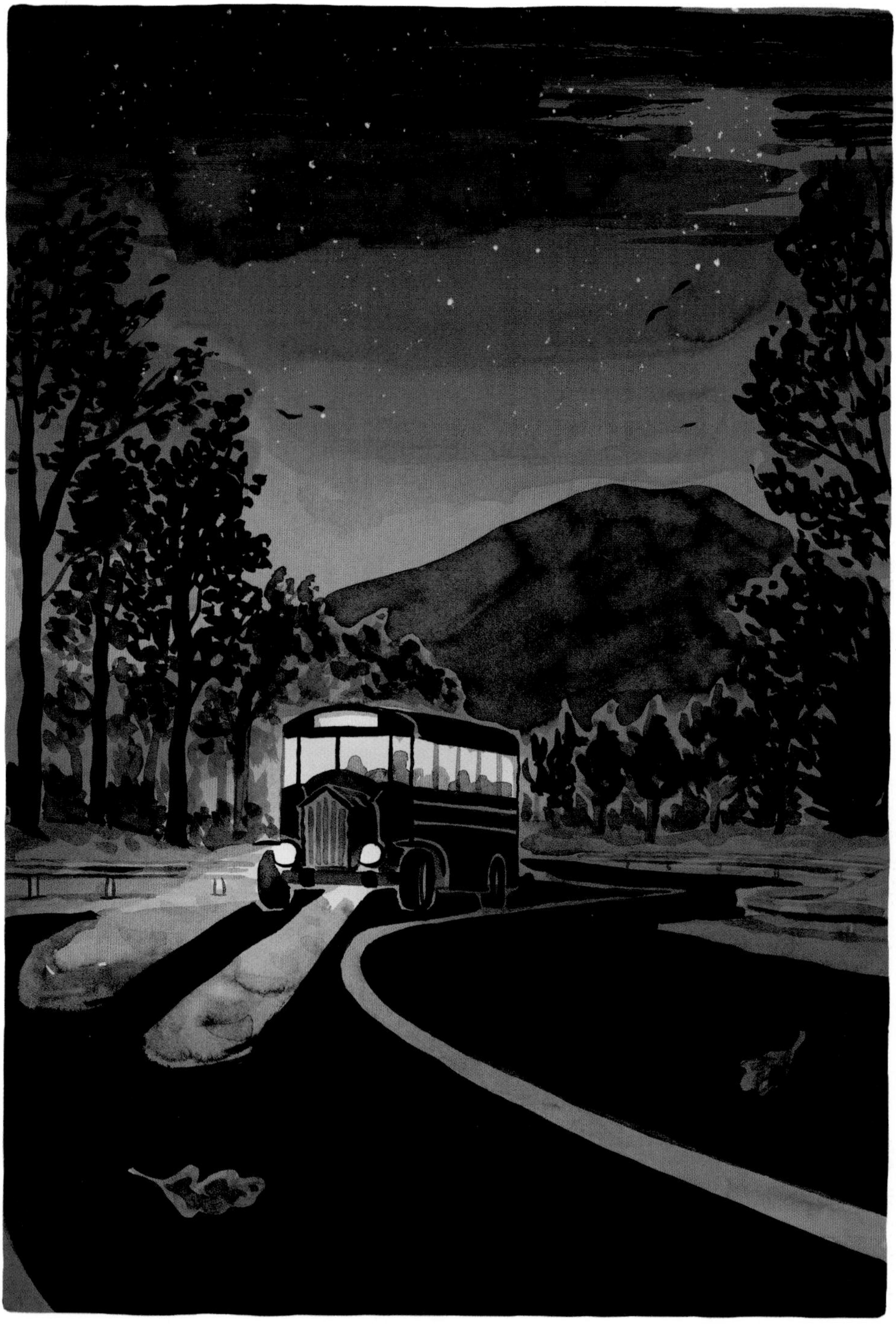

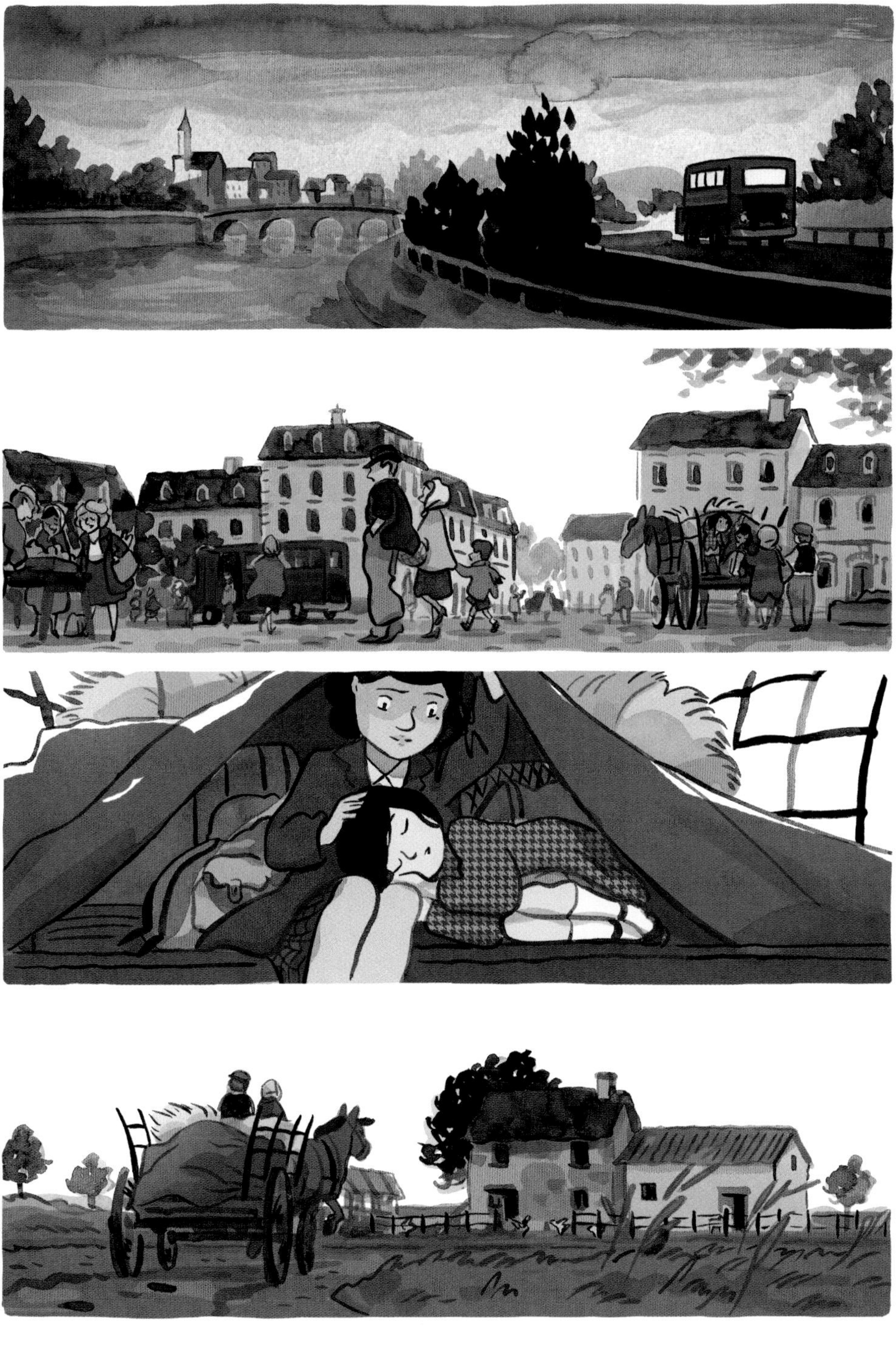

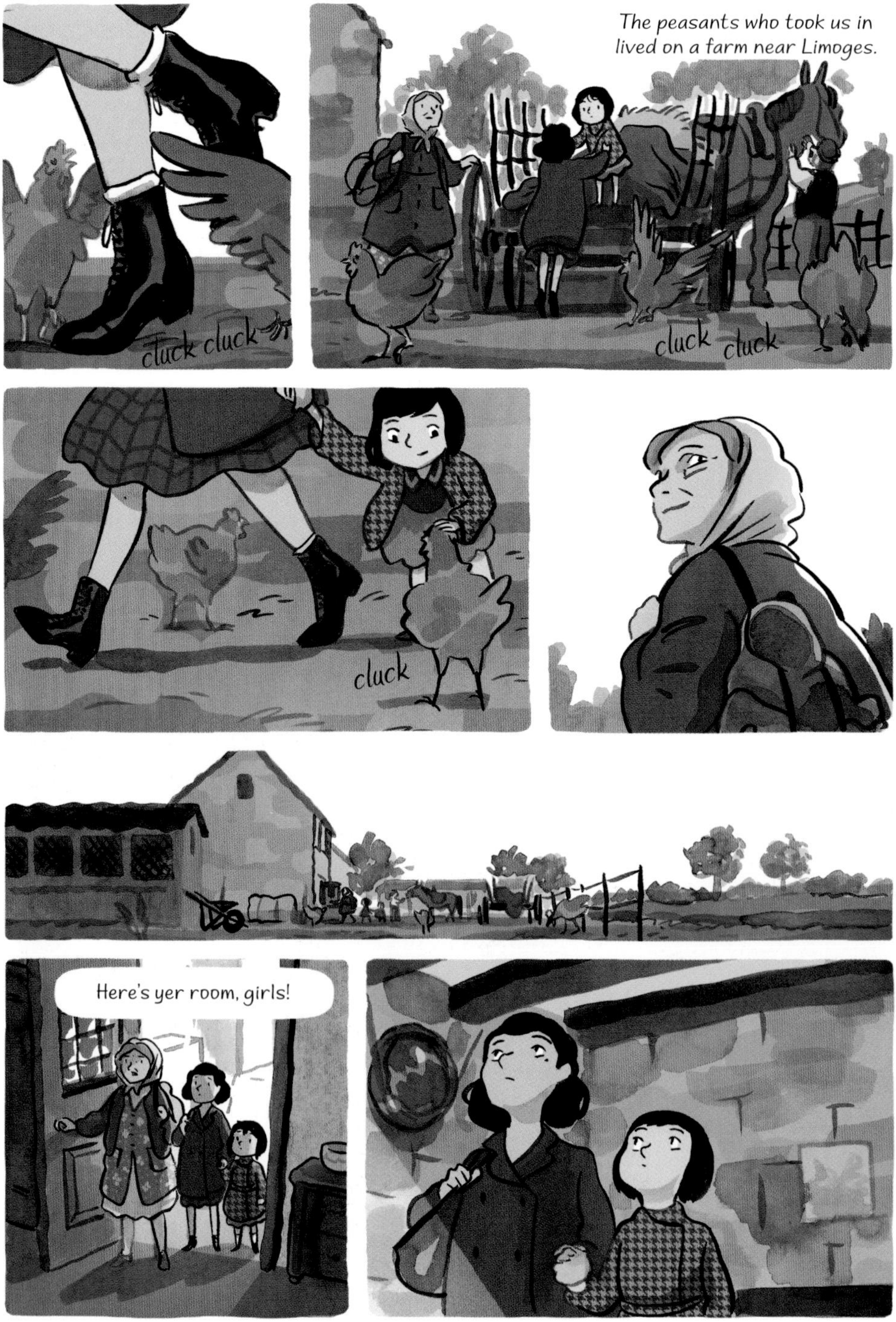

cluck cluck
The peasants who took us in lived on a farm near Limoges.
cluck cluck
cluck
Here's yer room, girls!

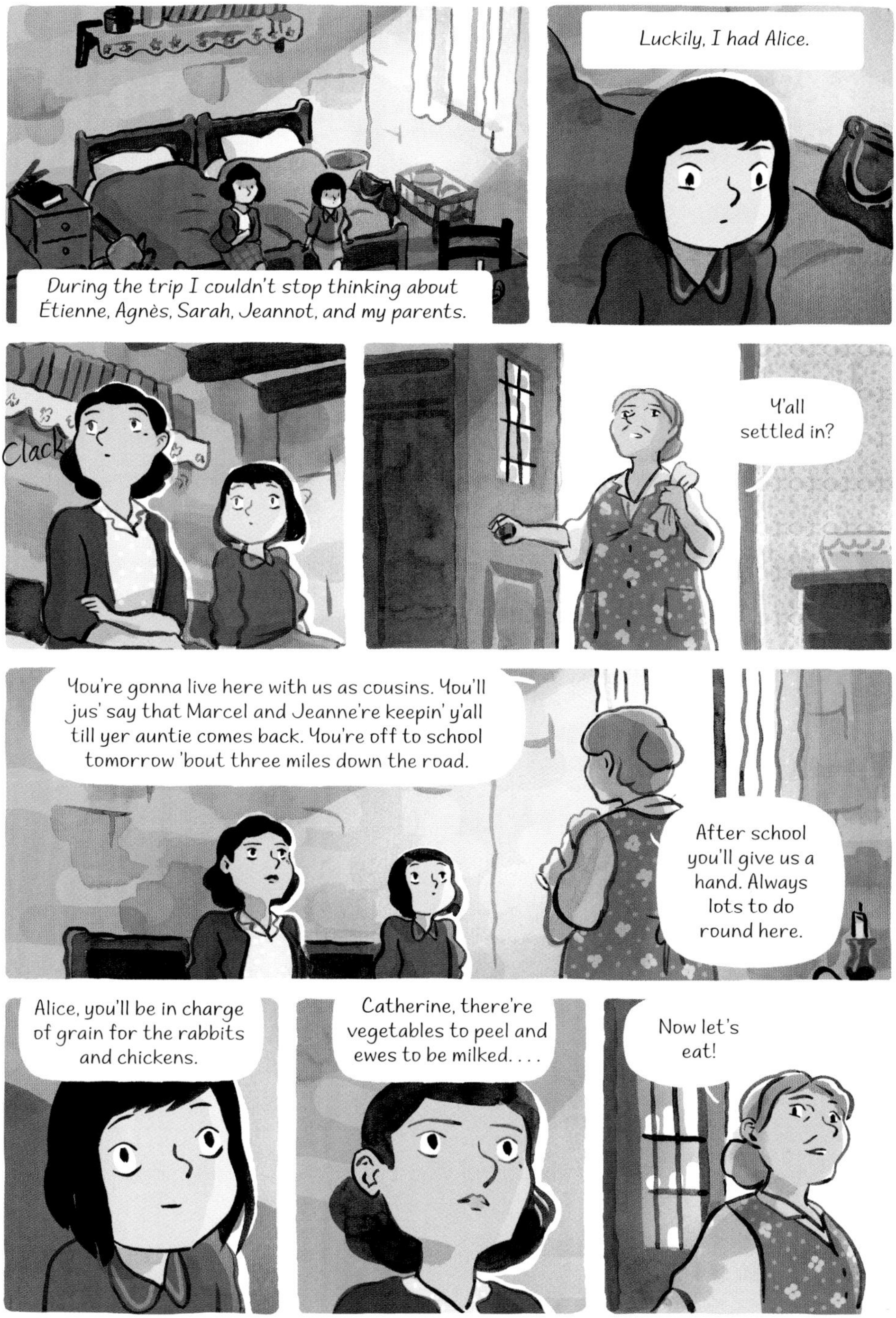
During the trip I couldn't stop thinking about Étienne, Agnès, Sarah, Jeannot, and my parents.
Luckily, I had Alice.
Clack
Y'all settled in?
You're gonna live here with us as cousins. You'll jus' say that Marcel and Jeanne're keepin' y'all till yer auntie comes back. You're off to school tomorrow 'bout three miles down the road.
After school you'll give us a hand. Always lots to do round here.
Alice, you'll be in charge of grain for the rabbits and chickens.
Catherine, there're vegetables to peel and ewes to be milked. . . .
Now let's eat!

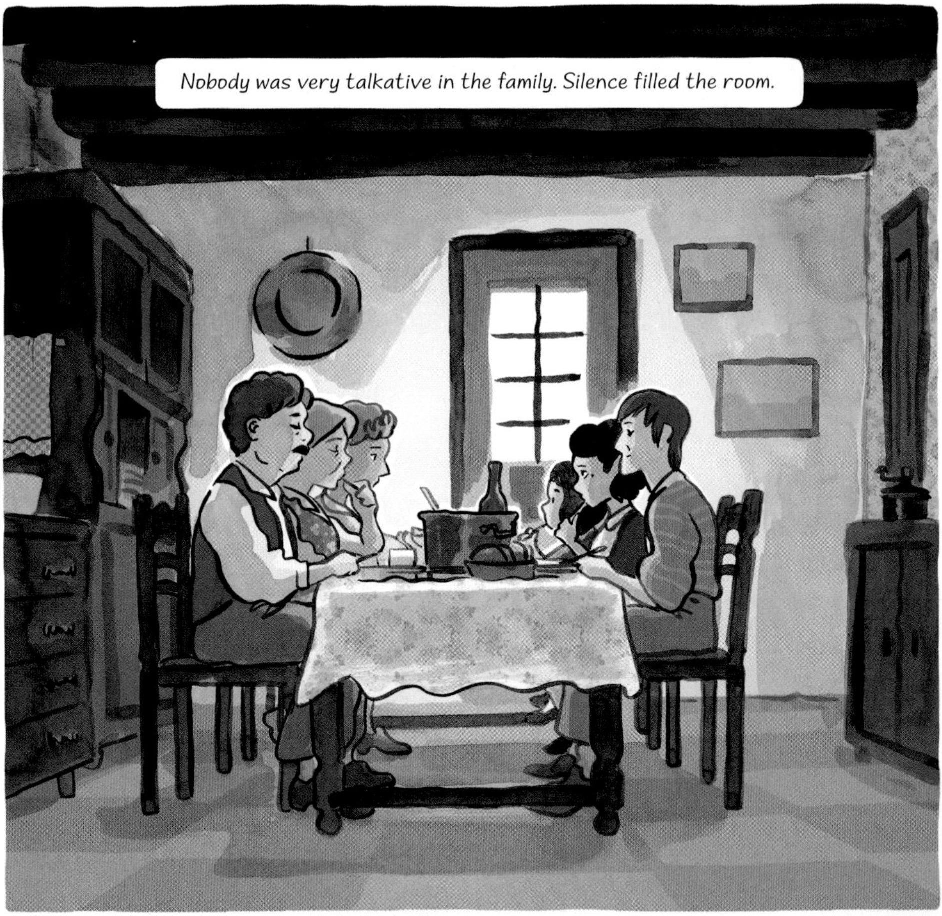
Nobody was very talkative in the family. Silence filled the room.

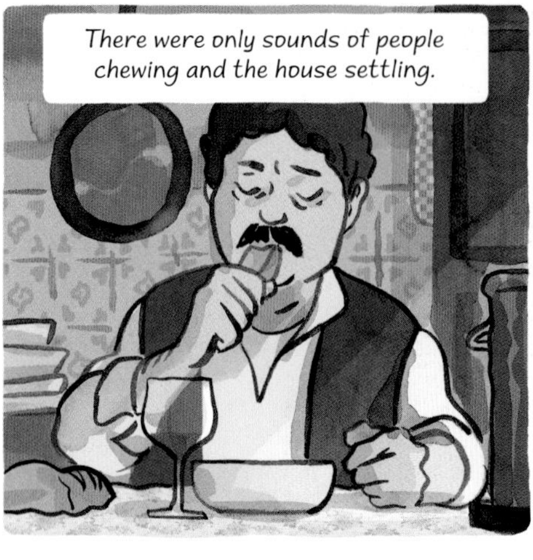
There were only sounds of people chewing and the house settling.

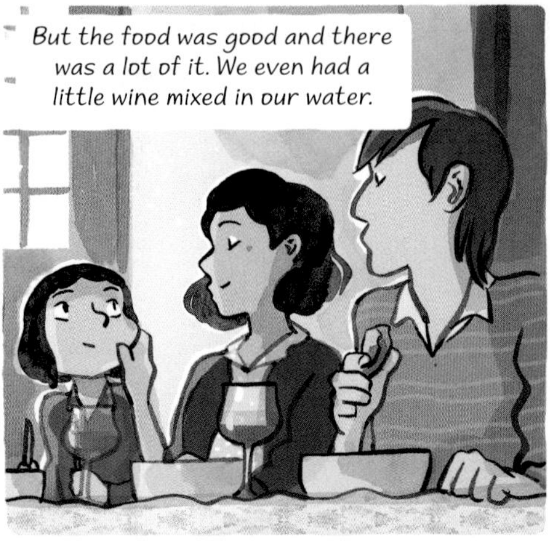
But the food was good and there was a lot of it. We even had a little wine mixed in our water.

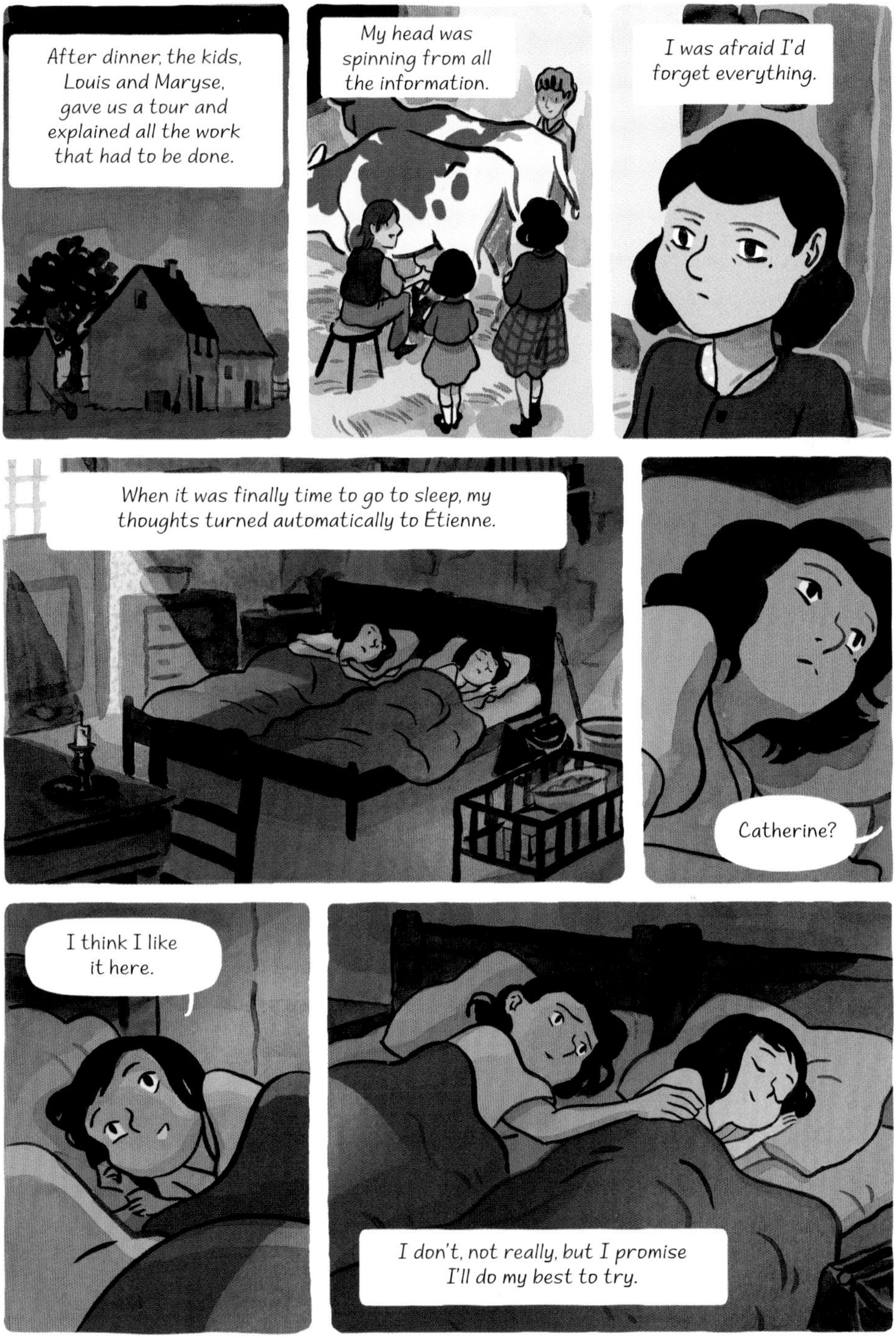

After dinner, the kids, Louis and Maryse, gave us a tour and explained all the work that had to be done.
My head was spinning from all the information.
I was afraid I'd forget everything.
When it was finally time to go to sleep, my thoughts turned automatically to Étienne.
Catherine?
I think I like it here.
I don't, not really, but I promise I'll do my best to try.

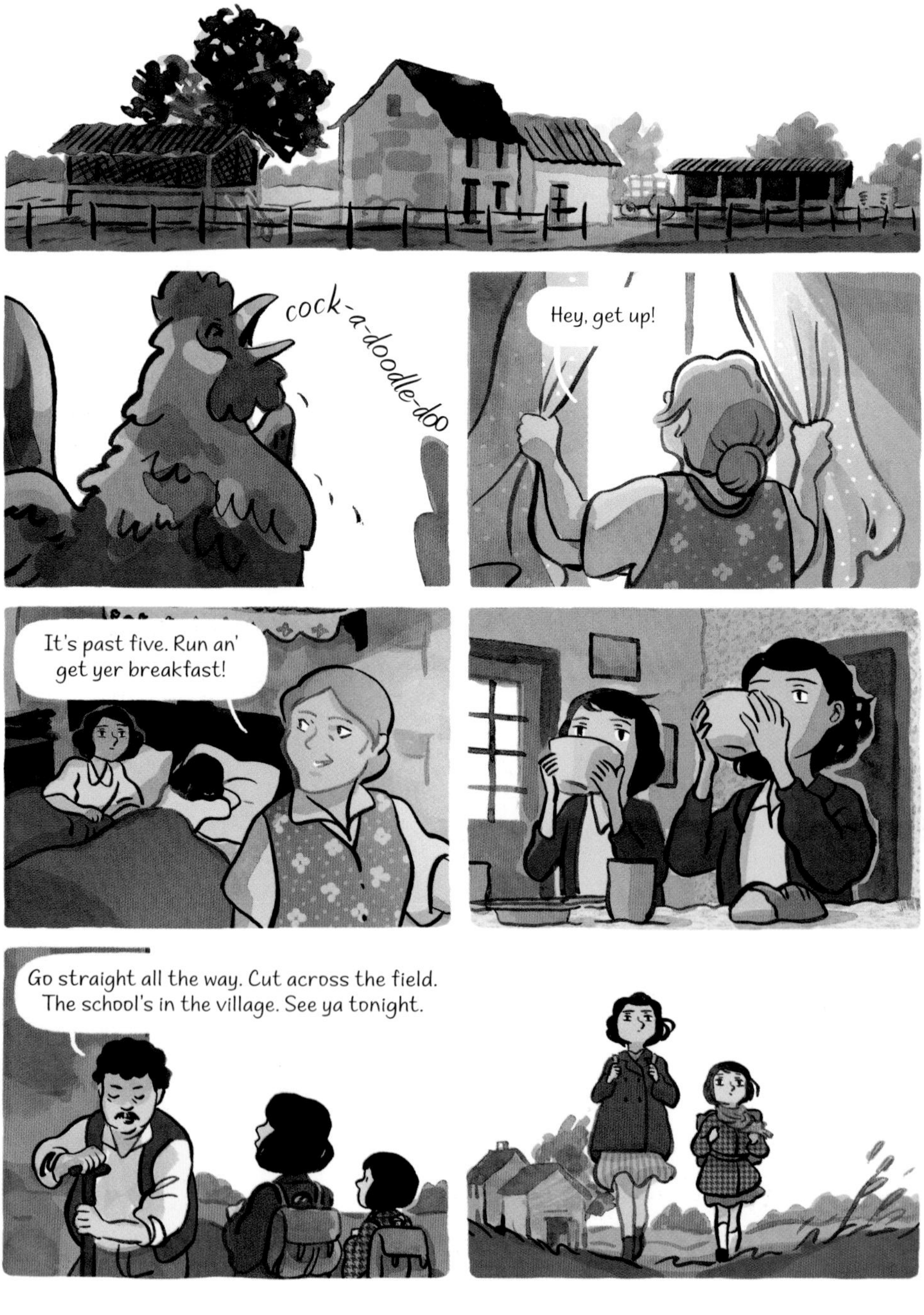

cock-a-doodle-doo
Hey, get up!
It's past five. Run an' get yer breakfast!
Go straight all the way. Cut across the field. The school's in the village. See ya tonight.

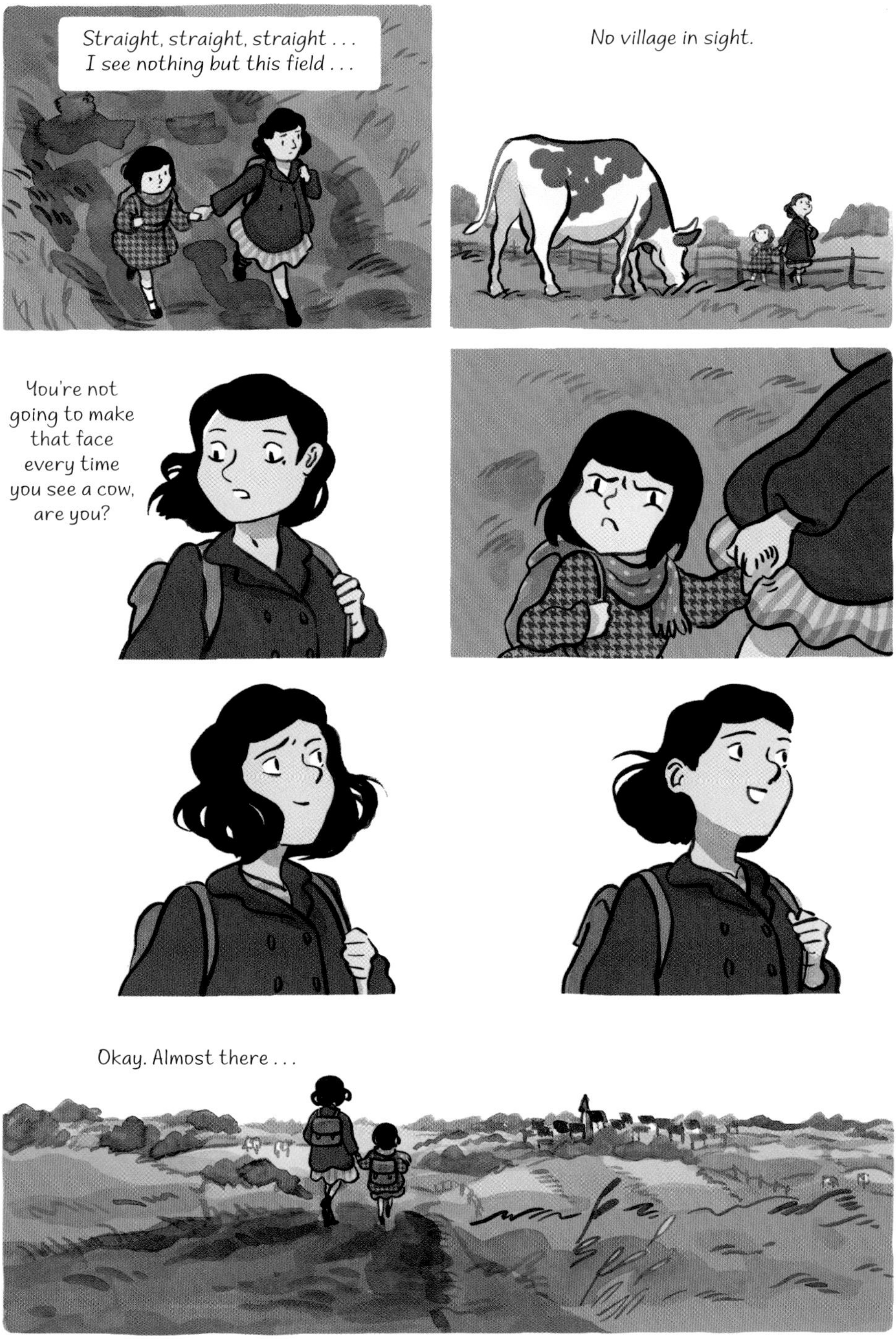

Straight, straight, straight . . .
I see nothing but this field . . .
No village in sight.
You're not going to make that face every time you see a cow, are you?
Okay. Almost there . . .

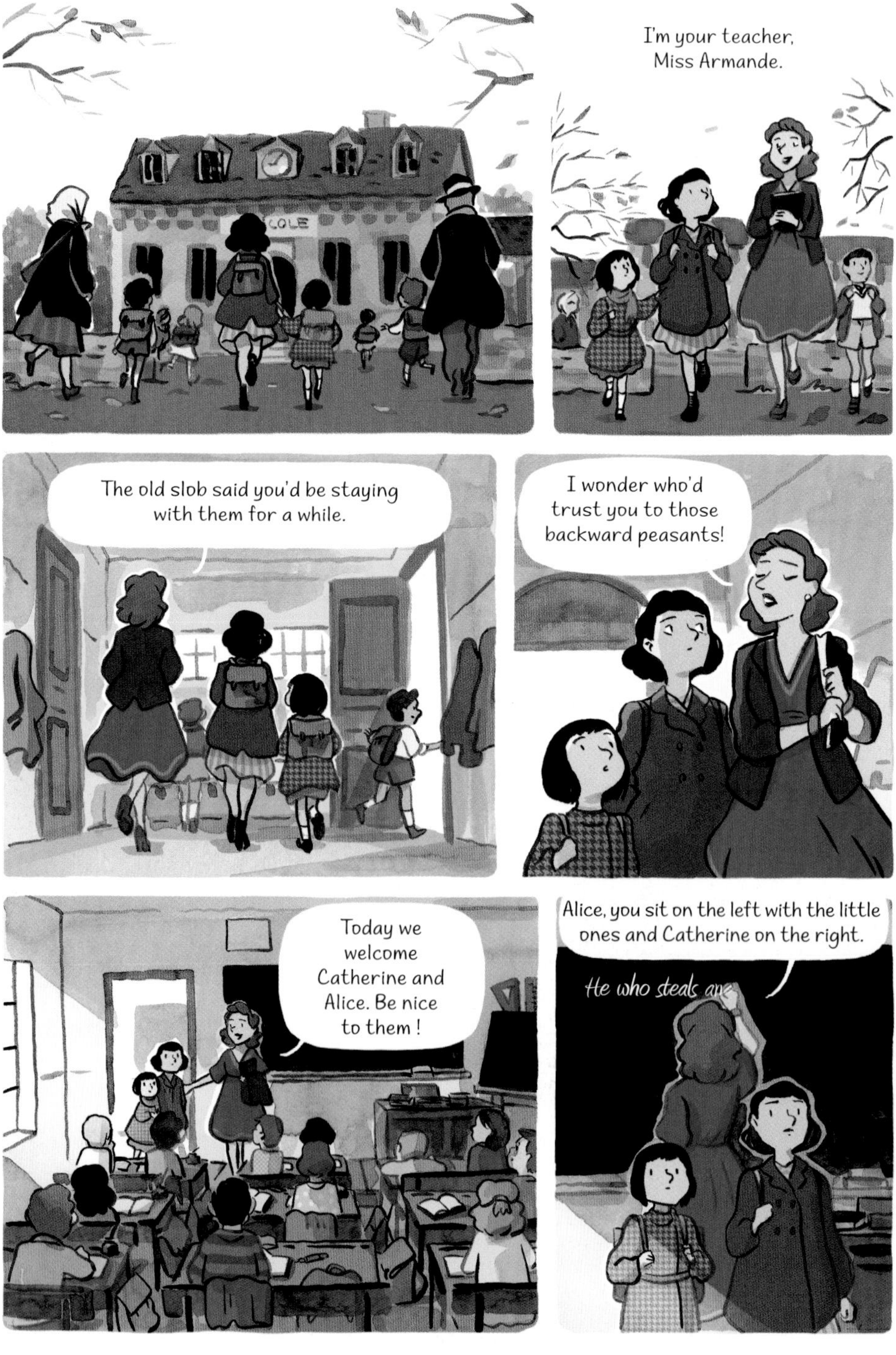

ÉCOLE
I'm your teacher, Miss Armande.
The old slob said you'd be staying with them for a while.
I wonder who'd trust you to those backward peasants!
Today we welcome Catherine and Alice. Be nice to them !
Alice, you sit on the left with the little ones and Catherine on the right.
He who steals an

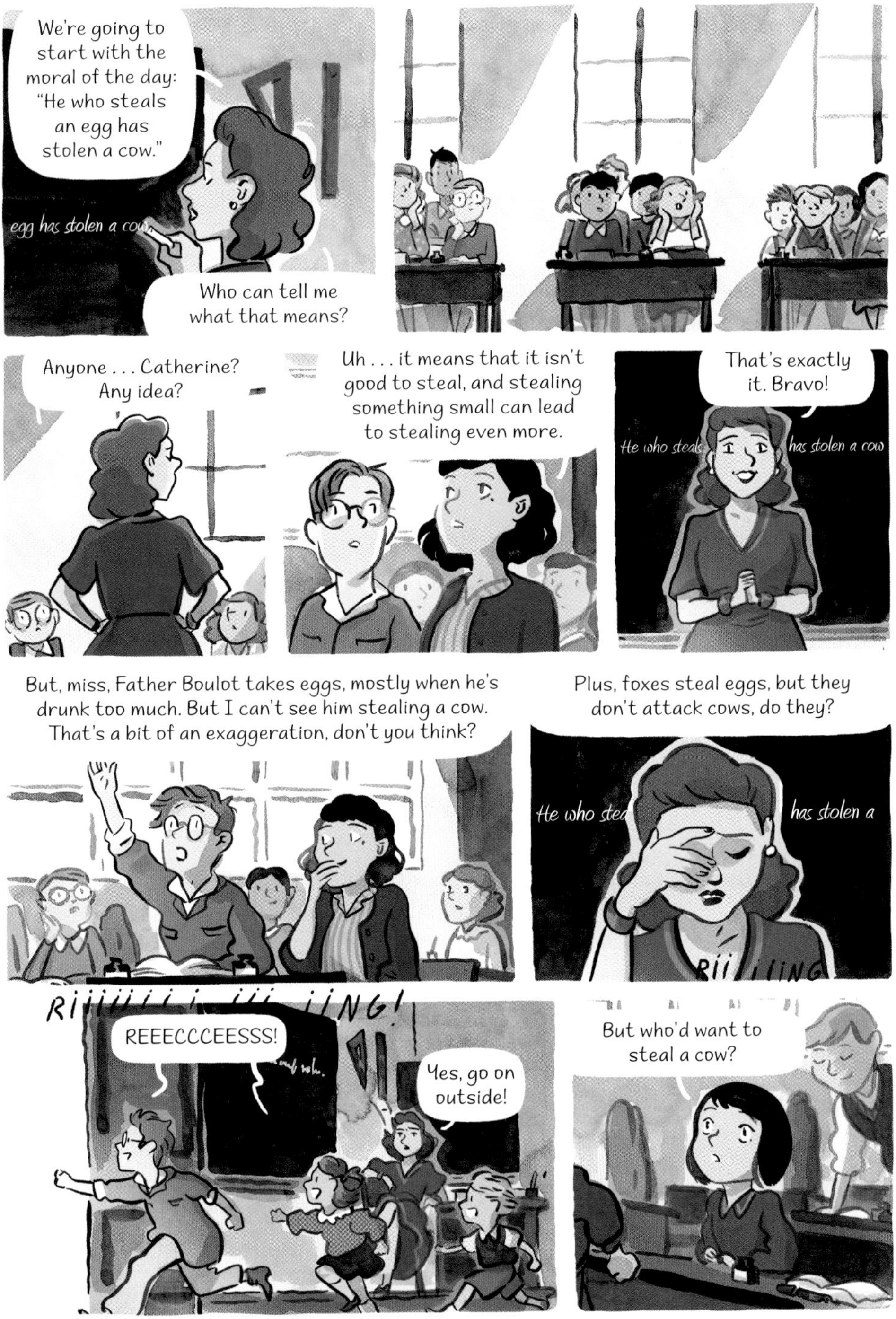

We're going to start with the moral of the day: "He who steals an egg has stolen a cow."
egg has stolen a cow
Who can tell me what that means?
Anyone . . . Catherine? Any idea?
Uh . . . it means that it isn't good to steal, and stealing something small can lead to stealing even more.
That's exactly it. Bravo!
He who steals
has stolen a cow
But, miss, Father Boulot takes eggs, mostly when he's drunk too much. But I can't see him stealing a cow. That's a bit of an exaggeration, don't you think?
Plus, foxes steal eggs, but they don't attack cows, do they?
He who ste
has stolen a
RIIIIING
RIIIIIIIIIIIIIING!
REEECCCEESSS!
Yes, go on outside!
But who'd want to steal a cow?

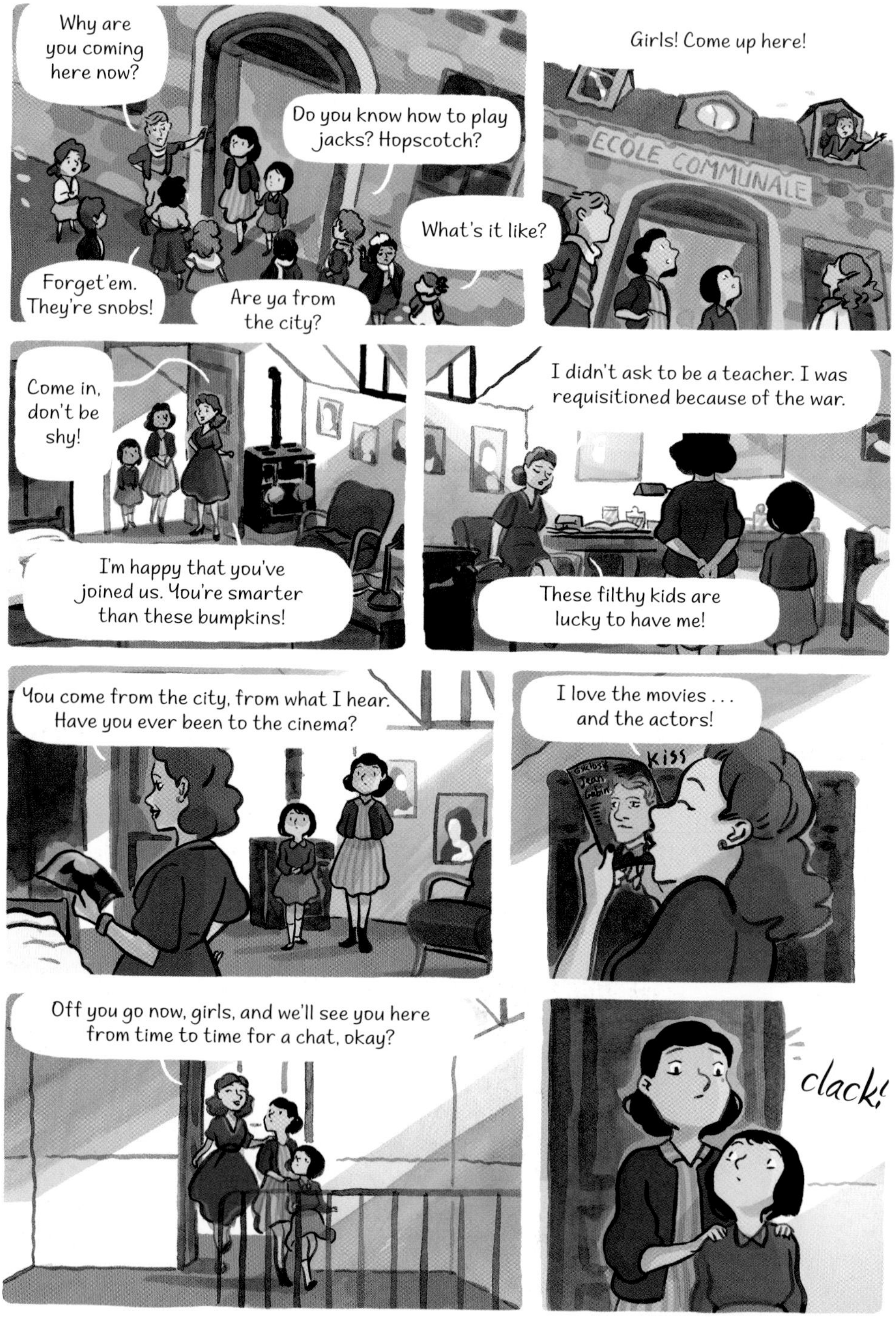
Why are you coming here now?
Do you know how to play jacks? Hopscotch?
What's it like?
Forget'em. They're snobs!
Are ya from the city?
Girls! Come up here!
ECOLE COMMUNALE
Come in, don't be shy!
I'm happy that you've joined us. You're smarter than these bumpkins!
I didn't ask to be a teacher. I was requisitioned because of the war.
These filthy kids are lucky to have me!
You come from the city, from what I hear. Have you ever been to the cinema?
I love the movies . . . and the actors!
KISS
Jean Gabin
Off you go now, girls, and we'll see you here from time to time for a chat, okay?
clack!

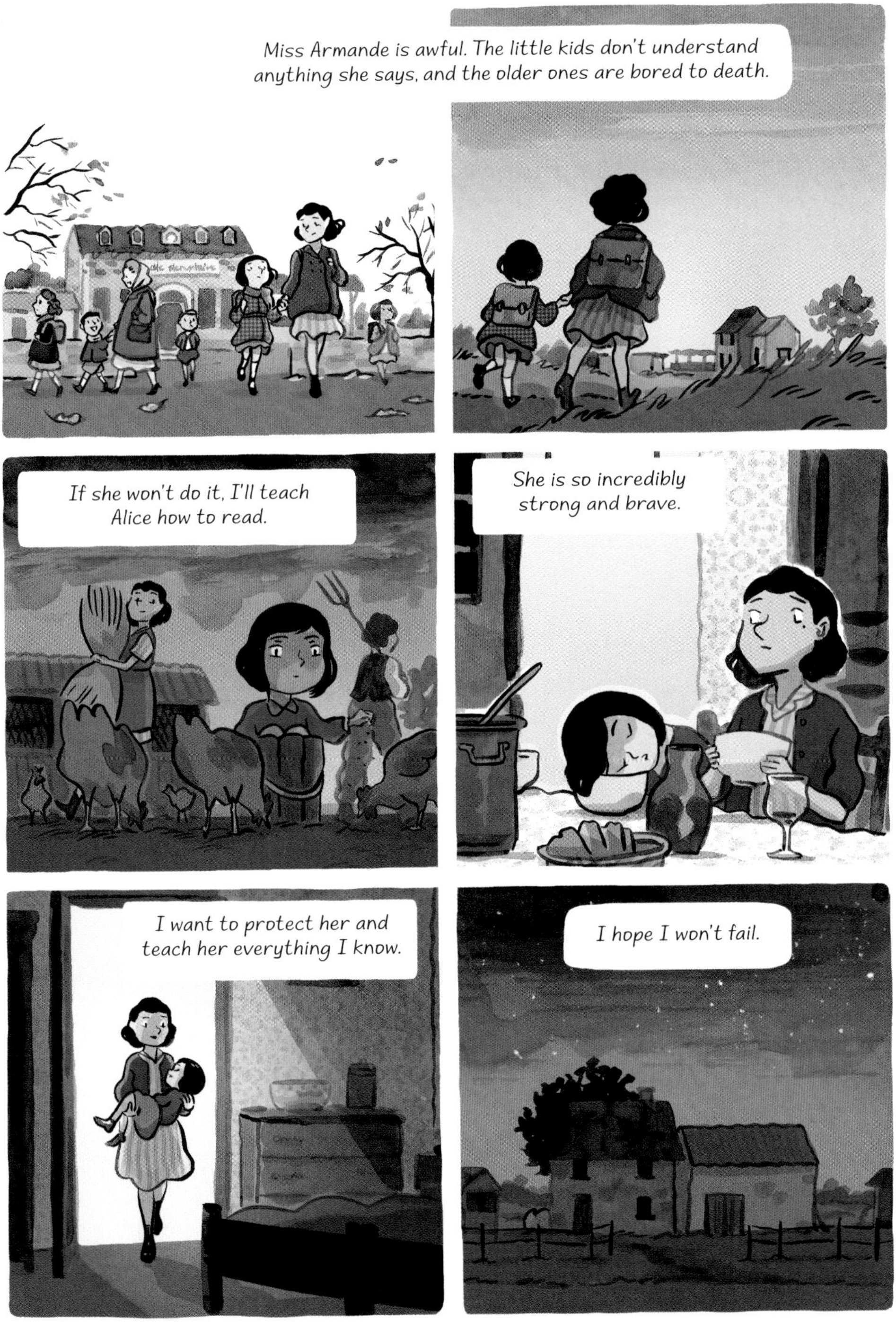
Miss Armande is awful. The little kids don't understand anything she says, and the older ones are bored to death.
If she won't do it, I'll teach Alice how to read.
She is so incredibly strong and brave.
I want to protect her and teach her everything I know.
I hope I won't fail.

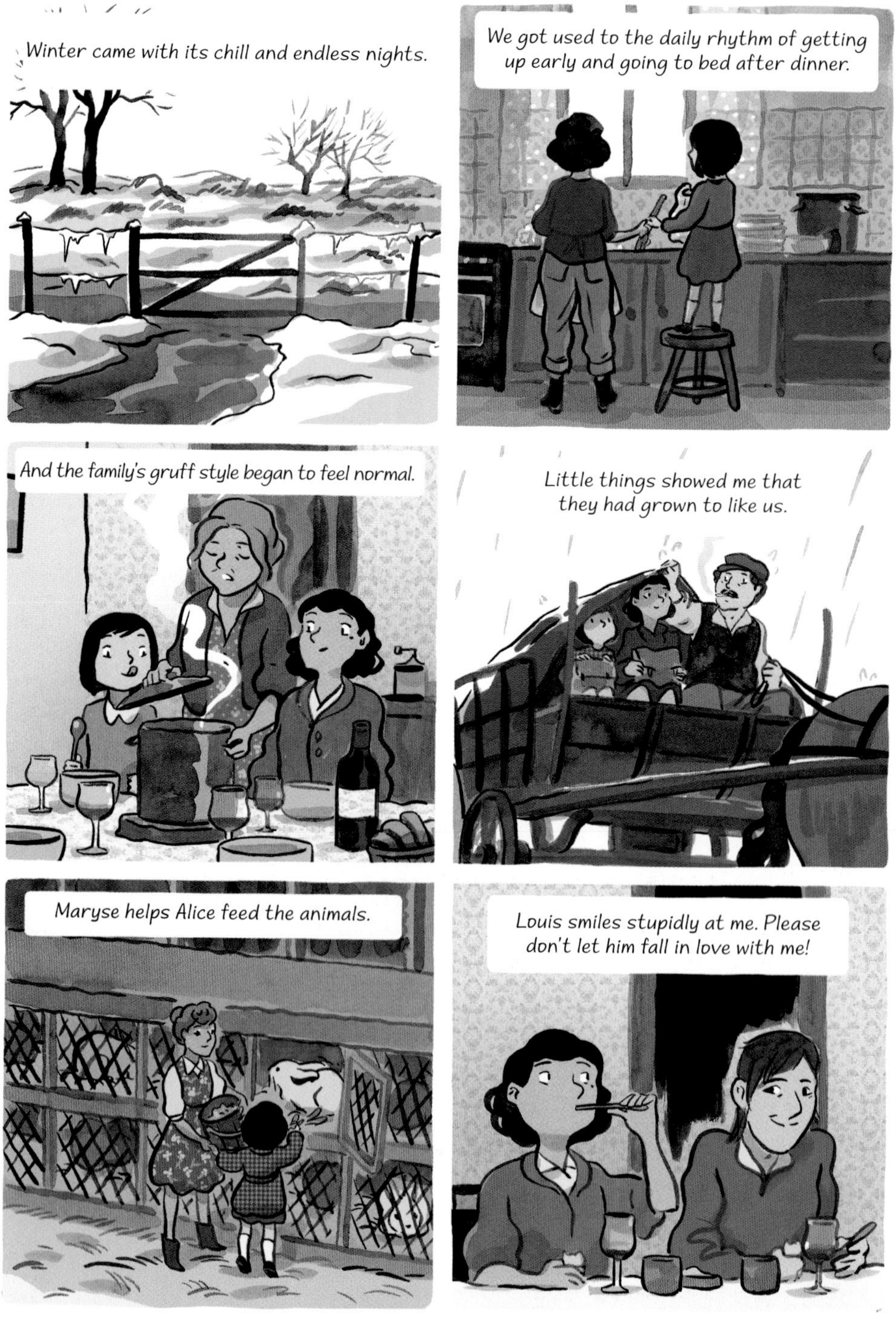
Winter came with its chill and endless nights.
We got used to the daily rhythm of getting up early and going to bed after dinner.
And the family's gruff style began to feel normal.
Little things showed me that they had grown to like us.
Maryse helps Alice feed the animals.
Louis smiles stupidly at me. Please don't let him fall in love with me!

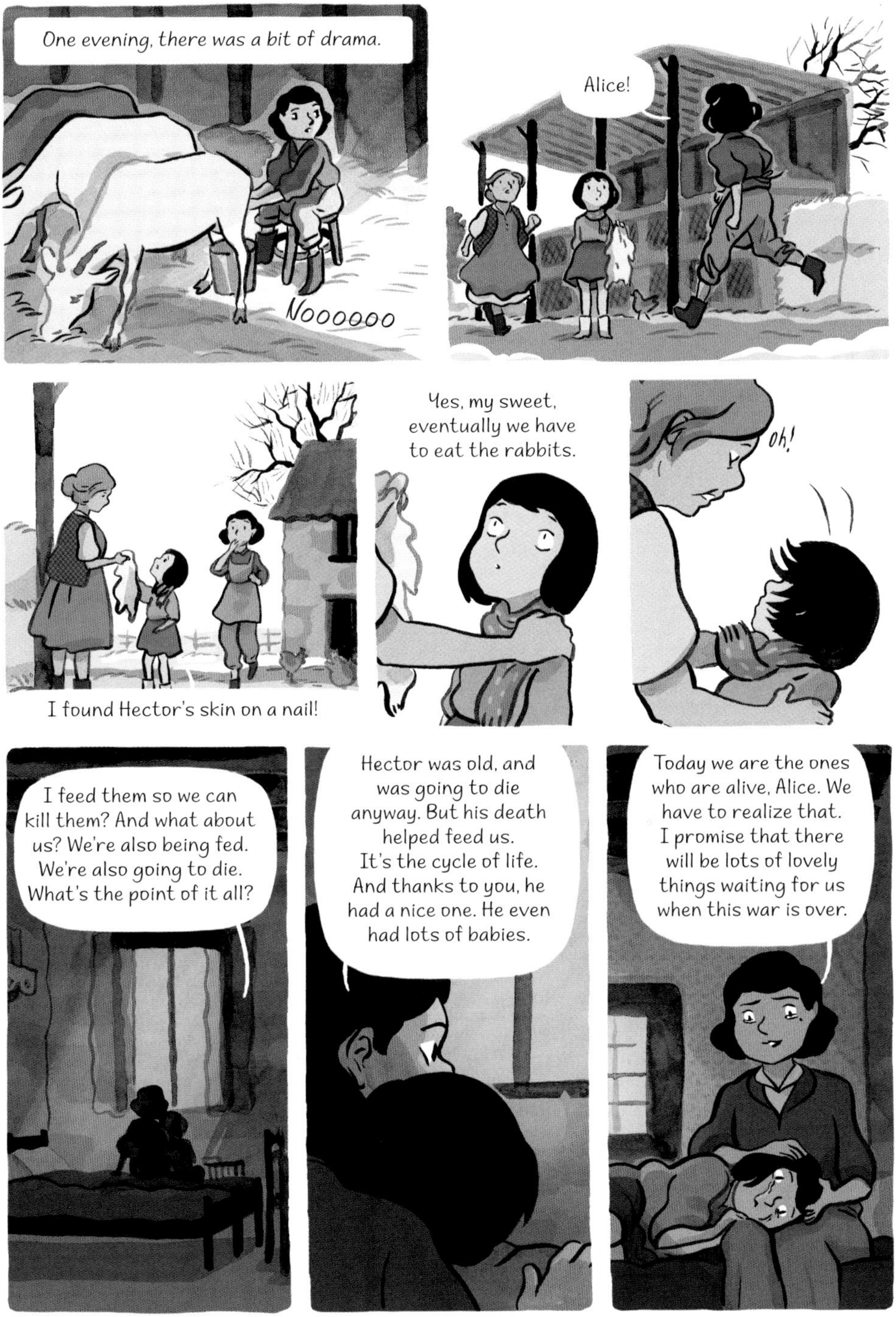
One evening, there was a bit of drama.
Noooooo
Alice!
I found Hector's skin on a nail!
Yes, my sweet, eventually we have to eat the rabbits.
Oh!
I feed them so we can kill them? And what about us? We're also being fed. We're also going to die. What's the point of it all?
Hector was old, and was going to die anyway. But his death helped feed us. It's the cycle of life. And thanks to you, he had a nice one. He even had lots of babies.
Today we are the ones who are alive, Alice. We have to realize that. I promise that there will be lots of lovely things waiting for us when this war is over.

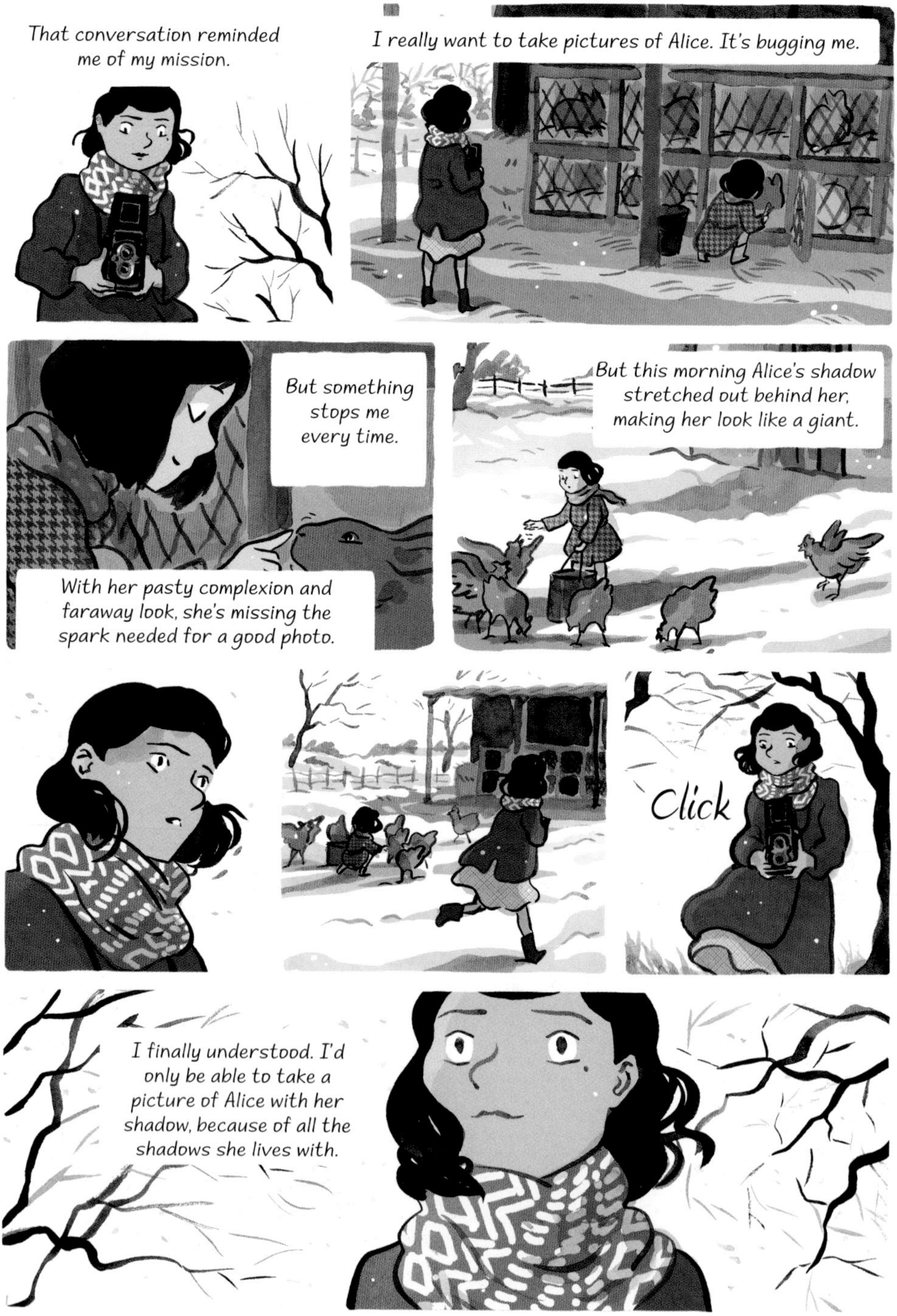
That conversation reminded me of my mission.
I really want to take pictures of Alice. It's bugging me.
But something stops me every time.
With her pasty complexion and faraway look, she's missing the spark needed for a good photo.
But this morning Alice's shadow stretched out behind her, making her look like a giant.
Click
I finally understood. I'd only be able to take a picture of Alice with her shadow, because of all the shadows she lives with.

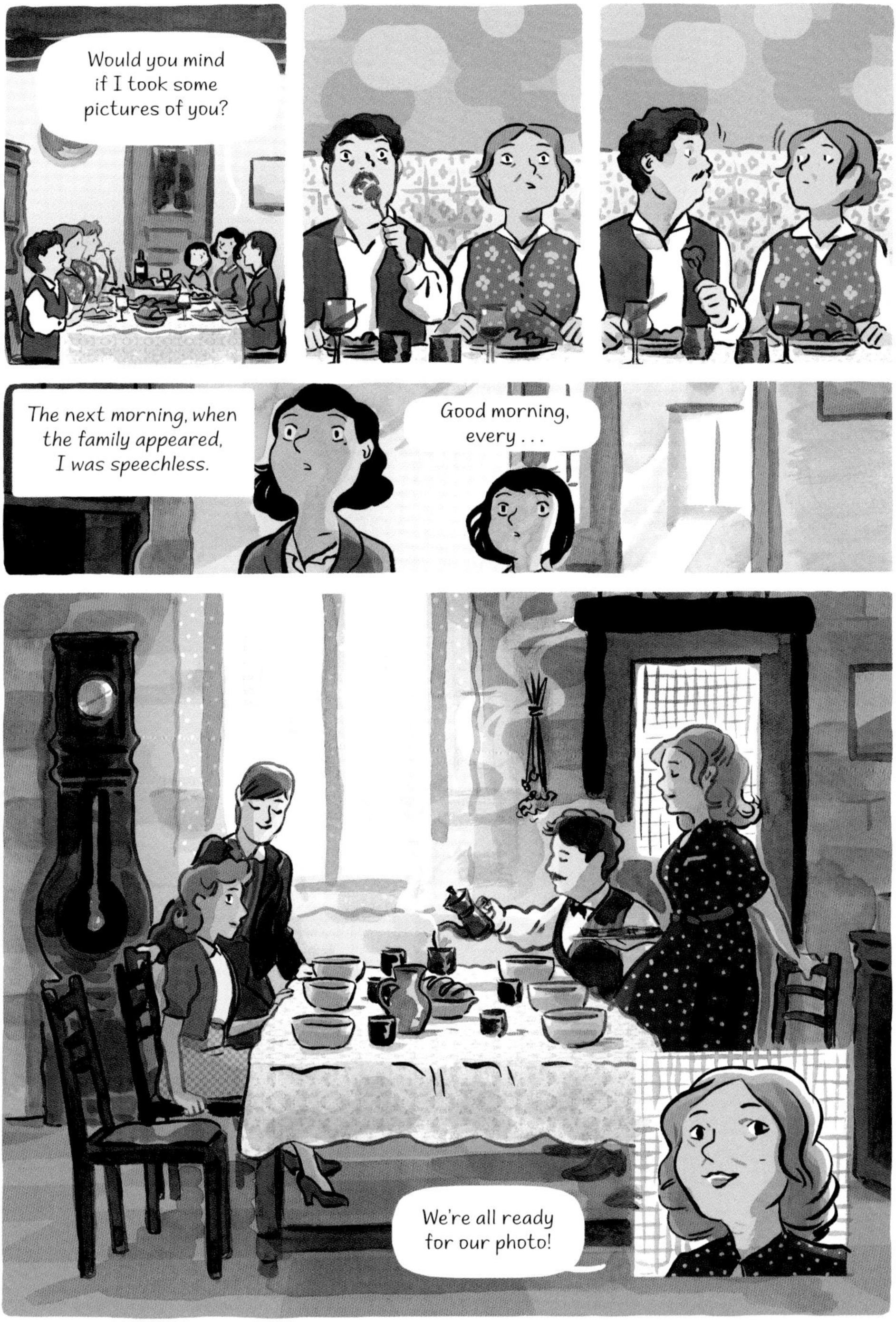
Would you mind if I took some pictures of you?
The next morning, when the family appeared, I was speechless.
Good morning, every . . .
We're all ready for our photo!

I remembered what Étienne had said.

People want to be captured in photographs looking their loveliest, and at a moment that feels like time has stopped.

Étienne draws out the pride from his subjects—men and women linked to the earth, its seasons, and its harshness.

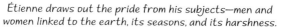

And that's where art is found— in life's little pockets . . .

. . . in the extraordinary.

Click

The farmers made a feast to celebrate.

I just hoped my work lived up to it.

Today made me feel like taking lots more photos—to keep learning how to shoot shadows . . . and framing, of course, like I could do with portraits.

I'll take the film to the village next Thursday.

I like printing my own photographs. I took classes and I'm pretty picky.

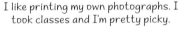

The photographer's wife has been running the shop since the war. Ask her if you can help.

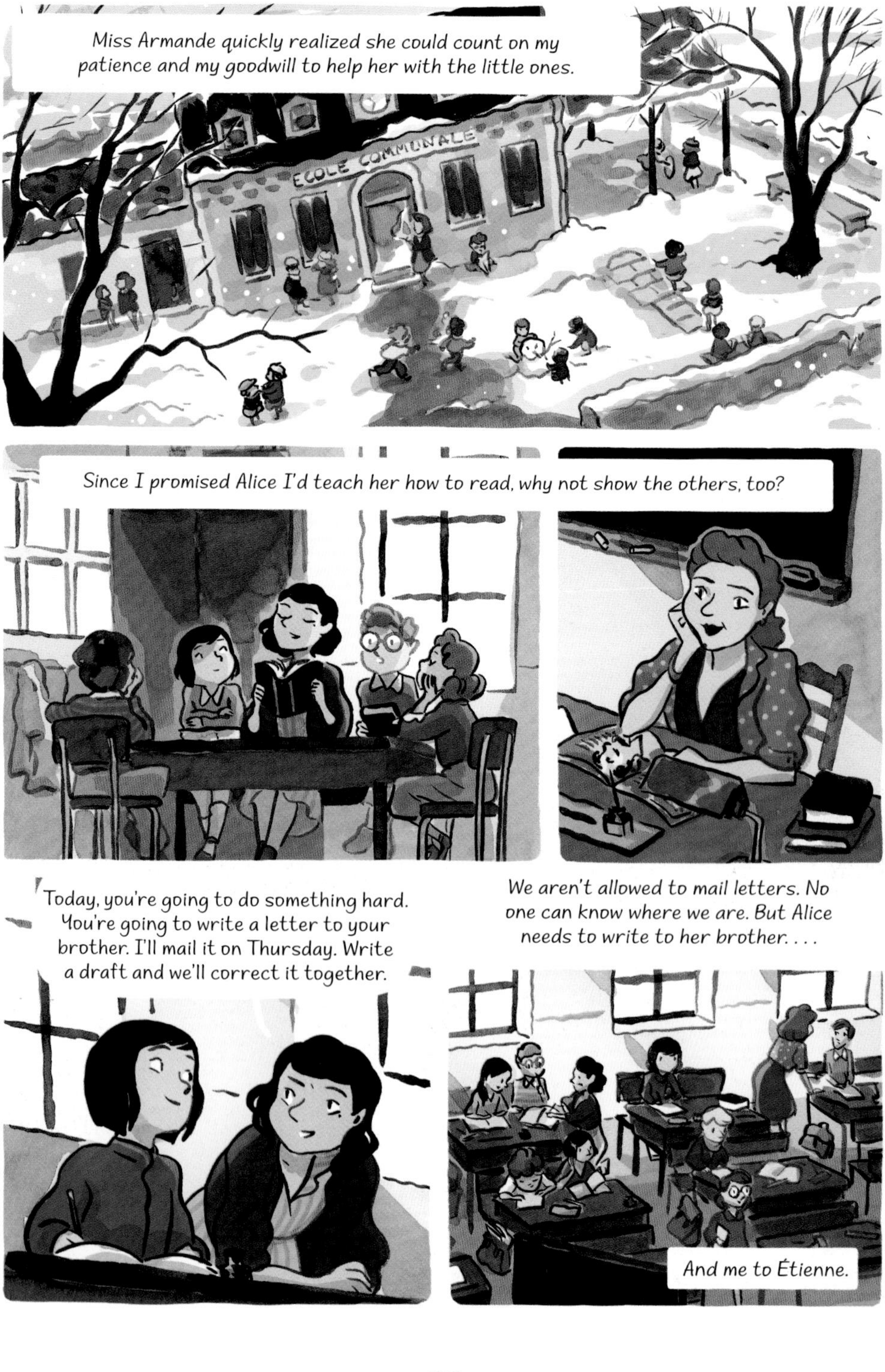
Miss Armande quickly realized she could count on my patience and my goodwill to help her with the little ones.
ECOLE COMMUNALE
Since I promised Alice I'd teach her how to read, why not show the others, too?
Today, you're going to do something hard. You're going to write a letter to your brother. I'll mail it on Thursday. Write a draft and we'll correct it together.
We aren't allowed to mail letters. No one can know where we are. But Alice needs to write to her brother. . . .
And me to Étienne.

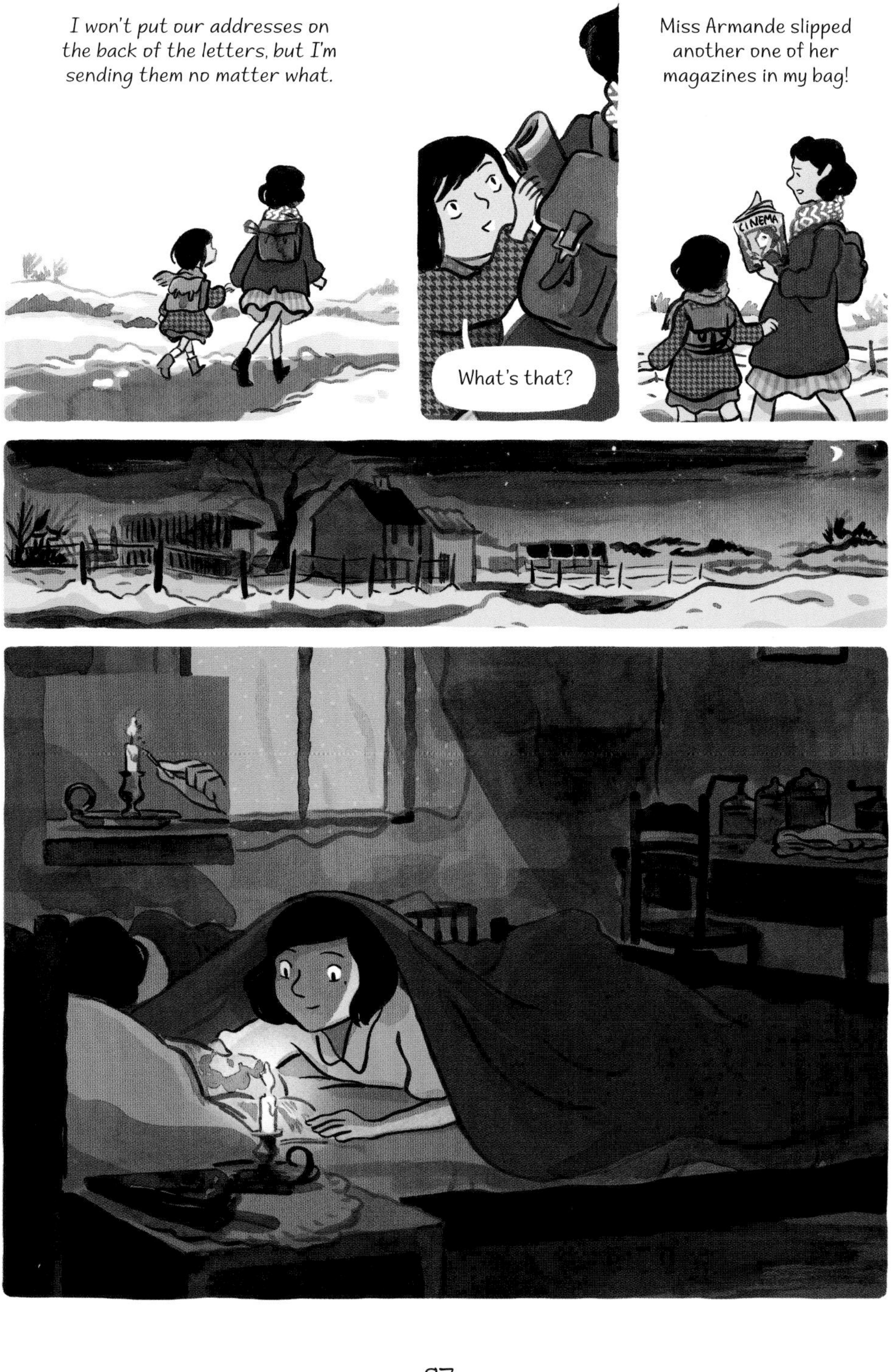
I won't put our addresses on the back of the letters, but I'm sending them no matter what.
What's that?
Miss Armande slipped another one of her magazines in my bag!
CINEMA

Thursday morning, at last!

Hello!

ding

Hello, how can I help you?

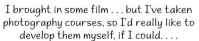

I brought in some film . . . but I've taken photography courses, so I'd really like to develop them myself, if I could. . . .

See how busy I am with my kids? I guess it's fine. As long as you pay for what you use, and you're careful.

I'll come back for you in three hours.

And just like that, I'm back in the magical darkroom.

Two hours later I ask the woman where to find the post office . . .

. . . and my mission is accomplished.

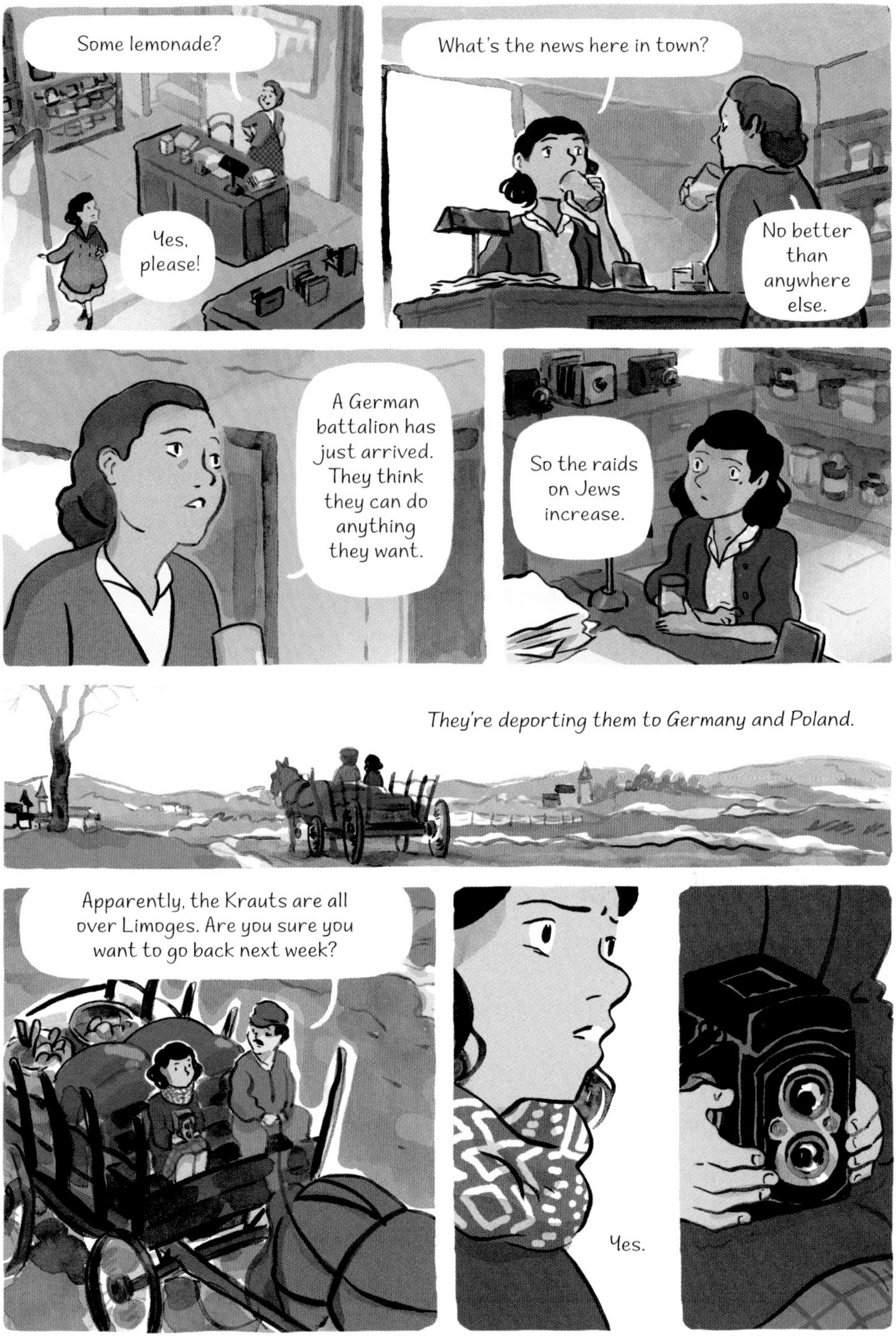
Some lemonade?
Yes, please!
What's the news here in town?
No better than anywhere else.
A German battalion has just arrived. They think they can do anything they want.
So the raids on Jews increase.
They're deporting them to Germany and Poland.
Apparently, the Krauts are all over Limoges. Are you sure you want to go back next week?
Yes.

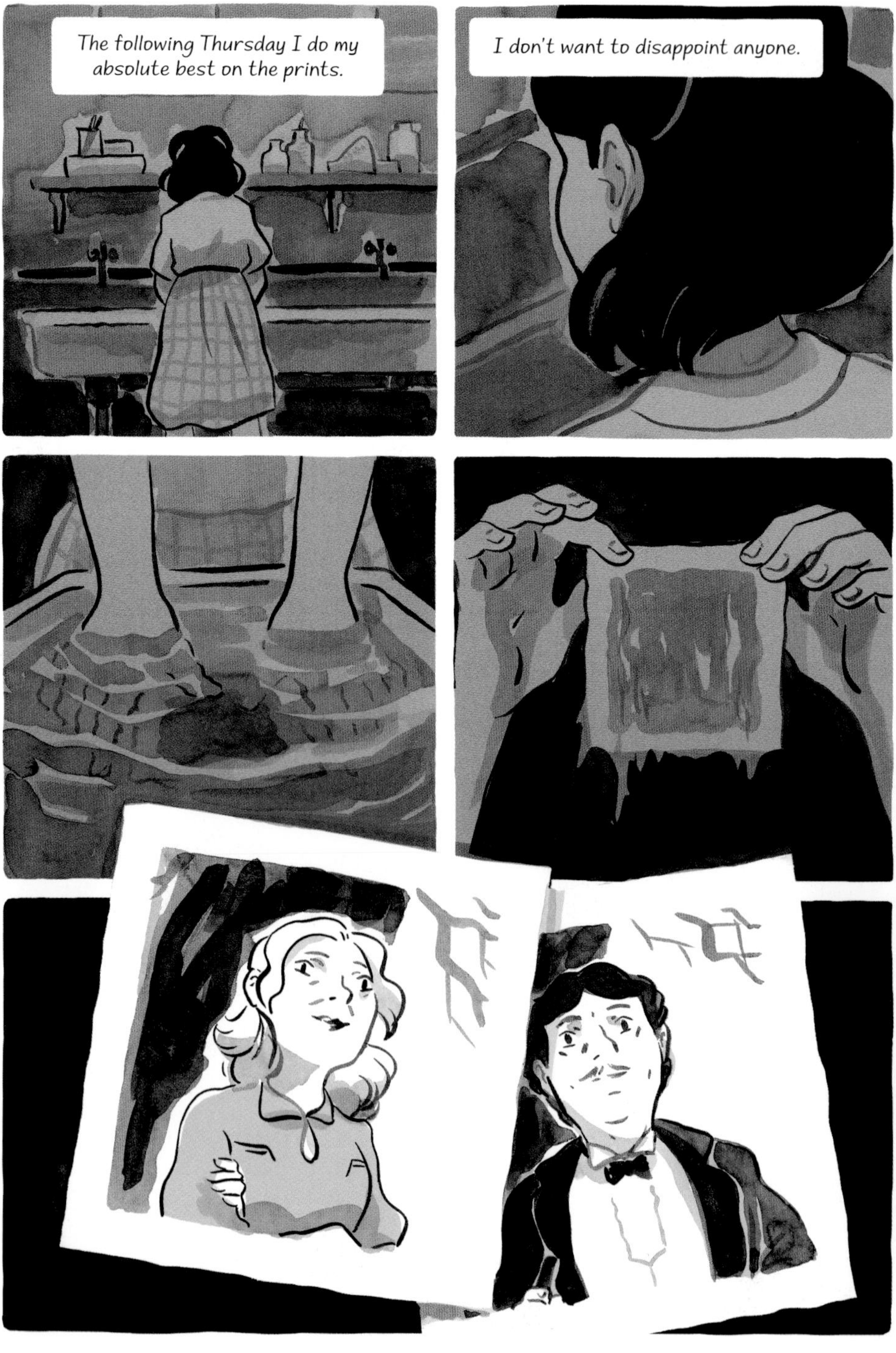
The following Thursday I do my absolute best on the prints.
I don't want to disappoint anyone.

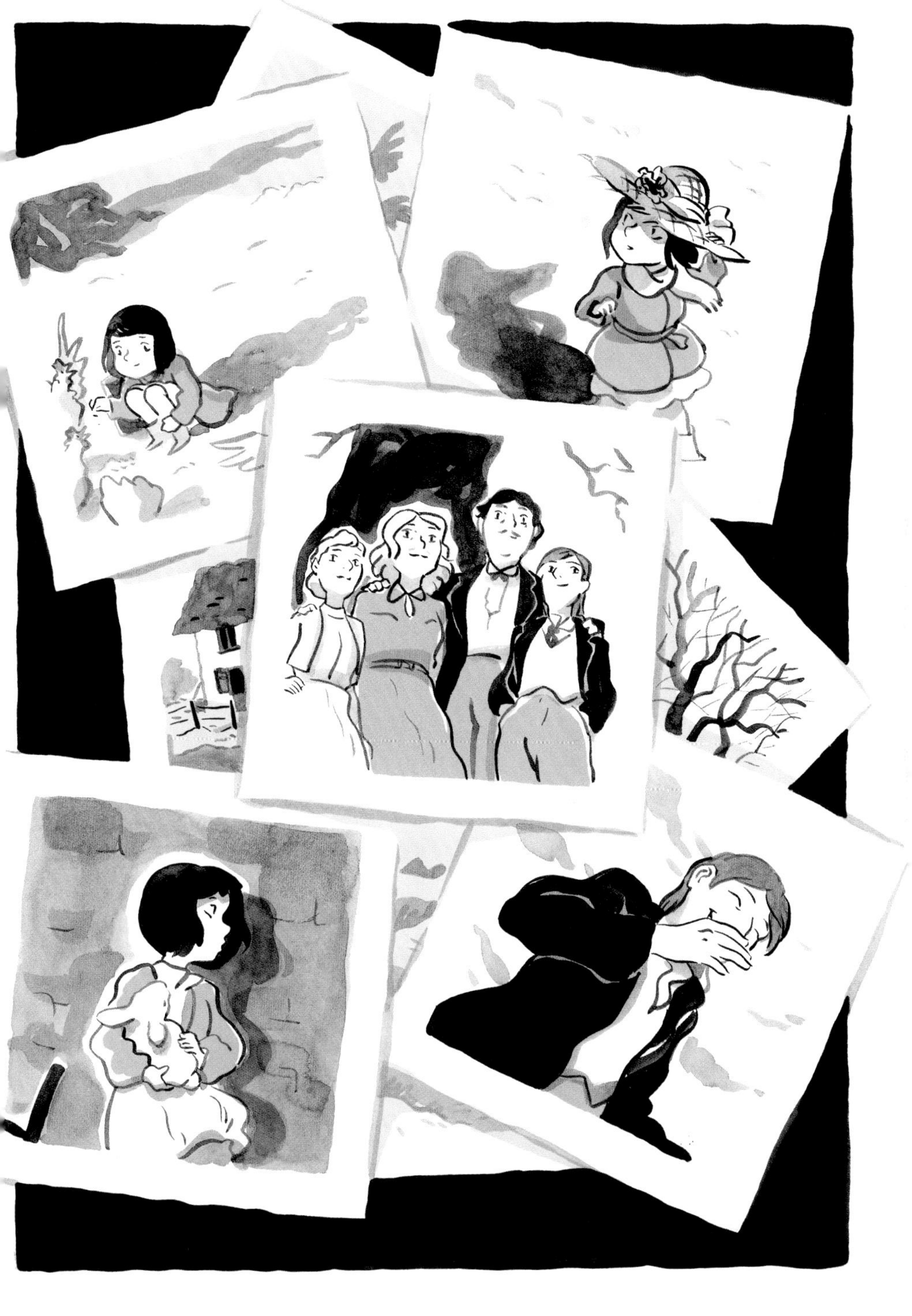

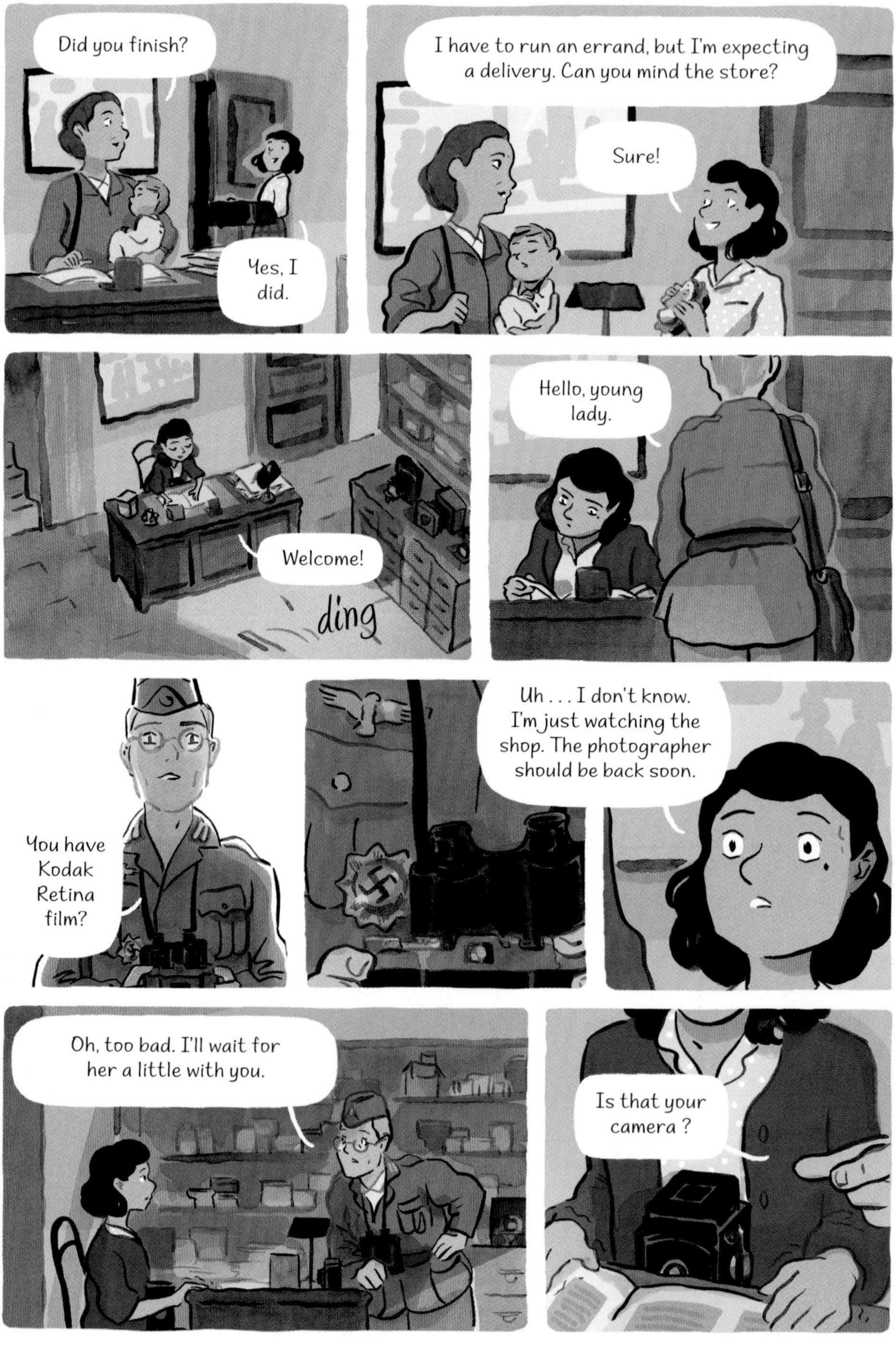
Did you finish?
Yes, I did.
I have to run an errand, but I'm expecting a delivery. Can you mind the store?
Sure!
Welcome!
ding
Hello, young lady.
You have Kodak Retina film?
Uh . . . I don't know. I'm just watching the shop. The photographer should be back soon.
Oh, too bad. I'll wait for her a little with you.
Is that your camera ?

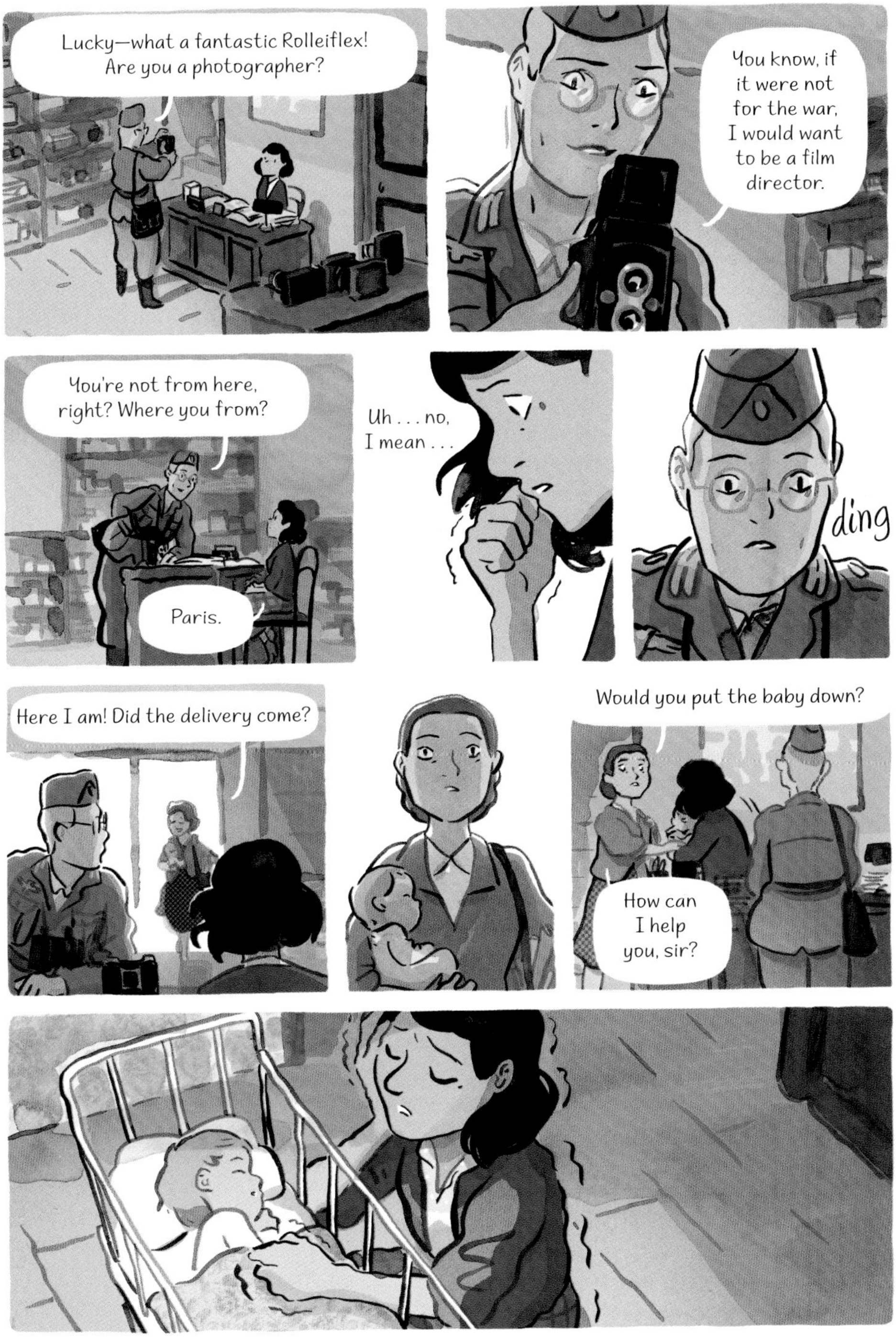
Lucky—what a fantastic Rolleiflex! Are you a photographer?
You know, if it were not for the war, I would want to be a film director.
You're not from here, right? Where you from?
Paris.
Uh . . . no, I mean . . .
ding
Here I am! Did the delivery come?
Would you put the baby down?
How can I help you, sir?

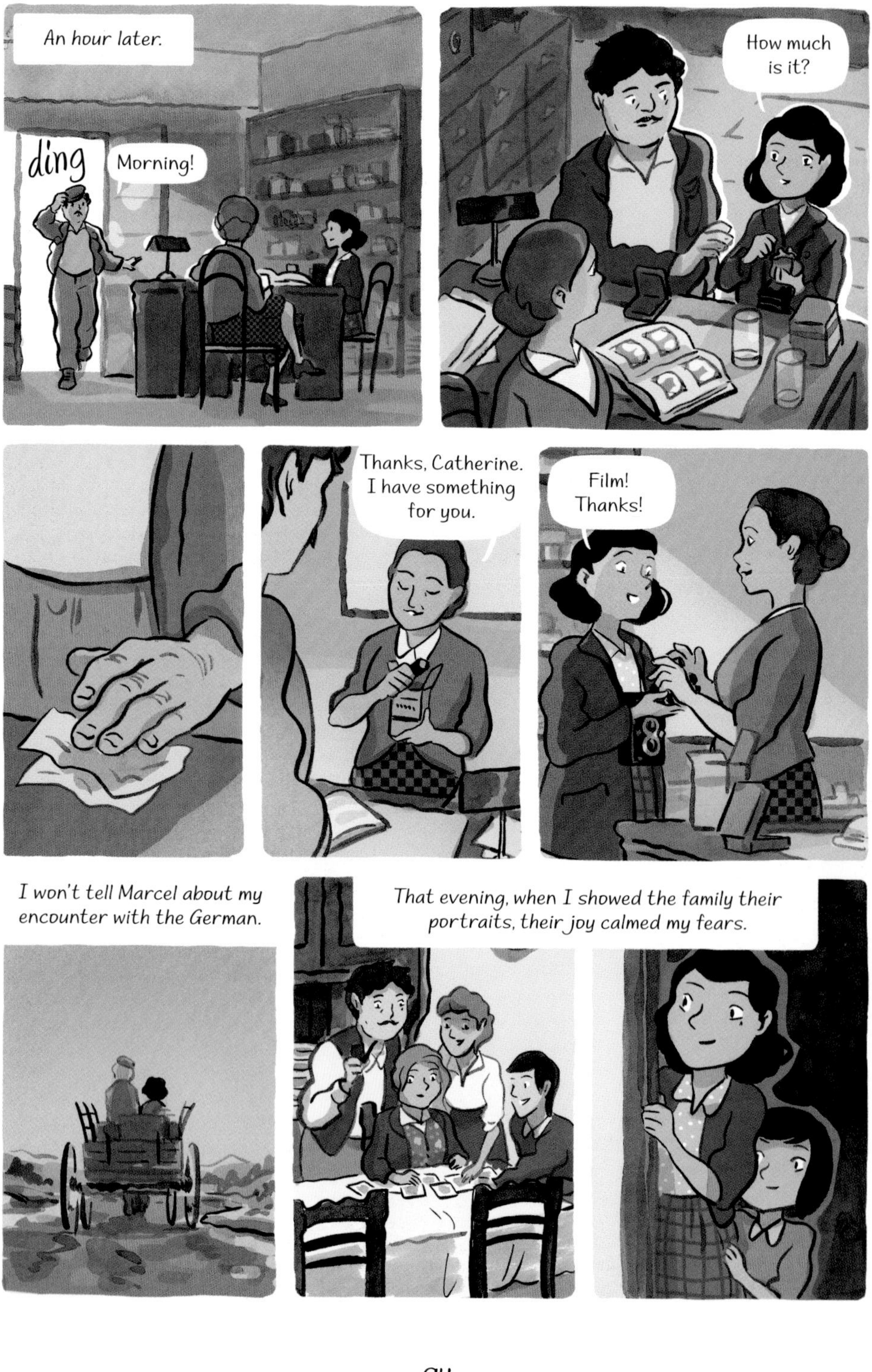
An hour later.
ding
Morning!
How much is it?
Thanks, Catherine. I have something for you.
Film! Thanks!
I won't tell Marcel about my encounter with the German.
That evening, when I showed the family their portraits, their joy calmed my fears.

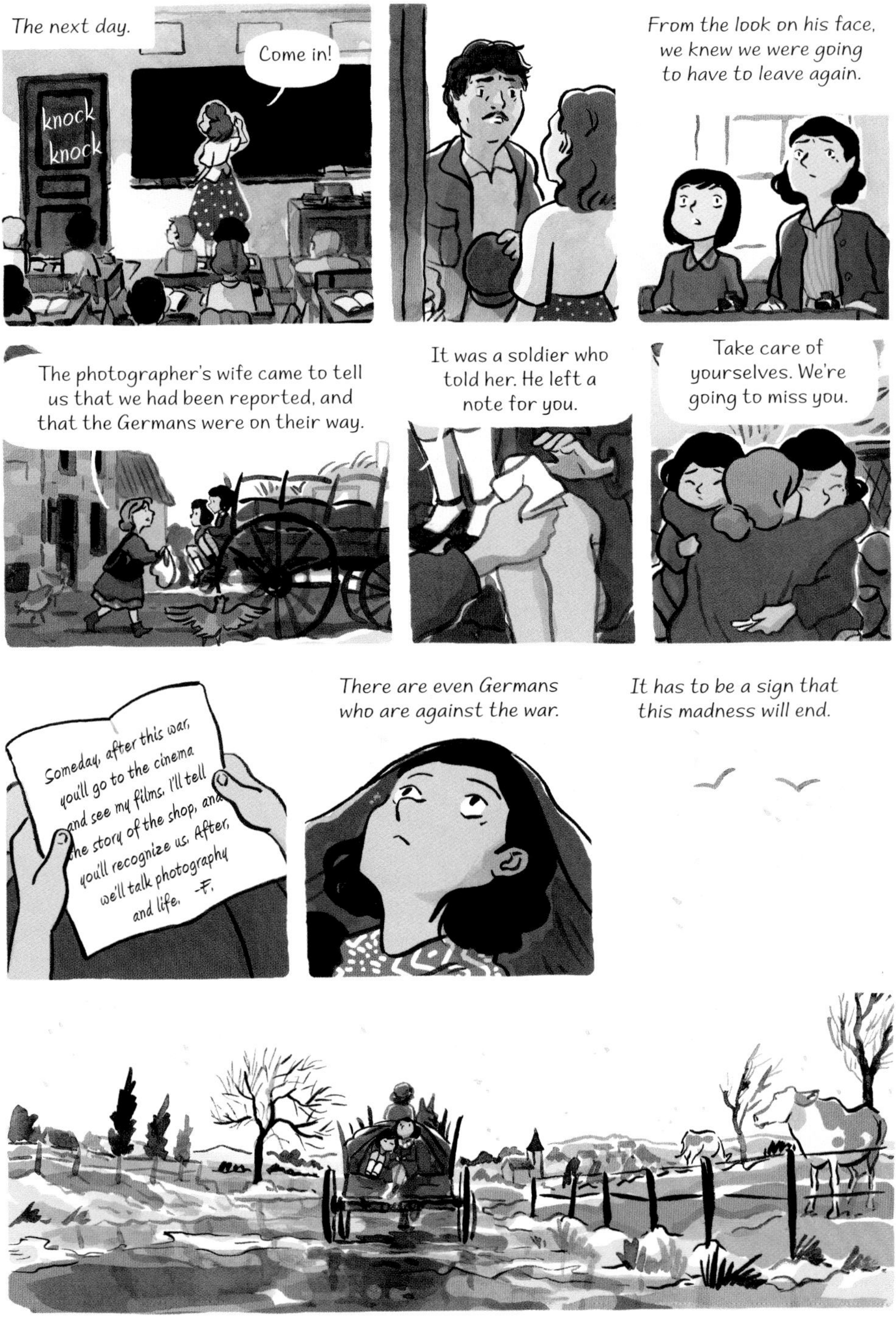
The next day.
Come in!
knock knock
From the look on his face, we knew we were going to have to leave again.
The photographer's wife came to tell us that we had been reported, and that the Germans were on their way.
It was a soldier who told her. He left a note for you.
Take care of yourselves. We're going to miss you.
Someday, after this war, you'll go to the cinema and see my films. I'll tell the story of the shop, and you'll recognize us. After, we'll talk photography and life. -F.
There are even Germans who are against the war.
It has to be a sign that this madness will end.

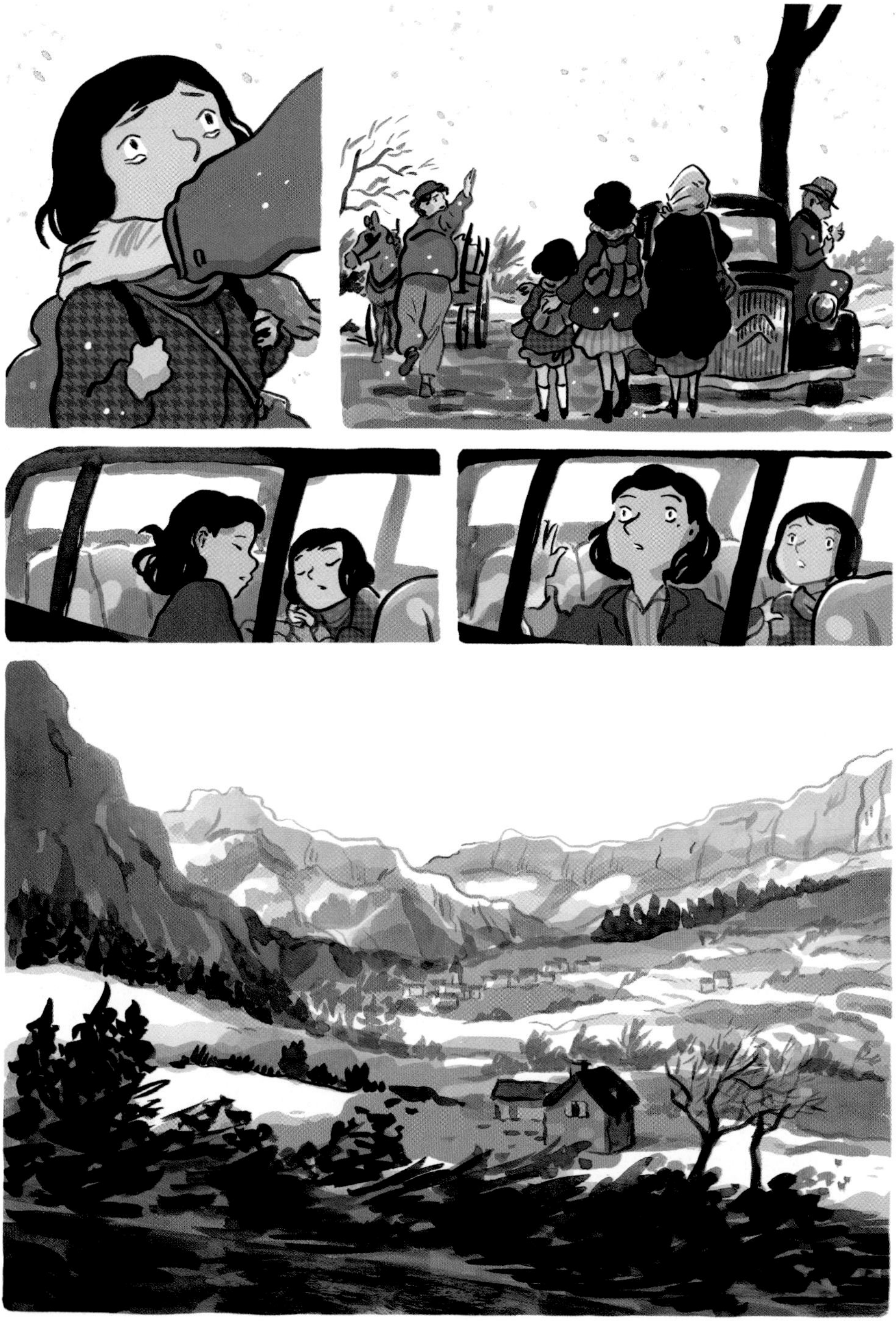

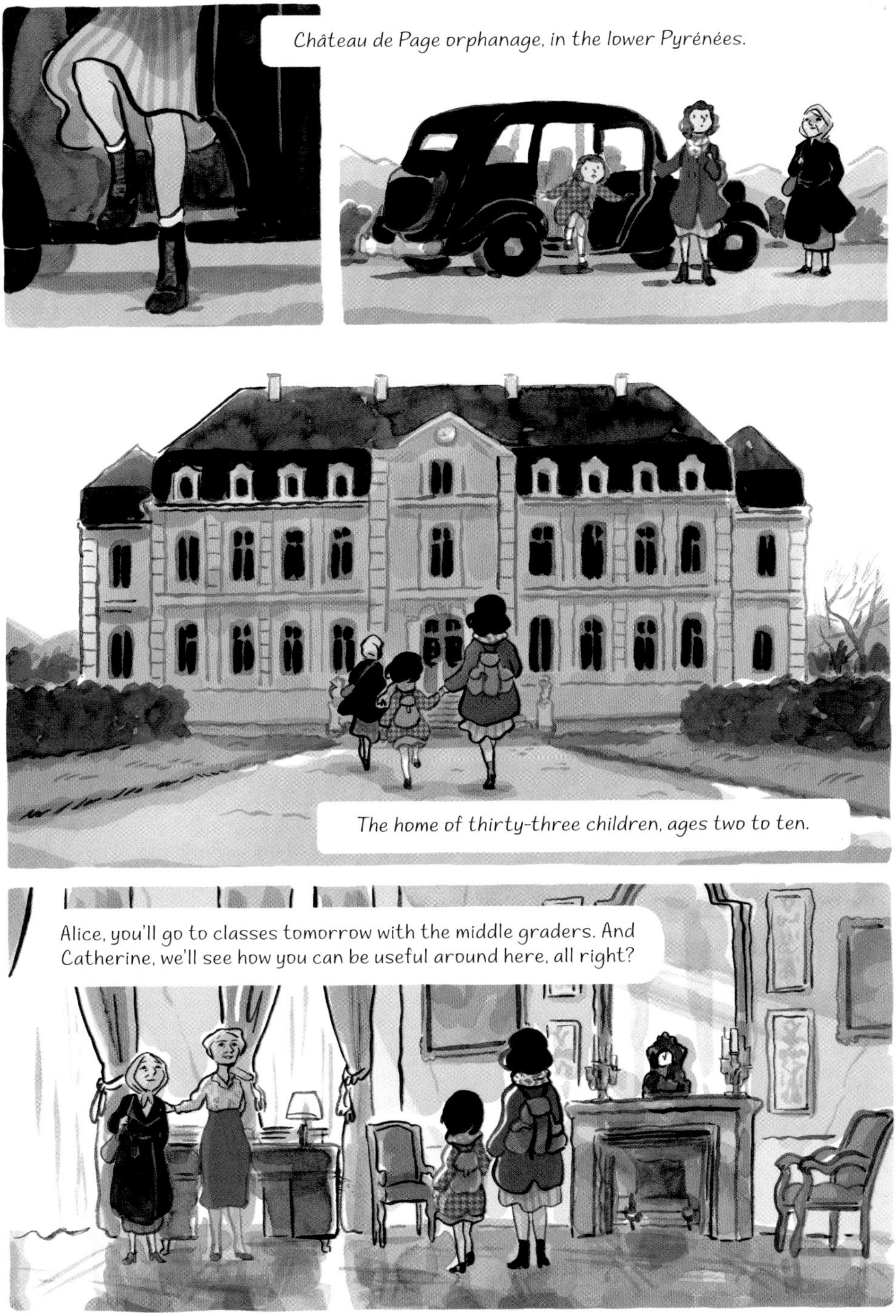
Château de Page orphanage, in the lower Pyrénées.
The home of thirty-three children, ages two to ten.
Alice, you'll go to classes tomorrow with the middle graders. And Catherine, we'll see how you can be useful around here, all right?

What's an orphanage?

It's . . . a place where children live.

Dinner was smaller than our stomachs had gotten used to.

Alice rejected the place completely.

Too many kids.

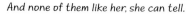

And none of them like her, she can tell.

She's shy, so the kids lose interest quickly.

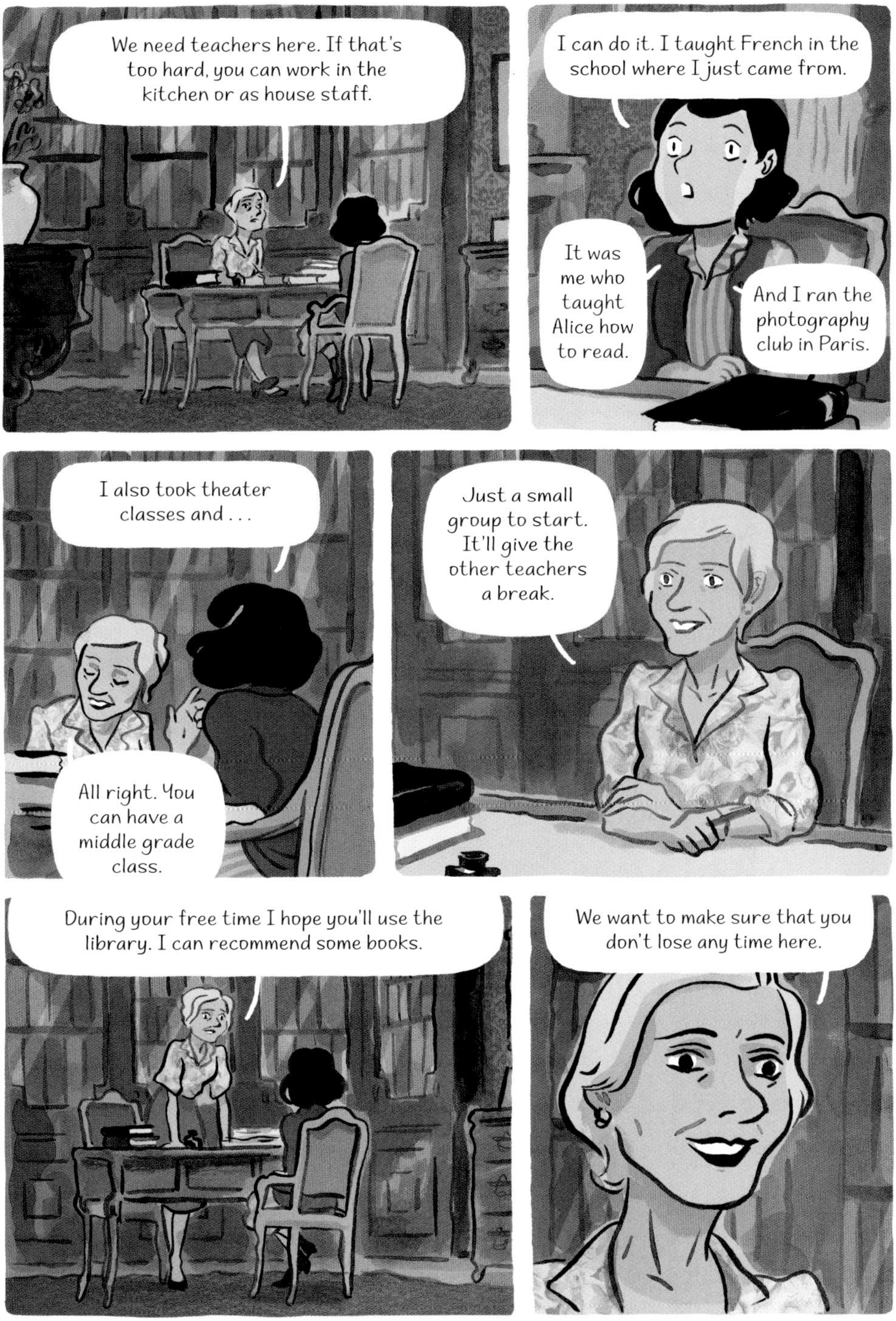
We need teachers here. If that's too hard, you can work in the kitchen or as house staff.
I can do it. I taught French in the school where I just came from.
It was me who taught Alice how to read.
And I ran the photography club in Paris.
I also took theater classes and . . .
All right. You can have a middle grade class.
Just a small group to start. It'll give the other teachers a break.
During your free time I hope you'll use the library. I can recommend some books.
We want to make sure that you don't lose any time here.

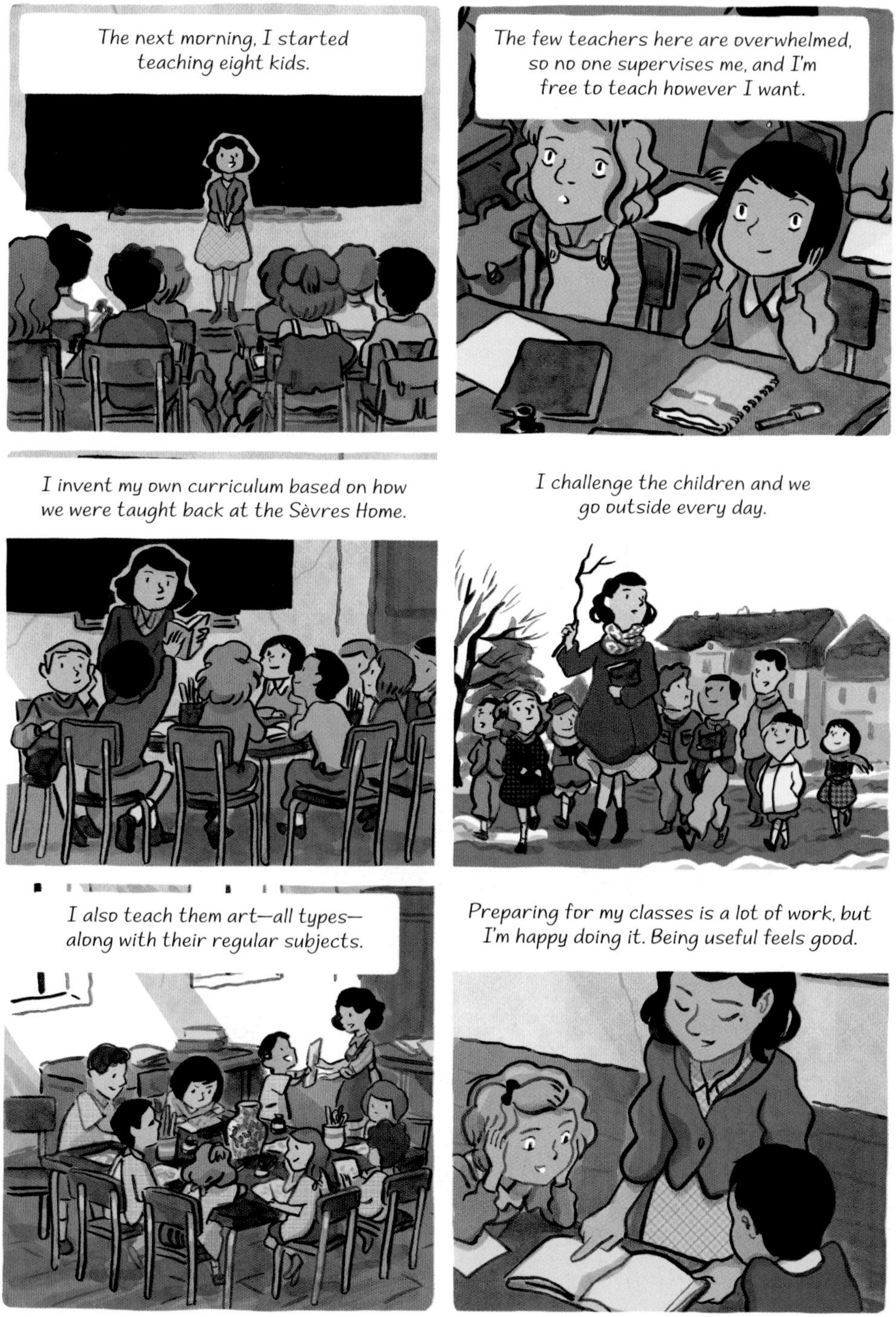
The next morning, I started teaching eight kids.
The few teachers here are overwhelmed, so no one supervises me, and I'm free to teach however I want.
I invent my own curriculum based on how we were taught back at the Sèvres Home.
I challenge the children and we go outside every day.
I also teach them art—all types—along with their regular subjects.
Preparing for my classes is a lot of work, but I'm happy doing it. Being useful feels good.

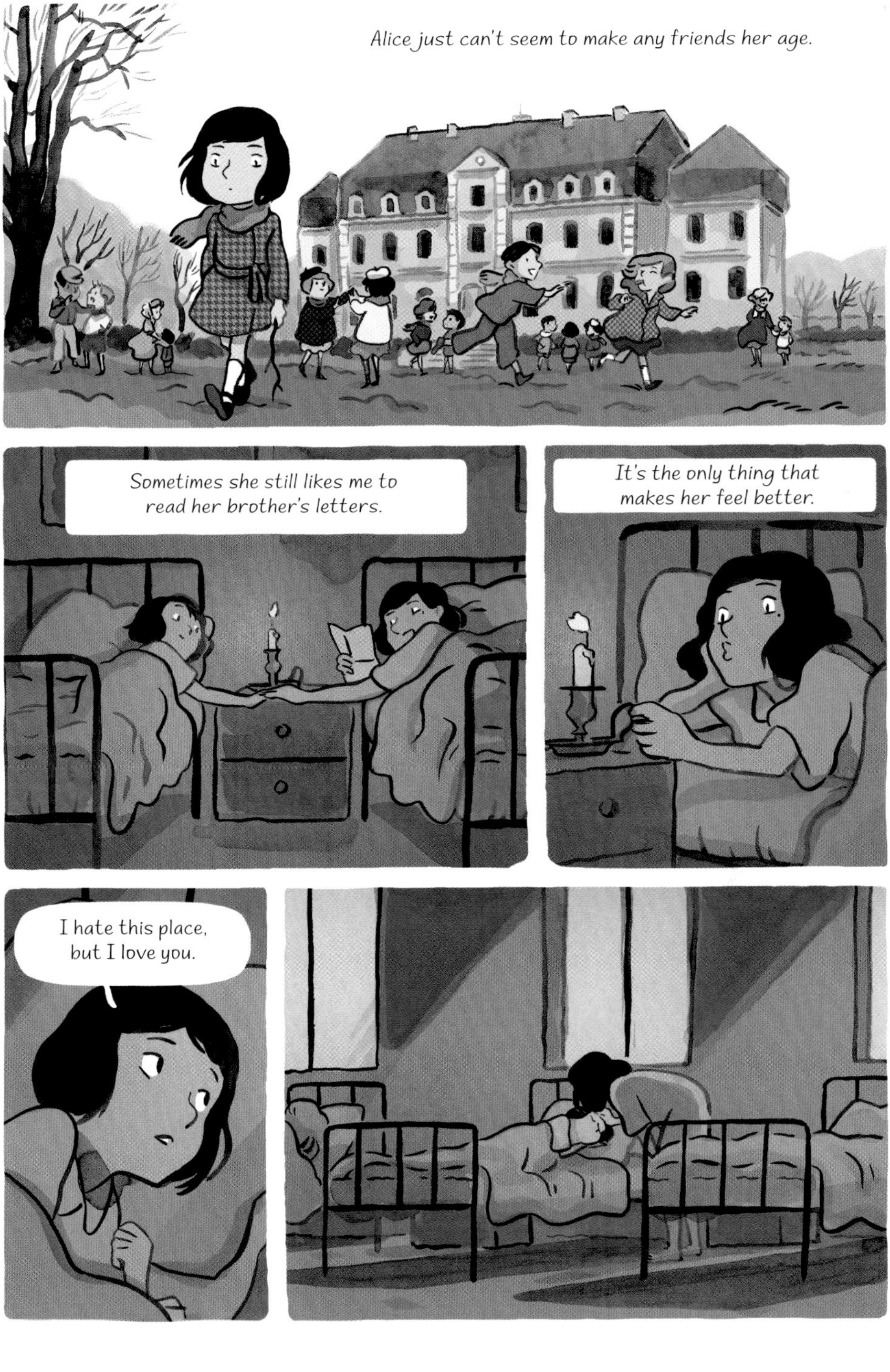
Alice just can't seem to make any friends her age.
Sometimes she still likes me to read her brother's letters.
It's the only thing that makes her feel better.
I hate this place, but I love you.

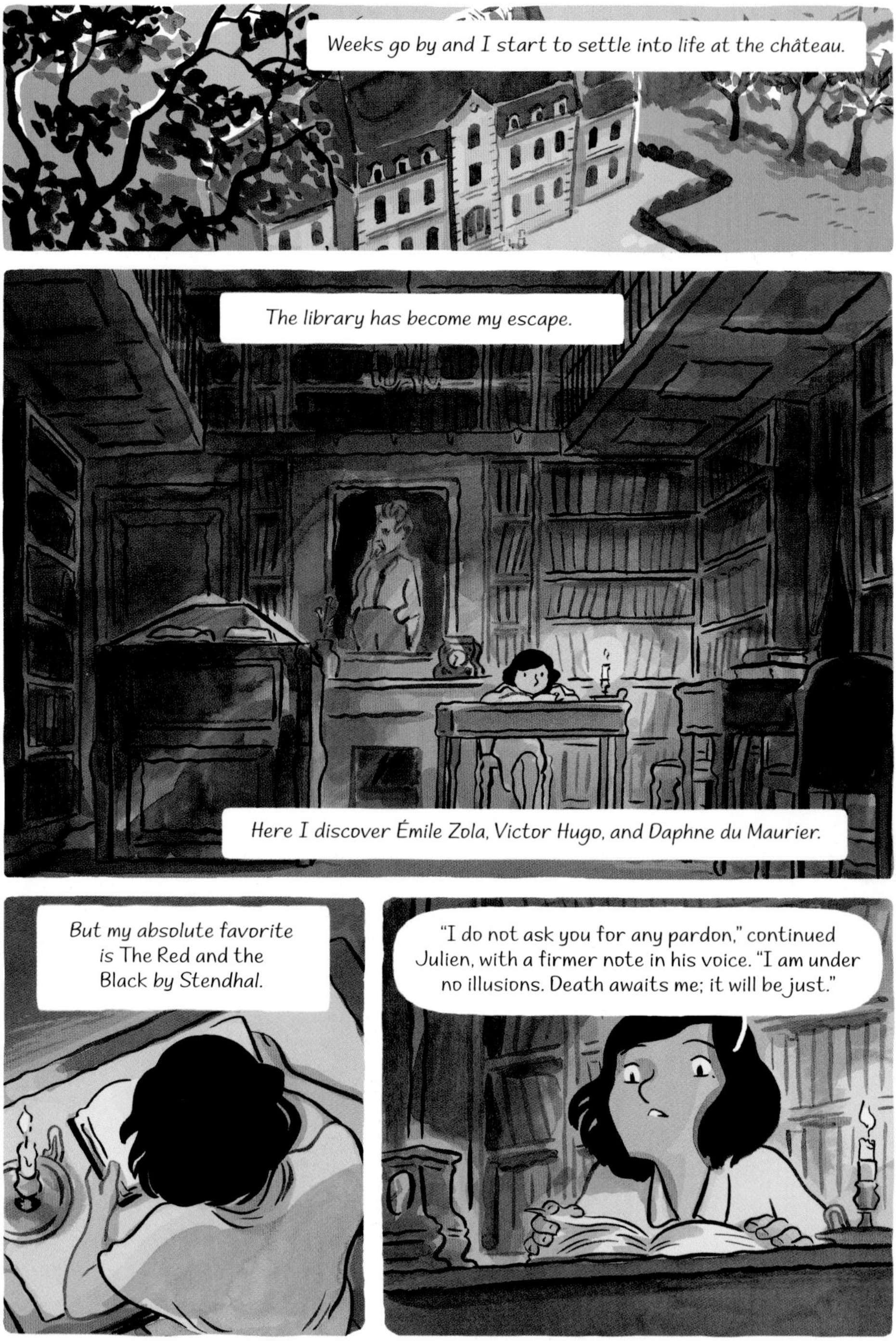
Weeks go by and I start to settle into life at the château.
The library has become my escape.
Here I discover Émile Zola, Victor Hugo, and Daphne du Maurier.
But my absolute favorite is The Red and the Black by Stendhal.
"I do not ask you for any pardon," continued Julien, with a firmer note in his voice. "I am under no illusions. Death awaits me; it will be just."

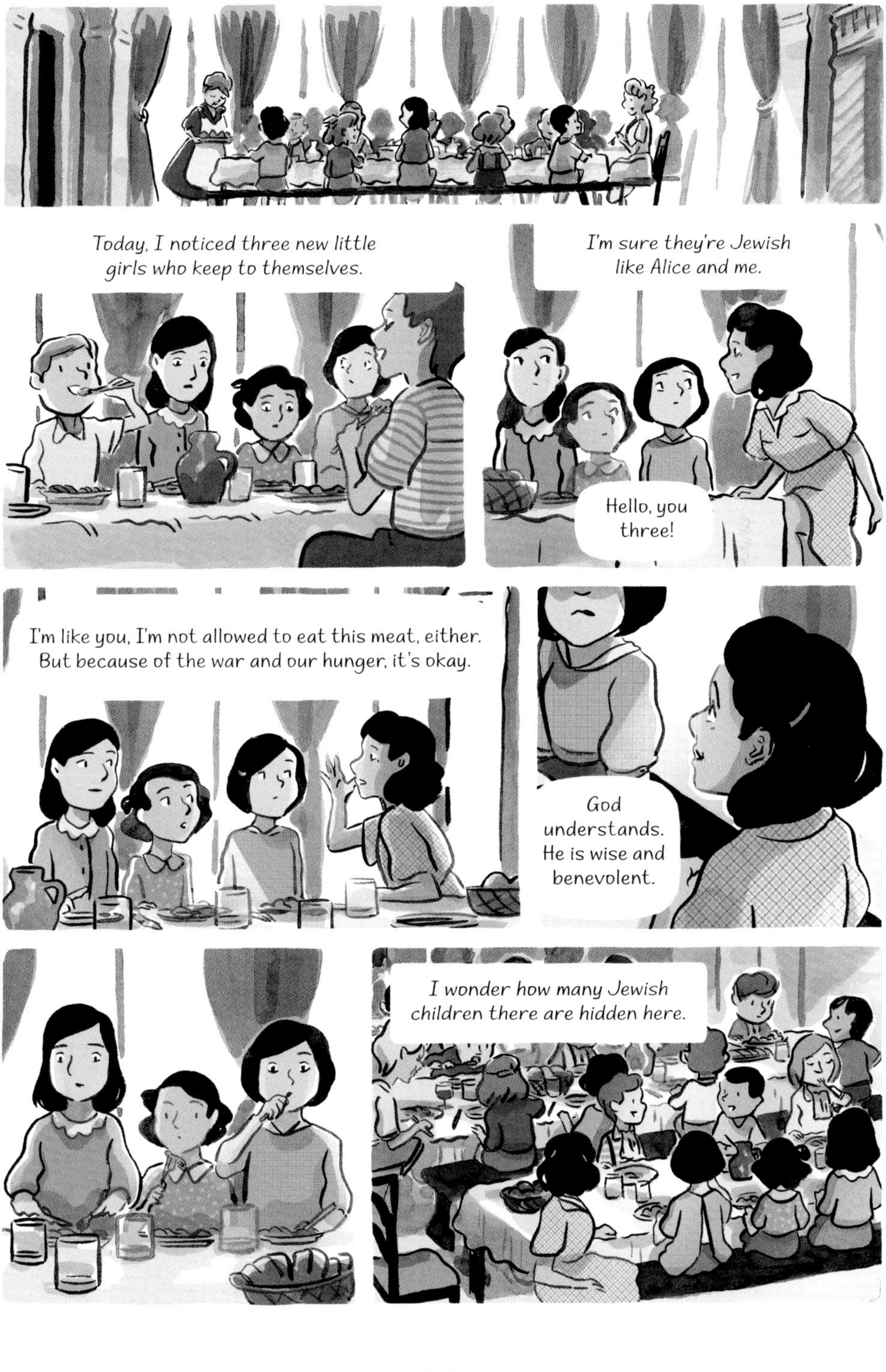

Today, I noticed three new little girls who keep to themselves.
I'm sure they're Jewish like Alice and me.
Hello, you three!
I'm like you, I'm not allowed to eat this meat, either. But because of the war and our hunger, it's okay.
God understands. He is wise and benevolent.
I wonder how many Jewish children there are hidden here.

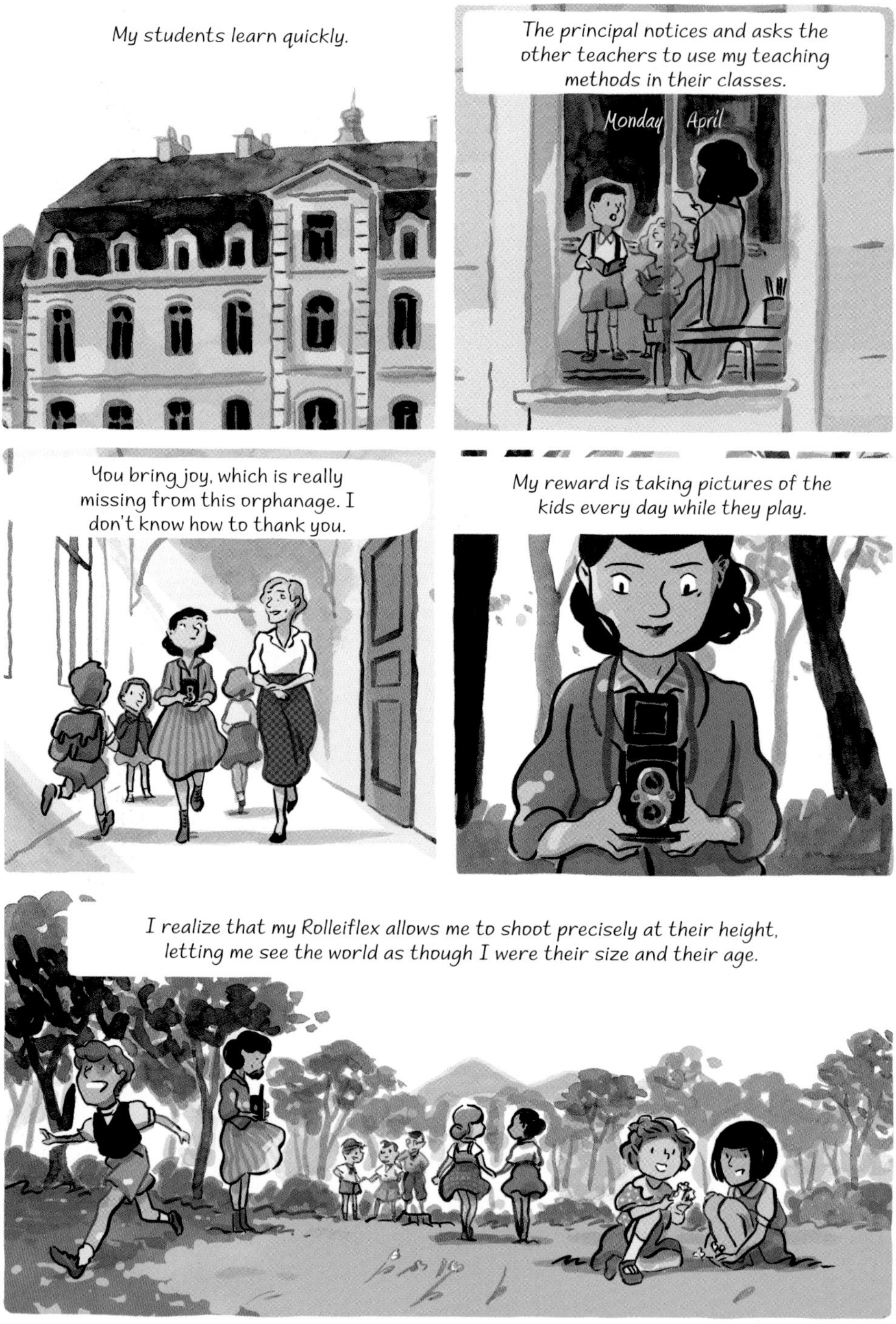
My students learn quickly.
The principal notices and asks the other teachers to use my teaching methods in their classes.
Monday
April
You bring joy, which is really missing from this orphanage. I don't know how to thank you.
My reward is taking pictures of the kids every day while they play.
I realize that my Rolleiflex allows me to shoot precisely at their height, letting me see the world as though I were their size and their age.

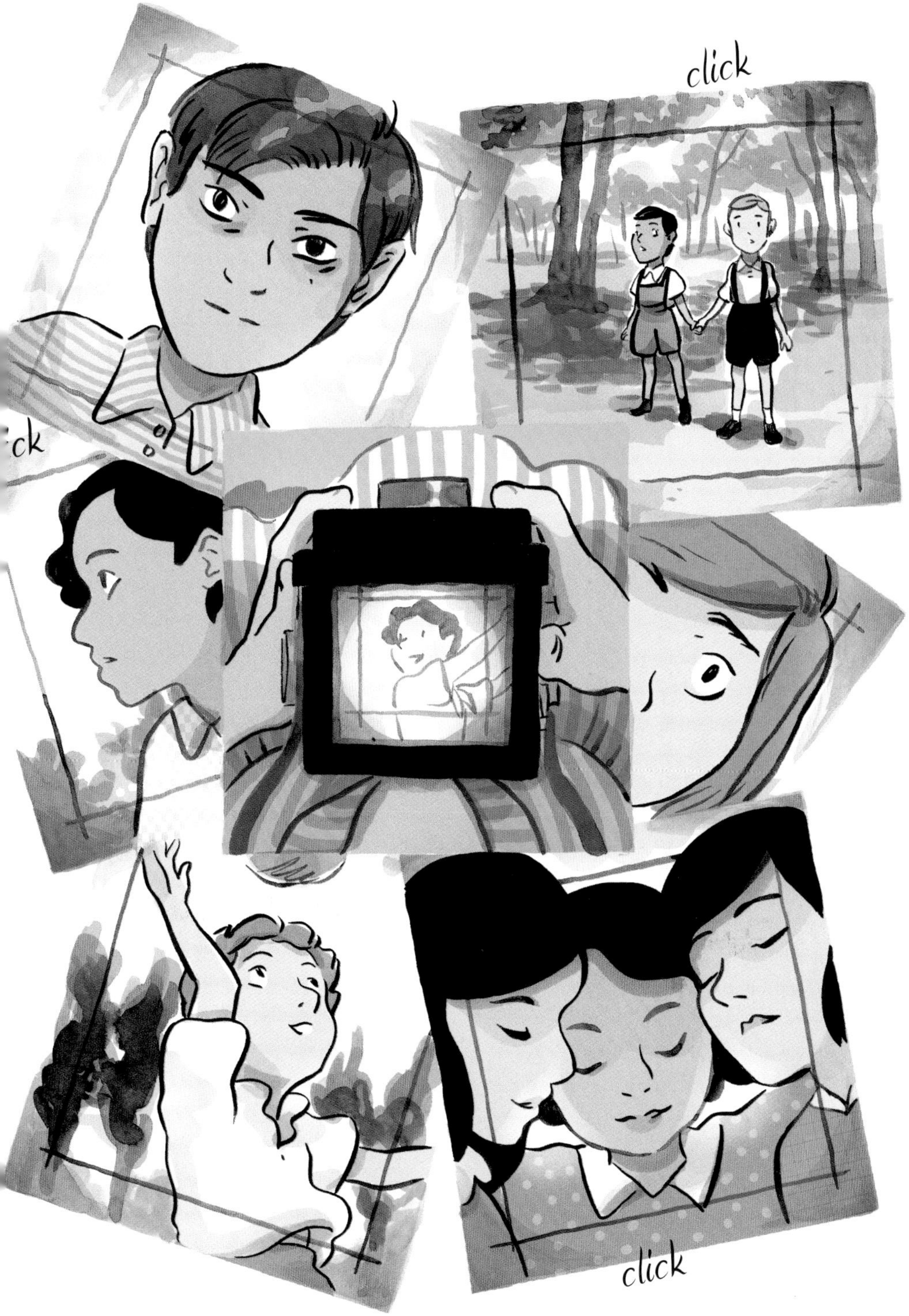
click
ck
click

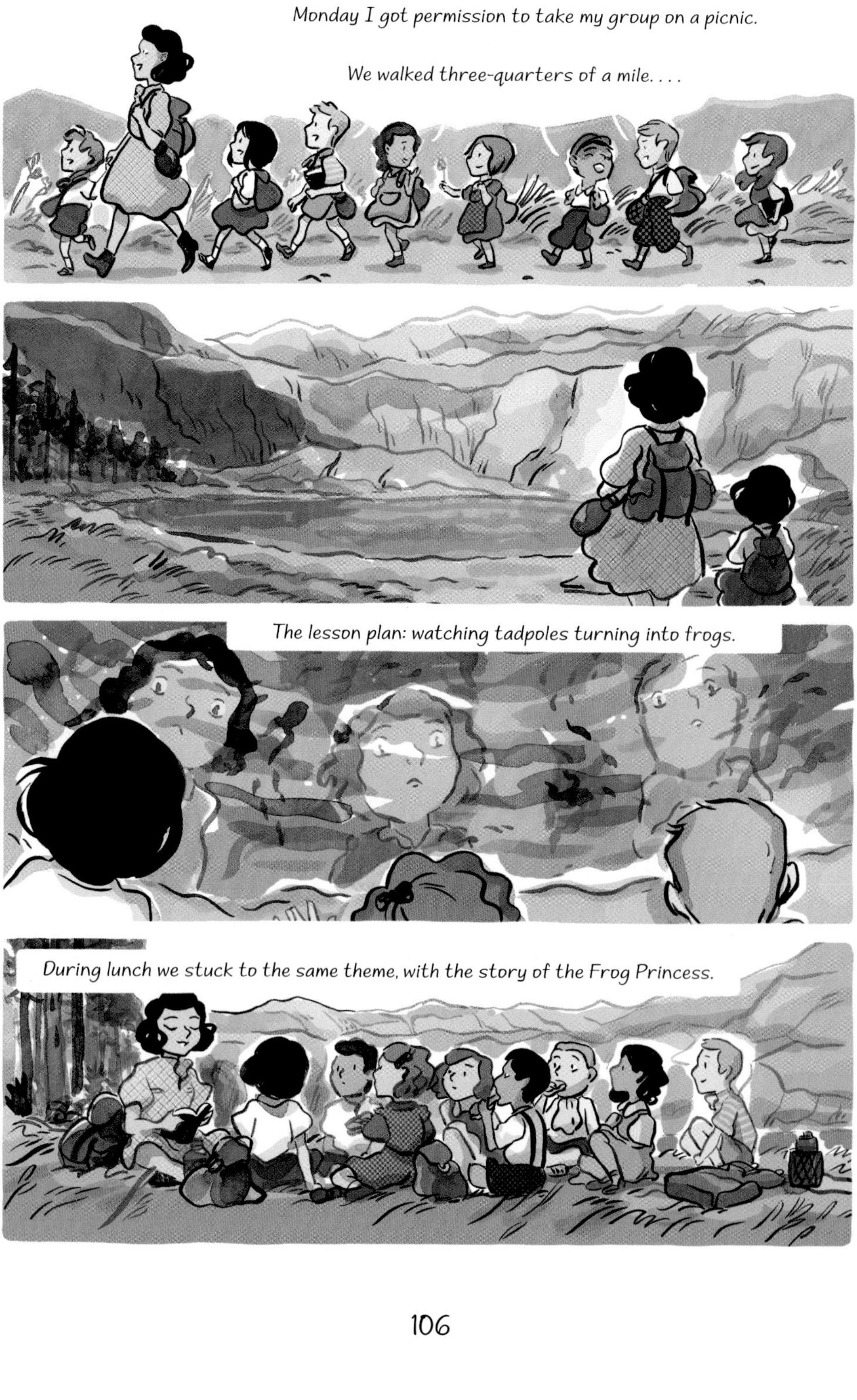
Monday I got permission to take my group on a picnic.
We walked three-quarters of a mile. . . .
The lesson plan: watching tadpoles turning into frogs.
During lunch we stuck to the same theme, with the story of the Frog Princess.

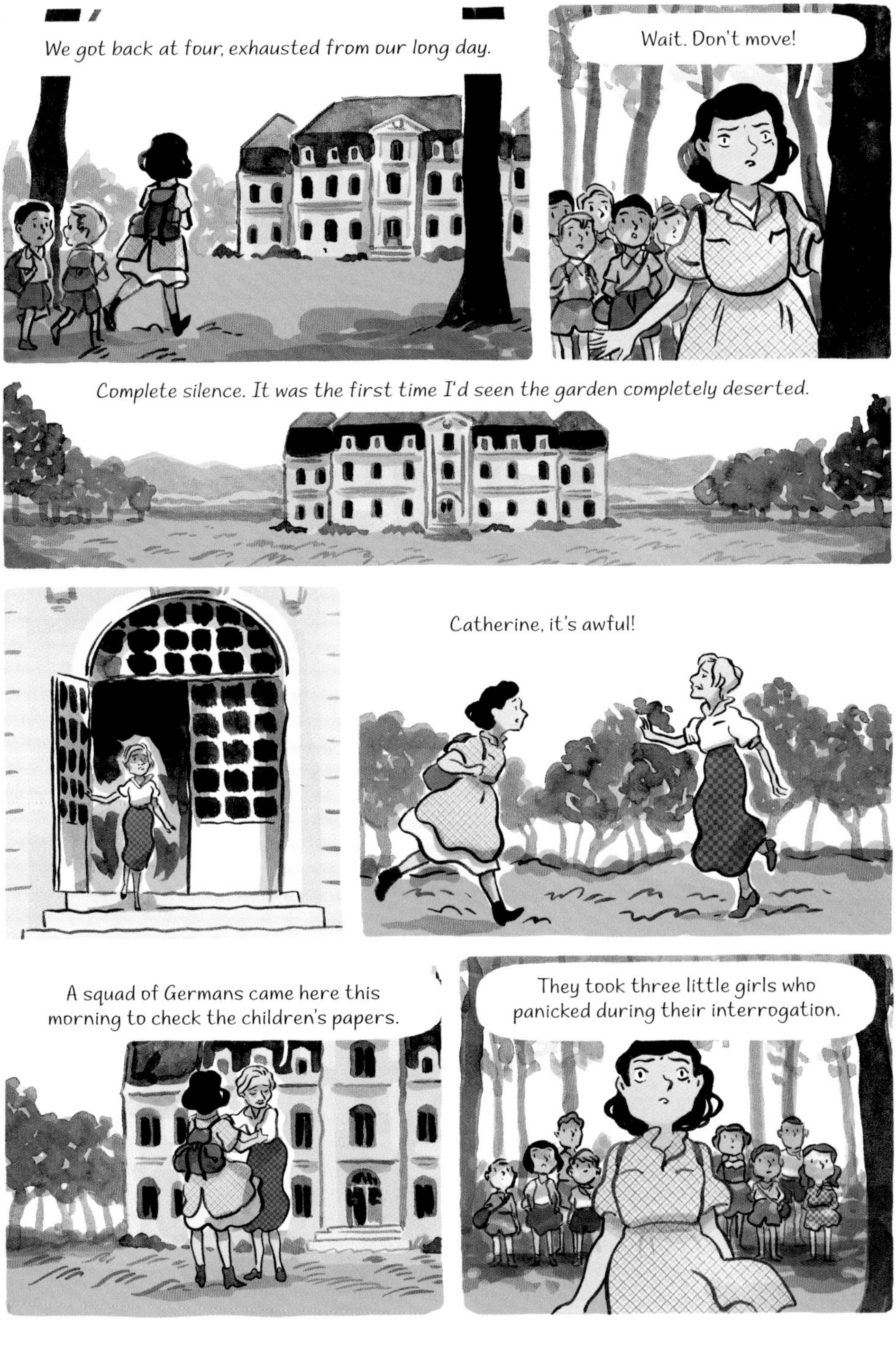
We got back at four, exhausted from our long day.
Wait. Don't move!
Complete silence. It was the first time I'd seen the garden completely deserted.
Catherine, it's awful!
A squad of Germans came here this morning to check the children's papers.
They took three little girls who panicked during their interrogation.

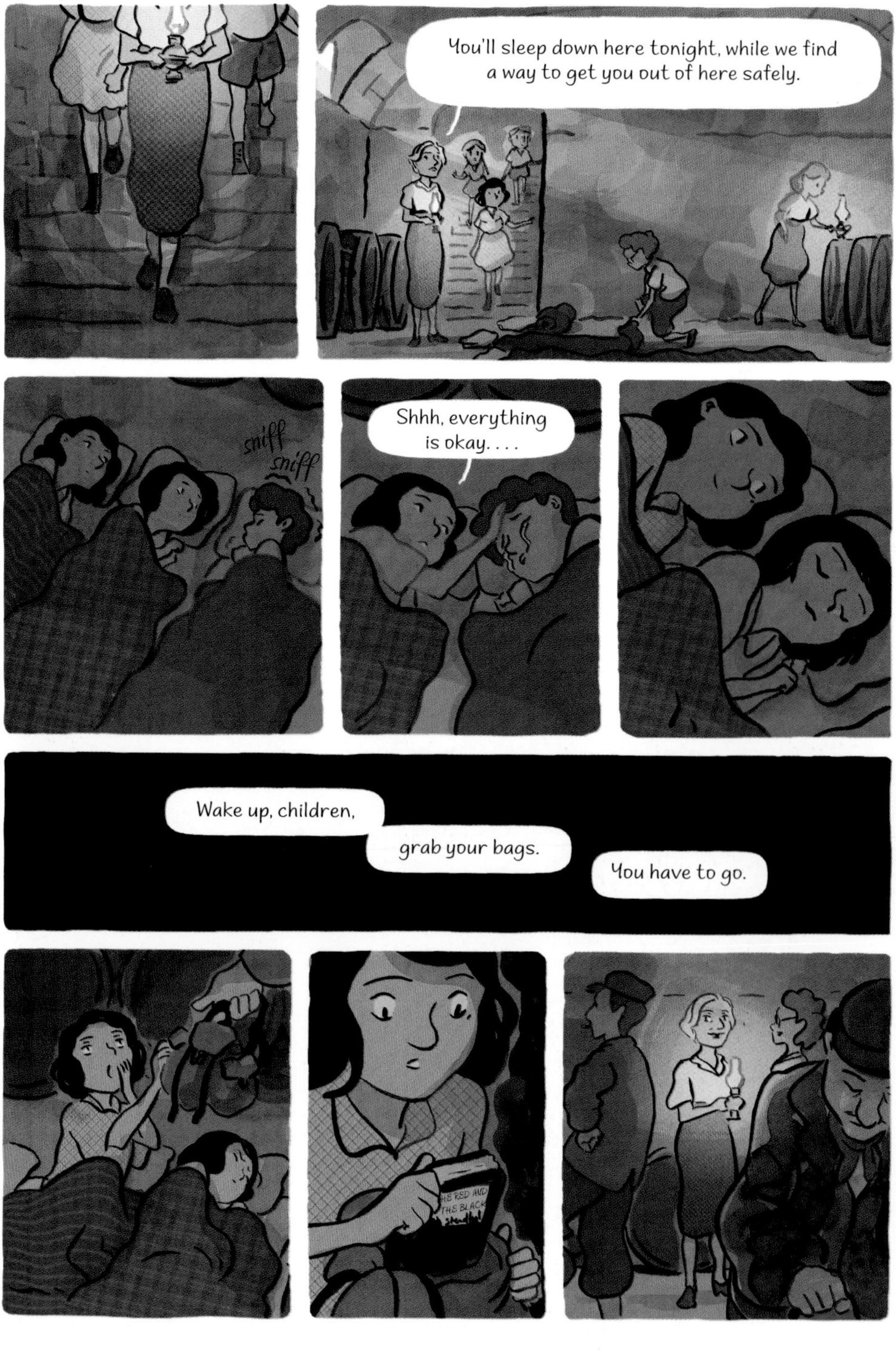
You'll sleep down here tonight, while we find a way to get you out of here safely.
sniff sniff
Shhh, everything is okay. . . .
Wake up, children,
grab your bags.
You have to go.
THE RED AND THE BLACK

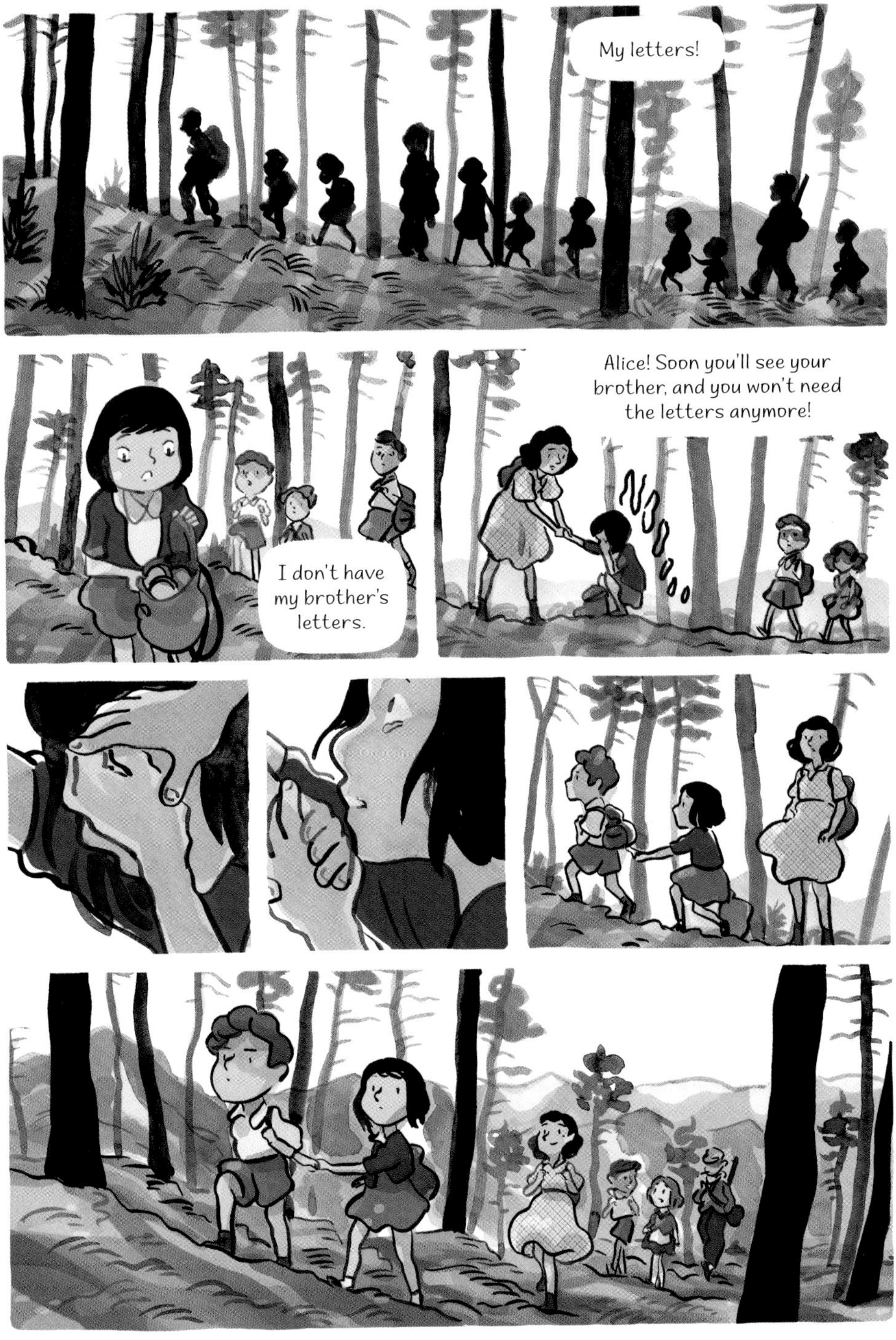
My letters!
I don't have my brother's letters.
Alice! Soon you'll see your brother, and you won't need the letters anymore!

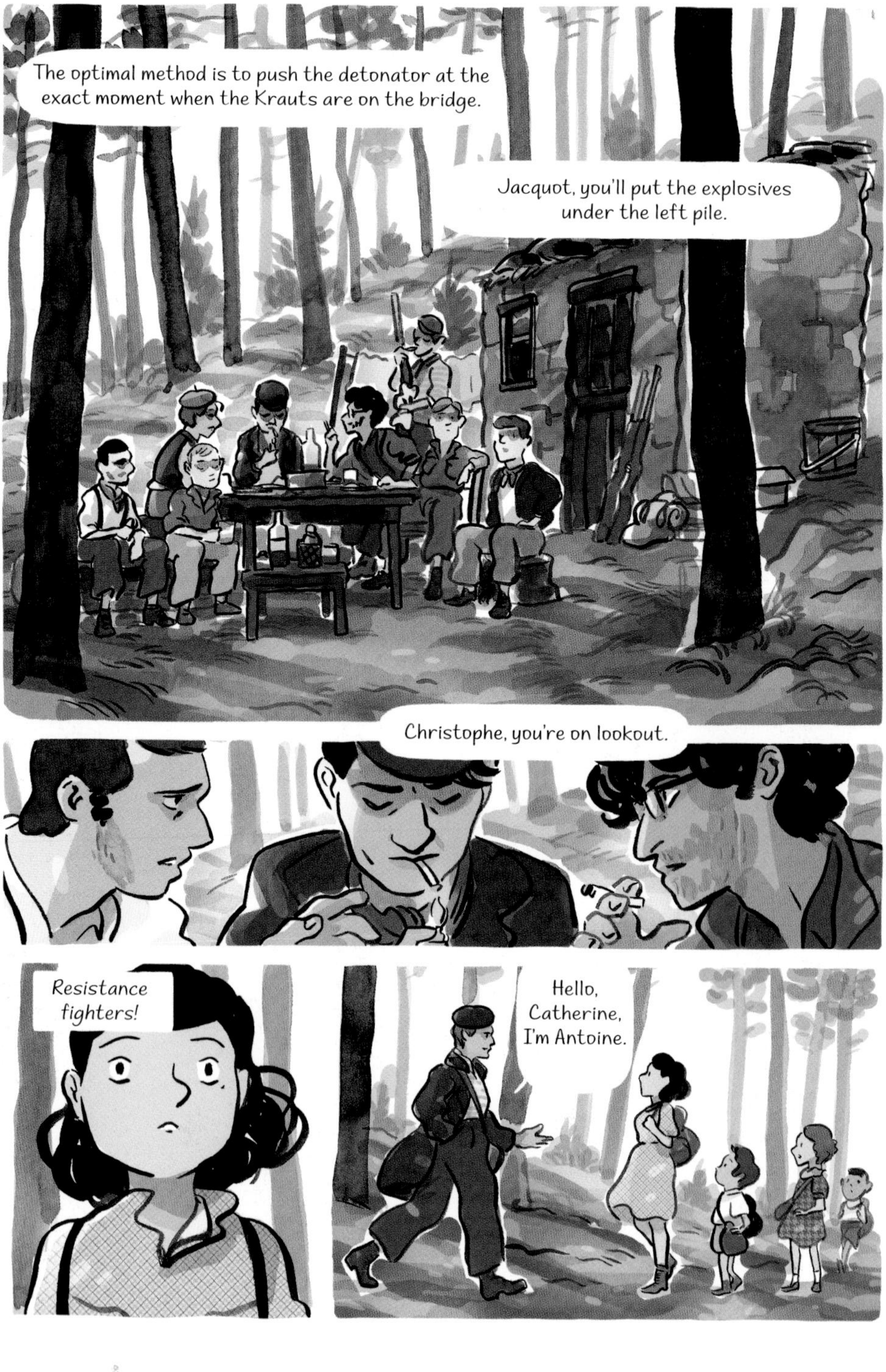
The optimal method is to push the detonator at the exact moment when the Krauts are on the bridge.
Jacquot, you'll put the explosives under the left pile.
Christophe, you're on lookout.
Resistance fighters!
Hello, Catherine, I'm Antoine.

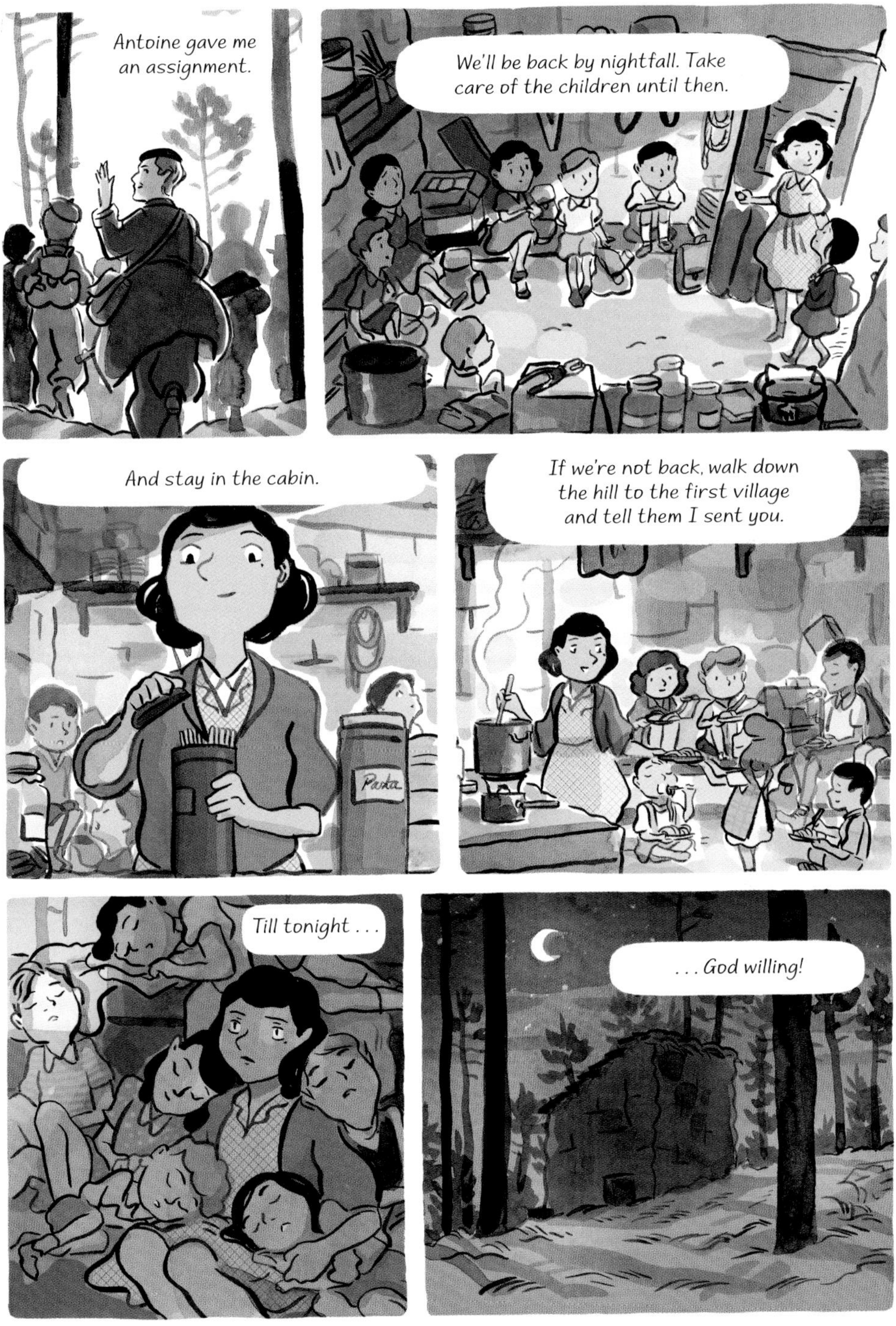
Antoine gave me an assignment.
We'll be back by nightfall. Take care of the children until then.
And stay in the cabin.
Pasta
If we're not back, walk down the hill to the first village and tell them I sent you.
Till tonight . . .
. . . God willing!

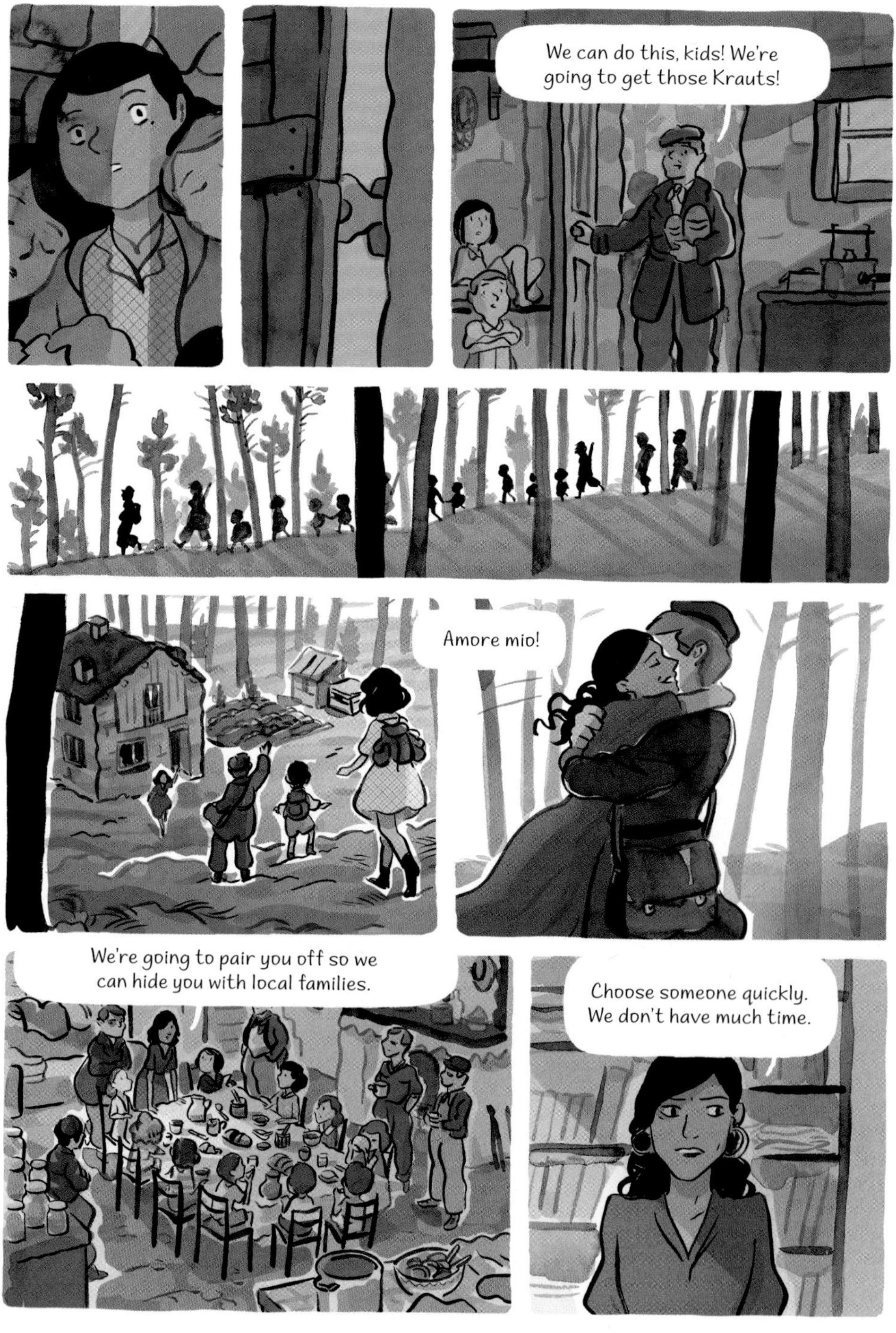
We can do this, kids! We're going to get those Krauts!
Amore mio!
We're going to pair you off so we can hide you with local families.
Choose someone quickly. We don't have much time.

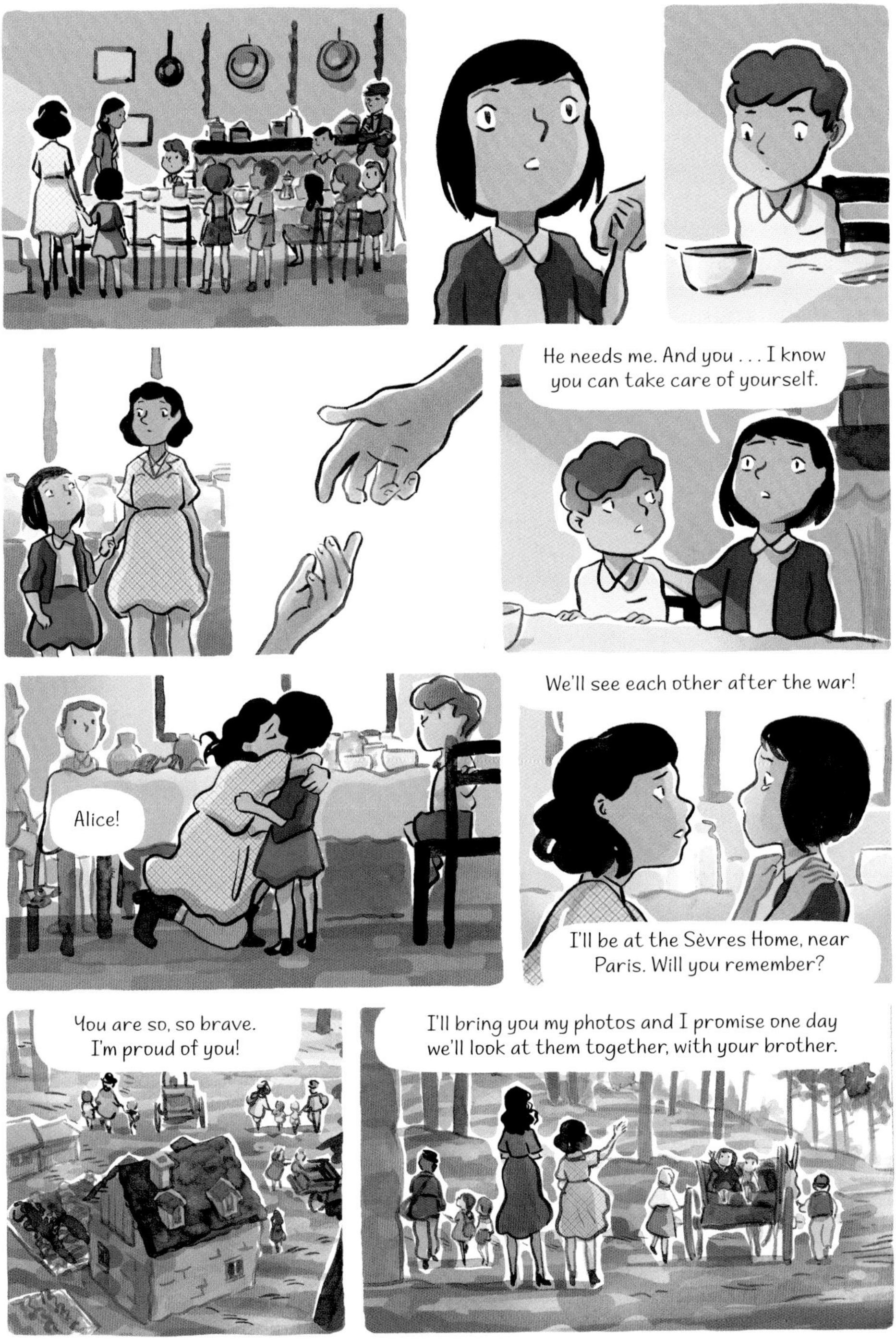
He needs me. And you . . . I know you can take care of yourself.
Alice!
We'll see each other after the war!
I'll be at the Sèvres Home, near Paris. Will you remember?
You are so, so brave. I'm proud of you!
I'll bring you my photos and I promise one day we'll look at them together, with your brother.

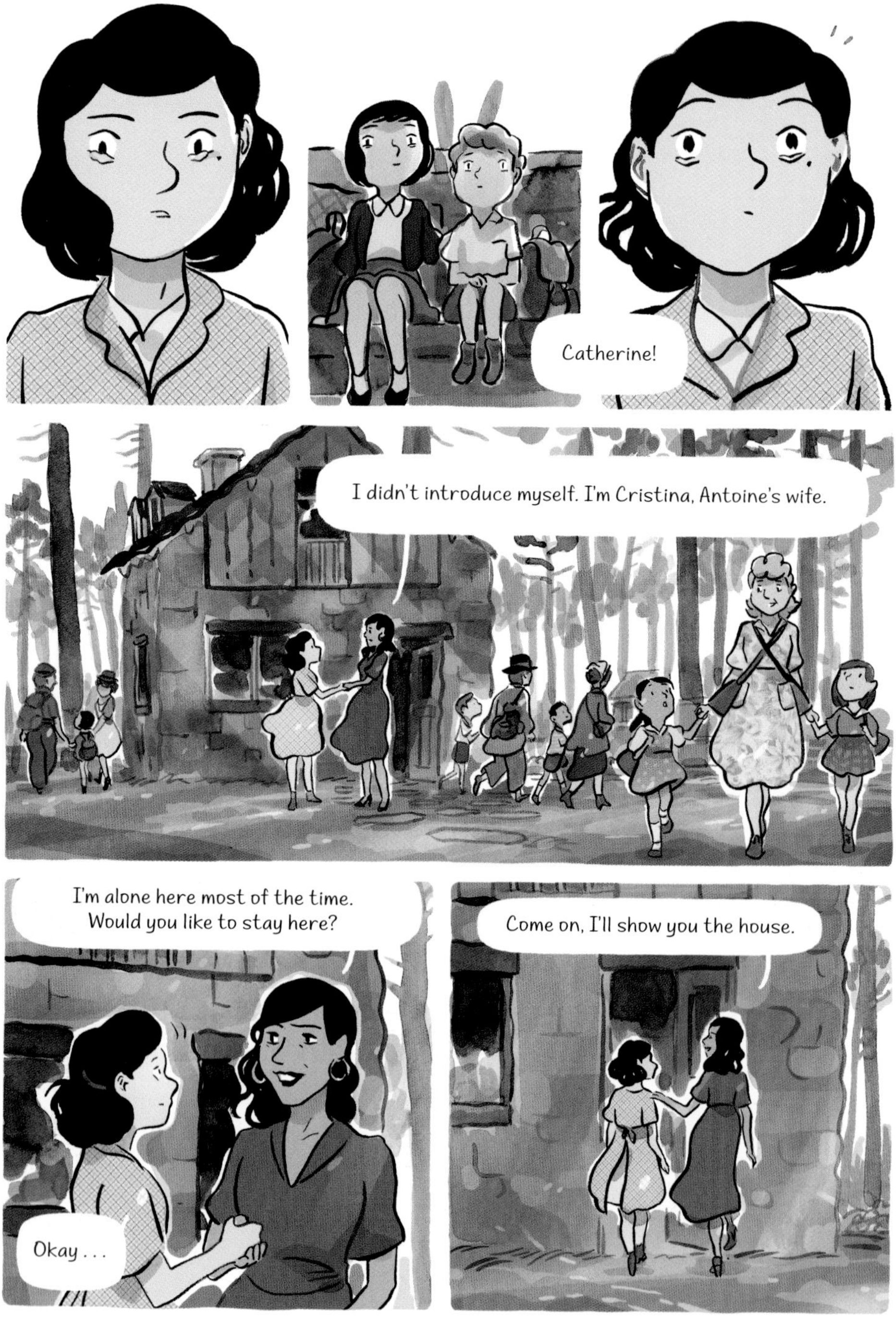
Catherine!
I didn't introduce myself. I'm Cristina, Antoine's wife.
I'm alone here most of the time. Would you like to stay here?
Okay . . .
Come on, I'll show you the house.

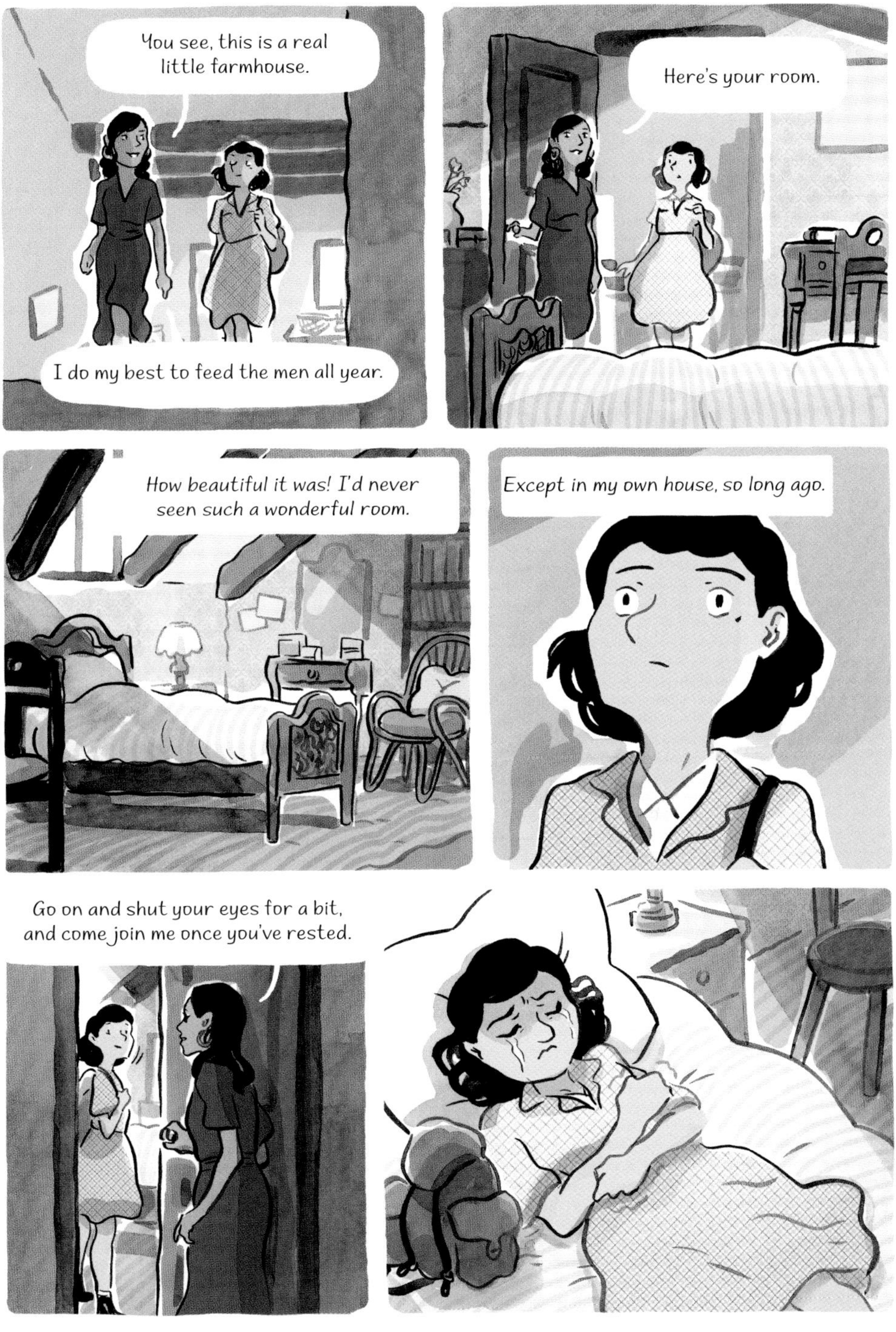

You see, this is a real little farmhouse.
I do my best to feed the men all year.
Here's your room.
How beautiful it was! I'd never seen such a wonderful room.
Except in my own house, so long ago.
Go on and shut your eyes for a bit, and come join me once you've rested.

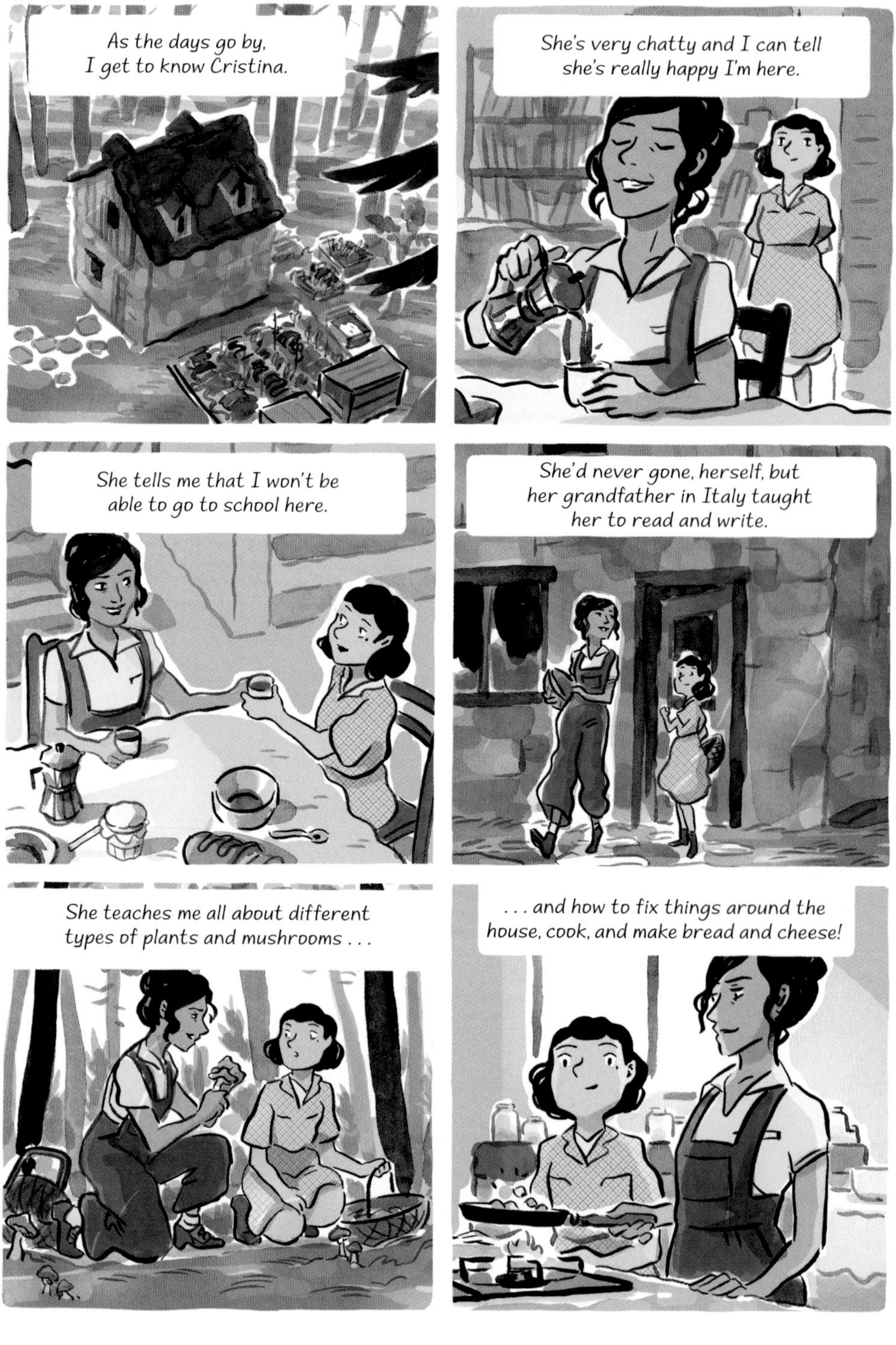
As the days go by, I get to know Cristina.
She's very chatty and I can tell she's really happy I'm here.
She tells me that I won't be able to go to school here.
She'd never gone, herself, but her grandfather in Italy taught her to read and write.
She teaches me all about different types of plants and mushrooms . . .
. . . and how to fix things around the house, cook, and make bread and cheese!

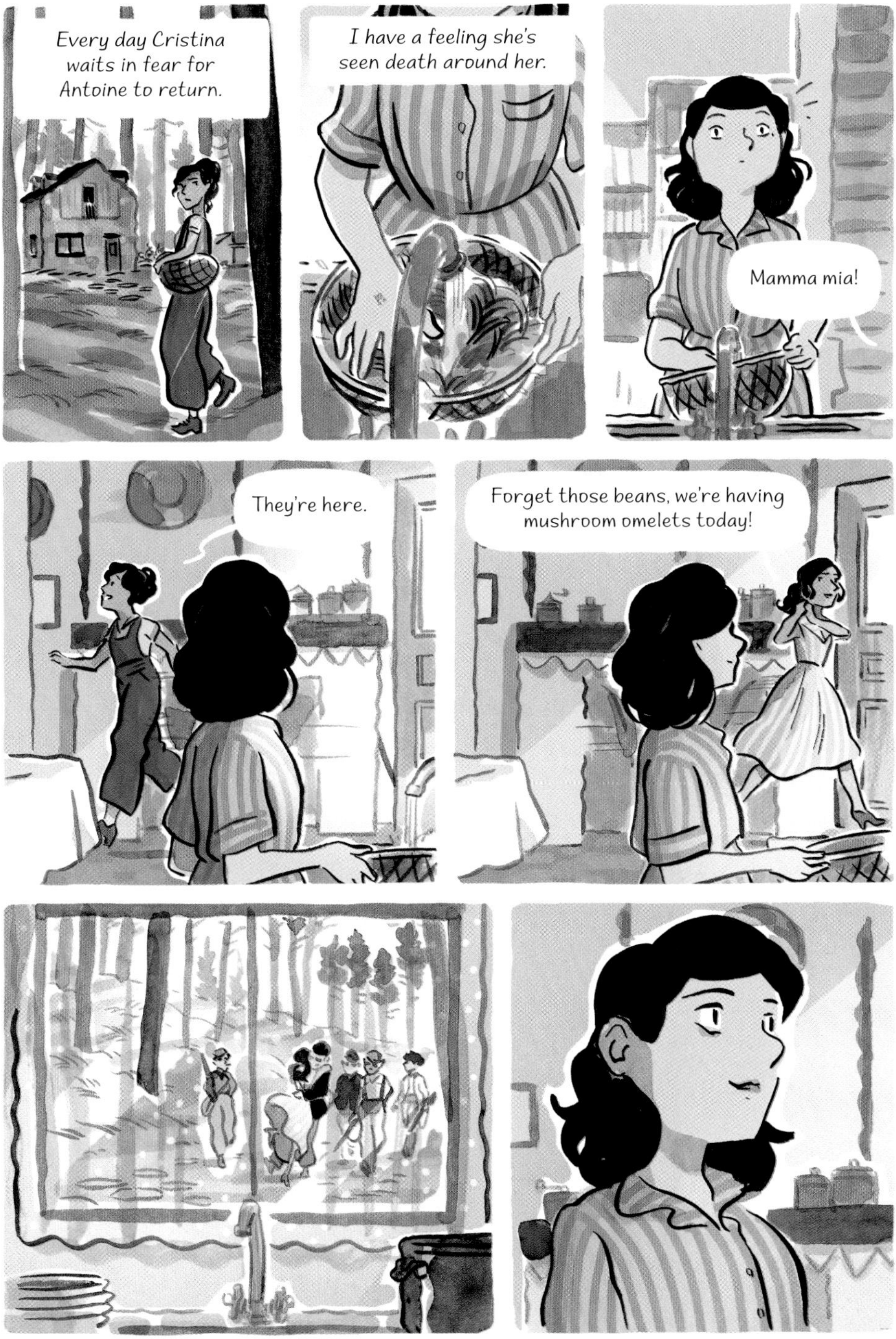

Every day Cristina waits in fear for Antoine to return.
I have a feeling she's seen death around her.
Mamma mia!
They're here.
Forget those beans, we're having mushroom omelets today!

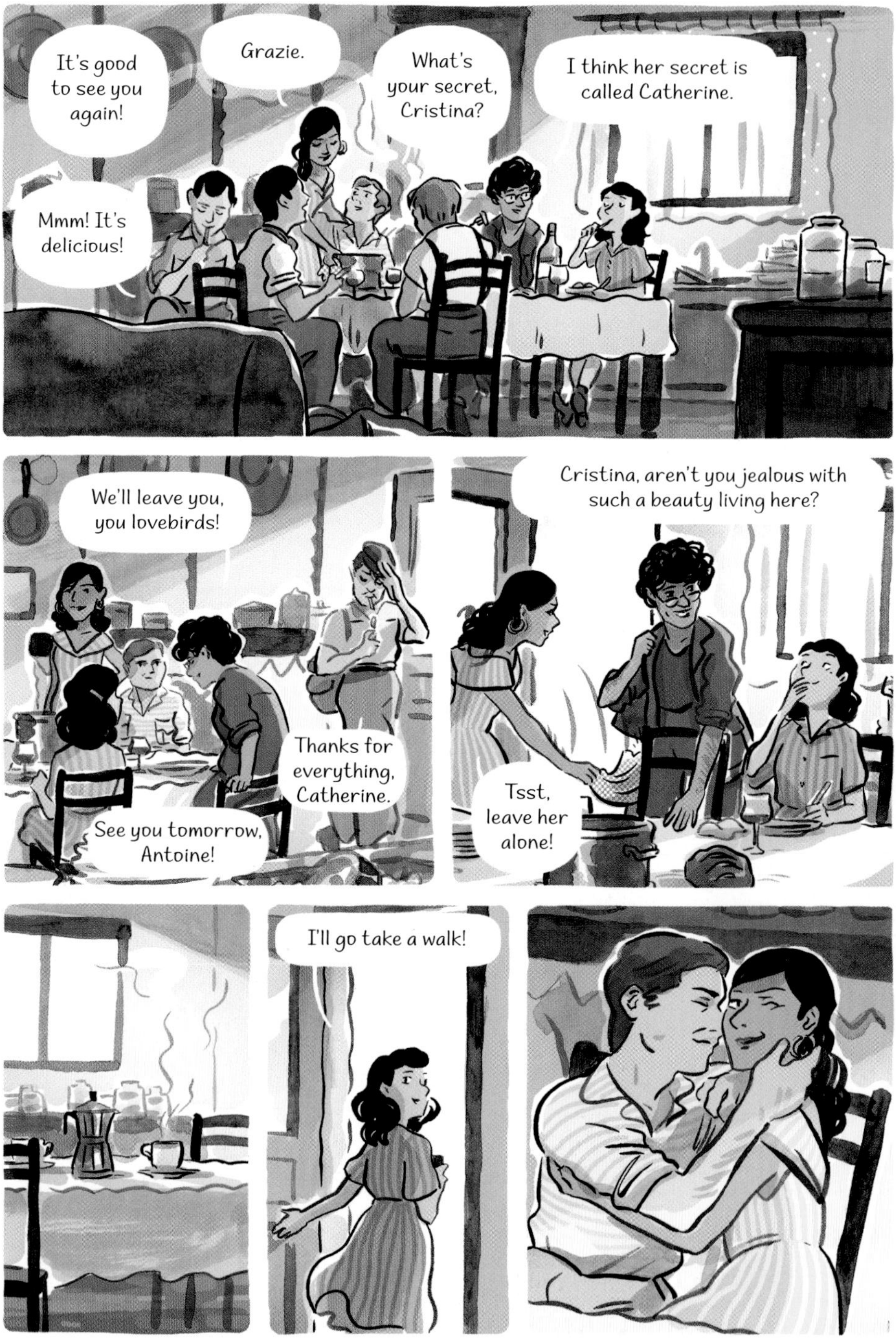
It's good to see you again!
Grazie.
What's your secret, Cristina?
I think her secret is called Catherine.
Mmm! It's delicious!
We'll leave you, you lovebirds!
Thanks for everything, Catherine.
See you tomorrow, Antoine!
Cristina, aren't you jealous with such a beauty living here?
Tsst, leave her alone!
I'll go take a walk!

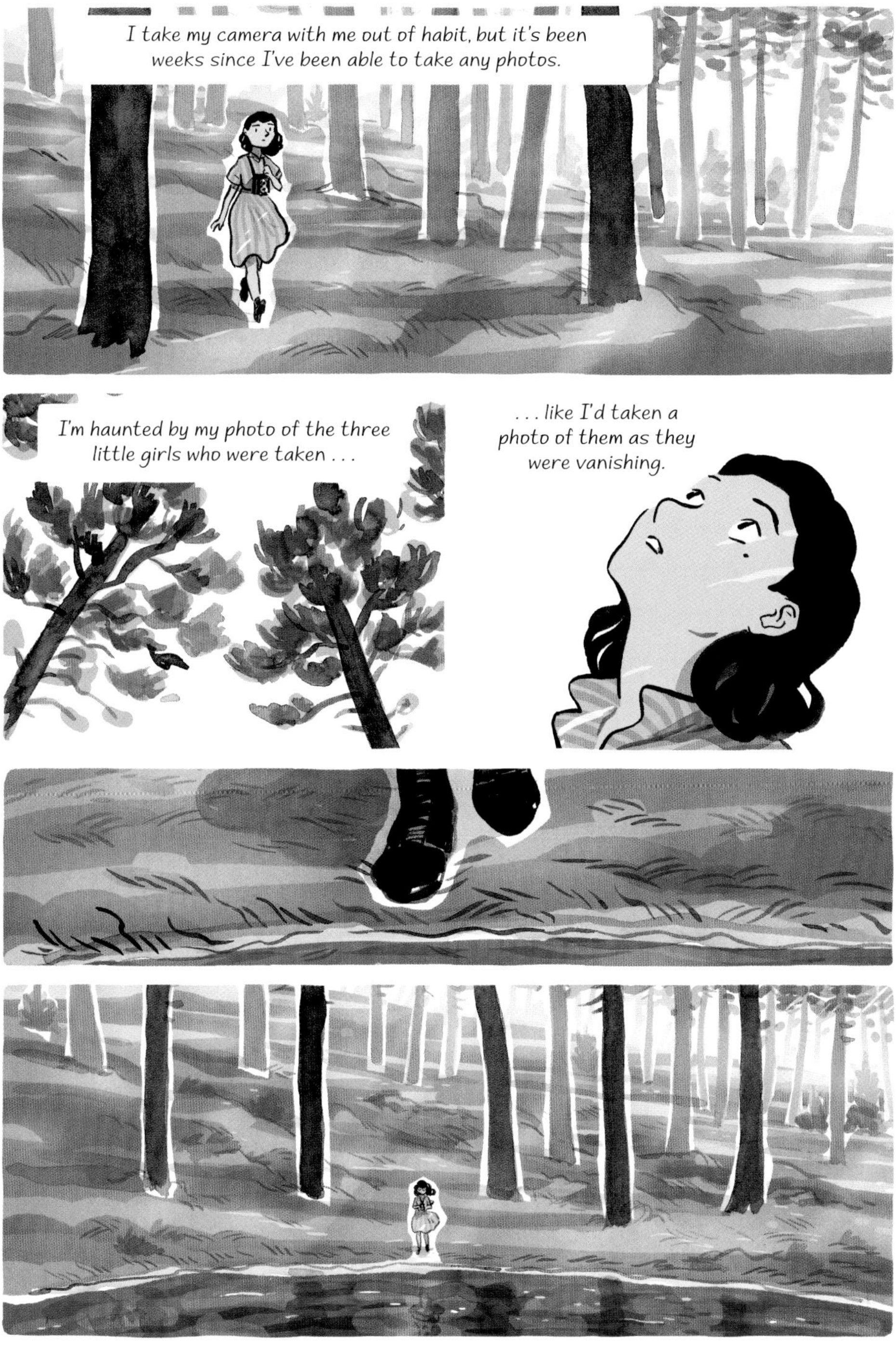
I take my camera with me out of habit, but it's been weeks since I've been able to take any photos.
I'm haunted by my photo of the three little girls who were taken . . .
. . . like I'd taken a photo of them as they were vanishing.

The lake reminds me of my last day at Château de Page.

So pretty.

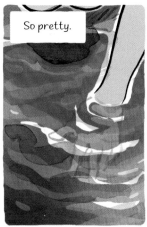

Suddenly, I want to take a picture. Without even thinking about it, the feeling has come back to me.

And like magic, I am back to looking at the world with a photographer's eye.

Seeing beauty everywhere . . .

. . . hidden in each reflection.

Click

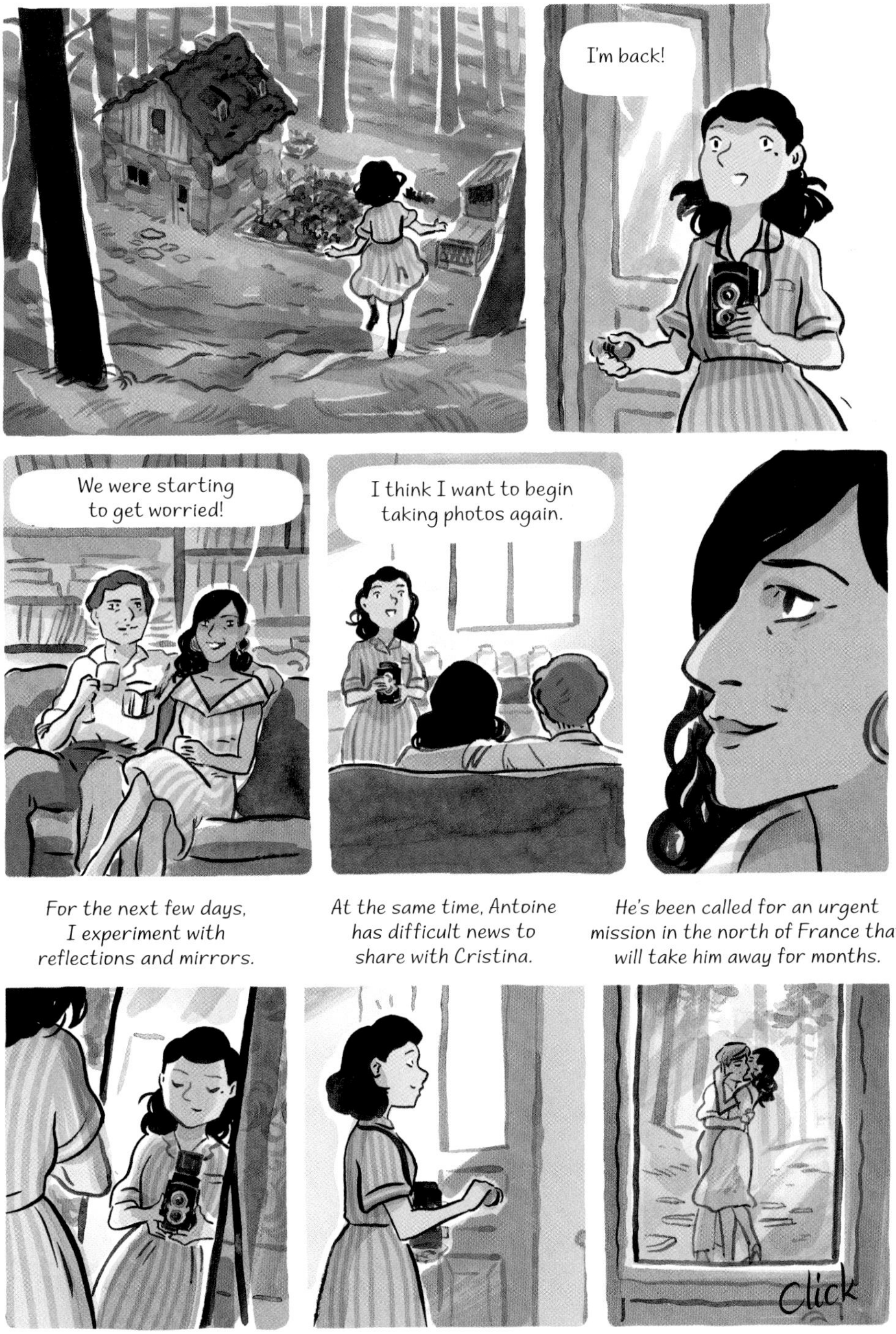
I'm back!
We were starting to get worried!
I think I want to begin taking photos again.
For the next few days, I experiment with reflections and mirrors.
At the same time, Antoine has difficult news to share with Cristina.
He's been called for an urgent mission in the north of France that will take him away for months.
Click

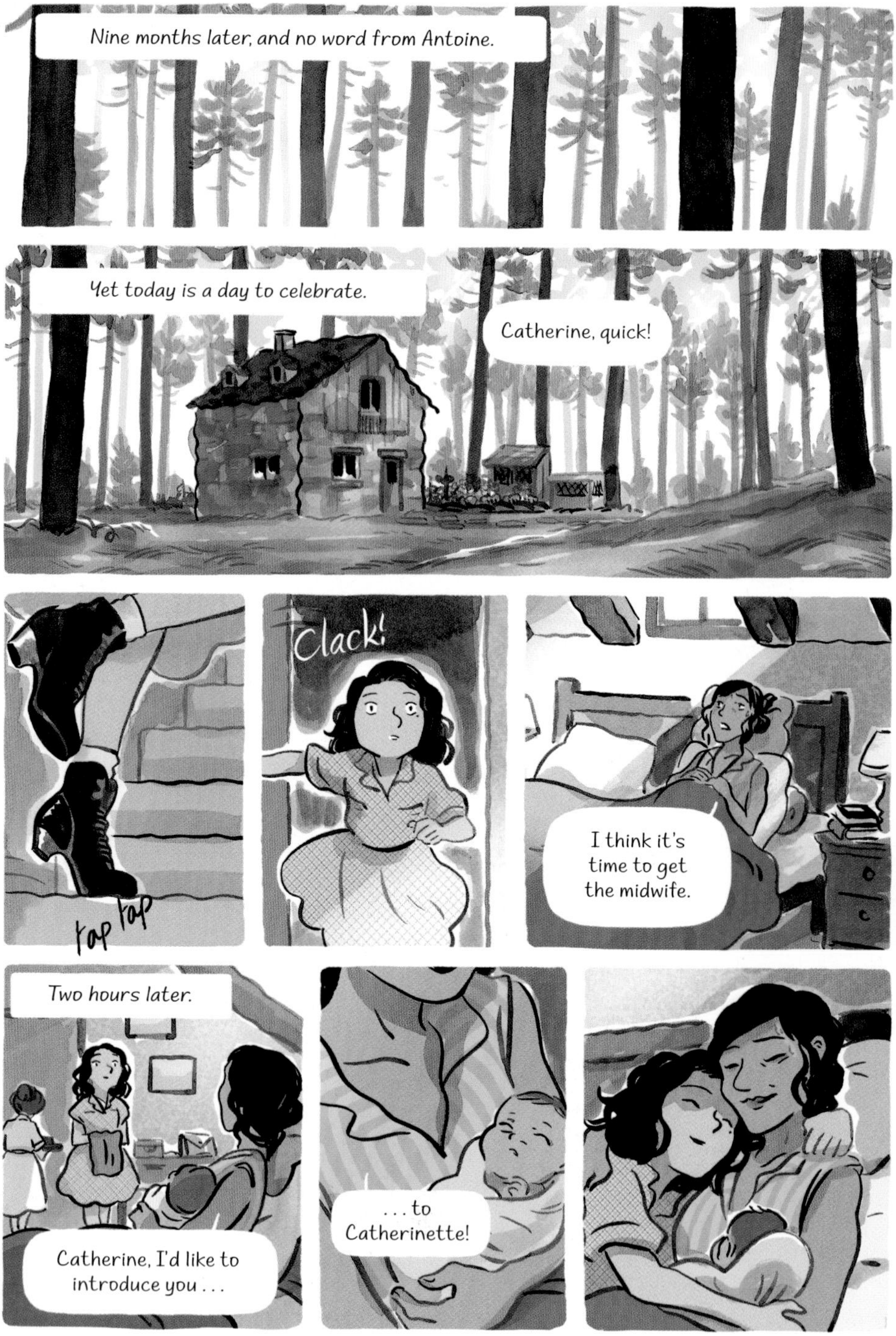
Nine months later, and no word from Antoine.
Yet today is a day to celebrate.
Catherine, quick!
tap tap
Clack!
I think it's time to get the midwife.
Two hours later.
Catherine, I'd like to introduce you . . .
. . . to Catherinette!

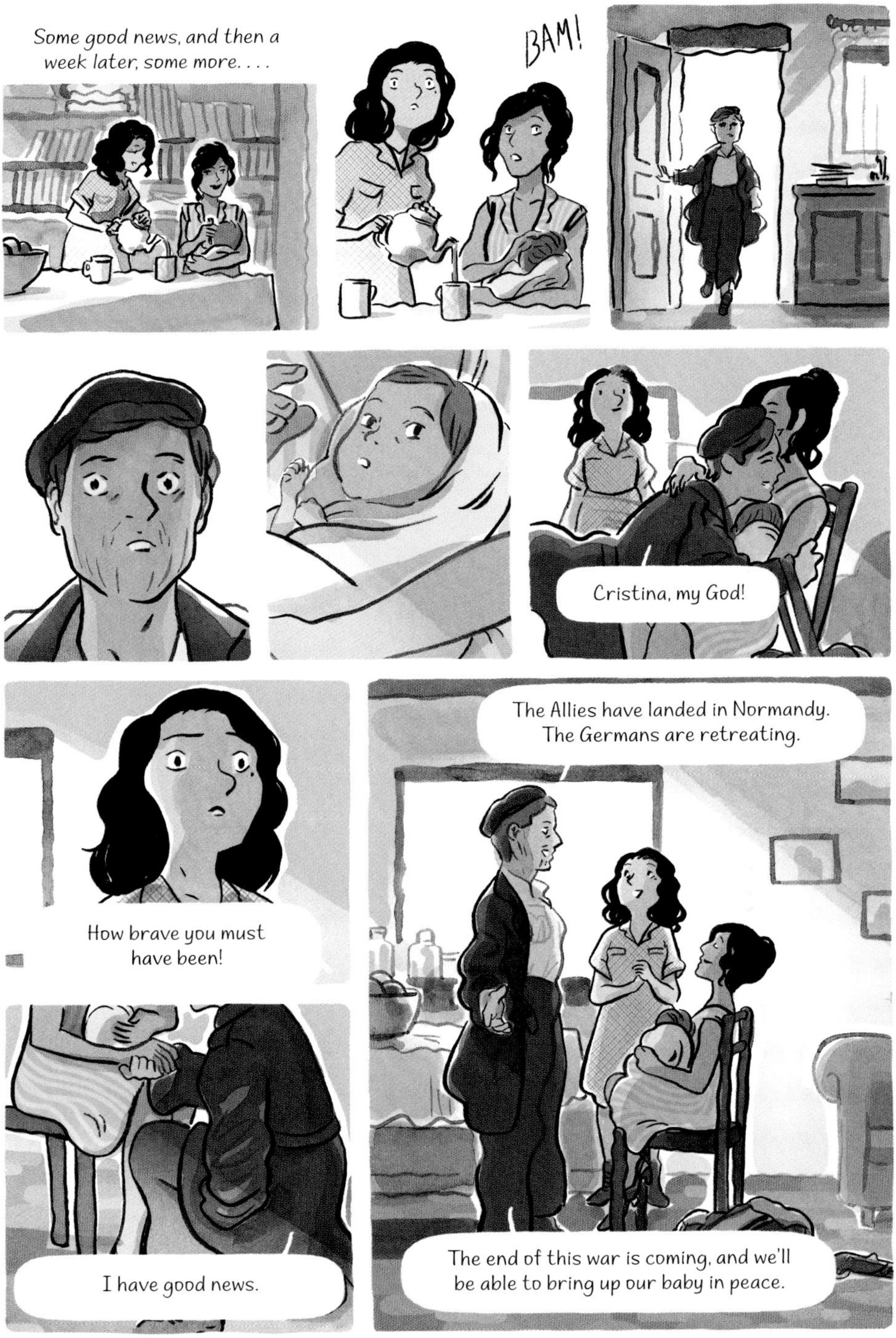
Some good news, and then a week later, some more. . . .
BAM!
Cristina, my God!
How brave you must have been!
I have good news.
The Allies have landed in Normandy. The Germans are retreating.
The end of this war is coming, and we'll be able to bring up our baby in peace.

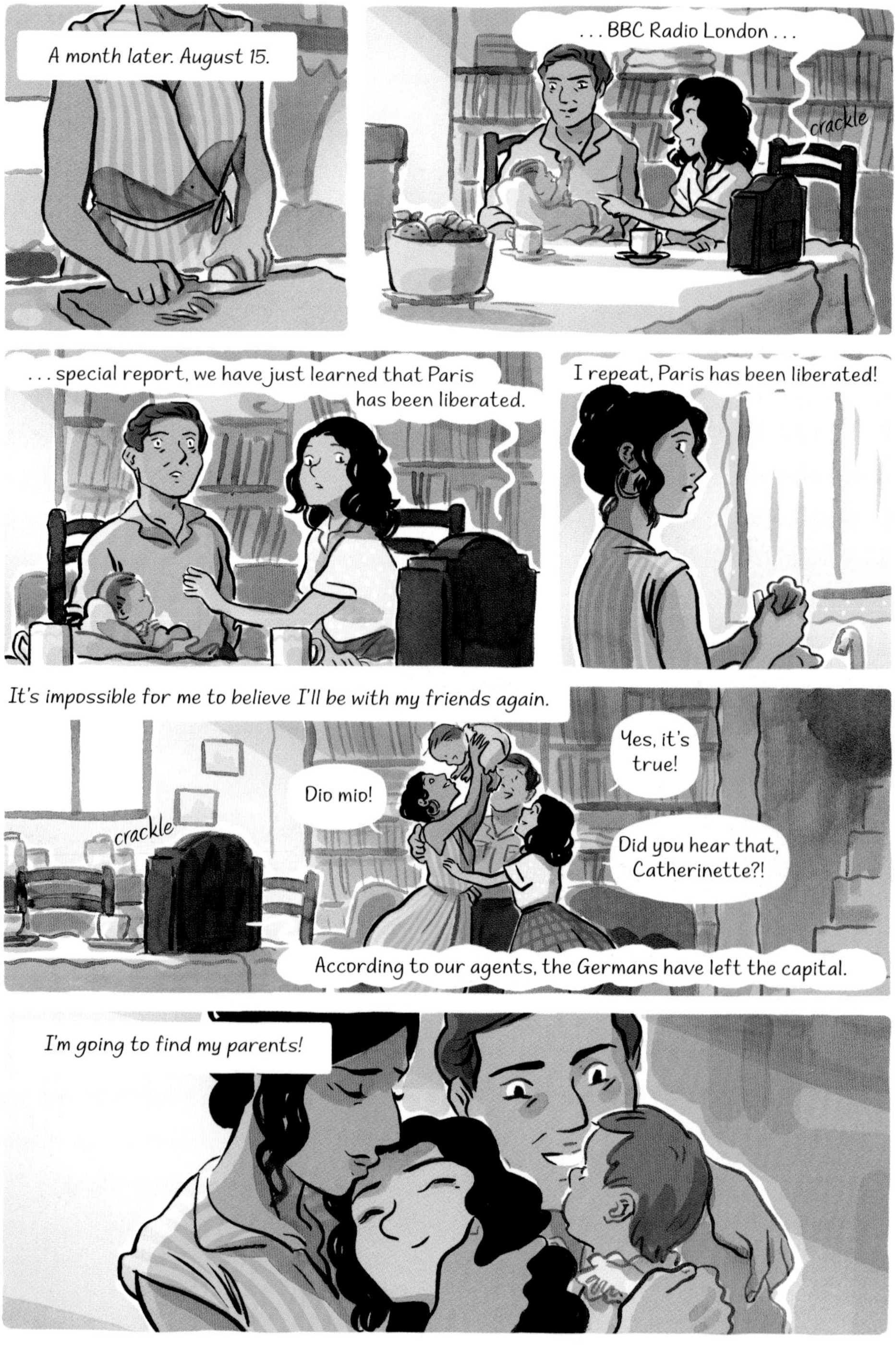
A month later. August 15.
. . . BBC Radio London . . .
crackle
. . . special report, we have just learned that Paris has been liberated.
I repeat, Paris has been liberated!
It's impossible for me to believe I'll be with my friends again.
Dio mio!
Yes, it's true!
crackle
Did you hear that, Catherinette?!
According to our agents, the Germans have left the capital.
I'm going to find my parents!

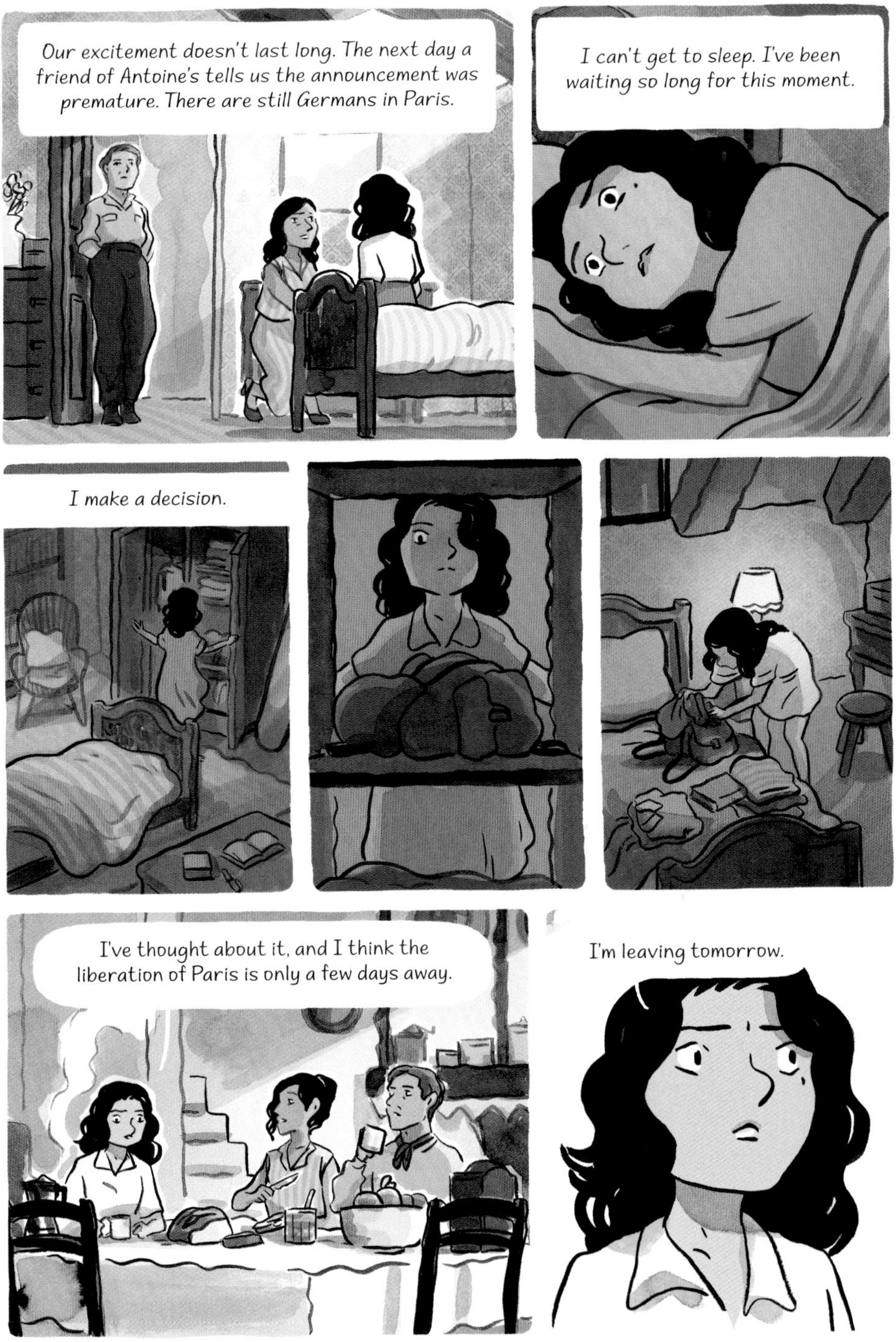
Our excitement doesn't last long. The next day a friend of Antoine's tells us the announcement was premature. There are still Germans in Paris.
I can't get to sleep. I've been waiting so long for this moment.
I make a decision.
I've thought about it, and I think the liberation of Paris is only a few days away.
I'm leaving tomorrow.

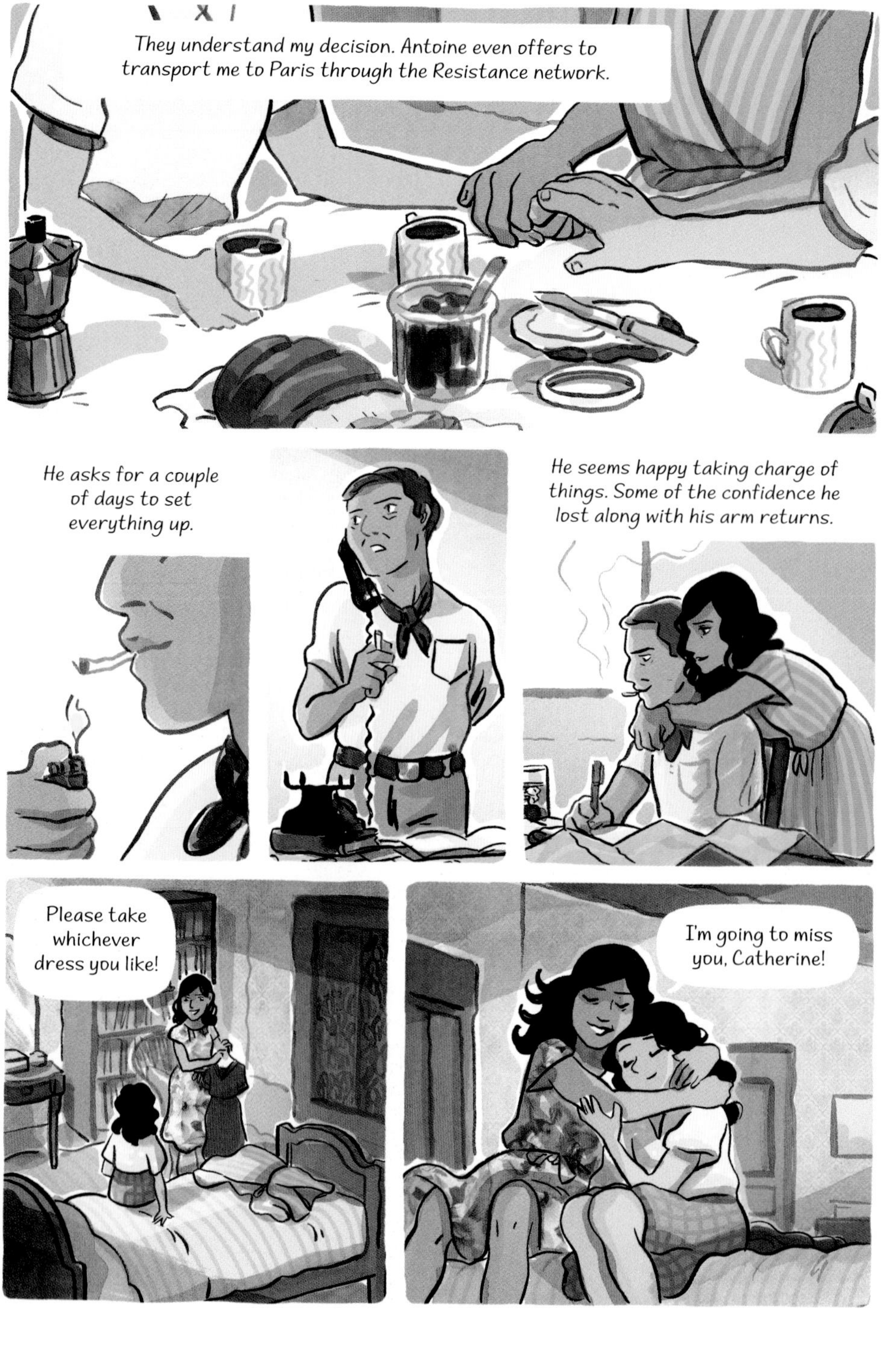
They understand my decision. Antoine even offers to transport me to Paris through the Resistance network.
He asks for a couple of days to set everything up.
He seems happy taking charge of things. Some of the confidence he lost along with his arm returns.
Please take whichever dress you like!
I'm going to miss you, Catherine!

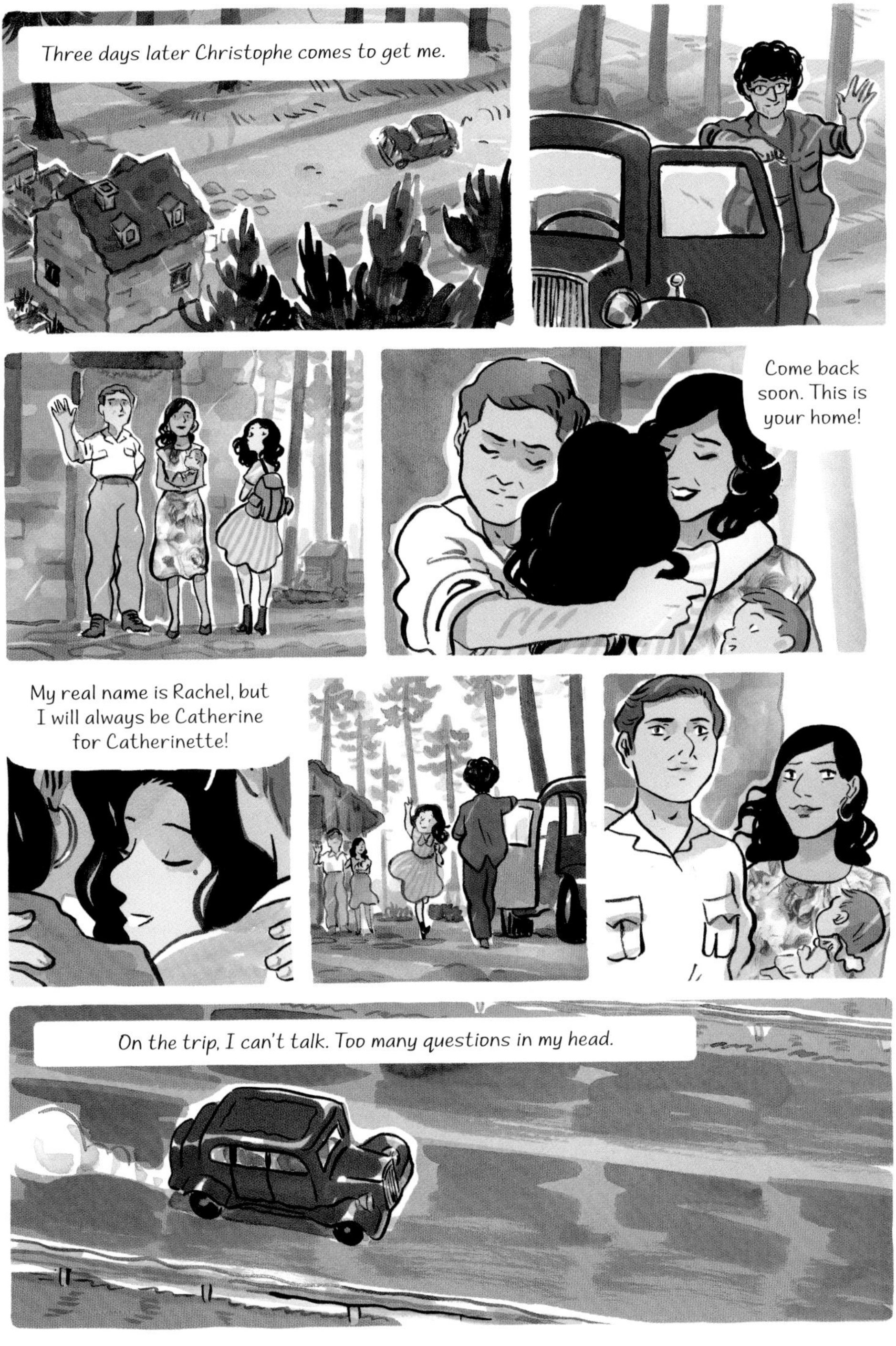
Three days later Christophe comes to get me.
Come back soon. This is your home!
My real name is Rachel, but I will always be Catherine for Catherinette!
On the trip, I can't talk. Too many questions in my head.

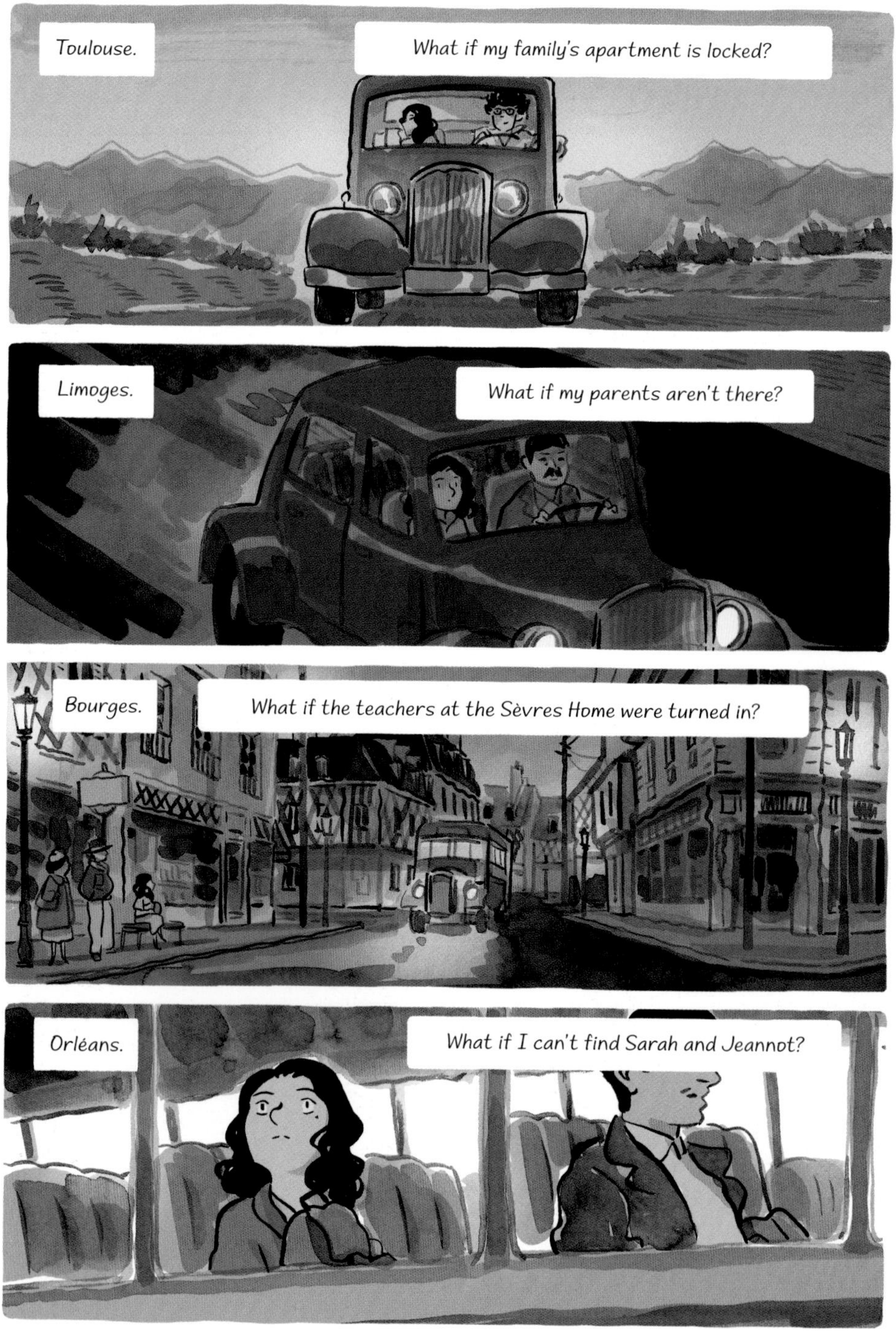

Toulouse.
What if my family's apartment is locked?
Limoges.
What if my parents aren't there?
Bourges.
What if the teachers at the Sèvres Home were turned in?
Orléans.
What if I can't find Sarah and Jeannot?

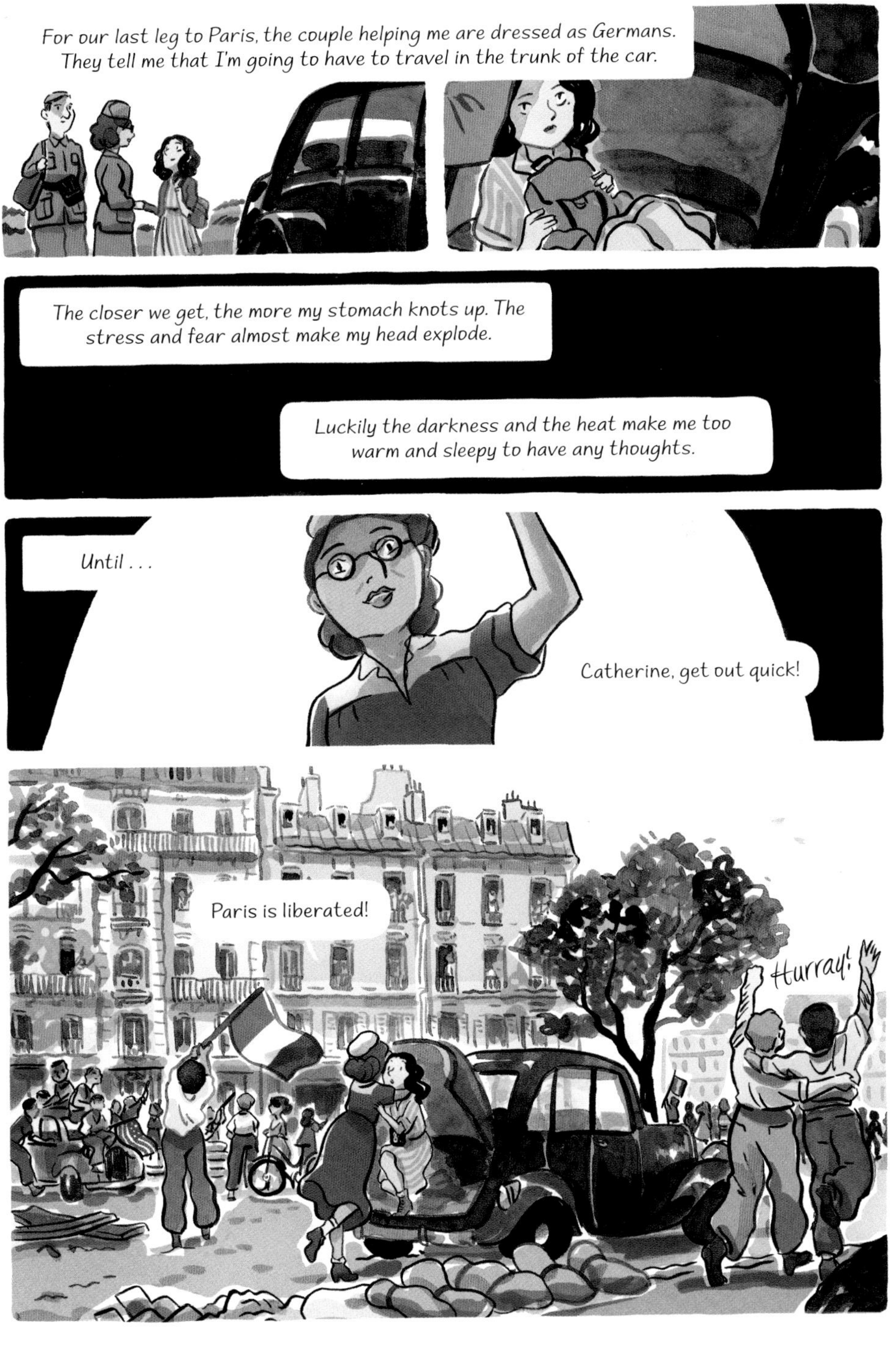
For our last leg to Paris, the couple helping me are dressed as Germans. They tell me that I'm going to have to travel in the trunk of the car.
The closer we get, the more my stomach knots up. The stress and fear almost make my head explode.
Luckily the darkness and the heat make me too warm and sleepy to have any thoughts.
Until . . .
Catherine, get out quick!
Paris is liberated!
Hurray!

August 20, 1944

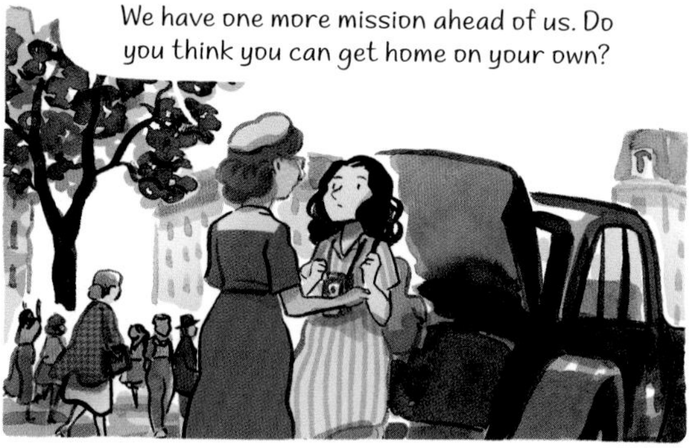
We have one more mission ahead of us. Do you think you can get home on your own?

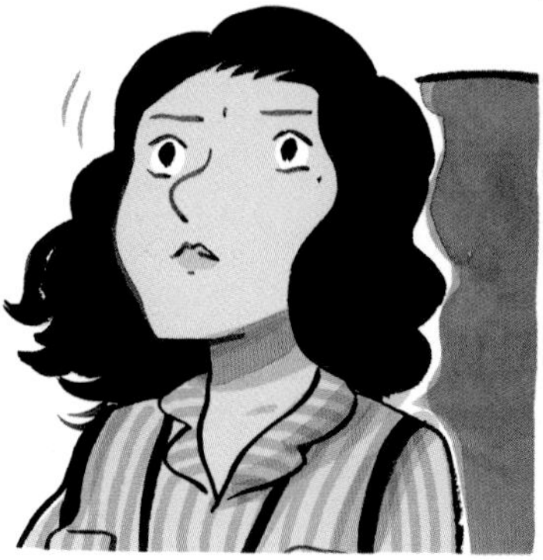

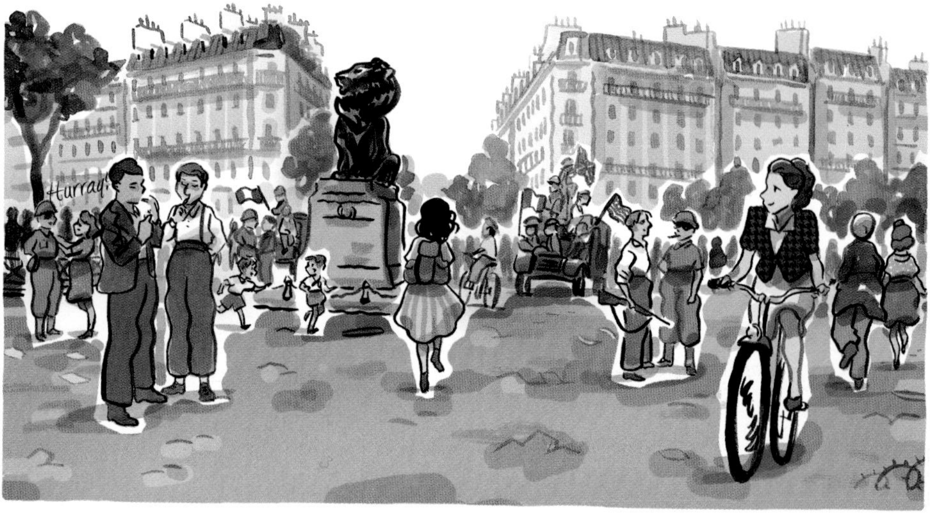
Hurray!

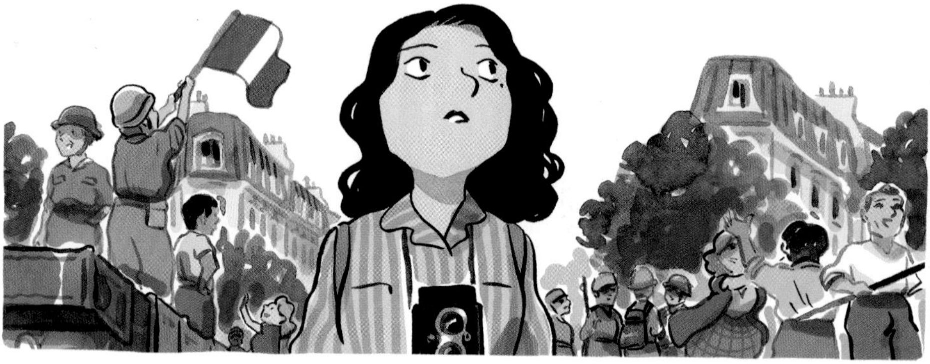

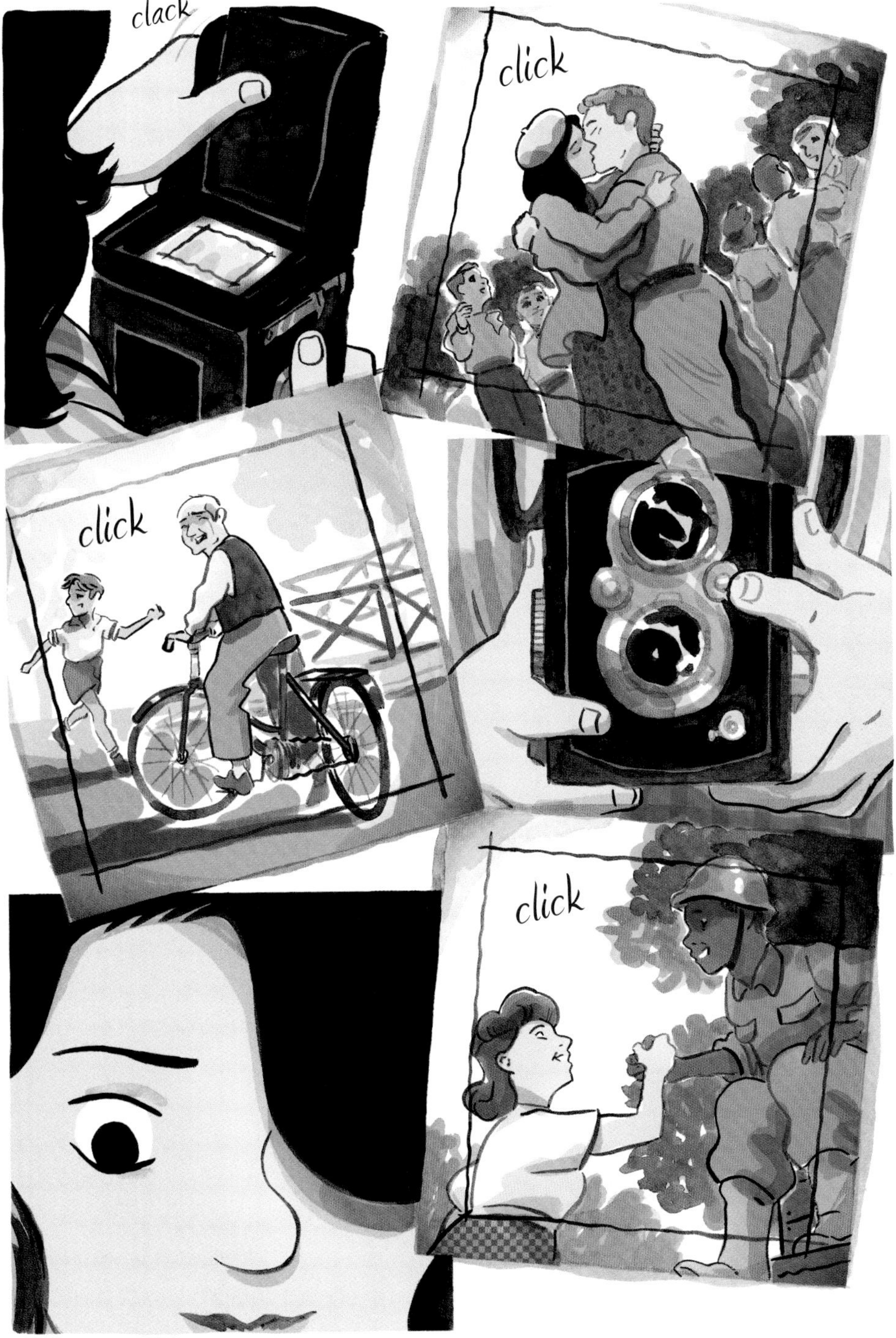
clack
click
click
click

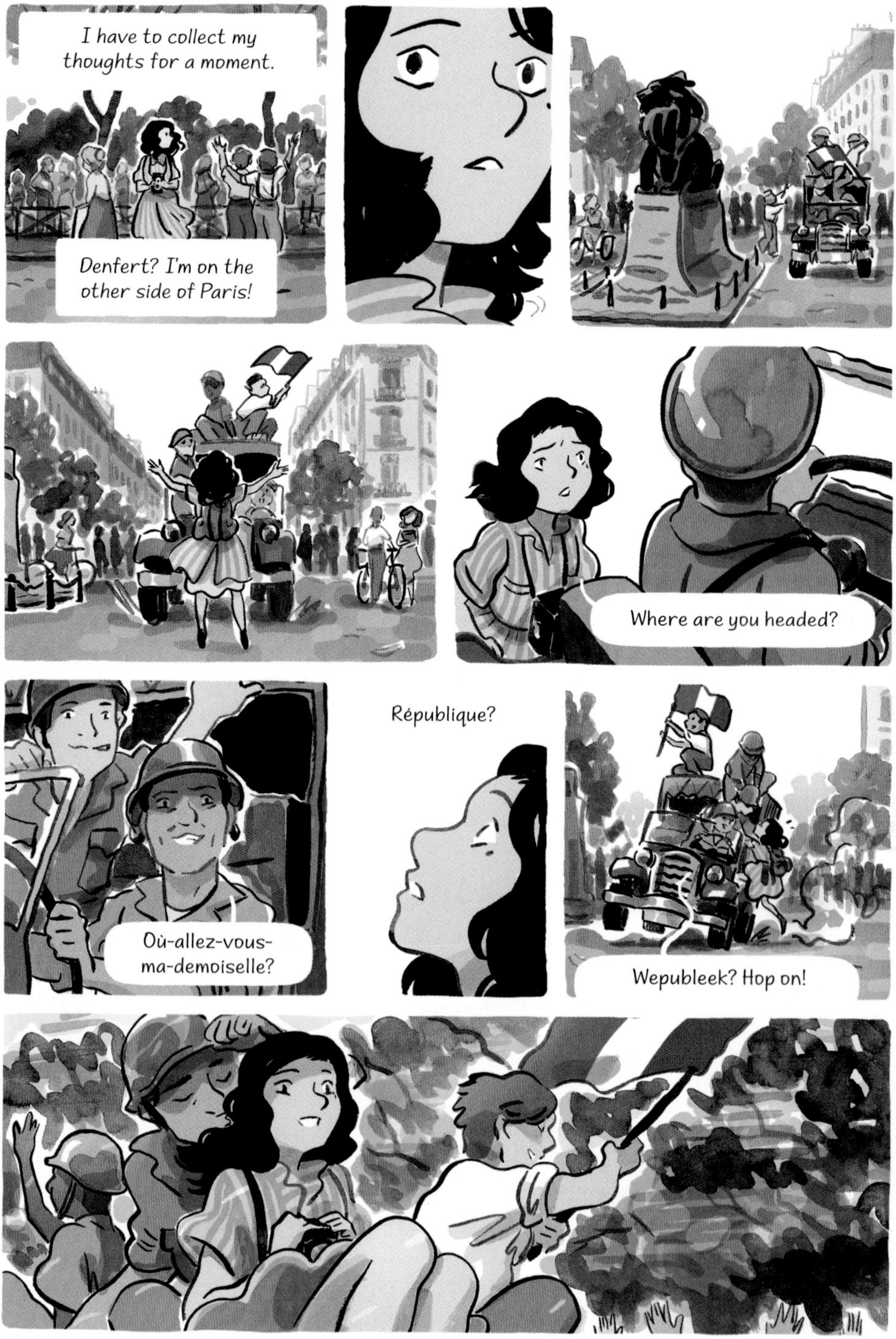
I have to collect my thoughts for a moment.
Denfert? I'm on the other side of Paris!
Where are you headed?
Où-allez-vous-ma-demoiselle?
République?
Wepubleek? Hop on!

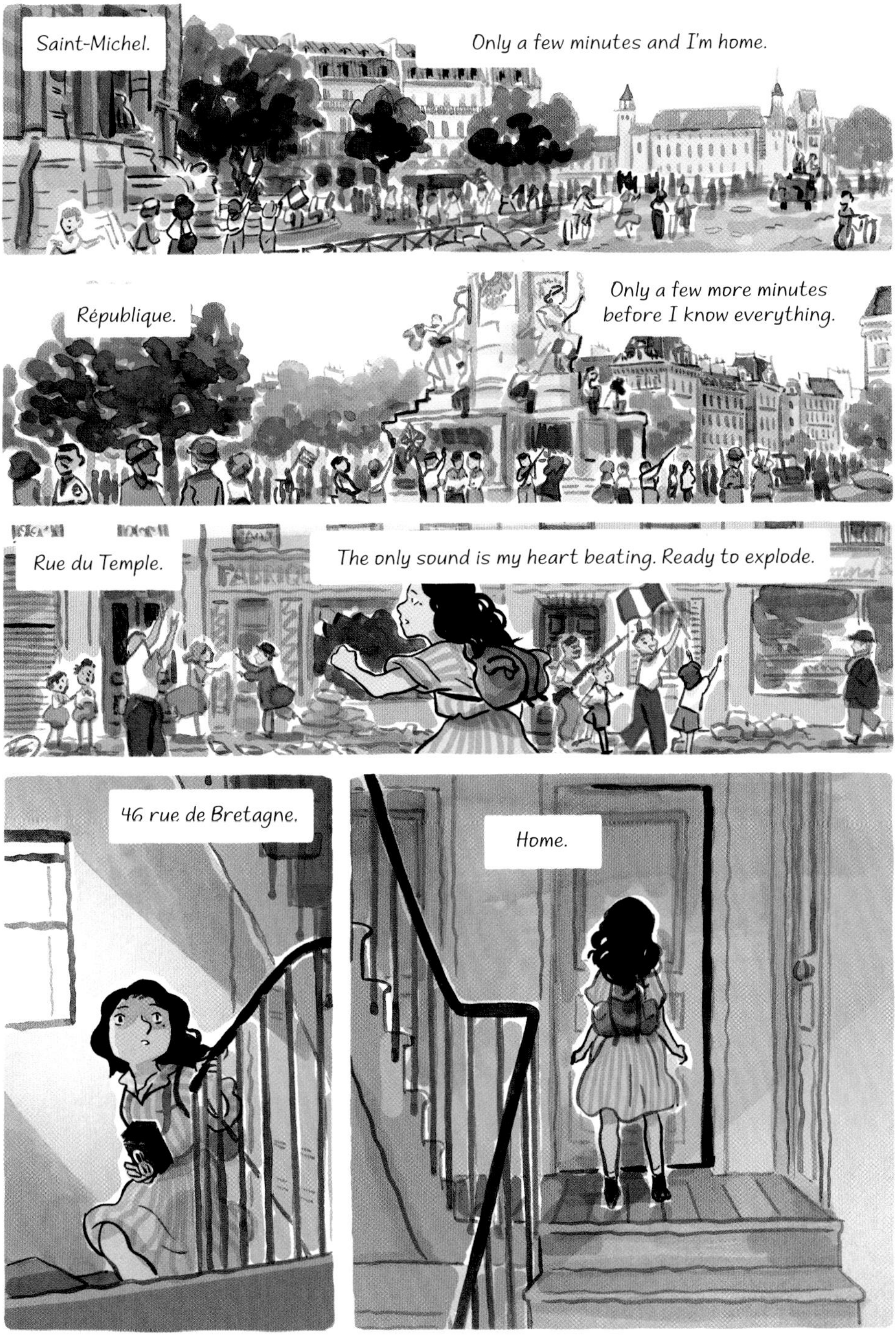
Saint-Michel.
Only a few minutes and I'm home.
République.
Only a few more minutes before I know everything.
Rue du Temple.
The only sound is my heart beating. Ready to explode.
46 rue de Bretagne.
Home.

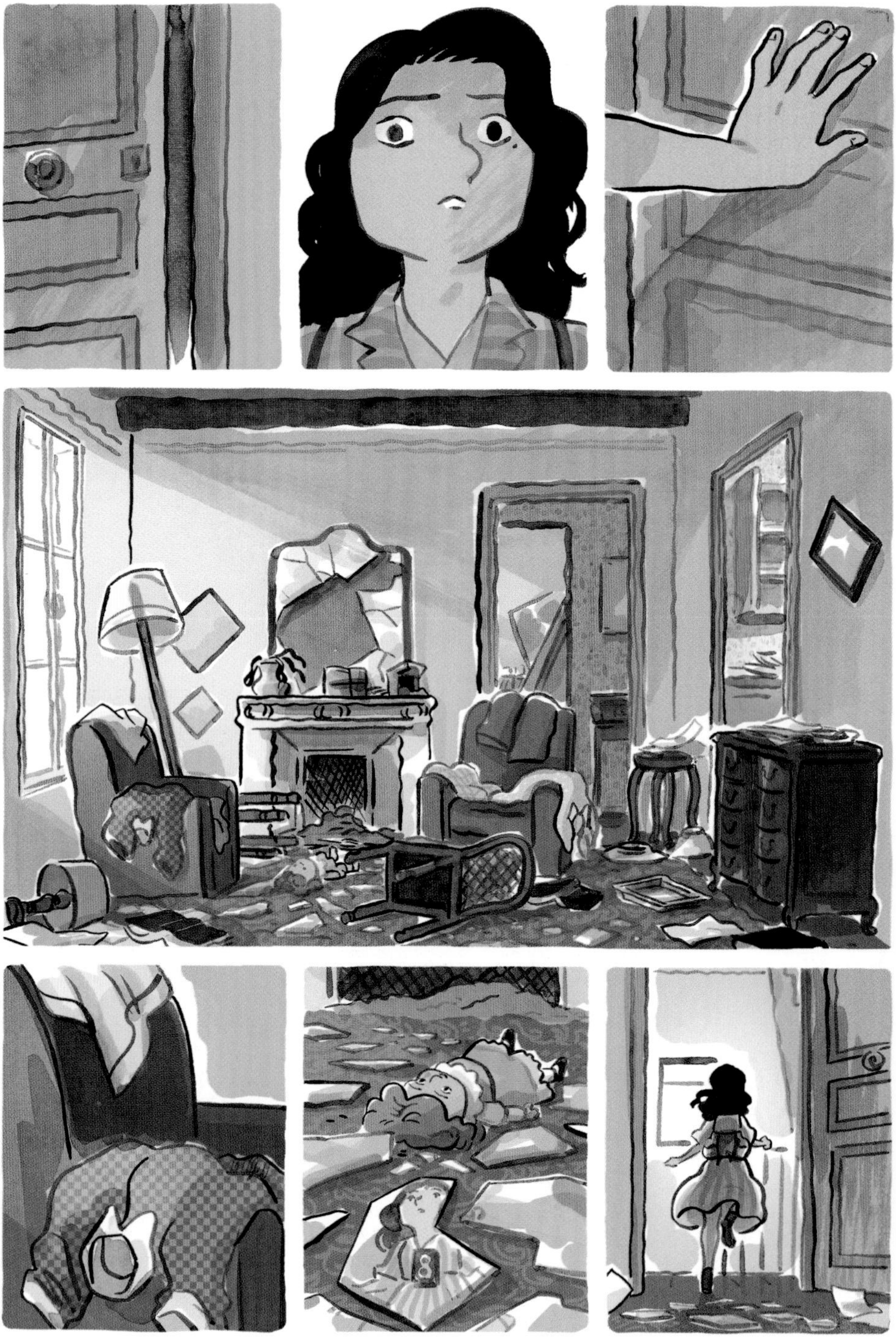

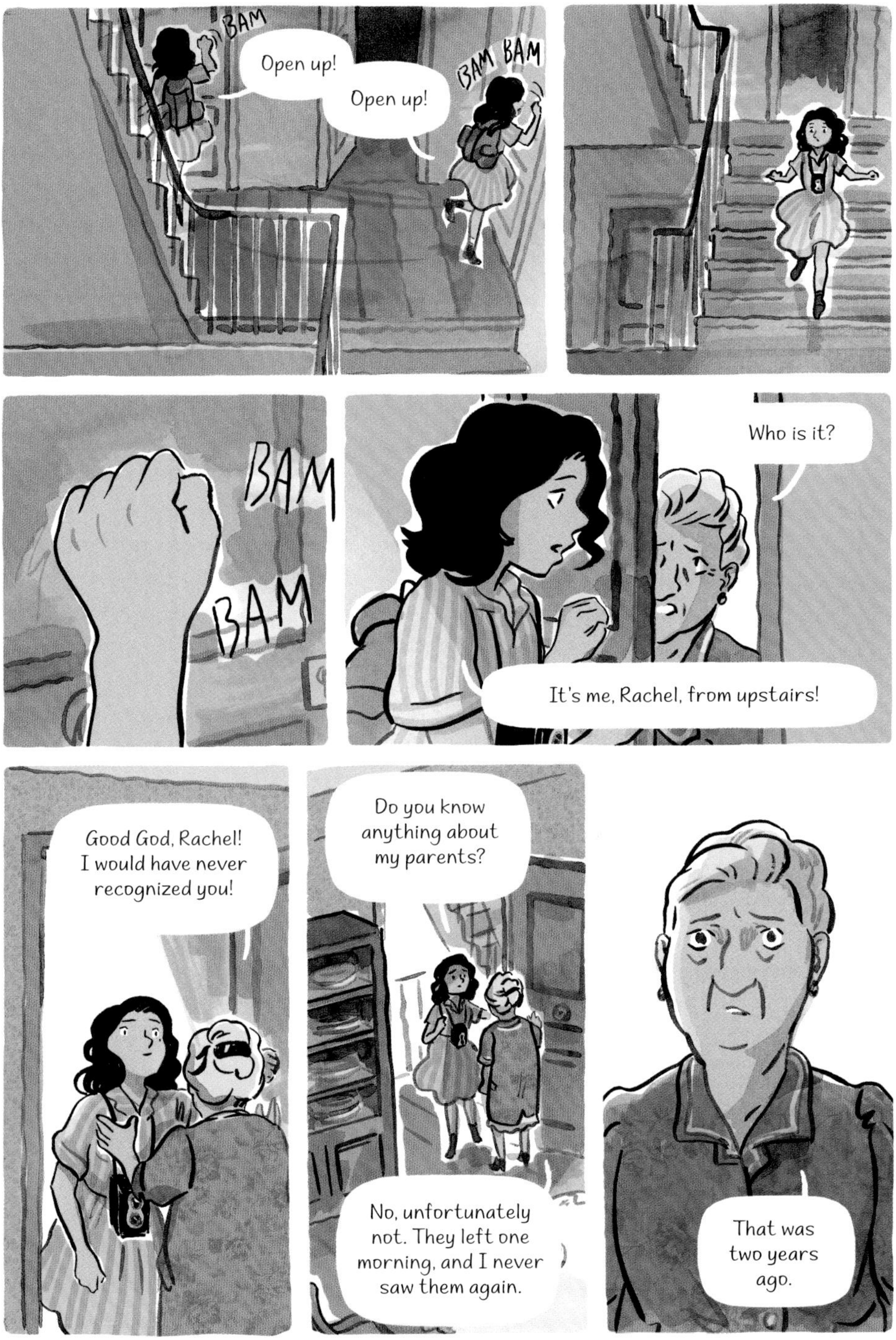
BAM
Open up!
Open up!
BAM BAM
BAM
BAM
Who is it?
It's me, Rachel, from upstairs!
Good God, Rachel! I would have never recognized you!
Do you know anything about my parents?
No, unfortunately not. They left one morning, and I never saw them again.
That was two years ago.

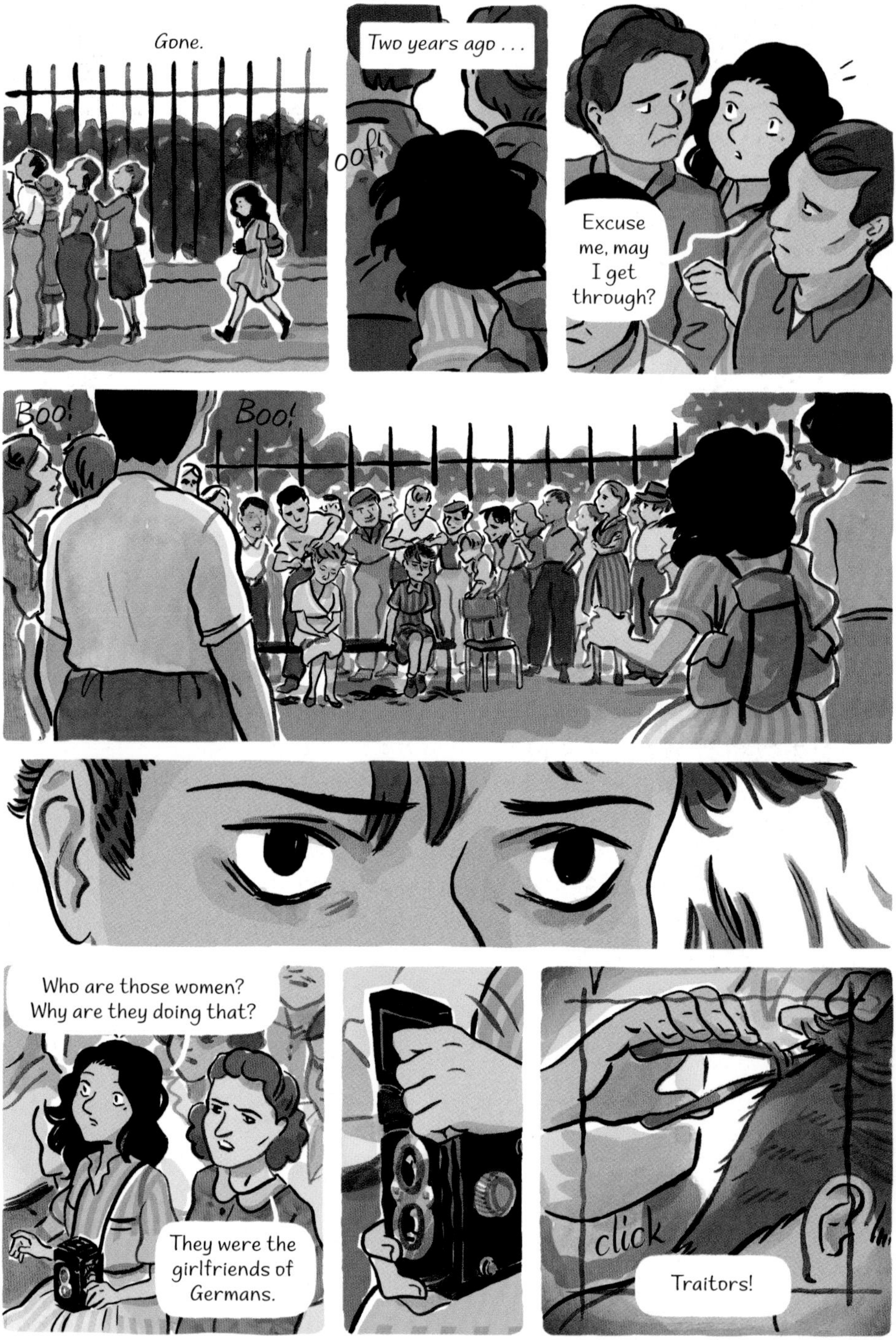
Gone.
Two years ago . . .
oof!
Excuse me, may I get through?
Boo!
Boo!
Who are those women? Why are they doing that?
They were the girlfriends of Germans.
click
Traitors!

Their hatred petrifies me.

I think of the German I met in Limoges.

Who knows what could've happened with him if things had been different?

I could've been one of them. . . .

These people want revenge . . . even the ones who would have reported my parents to the Germans.

beep! beep!

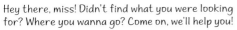

Hey there, miss! Didn't find what you were looking for? Where you wanna go? Come on, we'll help you!

You're our queen tonight!

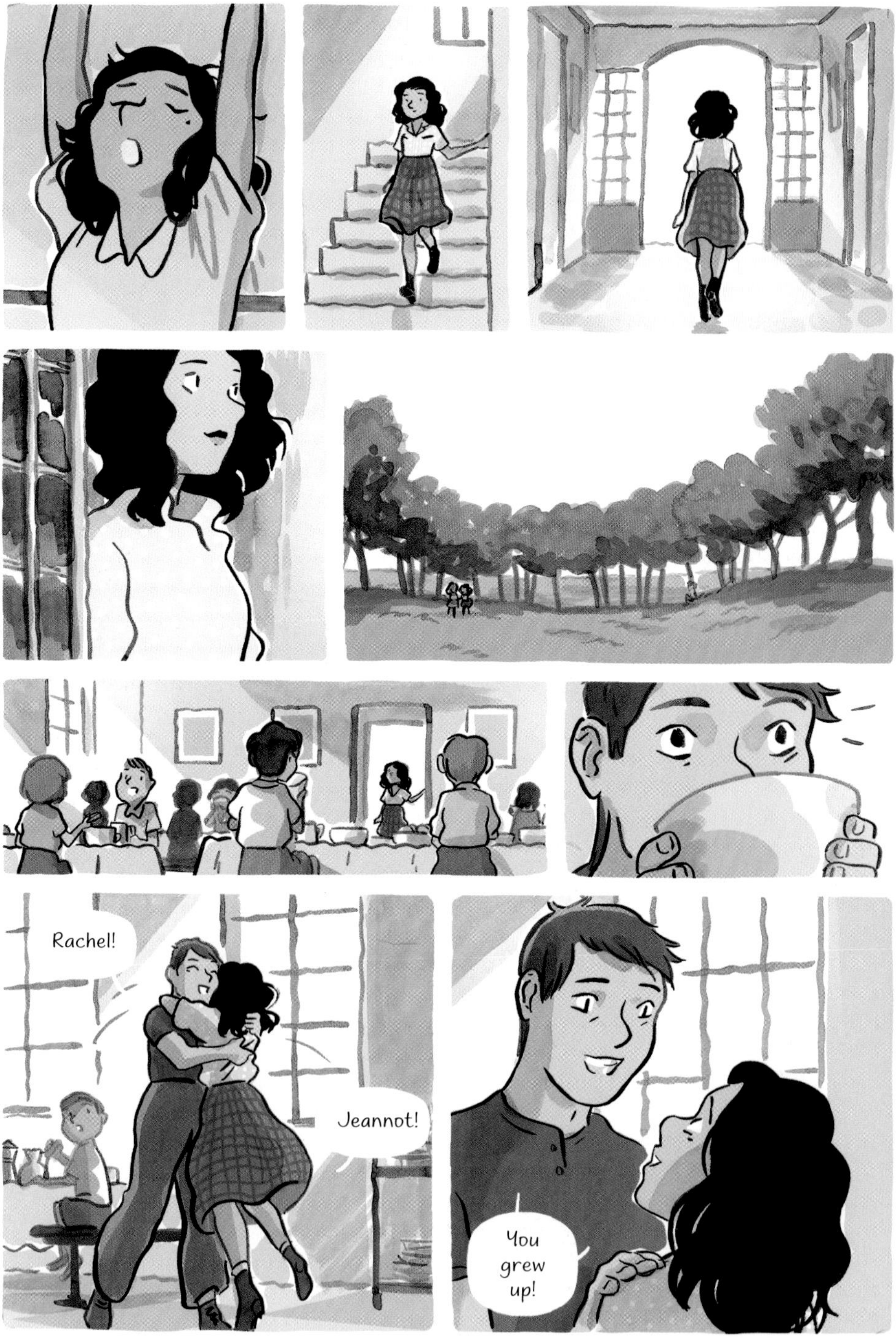
Rachel!
Jeannot!
You grew up!

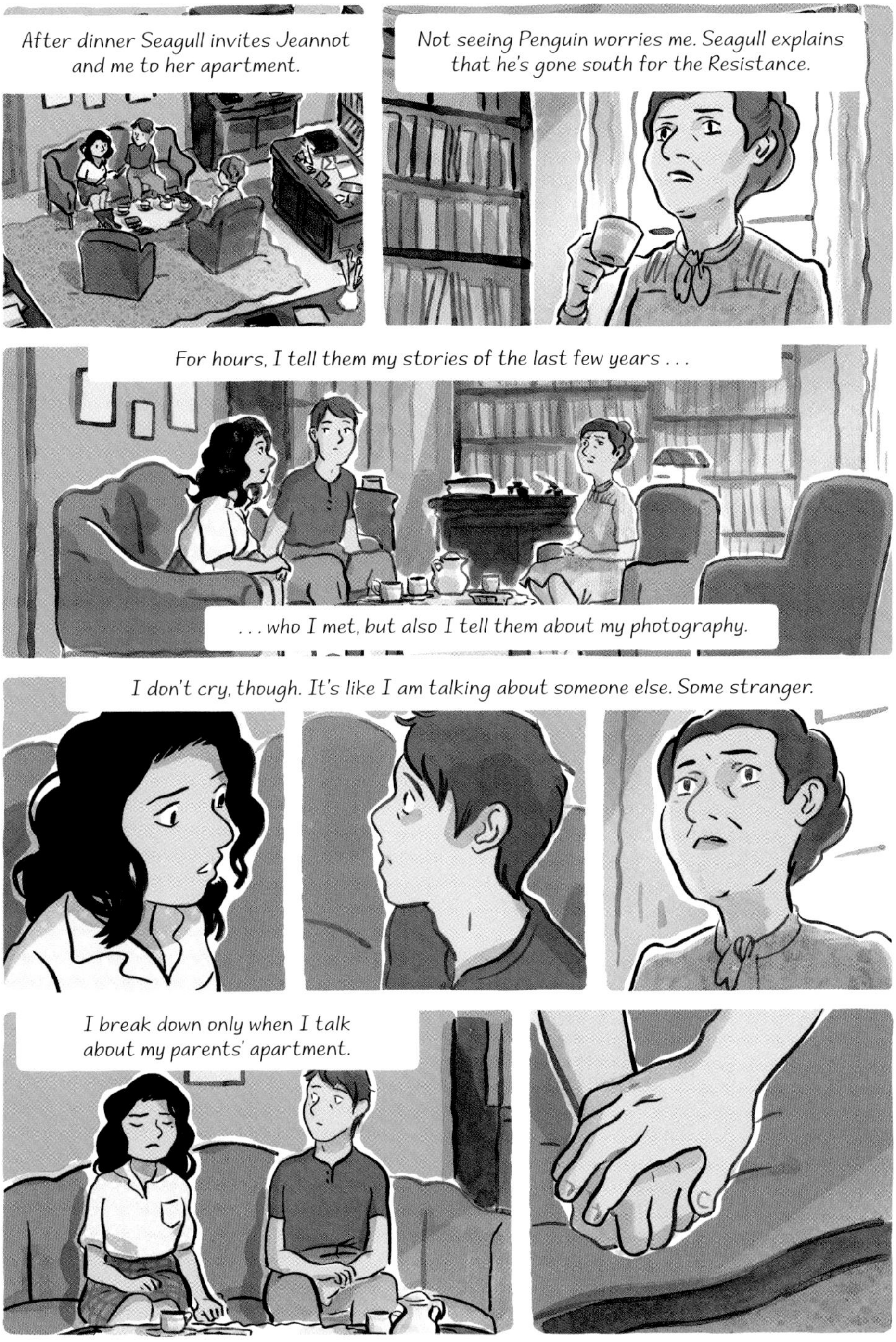
After dinner Seagull invites Jeannot and me to her apartment.
Not seeing Penguin worries me. Seagull explains that he's gone south for the Resistance.
For hours, I tell them my stories of the last few years . . .
. . . who I met, but also I tell them about my photography.
I don't cry, though. It's like I am talking about someone else. Some stranger.
I break down only when I talk about my parents' apartment.

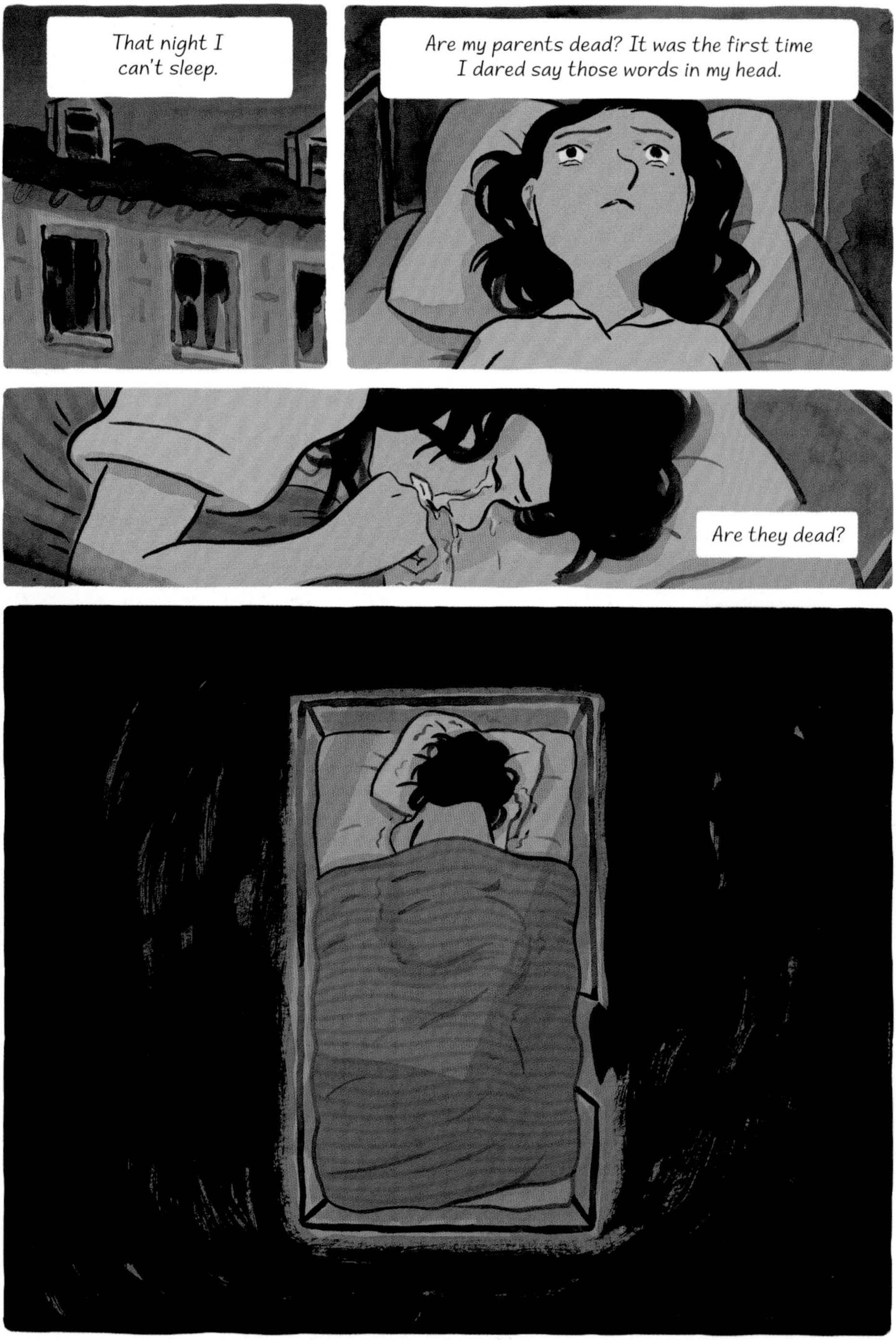
That night I can't sleep.
Are my parents dead? It was the first time I dared say those words in my head.
Are they dead?

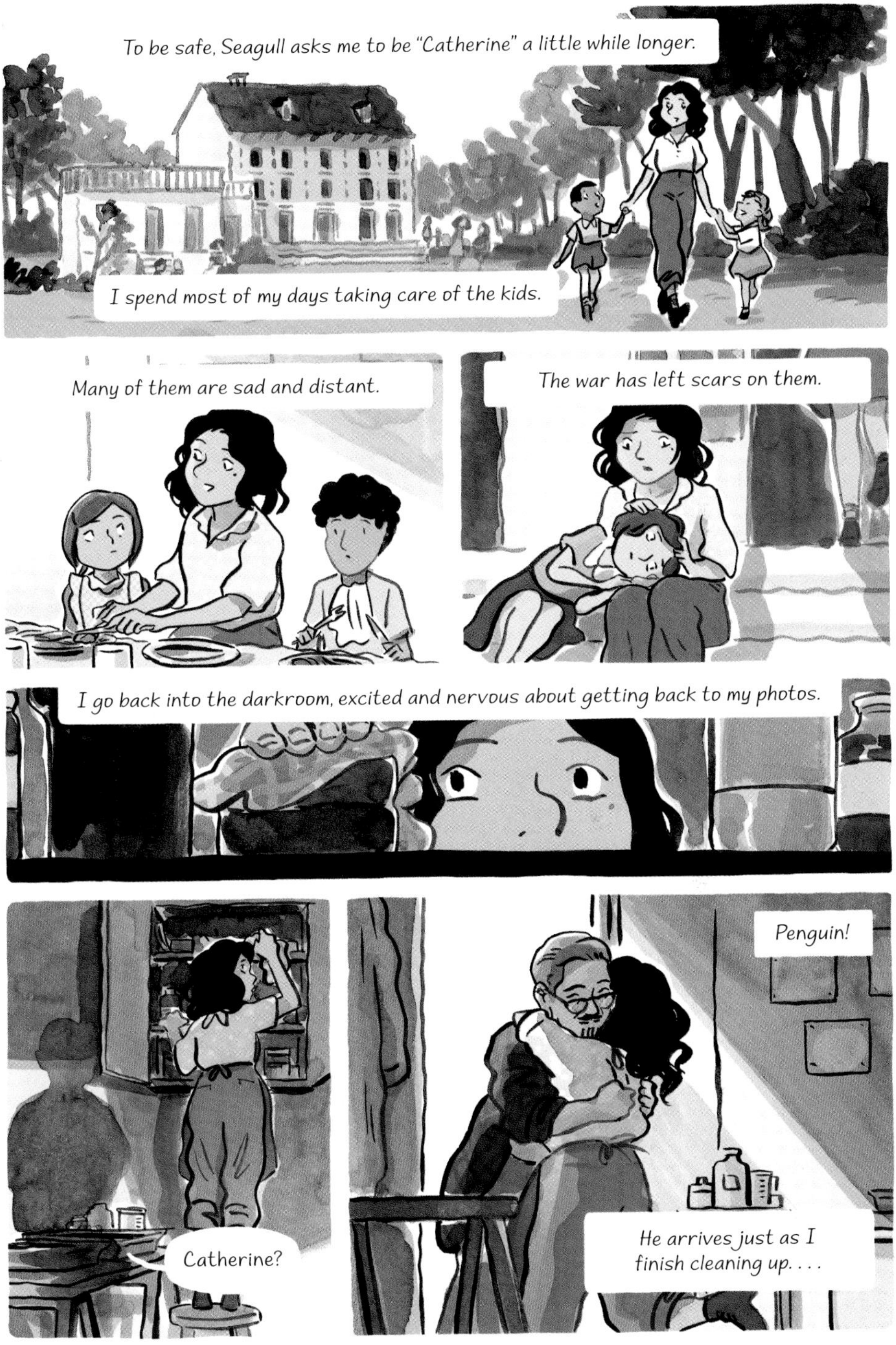
To be safe, Seagull asks me to be "Catherine" a little while longer.
I spend most of my days taking care of the kids.
Many of them are sad and distant.
The war has left scars on them.
I go back into the darkroom, excited and nervous about getting back to my photos.
Catherine?
Penguin!
He arrives just as I finish cleaning up. . . .

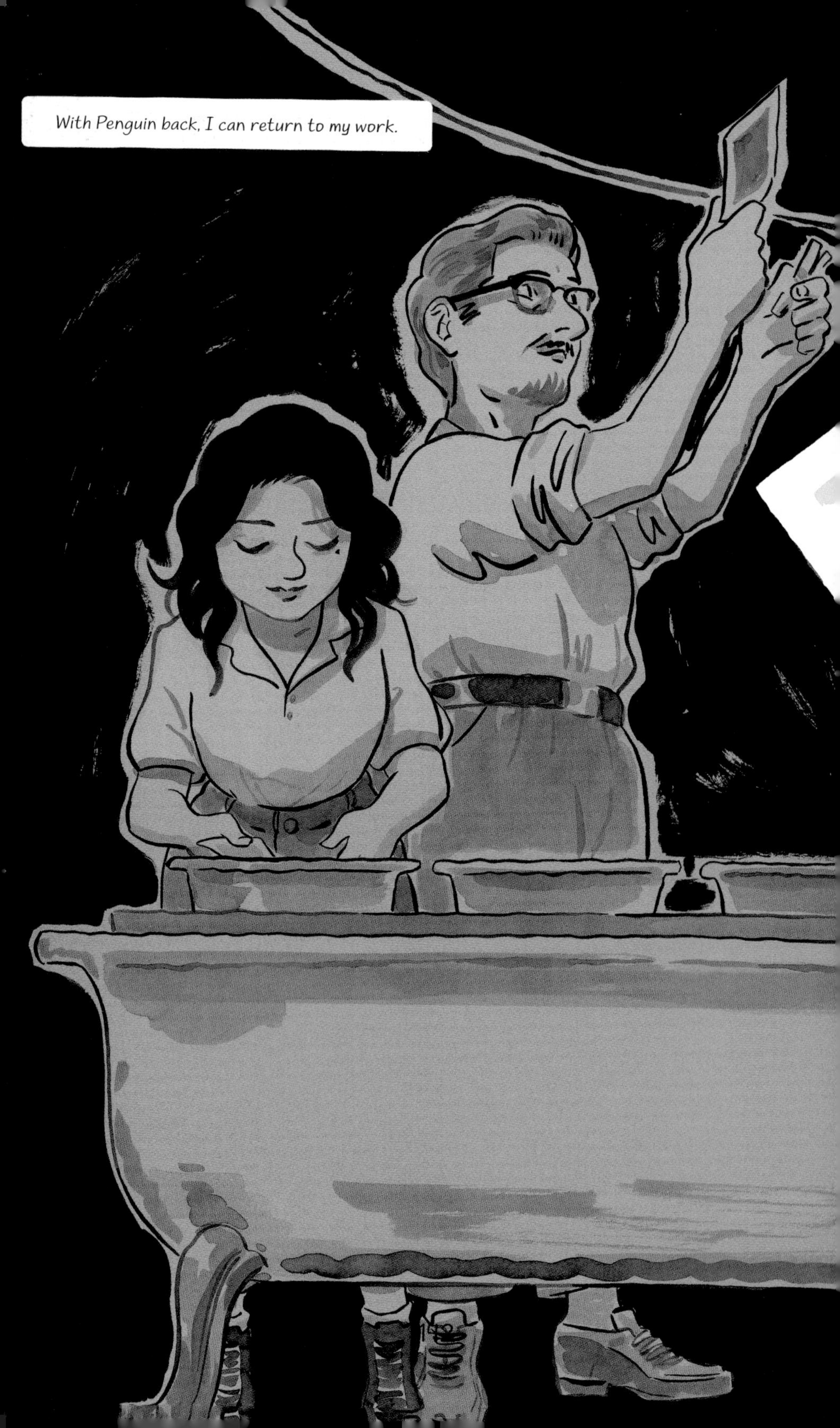
With Penguin back, I can return to my work.

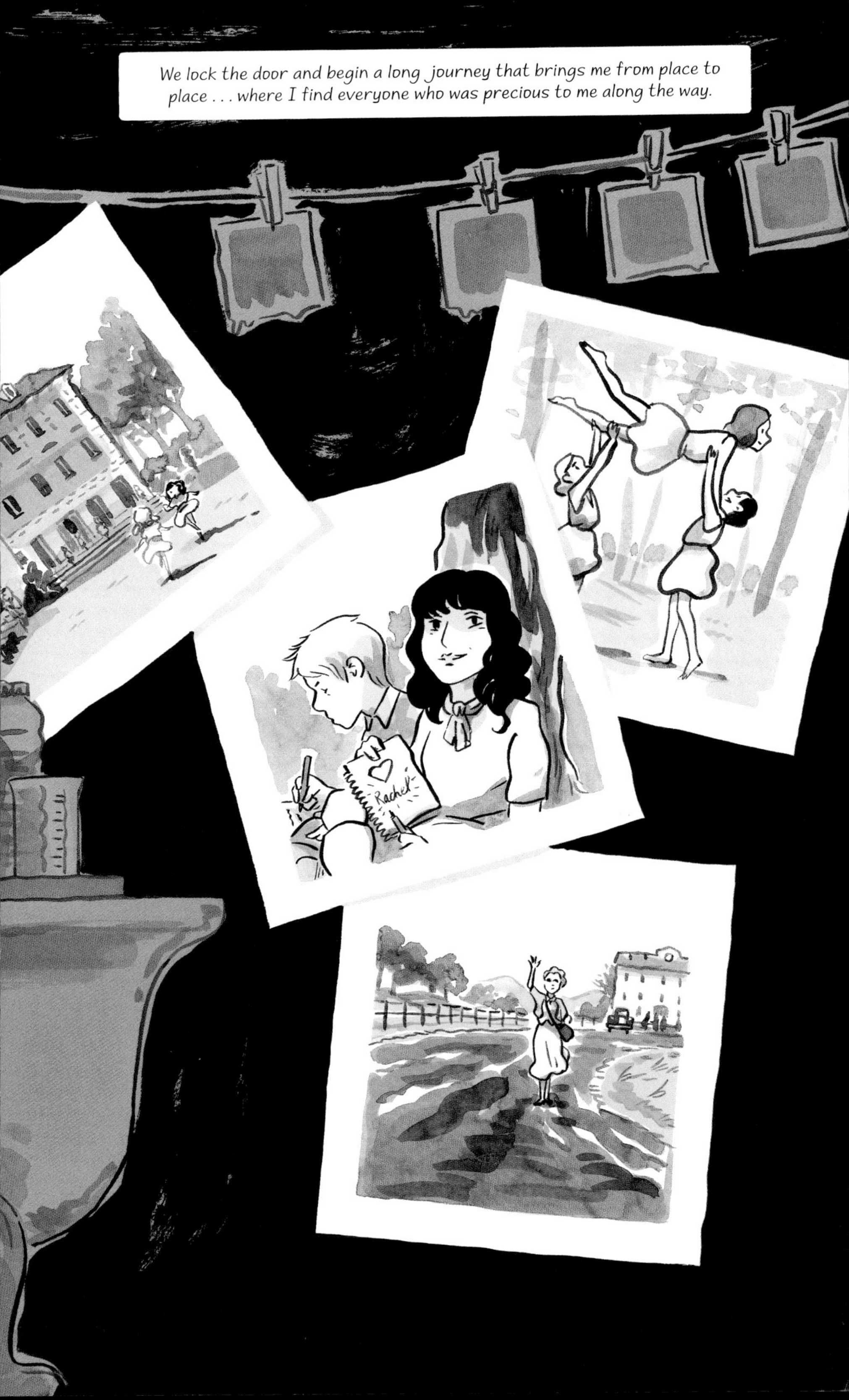
We lock the door and begin a long journey that brings me from place to place . . . where I find everyone who was precious to me along the way.
Rachel

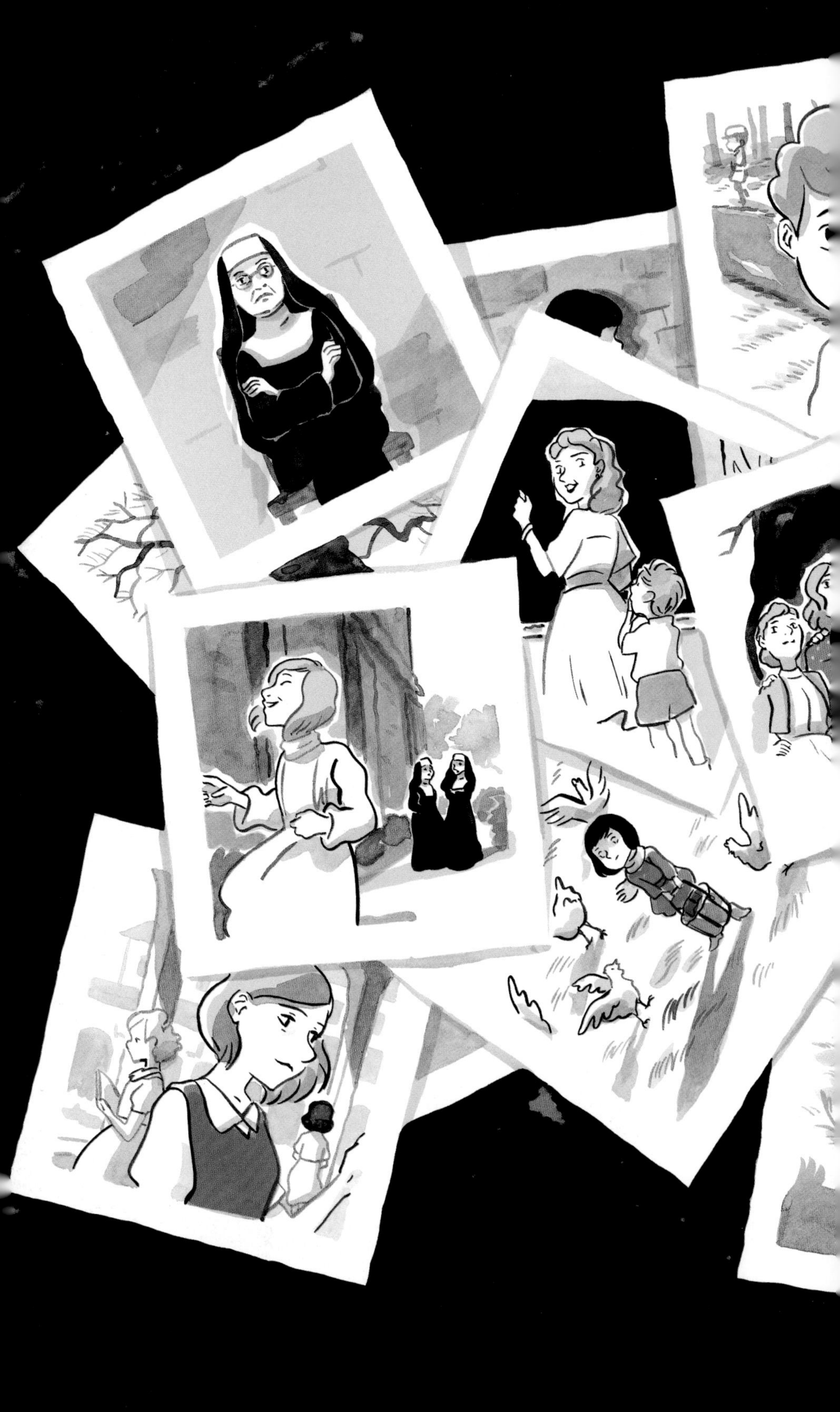

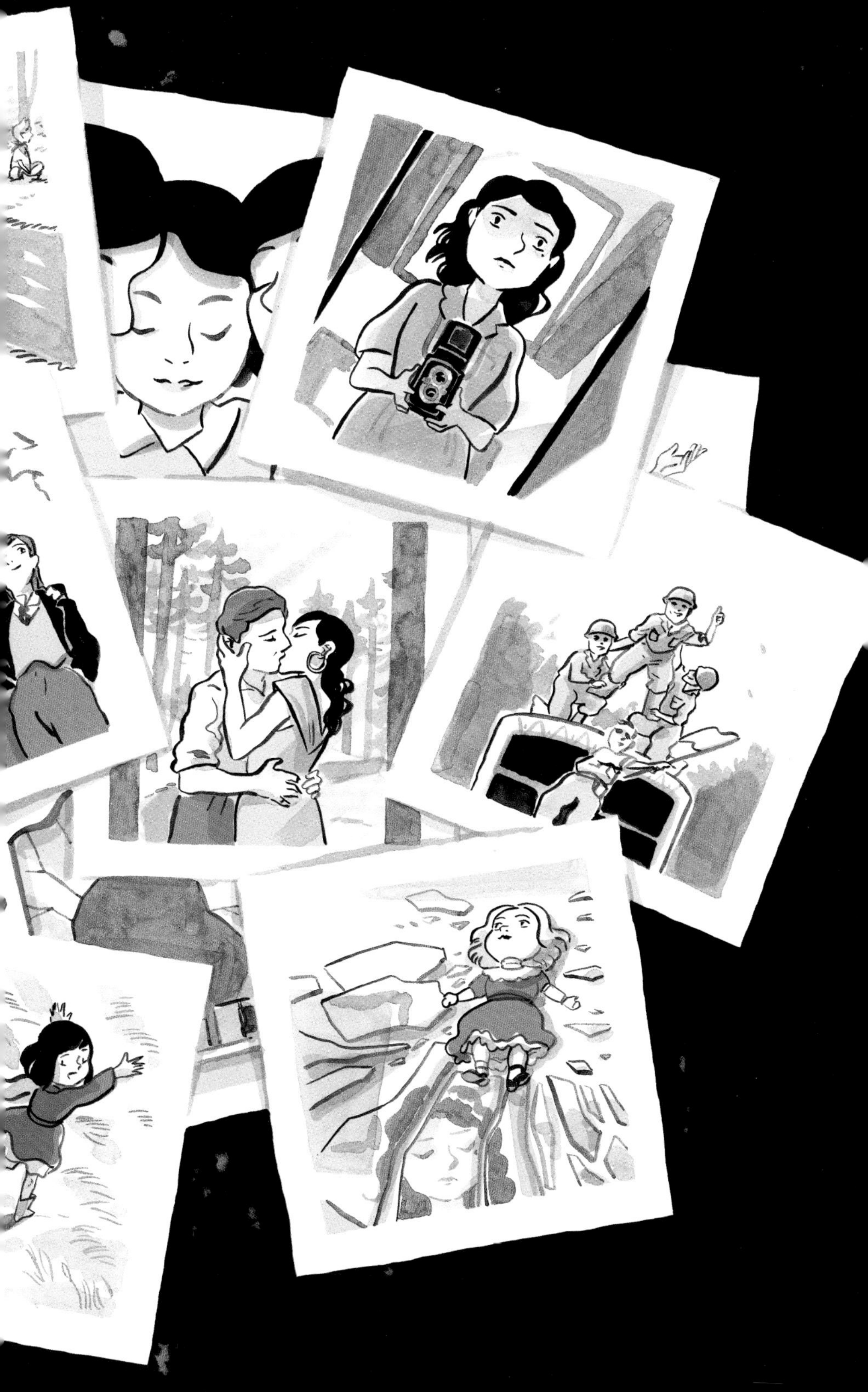

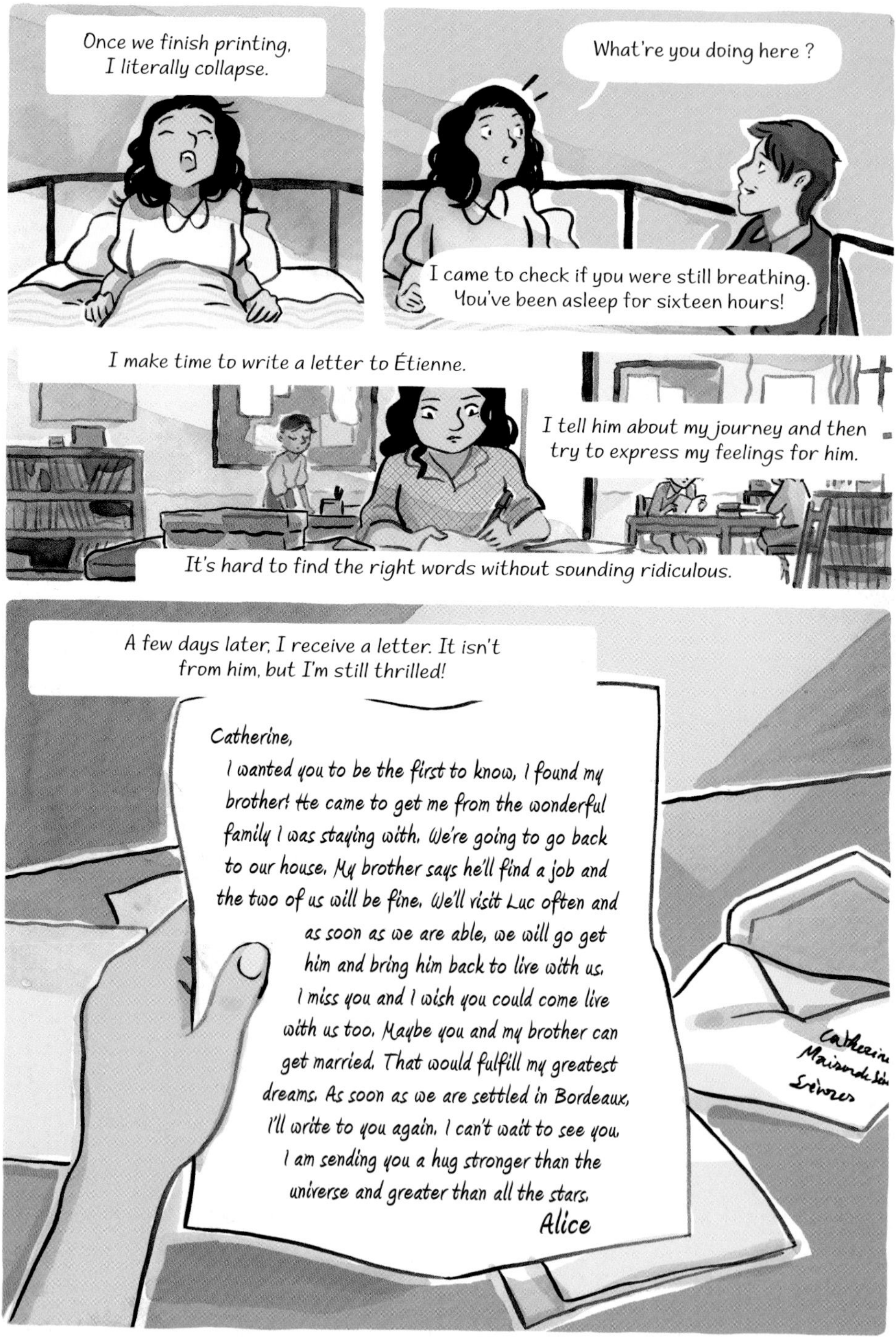
Once we finish printing, I literally collapse.
What're you doing here?
I came to check if you were still breathing. You've been asleep for sixteen hours!
I make time to write a letter to Étienne.
I tell him about my journey and then try to express my feelings for him.
It's hard to find the right words without sounding ridiculous.
A few days later, I receive a letter. It isn't from him, but I'm still thrilled!
Catherine,
I wanted you to be the first to know, I found my brother! He came to get me from the wonderful family I was staying with. We're going to go back to our house. My brother says he'll find a job and the two of us will be fine. We'll visit Luc often and as soon as we are able, we will go get him and bring him back to live with us. I miss you and I wish you could come live with us too. Maybe you and my brother can get married. That would fulfill my greatest dreams. As soon as we are settled in Bordeaux, I'll write to you again. I can't wait to see you. I am sending you a hug stronger than the universe and greater than all the stars.
Alice

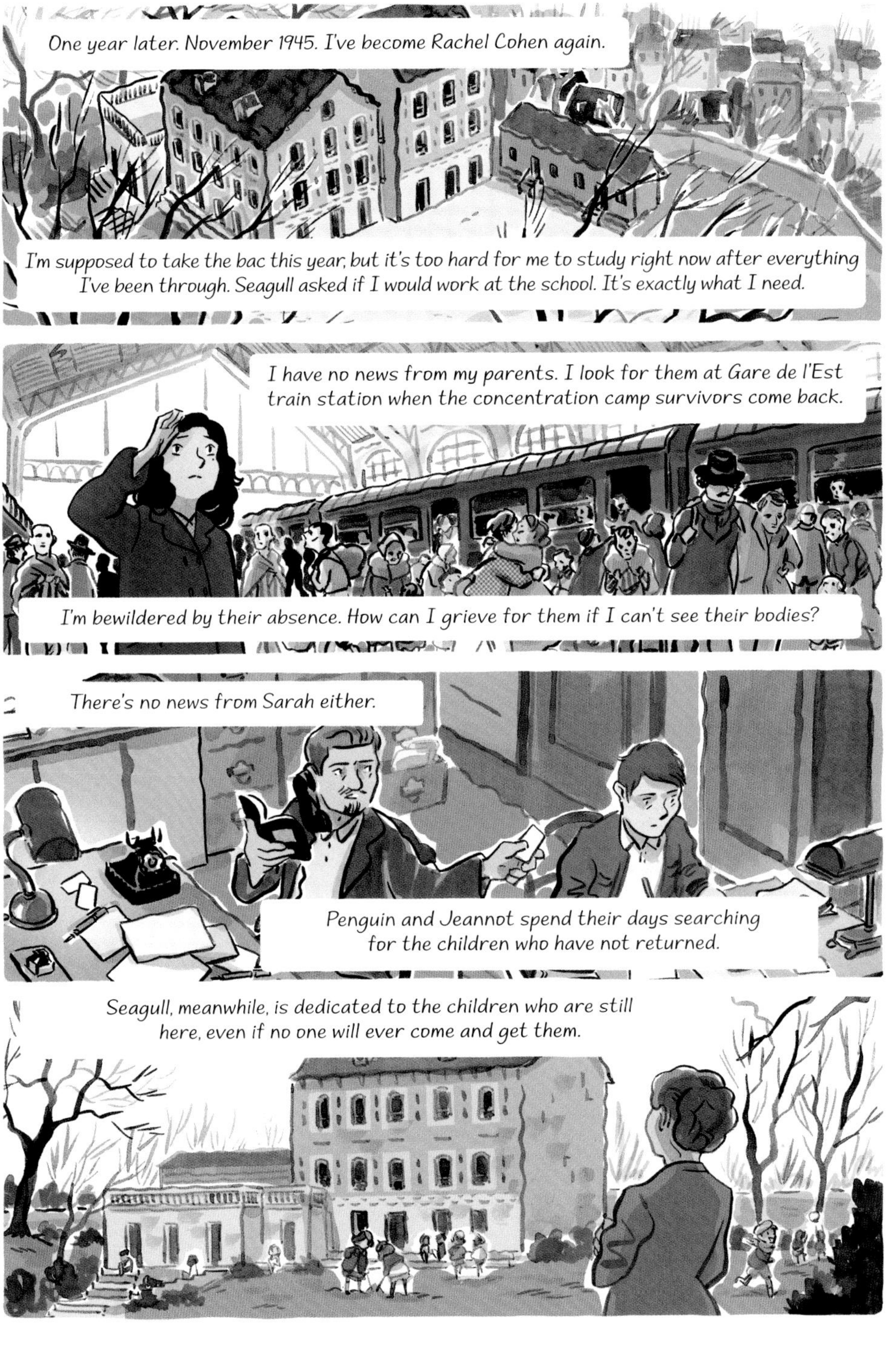
One year later. November 1945. I've become Rachel Cohen again.
I'm supposed to take the bac this year, but it's too hard for me to study right now after everything I've been through. Seagull asked if I would work at the school. It's exactly what I need.
I have no news from my parents. I look for them at Gare de l'Est train station when the concentration camp survivors come back.
I'm bewildered by their absence. How can I grieve for them if I can't see their bodies?
There's no news from Sarah either.
Penguin and Jeannot spend their days searching for the children who have not returned.
Seagull, meanwhile, is dedicated to the children who are still here, even if no one will ever come and get them.

I have my whole heart in her mission.

Psst, Rachel!

I showed your photos to some friends. One has a gallery in the Marais and wants to meet you.

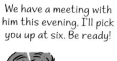

We have a meeting with him this evening, I'll pick you up at six. Be ready!

Ten minutes later.

Can you believe it? It's incredible!

I want to believe it, but...

...you're not going dressed like that?

Cristina's dress!

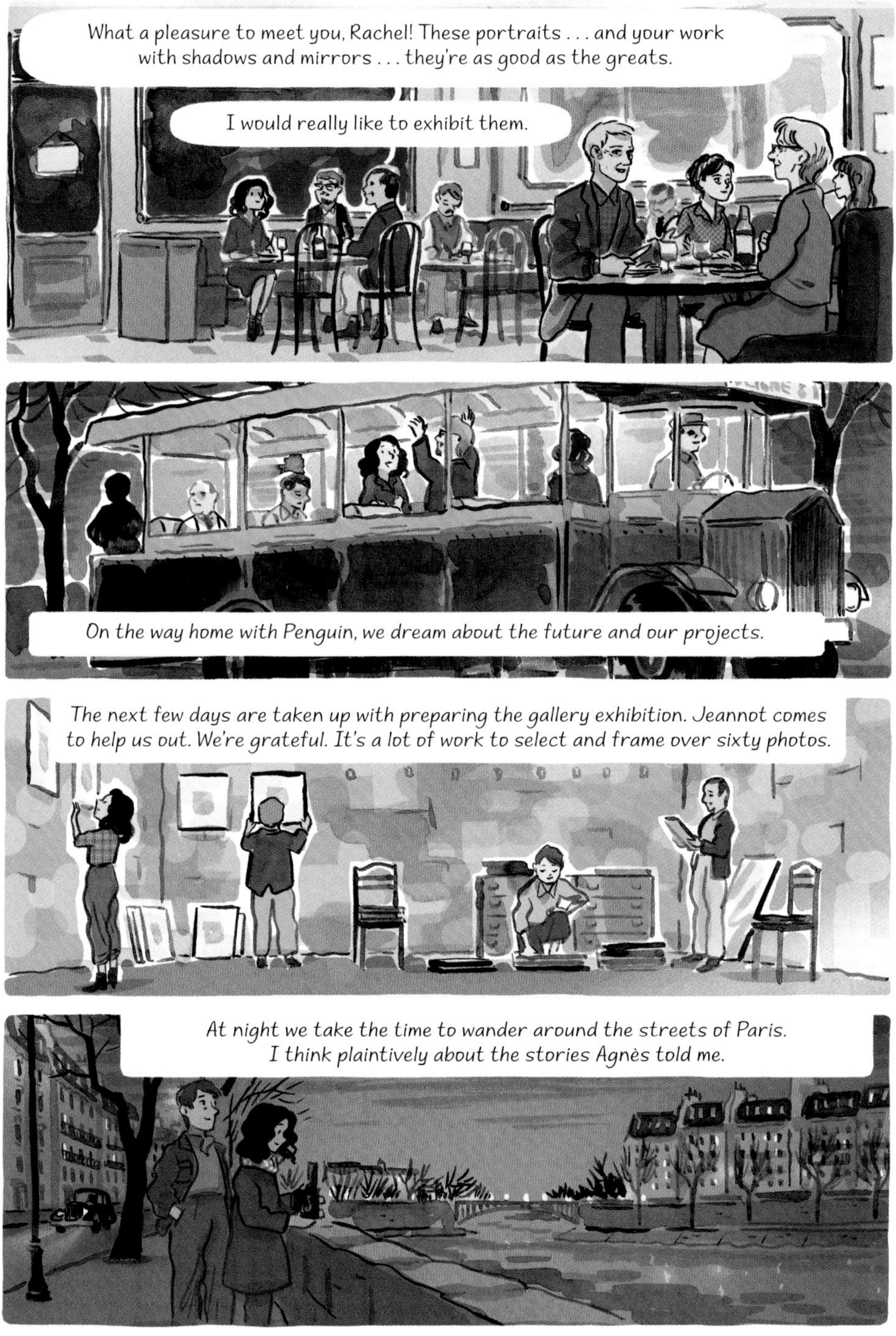
What a pleasure to meet you, Rachel! These portraits . . . and your work with shadows and mirrors . . . they're as good as the greats.
I would really like to exhibit them.
On the way home with Penguin, we dream about the future and our projects.
The next few days are taken up with preparing the gallery exhibition. Jeannot comes to help us out. We're grateful. It's a lot of work to select and frame over sixty photos.
At night we take the time to wander around the streets of Paris. I think plaintively about the stories Agnès told me.

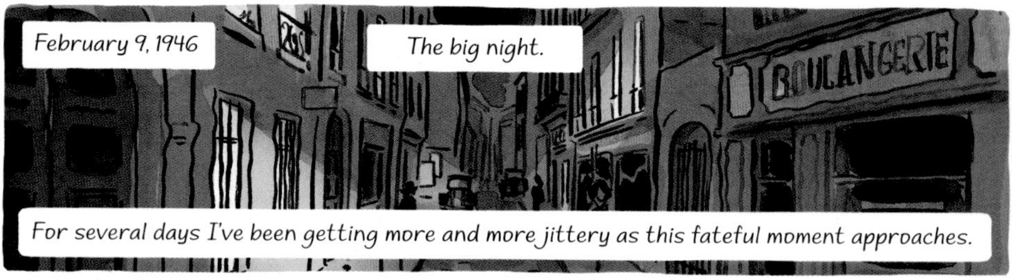
February 9, 1946
The big night.
BOULANGERIE
For several days I've been getting more and more jittery as this fateful moment approaches.

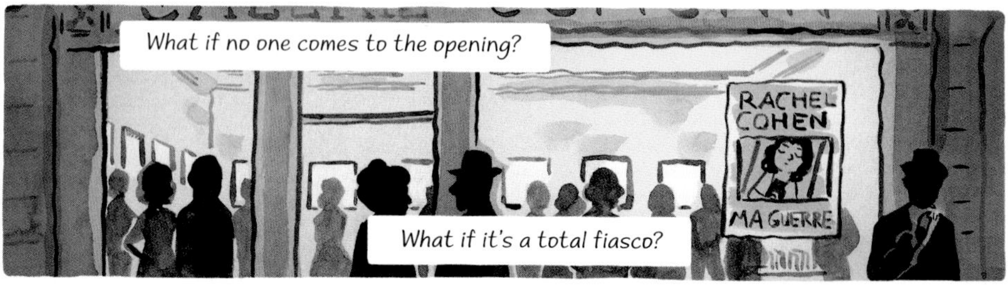
What if no one comes to the opening?
RACHEL COHEN
MA GUERRE
What if it's a total fiasco?

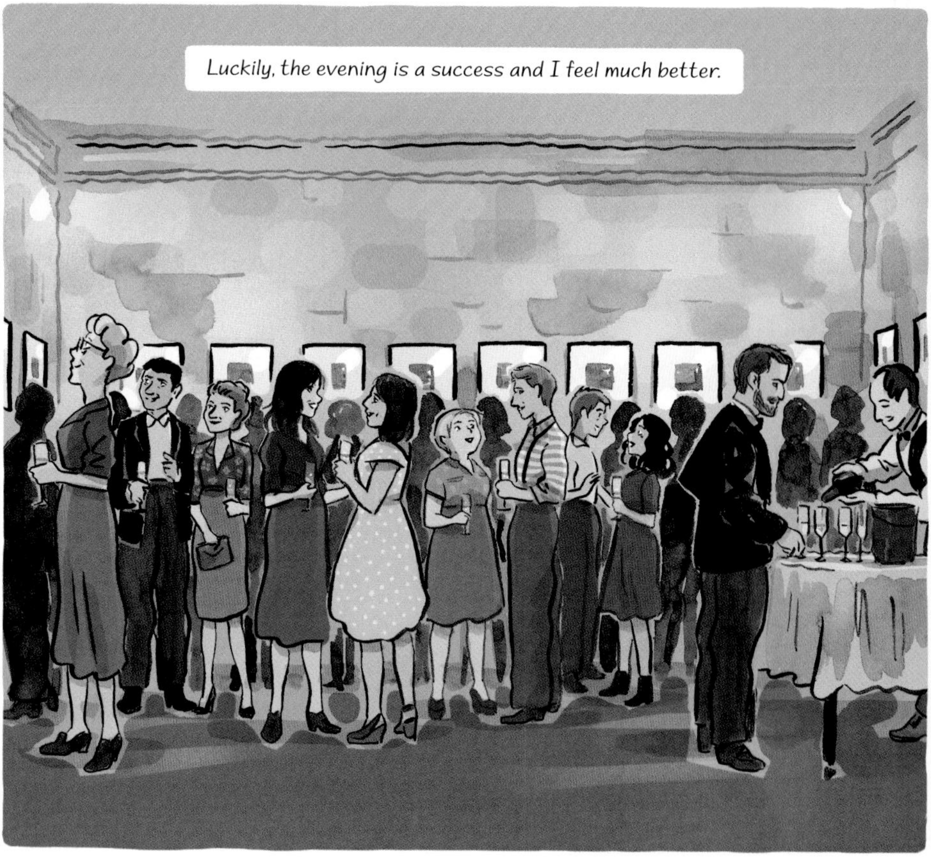
Luckily, the evening is a success and I feel much better.

I'm delighted to see all my teachers so proud of me.

Everyone in Paris who appreciates photography is here.

Journalists want to talk to me.

The champagne goes to my head, but I do the best I can to concentrate and enjoy a magical evening.

The following week, several journalists write about the exhibition.

Photo Show: *My War,* until March 3

A remarkable show that will transport you from Sèvres to the Pyrénées f...
with a truly

Portrait: Rachel Cohen

A young Jewish woman, rescued from the war, shares her story and her pictures–each one showing the world that buried and destroyed her until she lifted herself up.

st time a y...
ever photo...
e home fron...
utiful image...
to reflect the...
he many Fre...
o e force...
he n o...
, her...
ptured...
ring imag...
me front for...
ch citizens in th...
he German occu...

A you...
woman...
Rachel Cohen was...
are witness to d...
life in France un...
the occupation...
through her y...
eyes, and wi...
dued emoti...
Rachel tell...
her daily life.

Exposition:
My War by Ra... Cohen

A very young woman shares her story of the war in sixty photographs, and invites us to enter into the interior world of a teenager confronted with exile.

War
Rachel Cohen
In this rare event, a teenage girl shares her experience in France under the occupation. It's through the eyes of this young girl and

151

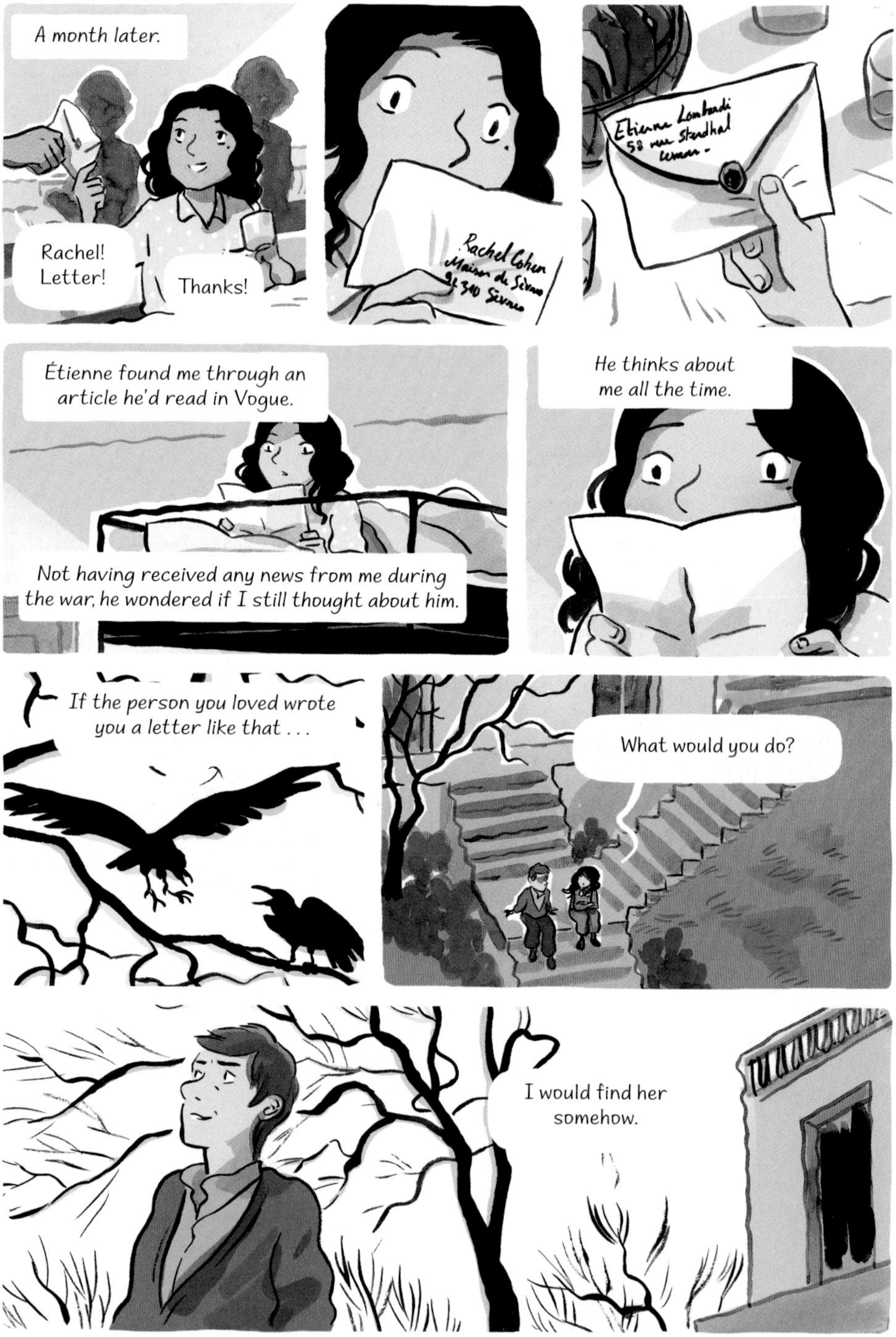
A month later.
Rachel! Letter!
Thanks!
Rachel Cohen
Étienne Lombardi
Étienne found me through an article he'd read in Vogue.
Not having received any news from me during the war, he wondered if I still thought about him.
He thinks about me all the time.
If the person you loved wrote you a letter like that . . .
What would you do?
I would find her somehow.

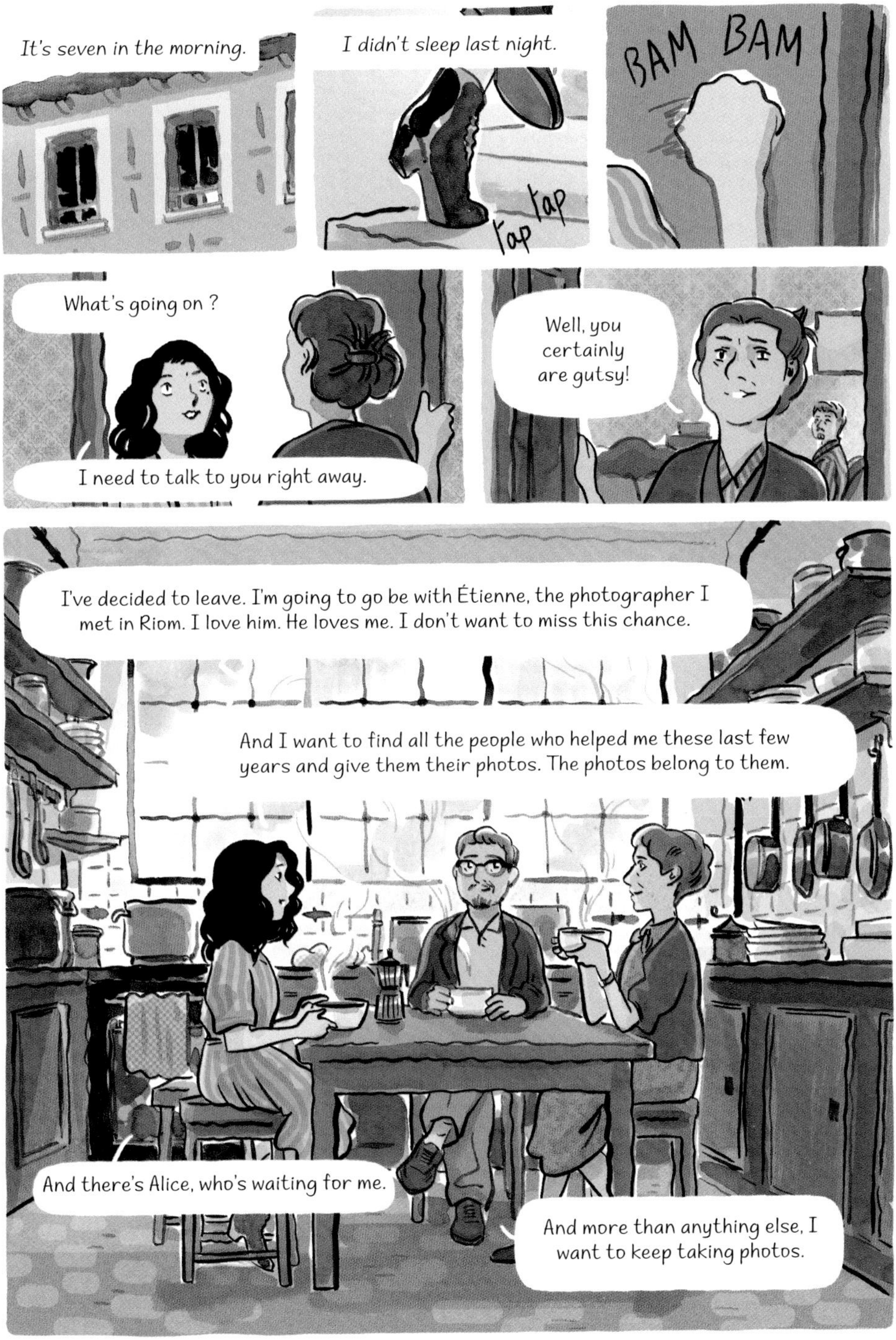
It's seven in the morning.
I didn't sleep last night.
tap
tap
BAM BAM
What's going on ?
I need to talk to you right away.
Well, you certainly are gutsy!
I've decided to leave. I'm going to go be with Étienne, the photographer I met in Riom. I love him. He loves me. I don't want to miss this chance.
And I want to find all the people who helped me these last few years and give them their photos. The photos belong to them.
And there's Alice, who's waiting for me.
And more than anything else, I want to keep taking photos.

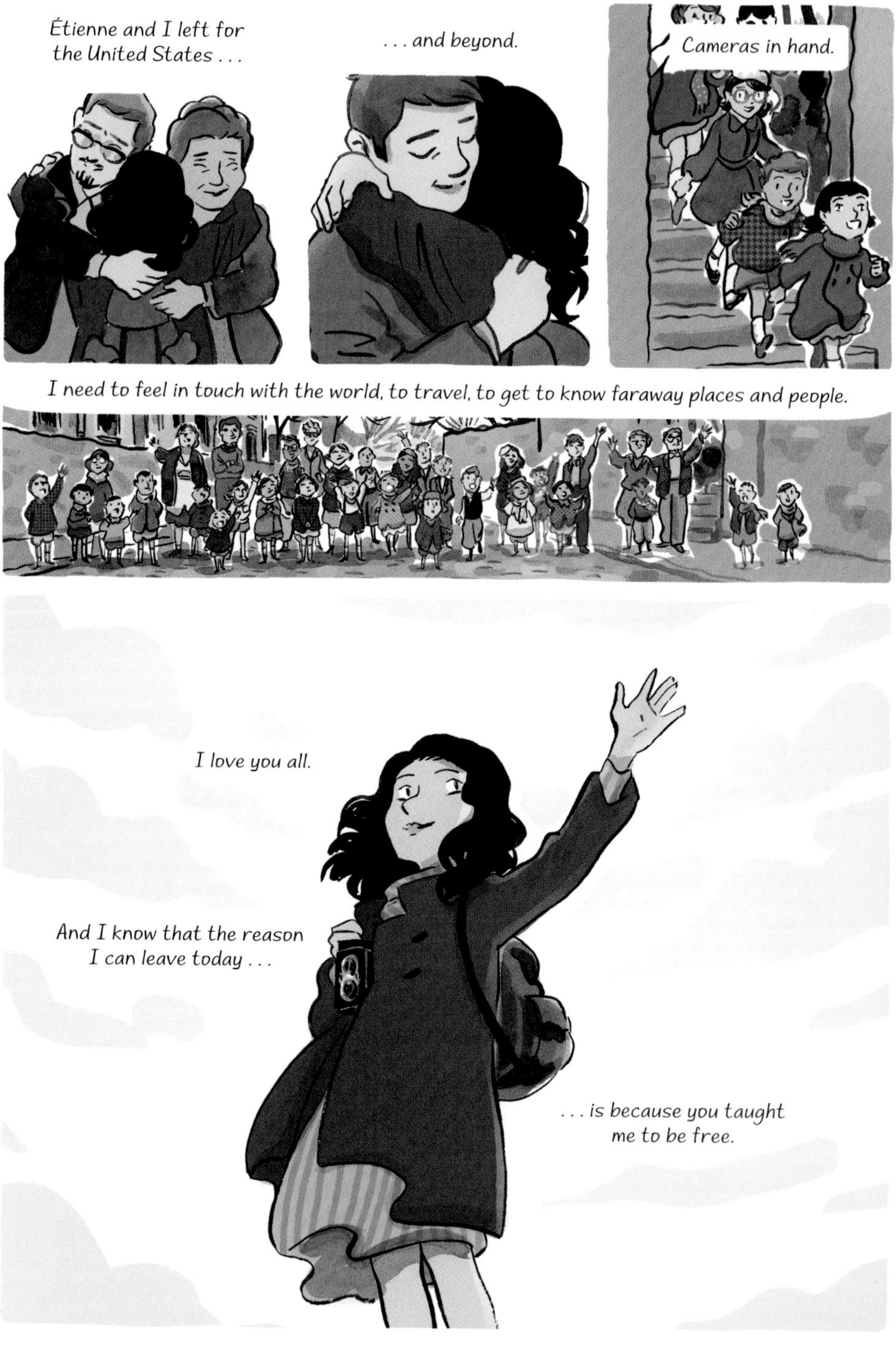
Étienne and I left for the United States . . .
. . . and beyond.
Cameras in hand.
I need to feel in touch with the world, to travel, to get to know faraway places and people.
I love you all.
And I know that the reason I can leave today . . .
. . . is because you taught me to be free.

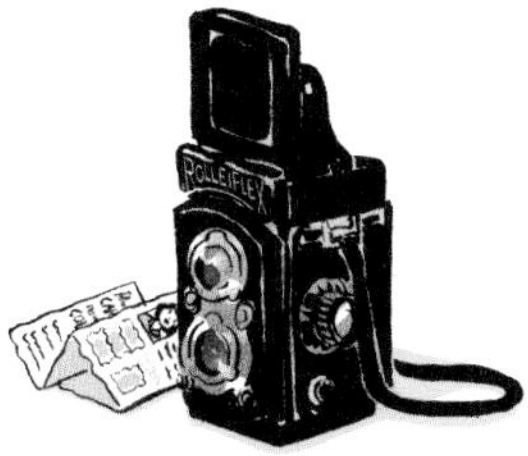
ROLLEIFLEX

Map of Catherine's Journey

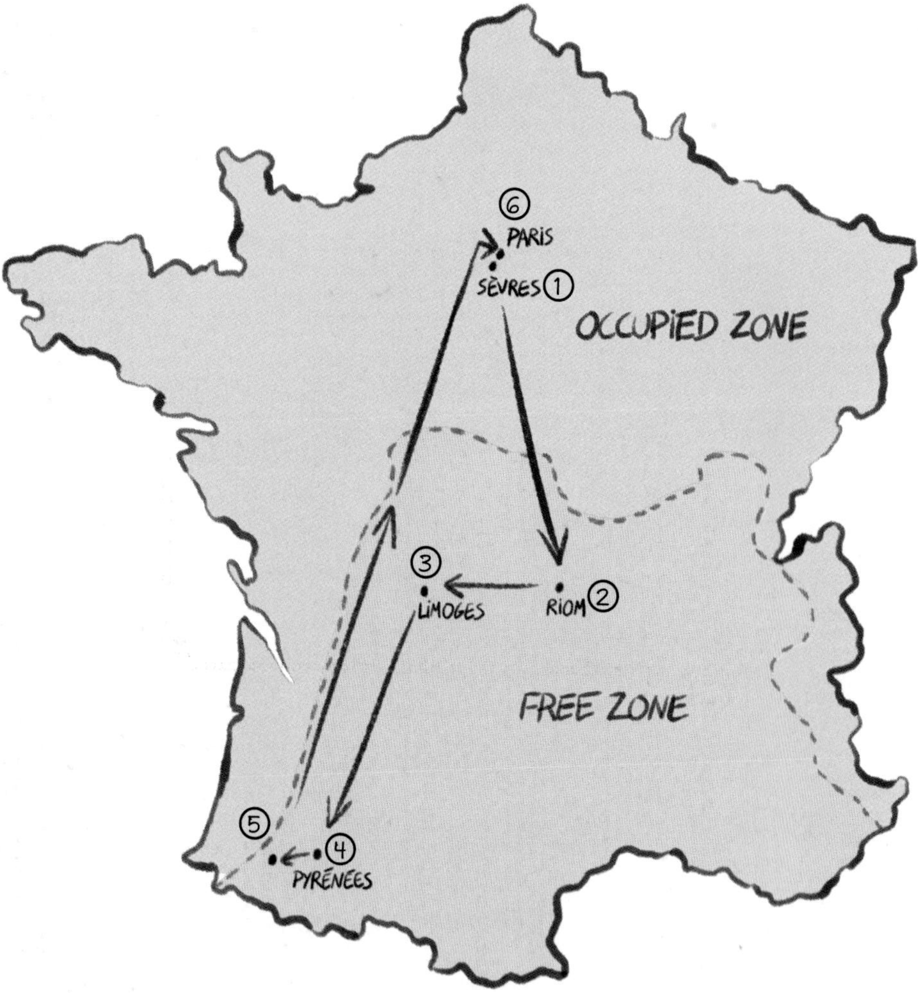
6
PARIS
SÈVRES 1
OCCUPIED ZONE
3
LIMOGES
RIOM 2
FREE ZONE
5
4
PYRÉNÉES

FRANCE 1942

1 – *The Sèvres Home near Paris.*

2 – *The old monastery in Saint-Eustache.*

3 – *The farm in Limoges.*

4 – *Château de Page orphanage in the low Pyrénées.*

5 – *Farmhouse in low Pyrénées.*

6 – *Rachel's home in Paris.*

Gallery of Photographs from the Sèvres Children's Home

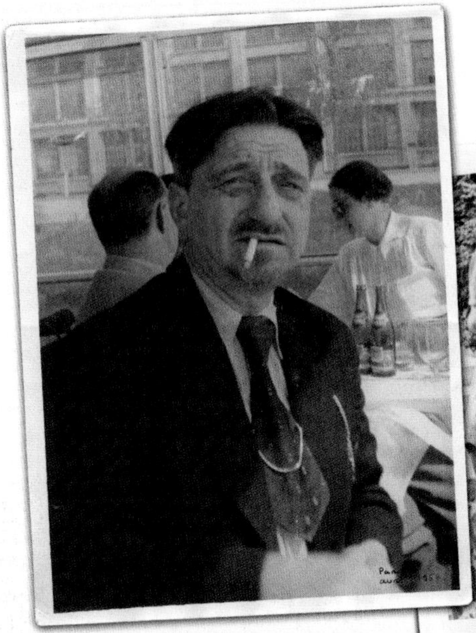

Penguin

Penguin and a group of big kids.

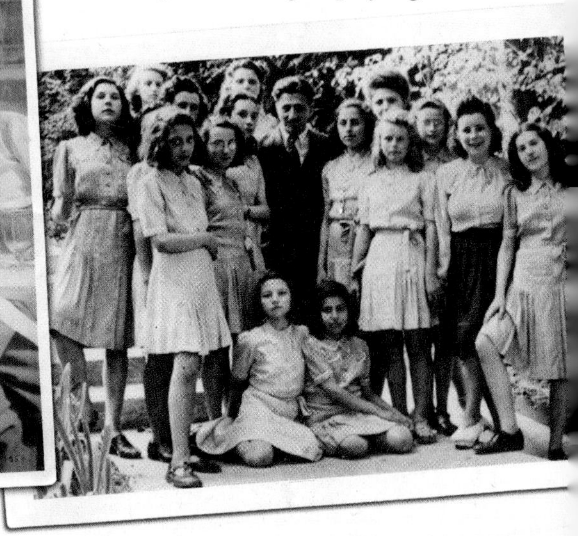

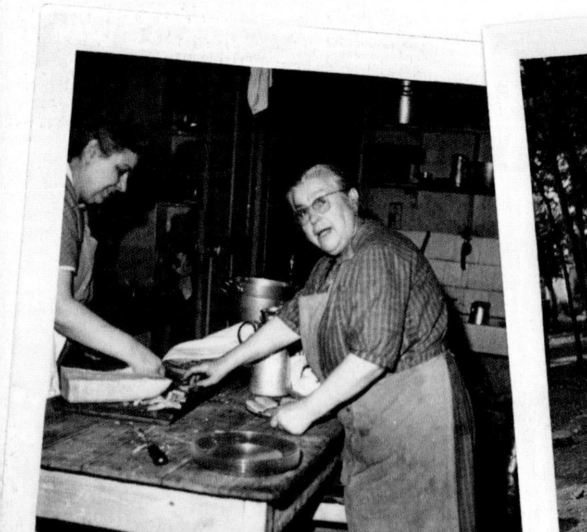

Madame Louise and Madame Lili prepare a meal.

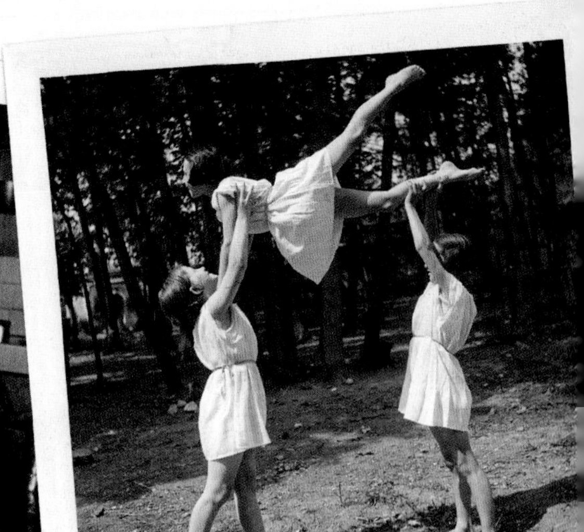

Middle graders do rhythmic dance.

Seagull

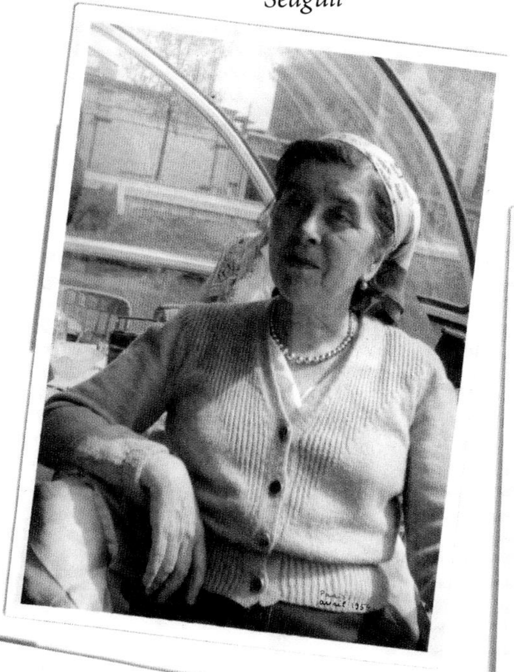

Catherine was inspired by the life of the author's mother. Her real name was Tamo Cohen. Here she is at the entrance to the Sèvres Children's Home.

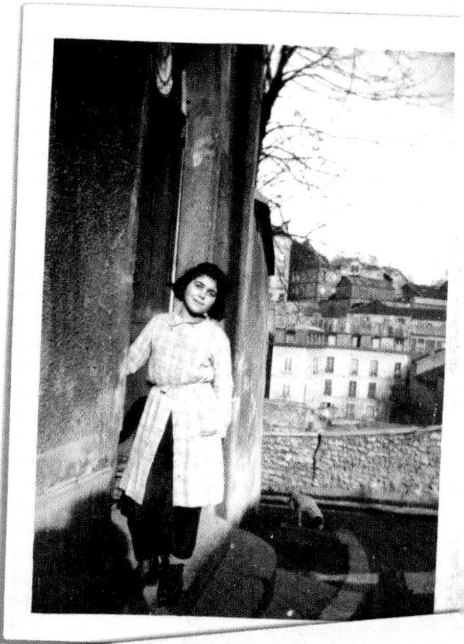

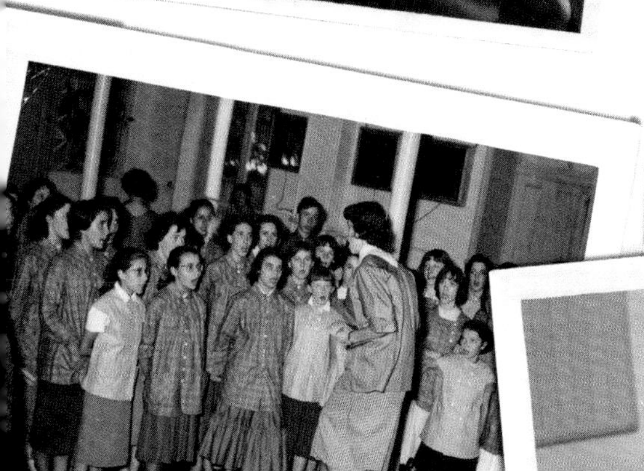

Gazelle conducts a chorus of little kids and middle graders.

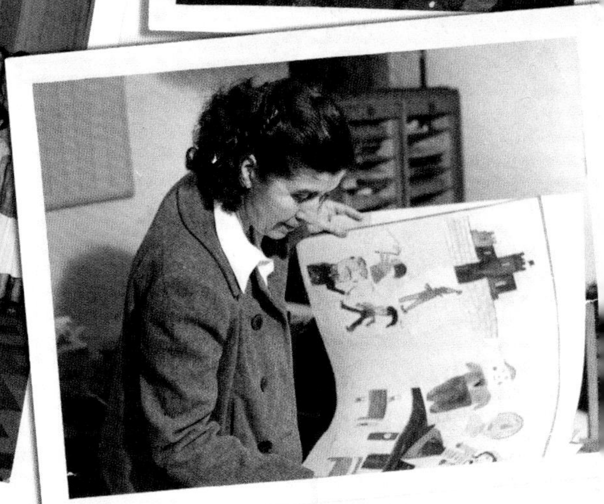

Seagull

A Note to the Reader

Dear Reader,

First, I am writing to tell you how proud and happy Claire Fauvel and I are that Catherine has crossed the ocean and come to you. She was born in France and now she is becoming a little bit American! You probably don't know that *Catherine's War* was a novel first, and that I am its author. A few years after its publication, an editor named Charlotte Moundlic, from Rue de Sèvres (a publisher in Paris) contacted me to ask if I would allow my novel to be adapted into a comic. I was immediately excited about the idea. Soon she contacted illustrator Claire Fauvel and asked her if she would draw the story. And that's how it began. Claire and I did not know one another before the book, but we became very close while working together.

Claire did a wonderful job. She read the novel and imagined all the drawings on these pages, creating a universe that feels very personal. I don't know what you think, but I love how she draws, her colors, the tenderness she puts in each panel—the way she tells this story.

Catherine's War now exists in two forms: a novel and a graphic novel, and it is translated into several languages. And who knows? One day, maybe it will be a movie? (That would be a great adventure!)

Thanks to Catherine, I met a lot of people both young and old: I went to classrooms, libraries, bookshops . . . and I was asked lots of questions about Catherine, about hidden children, and about the war. That's why I'm writing this letter. I may not have the chance to meet any of you, and I think it is important that you know a little more about the history of France during the Second World War. It will probably help you better understand details in the book. In the following pages, I have written down and answered the questions that I am often asked.

Please read ahead if you like. I hope my answers will give you some helpful perspective.

Yours truly,

Julia Billet

Questions from Readers

Why did Rachel and so many other Jewish children have to hide and flee throughout the war?

To understand it well, it is important to know that on September 1, 1939, German troops invaded Poland and then two days later, on September 3, France and the United Kingdom declared war on Germany. It was the beginning of what is known as the Second World War.

But in 1940, a French military hero of the First World War named Marshal Pétain, thinking that France was going to lose the war, decided to sign a peace agreement with German Chancellor Adolf Hitler. From then on, Marshal Pétain declared himself, "head of the French state," even though he had not been elected by France.

He changed France's motto "Liberty, Equality, Fraternity" to "Work, Family, Fatherland." Fatherland is another way of saying Germany. He forced all the schoolchildren of France to sing a song written in his honor:

> *Marshal here we are!*
> *Before you, France's savior,*
> *We swear, we, your men,*
> *will serve and follow your steps. . . .*

By signing this agreement with Germany, Pétain chose to collaborate with the Nazi regime. Collaborate means that he decided to help them win the war. Many French people did not agree at all with this man who helped Hitler.

What was the free zone in France?

When the peace agreement was signed in 1940, France was divided into several zones: those that were occupied by the Germans and the free zone. The occupied zone was in the northern half of France. Marshal Pétain settled in the free zone, in a town called Vichy. That is why this period, from 1940 to 1945, is known as the Vichy regime. The Sèvres Children's Home (less than six miles from Paris) was in the occupied zone: it meant there were many Germans all around.

What was the reason for World War II?

Hitler had decided to eliminate certain people, that means he wanted to make Jews, Communists, the disabled, homosexuals, and the Roma disappear from Europe. By collaborating with him, Pétain helped him to arrest men, women, and children, and send them to concentration camps in France, Germany, or Poland. Millions died in these camps under terrifying circumstances.

As early as 1941, the Germans wanted all Jews from the age of six to wear a yellow star that would be sewn onto their clothes. Marshal Pétain forced the Jews to respect the Nazis' orders. The Jews who obeyed were soon spotted and arrested. Seagull (from the book) categorically refused to permit the children of the Sèvres school to wear the yellow star. She decided right away that she would not obey such an unfair and dangerous law.

On July 16 and 17, 1942, the Vel' d'Hiv Roundup took place. It was called "Operation Spring Breeze." The Germans, aided by the French police, arrested over 13,000 people, including about 4,000 children, in and around Paris. They brought them to a big cycling arena where the Jews were deported to the concentration camp at Auschwitz. Only a few dozen people survived.

When did the people at the Sèvres Children's Home first decide to help the Jewish children?

It was when she heard this news about the raid in 1942 that Seagull called a meeting of the teachers and decided they must send the Jewish children away from Paris before someone denounced them, or turned them in.

At this time, Rachel, and many other Jewish children, were in great danger. They were at the children's home, in the occupied zone, with increasingly harsh laws against the Jews. That's why they were given new names—first and last—because certain last names demonstrated who was Jewish (Cohen, Levi), and some first names taken from the Old Testament were often used in Jewish families (Rachel, Esther, Rebecca).

In 1942, my character, Rachel Cohen, became Catherine Colin, and was brought to a free zone farther south, where the Germans were not yet settled. Except that the free zone gradually became an occupied zone. By 1943, everywhere in France and in all of Europe was very dangerous for the Jews.

The hidden children moved often throughout the war. No place was safe: Pétain asked the French to denounce the Jews, and some French did.

Others refused to do so because they thought it was wrong and would not collaborate with Germany and Hitler.

Seagull and Penguin were among those who refused to cooperate, and they also secretly welcomed children and families during the war. The sisters of the convent, the farmers, the director of the orphanage, and Cristina, as well, all took immense risks to protect Catherine. Had these adults been denounced, they would have been sent to concentration camps or to prison. They were the real heroes of the war because they refused to obey an unjust and cruel law.

For how long did children need to hide during the war?

Catherine would need to flee, and flee again, throughout the war. It was only in 1944, when the city of Paris was liberated from the Germans who were losing the war, that she would choose to return to the capital, then to Sèvres. The war in Europe was officially over on May 8, 1945.

Did anyone else in France try to save the victims?

General Charles de Gaulle, the military leader of France, did not recognize Pétain at all. That means that he thought Pétain was a traitor to France and that he took power without being elected by the French. Until the end of the war, de Gaulle fought against Pétain and against the Nazi party by organizing networks of "resistance" to save the countless people the Nazis were trying to exterminate. In 1945, Marshal Pétain was tried for high treason and ended his own life in prison. That was when General de Gaulle was elected by the French, as president of the republic.

Why are women being insulted and shaved on the day of the liberation?

On the day of the liberation, everyone in Paris celebrated. But on some streets, Catherine witnesses something strange: women sit on chairs, surrounded by angry mobs, and someone is shaving their heads bald. These women are treated as traitors because during the war years they fell in love with German soldiers. Yet none of them wanted a war. They were young and they were afraid to die. They needed love. These French women would continue to be shamed for years.

Catherine quickly understands that what she sees is not fair, and that she, too, could have fallen in love with the young German who saved her life. And she's probably wondering who these people shaving the women are, and why they are shouting at them with such anger. Did some of *them* not collaborate with the Germans and denounce Jews during the war? Didn't many people do far worse things than fall in love? Do these women deserve to be punished because they hoped that love could prevent war?

Who were Seagull and Penguin?

Seagull and Penguin were real people at the Sèvres Children's Home. They were the pioneers of a new way of teaching still considered revolutionary today. Many teachers and performers (such as Shrew and Kangaroo, whose real name was Marcel Marceau, and many others) participated in this great adventure. This wonderful book details Seagull's (real name Yvonne Hagnauer) work: *Pédagogie clandestine pour une école ouverte, La Maison d'enfants de Sèvres*. It was published by Seagull and Penguin's children in 2015, and is a testimony to how incredibly modern the school was and how progressive the people who made it work truly were.

Was there a real Rachel/Catherine?

Rachel/Catherine was inspired by my mother. My mother was one of the hidden children who was rescued with the help of the OSE network. Her real name was Tamo Cohen, and she spent the war using the name of France Colin. As a little girl, she traveled from place to place around France, and at the end of the war she returned to the Sèvres Children's Home.

How much of this story actually happened?

This story is based on facts and people who really existed and to whom I wish to pay homage. Penguin and Seagull were decorated with the Médaille des Justes (Medal of the Righteous) long after the war. My mother was much younger than my character, Catherine. But just like Catherine, she made her way, her eyes wide open to the arts and with an appetite for life that still lingers today.

Even though I relied on my mother's memories and Robert Leopold, an old student of Sèvres' remarkable site where he has brought together a host of incredible documents, my story remains a story.

I have indeed used quite a bit of artistic license; the characters and places are entirely of my own invention. I let myself be taken away through writing and words. It's a story that reminds us that even when the wolves are howling death at your door, there are women and men who are still faithful to mankind.

ACKNOWLEDGMENTS

I would like to warmly thank Claire Fauvel and Charlotte Moundlic. I loved our discussions, those moments bent over panels and dialogues, the words we struck out together, the doubts we shared, our laughter like light bubbles and also our enthusiasm and our curiosity. I loved the little words from here and there, and discovering with Charlotte, Claire's progress, both of us impressed by her talent as an artist; I loved our meetings, always cheerful and hardworking, listening to each other. I'm proud, really proud and happy to have shared this great and beautiful adventure with the two of them.

—J. B.

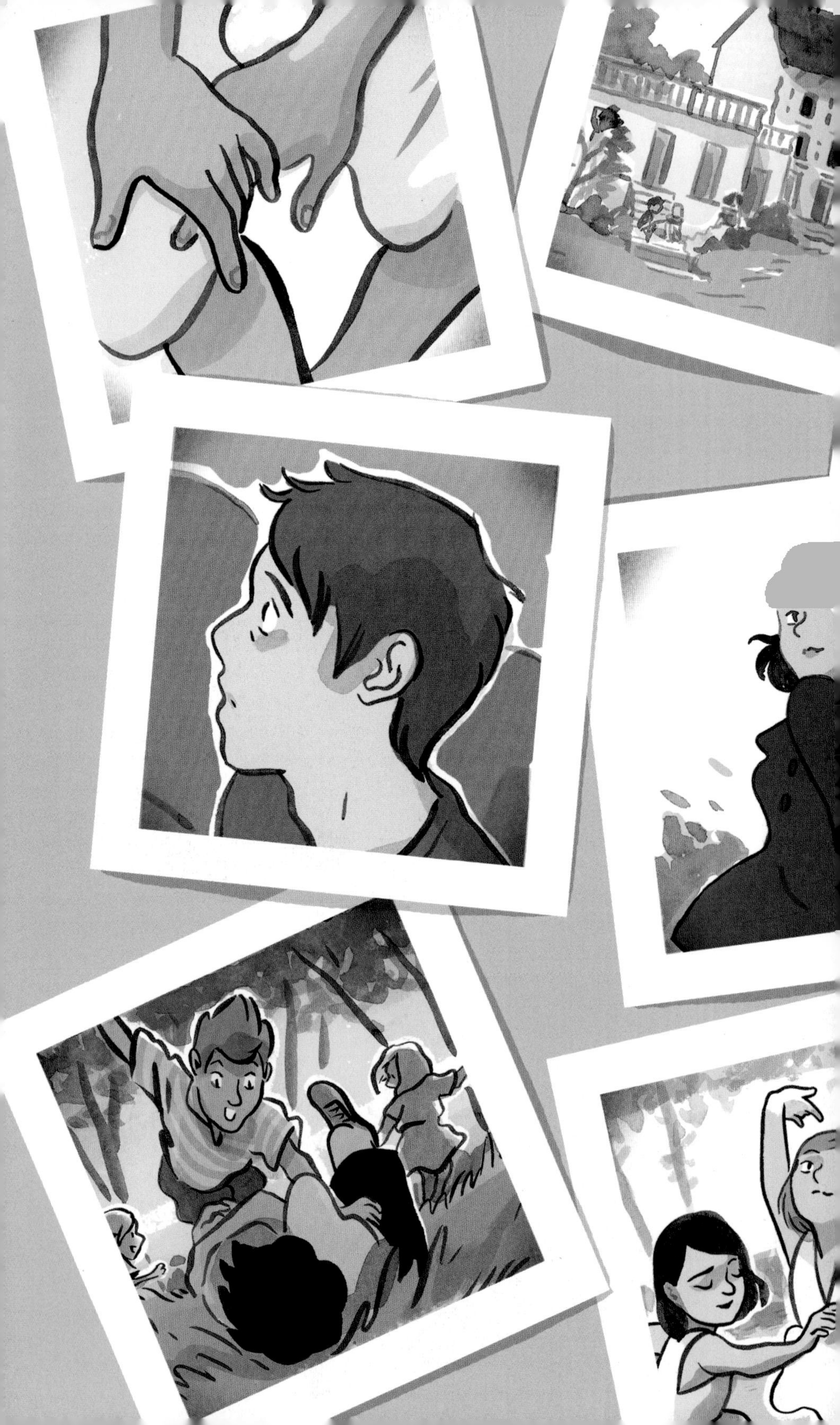